I0669886

KING OF THOL

BOOK 4 IN THE THOL SERIES

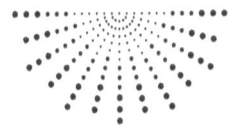

DAWN GREENFIELD IRELAND

ARTISTIC
ORiGiNS

CONTENTS

King of Thol by Dawn Greenfield Ireland

Published by Artistic Origins Inc.

Cover art by Yours Truly, me, the author

Interior layout by Yours Truly (me) Changes made 11/4/2022 and 8/12/2023, 6-26-2024,3-31-2026

The paperback cover was put together by Brandon White www.victorylau-rel.com

Danish crown scene break icon are Crown of Christian IV 1595 from Wikipedia.org

Map of Thol: Cartography by Scott K. Leslie www.theadventurerspack.com

Glossary of Thol by https://www.fiverr.com/ayshaarias

ISBN 978-1-940385-27-3 (eBook)

ISBN 978-1-940385-28-0 (paperback)

BISAC YAF056030

Dawn Greenfield Ireland

Artistic Origins Inc.

www.degreenfield.com

Please visit my website: http://www.degreenfield.com/ and sign up for my newsletter to get the latest news before the public.

Be kind = leave a review!

HINT: don't regurgitate the synopsis for your review. Just tell people what you liked, didn't like – that's what people want – your opinion.

❈ Formatted with Vellum

ACKNOWLEDGMENTS

Oh boy! I created the cover image using an AI program. It was touch and go for a while trying to figure out the program, but everything came together.

The paperback cover was put together by my oldest son, Brandon White www.victorylaurel.com

The beautiful Danish crown of Christian IV 1595 and scene break image came from Wikipedia.org.

I wanted a map of Thol, but I'm not even capable of stick figures. Thank you Scott K. Leslie www.theadventurerspack.com the cartographer who tackled the Map of Thol.

The glossary for the Thol book series was created by Ayshaarias from Canada. Man oh man, that gal had her work cut out for her, and she did a fabulous job. Many thanks that I found her! https://www."verr.com/ayshaarias

Creatures, creatures, creatures... A hearty thanks to Alex Gravalis (Fiverr.com) for Ghury, the Egrom creature; AskOrbin (Fiverr.com) for my diwal dog; and my son George White for Jakla Bosakin. The borjo creature was created by me via an AI program. YAY me for figuring this out!

Actions Appreciated

Please leave a review on the website where you bought the book. Reviews help authors get recognized, get the word out and sell more books. I will love you forever if you leave a review!

HINT: don't regurgitate the synopsis for your review. Just tell people what you liked, didn't like – that's what people want – your opinion.

Nonfiction	
The Puppy Baby Book	Mastering Your Money (2022)
Puppy Adoption and Beyond	Writers Preparation Handbook
Mastering Your Money (2008)	What's Breaking Your Budget
Online Classes	
Writers Preparation Handbook	How to Format Word Docs Like A Pro
Cozy Mysteries	**Sci-Fi-Fantasy**
The Alcott Family Adventures	**The Thol Series**
Hot Chocolate	Prophecy of Thol
Bitter Chocolate	Gifts From Thol
Spicy Chocolate	Love of Thol
Nutty Chocolate	King of Thol
Katz' Cat Series	Earth Calling Thol
Katz' Cat	**Sci-Fi Romance Adventure**
Bill Hill's Pills	Forced Dreams
The Detectives	**Dystopian**
The Pact	The Last Dog
	Texmexzona
Books by my Alter Ego ~ DG Ireland	
Bonded Shapeshifter Billionaire Series	
Bonded	
Tothars	
Tilted	
Unforeseen	
Connected	
Need A Notebook?	
See my 54 themed notebooks on my website	
www.degreenfield.com/notebooks	
Screenplays formatted as books	
Plan B (Dark Comedy)	Where's Ralphie? (Family Comedy)
The God Child (Action Adventure)	Standing Dead (Drama/Tragedy)
The Far Corner (Sci-Fi/Psychological/Creatures)	
Screenplays as TV Episodes	
Hot Chocolate ~ Episode 1	Prophecy of Thol ~ Episode 1
Bonded ~ Episode 1	
See my screenplays and awards on my website: degreenfield.com	
Filmfreeway, ISA Network	

CHAPTER ONE

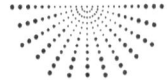

D'laine sneezed as she sat at a table in the massive library in the palace, with old, dusty scrolls from the mountain caves piled across the surface. Several scholars perused the shelves on ladders, trying to find anything related to the scrolls from the cave. Ebscalon's library content had been slowly rebuilt after the Great War of Taylon that occurred over fifty years ago. That war destroyed nearly all technology. All the great minds who authored or created the wonders that were Tholian inventions, perished in the war.

Luckily, the people of the former city known as Ciert, now named Ebscalon, which meant *knowledge*, were hoarders. They handed over scrolls that family members had authored before that horrible time, and placed them in trust with King Jor-Dan Bramstone.

As time passed and they recreated technology, they copied scrolls and the originals stayed in the library for safekeeping. Families were happy to receive copies of their ancestors work with the king's seal. They were proud that they could contribute to the rebuilding of not just their city, but their world.

Now, D'laine struggled to read through scrolls scripted in an older Tholian language, while she searched for information on the prophecy. She, her husband, Trakon, their unborn twins, and her father Lee Jackson, seemed connected to the Prophecy of Thol. So far, there didn't seem to be any mention of her brothers Brian and Jamie.

She looked up and stared at the container on the other end of the table. The trip to the cave at the crest of Ingosaquille in the Aguberro Mountains had been an eye-opener. Artifacts, such as the urn that stood on a nearby shelf, and the container on the table, surprised everyone.

The urn depicted D'laine, Trakon and the twins, while the container portrayed a picture of Lee. When Ghury, the Egrom elder of the Cember Forest, and D'laine's mentor, had boomed out that Lee was the direct descendent of King Jangston, it surprised everyone.

No one could overlook the similarities between the names.

Jangston and Jackson.

There was way too much of a coincidence in inter-dimensional language and pronunciation. D'laine and Trakon had been chasing the prophecy for two years, but nothing had them more hyped up than the discovery that images of their twins were in that cave.

What did it mean?

What were all of their roles?

How would this play out?

When Ghury informed them that King Jangston had been the King of Thol—the entire planet, not just Ciert—their heads spun. Not even the Visionary knew that at one time there was only one ruler.

The contents of the library only went back two or three hundred years, so there wasn't any historical data. No electronic files. No backups. Not even any crumbled pieces of paper. The Great War of Taylon had destroyed it all. They learned a valuable lesson that kept paying it forward.

Jor-Dan was the peacekeeper. All of the kingdoms turned to him for advice to solve their problems. There had been more than a few tense moments over the past few years that almost ended in war, but they diverted those incidents. The Plotals were now allies, having given up their wandering, warring, plundering, slaving ways. The Patrosyms would remain friends of the Ciertrons unless the princess somehow escaped her prison or the silencing helmet.

The only threat remaining was with Lee's mother-in-law, Augenta. The wicked woman seemed to have allied herself with the Trangula on the other side of Thol in the Valley of the Wailing Winds. While everyone was relieved she no longer lived in Ebscalon, no one had heard of the Trangula until Jakla Bosakin, the Plotal commander, told of their experience with them. Neska, Jakla's mate, lost her grandfather to the Trangula.

Augenta was no doting mother to her two daughters. Ilanda had chosen a husband far away so as not to have any contact with her spiteful mother. Ethaderia and Lee were now married, even though her mother looked down upon him as an alien. She had warned her daughter that if they had children, their half-breed spawn would never be accepted as Tholians.

Ditol, one of the Egrom elders, explained to Stanley Daigle, the Eartholian scientist who had returned to Thol with D'laine and her family, that the Trangula were not considered one hundred percent Tholian human.

They were *doski.*

Treikie Soluveia, Stanley's brainy scientist girlfriend, explained further the origins of the doski. They were subhuman creatures from the Calming Age—a mating between the extinct tree people and an early version of Tholian human's tens of thousands of years ago. The Trangula would never shrink that gap in their DNA.

Everyone in the palace speculated that Augenta must have petitioned and been turned away by friendly neighboring kingdoms. To move to the Valley of the Wailing Winds where the Trangula lived, after Jor-Dan expelled her from Ebscalon, seemed like a last-ditch effort to find anyone to accept her.

Ethaderia and Ilanda had a difficult time coming to grips with the thought that their mother would take up with sub-humans. But they knew their vindictive mother well, and now waited for whatever evil she had planned.

Trakon came into the library with Chatter on his heels. His diwal dog followed him everywhere. The prince plopped down onto a chair beside D'laine, removed the scroll from her hands and seared her lips with a kiss.

"Everyone's waiting for you. Did you forget it was lunchtime?" Trakon stood, took her hand and brought her to her feet. "Come on."

"Oh, all right," D'laine grumbled. She hated to stop the struggle with the translation. Old Tholian written language was more than a challenge for her.

Trakon wrapped an arm across her waist and led her out of the room. They walked to the dining salon and D'laine was happy to see her father, Ethaderia, and her younger brothers, Brian and Jamie, in attendance.

"Hi, daddy!" She rushed over and smooched her father on the cheek. Then she turned to Ethaderia and hugged her.

Brian eyed her warily. He wasn't going for any mushy stuff. He waved at her.

Jamie held his arms out and welcomed his big sister's affection.

"I'm sorry to keep everyone waiting," D'laine exclaimed. "I've been caught up with the scrolls again."

Treikie was in attendance, along with Victor Bennet, his wife Kara and their son Darren, who was between Brian and Jamie's age. The Bennet's were the last of the immigrants from Earth. And more significantly, Victor was the last of the original scientific team that had tried to find out where D'laine had disappeared to over two years ago.

The third member of their team was Ben Joplin. He now lived in the Cember Forest with the Kudaja in their tree city. The only remaining people on Earth who knew where any of them were, was Rosa, the Jackson's housekeeper, and her husband Erik. Al Jordan, a newspaper reporter and novelist was also in the know.

If anyone on Earth thought it was strange that Al became the caretaker of Victor and Kara's house in California, nothing had been mentioned—yet. They all waited for someone to connect the dots, but so far, their secret seemed safe.

Then there was the very strange aging algorithm that not even the scientists could figure out. When D'laine first disappeared, she had been seventeen. Victor and Stanley had been in their mid-twenties, and Ben Joplin had been in his fifties when their scientific team did their experiments.

On Thol, D'laine had conquered the invading robots from the Zan dimension. When Thol had aligned with Earth, she went through the portal, breaking Trakon's heart, to be reunited with her family. Her father and brothers returned to Thol with her within a few hours, along with Stanley, who had begged to go along.

Shortly thereafter, they discovered the weird aging difference when Kara was dying with cancer. Victor and Ben decided they had nothing to lose by going to Coronado Beach in California where Greg Claymore, the first Eartholian, had reappeared several times.

Victor and Ben slid a note across the sand hoping it would get to D'laine, wherever she was, to see if she could save Kara. That's when Buffy, the Jackson's beloved family dog that Victor and his family had taken in, jumped through the portal. Pup, Chatter and La'gar'ish, the diwal dogs D'laine had tamed, rescued Buffy from a pack of wild diwal dogs. Pup led Buffy back to the palace where she was reunited with her family.

The shock of the whole situation was that Stanley and Victor were no longer the same age. In the short time since Stanley came to Thol—within approximately one year, Victor had gained a wife and an eight-year-old son. Darren had not been adopted, hidden away or unplanned. He was Victor's natural son. And Ben was now sixty-two. No one could figure it out.

"Are you making any headway?" Kitry asked. D'laine's beautiful mother-in-law was the polar opposite of Augenta. All revered the queen. She had accepted D'laine as a match for her son, prince Trakon, and that was that.

"I know I'm missing a lot." D'laine seemed troubled. "The old language is difficult to translate. The scholars have found nothing on the shelves that point to the prophecy either. You'd think there was something hidden in those old books and scrolls."

"Why don't you ask the Egroms if they can tweak something in your head so you can read the old language?" Lee asked.

"Yeah, remember when you couldn't read Tholian at all? Ghury did something and suddenly, you could read it." Brian reminded her.

D'laine nodded, remembering. "That's worth a try. All this struggle weighs me down."

"We may have to make another trip to the cave," Stanley announced. "I think we only scratched the surface. There're most likely other artifacts and things we should look at."

"The cave is enormous." Lee recalled. "We were too excited with what we found, then got distracted with the borjos."

"When we go back, we should split up to cover more area," Trakon suggested.

The majordomo sent a silent message to chef Grubio in the kitchen to let him know that all were present and accounted for at the dining table. Within moments, the food arrived. The servers presented platters and bowls of an assortment of vegetables and meats to everyone at the table.

Ethaderia's sharp eyes noticed that Jamie shook his head at the two vegetable bowls the servers offered. "Jamie, why aren't you taking any vegetables? Don't you want to grow up strong and tall like your brother?"

"They're gross!" Jamie exclaimed.

"You ate them the other day," Lee said. "When did they become gross?"

Jamie squirmed in his chair with everyone's eyes on him. He let out a huff of exasperation. "They make me poop."

The Tholians faces showed they didn't understand what he said.

"What does 'poop' mean?" Jor-Dan asked.

"He means they give him gas." Lee muttered. He turned to his seven-year-old. "Are you sure the vegetables are giving you gas and not something else?"

Jamie's face lit up bright pink. "Do we really have to discuss this NOW?"

Brian and Darren snickered, which gained them parental stink-eyes. They got themselves under control.

"Jamie, you have to eat vegetables," Kitry said, determined. "You can't live on meat and fruit alone."

"Take one vegetable and see how your stomach is after lunch," Ethaderia suggested. "Maybe there's a particular vegetable that doesn't agree with you."

Jamie let out another huff. "Okay."

The server with the vegetables returned to Jamie's place and offered one of two bowls. Jamie looked them over and chose the adpe, which was like a wide Italian green bean. The server spooned them onto Jamie's plate.

Jamie grabbed his fork and shoved several adpe's in his mouth. "Is everyone happy now?"

"Honestly, you're such a little kid," Brian chided.

"I am not! I just turned seven! Remember when you were seven? I'll bet you were just like me, pooping all over the place," Jamie spat.

"If you don't get ahold of yourself real quick young man, you're going to find yourself standing in that corner behind you while the rest of us eat in peace," Lee announced. Then he turned his frosty eyes at Brian. "And you, young man, button your lips unless you have something good to say."

Brian shot dagger eyes at his brother.

Darren looked from Jamie to Brian, not even willing to jump into the fray. He felt his mother's eyes on him and refused to make eye contact with her.

La'gar'ish, Jor-Dan's diwal dog that rarely left his side, stuck his nose up at the edge of the table and sniffed.

"What do you think you're doing?" Jor-Dan flicked the dog's nose with his fingers. "No!"

"Testing the waters," Stanley said.

Everyone finished lunch and the three boys asked to be excused. They shot out of the dining salon and out of the palace before anyone cornered them into anything that resembled a chore.

There were chuckles and heads shaking around the table.

"I have good news," Kara whispered. There was a twinkle of excitement about her.

"Is it about chocolate?" Trakon asked, hopefully.

"Honestly, is that all you can think about?" D'laine nudged him.

Trakon gave her a smoldering look. "Noooo."

Kara cleared her throat. "Sorry, Trakon." She turned to face Lee. "I've been working with Adrum and Drusta and we've perfected the educational mind movies!"

"That is good news," Lee said. "Are they going to come here, or do we ship the boys off to the Egrom village?"

"Neither. Adrum and Drusta have come up with a way to

integrate the movies into the boys' translators!" Kara's eyes were blazing with excitement.

"I wonder how they managed that?" Stanley asked.

"Oh, wow. I wonder if they have a separate movie for those college courses and advanced subjects?" D'laine asked. "I'd like to continue my Earth education."

"That's downright sneaky." Victor snickered. "They'll be learning without even knowing it!"

"Not only that, but no one gets stuck with listening to them bellyache about school." Lee smiled happily.

"But they'll still be running wild," Ethaderia reminded them.

"Brian is practically a documentarian," Jor-Dan said, with pride. "He spends several hours a day with us, and he is very proficient at documenting the petitioners alongside Marrak."

"I'm happy to hear that," Lee said, surprised.

"Remember, Jamie spends quite a bit of time with Jugdaak training the pakows," Kitry said, knowingly. "And don't forget, he's our little diplomat among the kingdoms making sure everyone knows how to communicate with the pakows. Even the Plotals talk to their pakows now."

"So, I guess while they run wild across Thol, at least they're learning something?" Victor asked with a hint of sarcasm. "What about Darren? What's he going to contribute to Ebscalon, or Thol?"

"I've seen him hanging around some Youngmen," Trakon shared. "They were showing him how to protect himself, and he was demonstrating how he shocked that creature."

"So, what does that mean? He's going to train to be an Earth-olian Youngman?" Victor asked.

Trakon shrugged.

"Don't worry about it," Jor-Dan suggested. "You haven't been here all that long. He still has time to determine what he wants to do with his life."

"Let's go sit in the small salon," Kitry suggested.

"I want to go see Ghury," D'laine announced.

"We're going to see Ben," Victor said, as he, Lee and Stanley stood.

"Can I come with you?" Trakon asked. "I want to see Herish." He turned to D'laine. "Are you ready to go now?"

D'laine stood. "Let's go. I'm eager to be able to do a better job on these scrolls."

Jor-Dan stood. "Petitioners…"

Treikie and Kara stood. "We'll join you in the salon, Kitry," Treikie said.

CHAPTER TWO

*T*he mid-sized crestrider landed at the edge of the Cember forest, and everyone trooped down the escalator to the spongy, moss-covered ground.

Lee tapped the communicator device on his Tholian suit, which looked like something Arnold Schwarzenegger would wear in a sci-fi movie. "Ben, we're here. Are you at your place?"

The group headed into the forest, walked several yards, then climbed the stairs that were built into the side of one of the mighty agrin trees. They climbed to the boardwalk overhead that connected all the buildings and dwellings in the tree city.

Ben trotted down the boardwalk and waved when he saw them. "Hey!" The older scientist greeted his friends. They had to move out of the way so people could get by. "Let's go back to my place."

"Ben, if you had a bow and arrow you'd look like Robin Hood," Lee chuckled. Every time he saw Ben in the Kudaja clothing, it brought a smile to his face.

"You know, the wyre energy bow would have been so much better for Robin Hood. He wouldn't have had to lug all those arrows around," Ben determined.

Everyone followed Ben down the boardwalk which reminded D'laine of the Ewok city from one of the *Star Wars* movies.

A woman called out from a crosswalk. "D'laine!" She waved and approached the group.

"Hi, Meeri! I tagged along with the guys so I could go see Ghury," D'laine shared.

"Where's Herish?" Trakon asked

"He's with the king, but will be along in a few moments," Meeri explained. "How are the twins?"

Trakon turned to the men. "I'll catch up with you later."

Ben, Lee, Stanley and Victor waved and continued on their way to Ben's house.

"Their shells are expanding. I can't wait until I have them in my arms." Not thinking, D'laine asked, "What about your baby?"

"Baby?" Meeri scoffed. "We're not Earthlings or Eartholians. My little prince of a warrior, or princess, is this big." She held her hands to the size of an acorn squash. "In a little over two completed years he will take his place in society."

They walked over to the palace and Meeri led them to her and Herish's suite. Right away, D'laine noticed the beautiful new wall hanging.

"Oh, Meeri, this is beautiful!" D'laine ran her hand over the surface of the soft material that was a realistic depiction of a boardwalk in the trees. "You could practically step on this boardwalk. Did you make this?"

Meeri joined D'laine at the wall hanging. "Yes. My mother raised me at the foot of her loom. I remember all the colorful yarns in the weaving room."

"Can you make us one?" Trakon asked.

The door opened and Herish came inside. He and Trakon whacked each other on the back playfully. D'laine and Meeri shared knowing looks. Their husbands were like little boys when they were together. D'laine had to shake her head. There was a point when they were practically mortal enemies as they each vied for her affection. She was glad that had been settled, and Herish found Meeri so they could all be friends.

The Kudaja prince was D'laine's first human friend on Thol. Then, when she and Trakon met, in the flesh, outside their dreams that were part of the prophecy, Herish felt left out. He thought he had lost his friend. Trakon had been insanely jealous, and he and Herish duked it out on more than one occasion.

Herish and Trakon joined their wives. Herish gave D'laine a hug.

"How are you doing?" Herish asked her.

D'laine brought them up-to-date on the scrolls, the old language, and the upgraded translators the boys would get soon.

"We captured a Trangula in the marketplace!" Trakon exclaimed.

Meeri steered them over to the sofas where the men flopped down unceremoniously, to their wives' chagrin.

Herish's forehead creased in confusion. "Trangula? I sort of remember that word…"

"Remember the old doski from our history lessons?" Meeri asked him. "Those Trangula's live on the other side of Thol in the Valley of the Wailing Winds. I wonder what it's doing in Ebscalon?"

That started a whole explanation about Augenta.

Meeri was open-mouthed. "She went to the Trangula? Is she crazy? They're not even humans!"

D'laine shrugged. "To each his own, I guess."

"We're keeping watch," Trakon said. "I seriously doubt they sent just one Trangula to spy on us."

"Where are you keeping it?" Herish asked.

"What do they eat?" Meeri asked.

"It's down in the holding area," Trakon explained. "We thought since they were descendants from the tree people they'd eat fruit, vegetables and leaves. But after a few days, he demanded meat. That's when we noticed that they have pointy teeth."

"Huh," Herish and Meeri said at the same time.

"I've got to head over to the Egrom village," D'laine declared.

Meeri hugged D'laine. "I'm so glad you stopped by."

They all walked to the door.

"Let's go see what Ben and the guys are up to," Trakon said.

D'LAINE WALKED OUT OF THE FOREST ON THE OUTSKIRTS OF THE Egrom village. The gigantic mushroom houses amazed her every time she saw them. She needed to ask Stanley exactly how big they were. She estimated the stems were forty or fifty feet high. They were exactly like the mushrooms you'd find in a grocery store back on Earth. But these mushroom caps were as wide as a house back home.

As she walked toward the village, an Egrom boy ran toward her wildly swinging his four arms.

"Hi, Chacoodi!" D'laine called out.

He looked toward the forest as if expecting company. "Where's Brian, Jamie and Darren?"

"Sorry to disappoint you, but they're back home. I came with my father, Stanley, Victor and Trakon. They're visiting Ben and Herish."

A female Egrom walked across the moss toward them. D'laine waved when she recognized Kestrum. "Hi, Kestrum!"

The Egrom waved both of her right hands in greeting, having adopted the Earth custom.

Female Egroms were daintier than their male counterparts. Kestrum stood just under seven-feet tall with a face shaped slightly different from the males. Aside from the marsupial pouch and their smaller frame, at first glance it was difficult to tell the Egroms apart until you took time to study their faces. Then you noticed that no two Egroms looked alike.

"Hello, D'laine," Kestrum said, as she stood towering over her human friend.

"Hi, Kestrum. Would you be able to make a change so I can read the old Tholian language? I'm having a hard time trying to translate the old scrolls."

"Ghury will help you," Kestrum announced. She hooked one of her hands through D'laine's arm and they walked side by side to the village while catching up on events.

Kestrum shook her head when D'laine told the story about Jamie and the vegetables. "That should not be. There must be something going on in his belly for vegetables to give him gassy bowels. We will discuss this with Ghury."

"Oh, no! We thought it was something normal. Back home people get gas in their stomachs when they eat certain foods, like beans," D'laine explained. A frown crossed her face as she wondered what was wrong.

They approached Ghury's mushroom house, but he wasn't there. They found him at the circle where the elders congregated, and where they ate their meals.

"Greetings, D'laine," Ghury exclaimed. "Join us."

"Hi, everyone!" D'laine sat in a vacant place on the moss, in-between Ghury and Adrum.

"I will adjust your brain so you can read the old language," Ghury said, stepping into place in front of her.

It didn't surprise her that he knew why she was there. That was the way of the Egroms.

He placed one hand on the left side of her forehead, another hand covering the rest of the left side of her head, then a third hand on the crown of her head. He studied her head for a bit, then settled his fourth hand toward the rear of her head.

"Adrum, close the gap with your hands," Ghury requested.

Adrum placed two of his hands on the right side of her head, one toward the front right forehead area, and the other on the right side of her head.

D'laine felt a buzzing in her head. When they removed their hands, the buzzing stopped.

"You should have no problem with languages now," Ghury announced.

Adrum nodded. "You will now have the ability to speak and read any Tholian or Earth languages."

"Gosh, where were you when I was in high school?" D'laine said, as she rubbed the top of her head.

"There is a possibility that Jamie has parasites in his intestines," Ghury said, in that Egrom emotionless statement.

"Parasites?" D'laine asked, alarmed.

"It will not be a pleasant experience," Adrum admitted. "We should scan him immediately."

"Oh, no. Let me call our father. He's with Ben," D'laine said. She pressed her communicator, chose his name in the address book and sent him a chime.

THE GUYS ENTERED BEN'S HOUSE. SOMETHING LEAPT FROM THE top of a bookcase and landed on Ben's shoulder. Little dark brown furry hands wrapped around his head, hanging on, and a long tail wrapped around Ben's upper arm. Wide eyes stared at the strangers.

"What the…" Victor began.

"This is Brownie, my new pet," Ben said, joyfully.

"What is it?" Stanley asked.

"It's a gippe," Ben explained.

Lee's communicator signaled an incoming call. "What's up?"

"Daddy, Ghury and Adrum said Jamie may have parasites. They need to scan him," D'laine explained.

"Oh, no! I'll be right there," Lee said, then disconnected the call. "I'll catch up with you back at the palace. See you later, Ben."

A few minutes later, Lee came out of the woods at a jog, and joined the group around the circle. "Parasites? You don't think it's just gas?" he asked.

Ghury shook his head. "There is no reason for everyday vegetables to produce a gassy stomach. Parasites can become very painful and may require an unpleasant treatment."

"I'll let everyone know we have to go back to the palace," Lee said, his mind far away lost in thought about this latest issue.

"There's no reason for your friends to shorten their visit," Ghury determined. "Adrum and I will step you and D'laine to Ebscalon."

Lee sent a mental message to Stanley letting him know what was going on, and that he would see them back at the palace later.

"Okay, I'm ready," Lee announced.

The four stood, and within a blink, they disappeared.

When they stepped into the palace, they found Jamie looking slightly green in Ethaderia's arms. She rocked him, trying to soothe him as he moaned pitifully. The four dogs hovered at her feet, clearly upset that their animal communicator was sick. It was a surprise to see La'gar'ish away from Jor-Dan. The dog rarely left the king's side. And Pup guarded the twins in the tower. Typically, he left only to go to relieve himself, hunt, or beg for scraps in the kitchen. Chatter and Buffy's faces were creased with worry.

Lee rushed over to Ethaderia. "Jamie?" He looked at his wife. "When did he get so sick? He was fine at lunchtime."

"He came stumbling into the palace and could barely make it to the bathroom," Ethaderia sobbed out.

Stanley stepped Victor and Trakon into the salon just as Kitry came through the doorway.

"Oh, no!" Kitry rushed over to the sofa and placed her hand on Jamie's forehead. "He's burning up."

"All will be well," Ghury explained. "We need to scan him. Would you place him on the sofa and move away? We need to scan only him."

Lee helped straighten Jamie out on the sofa.

"It hurts," he moaned, trying to curl back up on his side again.

"Try to straighten out so the Egroms can scan you," Kitry said in a motherly voice.

They all moved away and let Ghury and Adrum step in and take over.

Eight large, white, furry hands spread out just above Jamie's body. After several long moments, the Egroms straightened up and turned to face the humans.

"It is as we suspected. Jamie is infested with parasites," Ghury declared .

"What can you do to get rid of them? Can D'laine pull them out of him?" Lee asked. He was clearly distressed over Jamie's condition.

Ghury and Adrum shook their heads.

"No. They are spread throughout his intestines. He will have to drink jiffaberra tea," Adrum said.

Trakon's eyes widened. He slapped a hand over his mouth and ran from the room making gagging noises.

Stanley and Victor were wide-eyed as Trakon sped past them.

"Trakon?" D'laine started to go after him, but Kitry stopped her.

"He recalls when he had to suffer through jiffaberra tea when he was a little boy," she shared. "He may lose his lunch."

Everyone looked over to Jamie, then the Egroms.

"Is it that bad?" Lee asked.

Trakon stumbled into the room, looking a little pale. "Yes! He's going to suffer, but there's nothing you can do about it."

D'laine slipped her arm across Trakon's back and patted him. "It must be bad for you to have that reaction to just hearing the name of the tea."

"That was the worst experience I've ever had. I'm rarely ill, and I swear the treatment is worse than the stomachache," Trakon spit out.

Ghury instructed them how to proceed. "For the next three days, keep him in his bed. This will not be difficult because he will be very sick. Do not feed him any solid food. You will prepare a large batch of the tea and have him drink it every two or three hours. It may be cold or hot."

"Where do we get the tea?" Ethaderia asked, her eyes wide.

"The marketplace," Kitry said. "There's a stall that sells herbs and remedies."

The Visionary entered the room holding a large basket of leaves. "I have what you need here." He nodded to Victor.

"Thank you so much. How do I prepare this?" Ethaderia asked, taking the basket.

"I'll come with you and show you," Kitry said. "Basically, you soak the leaves for several hours until the water turns a dark, murky color. Then, you scoop the leaves out of the container— you can make one more batch of tea, but after that, they need to be discarded. Then you can either heat the water to make a warm tea, or serve it cold. Whatever way you can get it down him."

"It's the most disgusting stuff that will ever pass your lips, I guarantee it," Trakon vowed. "But don't worry, for the first two or three days, Jamie will be too sick to even taste the stuff."

"What about after the three days?" Lee asked the Egrom.

"When his fever breaks, recovery will be speedy. He will continue the tea for another day, then ease his stomach back to solid food," Adrum explained.

LEE HAD TO REMOVE THE CRESTRIDER MODEL THAT HUNG FROM the ceiling that moved with the breeze over Jamie's bed. The motion of the model made him more nauseated.

They replaced Jamie's linens often because of the fevered sweats. There were several instances when he could not get his head over the edge of the bed in time to vomit into the bucket on the floor. He was a pathetic sight.

Lee held him as Ethaderia and Kitry or D'laine stripped the sheets off the bed and replaced them. He was no better by the end of the third day and they called Ghury back for a consultation.

The Egrom scanned Jamie in his bed while everyone hovered nearby. When he finished the scanning, he joined the family.

"You must make a new batch of tea. Let it boil down until it has thickened, then spoon feed Jamie as if it were pudding.

D'laine noticed Trakon beginning to have a reaction to Ghury's words. She shoved him out the door of Jamie's room to the bathroom. They made it just in time before Trakon lost all that was left in his stomach from breakfast. Once he recovered, D'laine ran a cool washcloth across his face.

"Jamie will never eat pudding again!" Trakon wailed. "Just the thought of it makes me green."

"I hope I never have to take that remedy," D'laine whispered.

They returned to the sickroom just as everyone was heading

toward the kitchen. Trakon leaned down and kissed D'laine on the cheek.

"I can't be in the same room with that vile stuff, so I'm going over to the shop," Trakon said, feeling slightly off.

"I understand." D'laine patted his back and watched as he left the house.

Ethaderia and Lee went about making another batch of the jiffaberra tea. After a couple of hours it was still thin tea.

"This is going to take a while for it to boil down and thicken up," Lee figured.

"It must really be nasty for Trakon to have such a violent reaction with just the mention of it," Ethaderia exclaimed.

Kitry wandered into the kitchen. "Jamie's sleeping, but it's fitful." She shook her head.

They heard conversation at the front door, then Kara, Victor and Stanley entered the kitchen. Ben followed a few hours later.

"Still no change?" Kara asked.

Brian and Darren thundered inside and ran to Brian's room.

Lee excused himself from the group and headed to his errant son's room. He hovered in the doorway. "Listen, your brother is very, very sick, and you need to be quiet. Do you remember how everyone tiptoed around the house when you were sick back on Earth?"

Brian appeared guilt ridden. "Sorry, daddy. When's he going to be better?"

"We don't know," Lee said with a shake of his head. "Just be mindful that he's very sick, okay?"

Brian and Darren echoed each other. "Okay."

Lee returned to the kitchen.

"Let's go sit down," Ethaderia suggested. "This process will take a while."

They all headed to the main salon and settled onto the comfortable sofas and chairs. Duncts later, Eglabado, Ethaderia's manservant, showed Marrak, Dannin and Jugdaak into the room.

"Any change?" Jugdaak asked. Jamie spent a lot of time at the pakow pens with the man.

"Nope. We're about to go into phase two," Lee explained.

"They have to make a stronger batch of the tea," D'laine told the pakow handler. "It's thick like pudding."

"That doesn't sound too bad," Dannin thought out loud.

"Don't mention it around Trakon," Kitry announced. "He can't even hear the word jiffaberra, let alone smell it."

A loud clattering came from down the hall.

"What the heck?" Lee exclaimed. He jumped up and took off down the hall and up the stairs, expecting to clobber Brian. Everyone followed.

As he got to the boy's bedrooms, Lee couldn't believe his eyes. Ekka, Jamie's borjo, was trying to claw his way into the bedroom.

"Ekka! No! Back!" Lee yelled.

D'laine scurried into the room around the group. She rushed to the window and patted the distraught borjos snout. "It's okay, Ekka. Jamie is sick. He can't come out to see you."

The borjo snuffed loudly, steam escaping through his flared nostrils. His claws were sunk into the window ledge, holding him steady so he could see his human.

D'laine patted the borjo again. *Return to your tower. Jamie is sick. Like when you were sick with the queper.*

The animal looked over to the bed, then back to D'laine. He pushed off, took to the air, and they all watched as he flew back to his tower.

"I told him Jamie was sick like when he was sick from the queper," D'laine explained. "He understood."

"Let's hope the og and the bobboes don't show up next!" Dannin said, with a snicker.

"I'd better get back to the palace," Marrak said, as he left the group and headed to the front door.

Lee, Victor and Stanley examined the window ledge. They didn't see any structural damage from the large dragon-like borjo.

"Just think of the damage he would have done if he had gotten in here," Stanley said.

"If that isn't devotion, I don't know what is," Kara announced.

Ethaderia left the room to check on the tea. She returned a few minutes later. "Why don't we go back to the salon." She ushered everyone out of the room and down the stairs.

OVER THE NEXT TWO DAYS, LEE, ETHADERIA, KITRY, KARA AND D'laine took turns spooning jiffaberra pudding into Jamie's mouth. Brian became a little bratty because all the attention was on his little brother. He snuck a bowl of the pudding when no one was looking and hid in his room to eat and gloat. All he did was stick the spoon into his mouth, with a snide expression on his face. He immediately spit the gross concoction out of his mouth and ran to the bathroom, hacking, coughing and spewing.

Ethaderia rushed into his bedroom, saw the bowl in the middle of the bed. There were pudding streaks on his bedding, and she had to force herself not to laugh out loud. She grabbed up the bowl and the spoon and quietly left the room.

Lee caught up with her as she returned the bowl to the kitchen and used a clean spoon to scrape the pudding into the larger bowl.

"Brian must have thought Jamie was getting something yummy, so he made himself a bowl," she explained. "I think he's in the bathroom washing his mouth out."

Several moments later, Brian waltzed into the kitchen looking a picture of innocence.

"Want another bowl of that pudding, son?" Lee asked.

Brian huffed. "I didn't know, okay?"

"Haven't you seen Trakon practically turn purple at just the mention of jiffaberra?" Lee asked. "It isn't a treat. When your brother feels better, it will be a challenge to get him to eat it. We may have to call in the entire army to hold him down and pry his mouth open."

"I hope I never get that sick!" Brian exclaimed.

Ethaderia patted his back. "Have you changed your bed?"

"Yes," Brian huffed out. "I hung things in the smart closet, but there's not a lot of room for everything."

"Have Eglabado show you where the larger linen smart closet is located," Ethaderia suggested.

"Oh, I didn't know we had one." Brian took off to find the manservant.

THE NEXT DAY WHEN KARA WAS FEEDING JAMIE, EKKA CAME TO visit. This time, the borjo stuck his head through the window as he hovered like a dragonfly; he didn't try to climb inside.

Kara crossed the room to the window. She had never been very close to one of the dragon-creatures. She swallowed her fear, reached out and stroked his velvety snout as steam billowed out.

"Jamie's still sick, Ekka," she cooed. "Don't worry. He will get better soon."

The borjo nudged her with his snout for another rub, then he pushed off from the wall and flew away.

Kara let out a huge sigh of relief at overcoming her fear.

Ethaderia stopped by and noticed the borjo flying in the distance. "Did Ekka try to get inside again?"

"No, he seems to understand he can't get through the opening. I patted him and that seemed to do the trick," Kara explained. "He's so big! I don't understand Jamie's relationship with the animals, but I'm glad Ekka is a friend."

"I would hate to be on the receiving end if that borjo felt threatened, or got mad," Ethaderia said, with a worried expression across her face.

"Want to help me give Jamie a sponge bath?" Kara asked.

"I'll get a bowl of warm water and some wash cloths," Ethaderia said. She left the room and returned with two washcloths and the bowl.

ALMOST A FULL WEEK PASSED BEFORE JAMIE'S FEVER BROKE. NOW that he was aware of everything, he rebelled against the pudding.

"Don't come near me with that horrible stuff!" he cried out when his father entered the room with a bowl and a spoon.

"Son, you have to eat the pudding, or drink the tea so the parasites don't come back," Lee declared.

"No!" Jamie screamed at the top of his lungs. He ducked his head under the covers.

Ethaderia and Kitry rushed into the room.

"What's going on in here?" Kitry asked.

"He's better," Lee said. "He won't eat the pudding."

"Perhaps we should summon Ghury and see how to proceed, now that he's somewhat better?" Ethaderia asked.

Lee hit his communicator and called D'laine. He explained what the problem was, and she contacted the Egrom. Before he could tell his wife anything, the Egrom materialized in the room.

"Your patient is better?" Ghury asked.

"He refused the pudding, so it seems he's over the worst of it," Lee announced.

Ghury placed a hand on the lump under the covers. "Jamie, come out so I can scan you."

Jamie stuck his head out and took in everyone's positions in the room. He glared at his father who was holding the bowl and spoon. "I'm NOT going to eat that stuff!"

"Settle down so I can determine whether the parasites have all passed through your body," Ghury scolded.

Jamie crawled out of the covers and flopped onto his back.

Ghury spread his four hands over Jamie's body and focused. Duncts later, he patted the boy on the head. "It appears you are free from the parasites."

"Can I eat real food now?" Jamie asked. "I'm starving."

"Begin with soup and soft foods," Ghury advised. "Your digestive system is weak and it will take several meals before you can eat heartily again."

"As long as I don't have to eat that pudding, or drink that tea ever again!" Jamie shouted. "I don't even know how I got those parasites in the first place."

"Son, it's like getting the flu or a cold, back on Earth. It just happens. Things are in the air and on surfaces. You can't see them," Lee said.

Jamie yawned widely. "Can I sleep in the salon? I'm sick of my bed!"

"Go lie down on the sofa. We'll change your linens," Ethaderia told him.

CHAPTER THREE

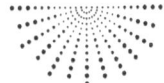

*J*amie spent two days resting on the sofa in the small salon. Then he dragged an old blanket to Ekka's tower and napped with the borjo on his bed of gauze. The dragon-like creature took comfort with his human close by.

The new borjos from the Aguberro Mountains settled into their new positions as defenders of the kingdom. When they flew, they were like geese or ducks on Earth, with Ekka in the lead. For the most part, they all accepted Ekka's domination. Trakon's borjo, Ehtuta, might have felt a little privileged because he was the Prince of Ebscalon's borjo. Ekka had to put him in his place to let him know he was the boss.

Trakon and Jor-Dan were thrilled to ride the beasts. At first, Jor-Dan rode with Trakon on Ehtuta. His improved confidence kept him from falling off or having miscommunications with Dundo and Grasko, the only two borjos he rode.

Many of his subjects waved as they saw their king gliding through the sky on the back of the borjo. Kitry thought it was the best stress reliever she had ever seen. Jor-Dan was much more relaxed these days.

When Jamie fully recovered from the parasite ordeal, he and Ekka flew for the first time in over a week. Cruising over the mossy fields near the Cember and Ikley forests at the edge of Ta'Byu'Vohon, Ekka dove suddenly after spotting something on the ground. Jamie gave a scream of half-fear and half-exhilaration on the swift descent. The only control he had was to hang on for dear life.

Plotals looked up and saw the borjo swooping toward the ground and Jamie hanging on. The borjo scooped up his prey and flew over the Plotal city with a creature clutched in its claws.

Jakla heard the commotion outside and joined the guards who pointed to the sky. The Plotal commander shielded his eyes to see what the borjo carried.

"Trangula!" Jakla shouted. He hit his communicator and called to Jamie. "Your borjo caught a Trangula. Have him hover near the ground and release the doski. We will take him into custody and I will call Jor-Dan."

Orongo, one of Jakla's advisors and a keen military strategist, barked out orders in his communicator. "I need two units over here, on the double!"

Jamie waved to Jakla. "Ekka, fly real low and drop the Trangula over by the Plotals."

Ekka hovered close to the Plotal guards and Jakla, his mighty wings stirring up loose dirt and moss. He released his prey, and the doski dropped to the ground with a painful grunt. The Plotals grabbed the creature before he could get away.

The borjo flew around thirty feet away and landed so that Jamie could dismount.

"Go hunt, Ekka. If you see any more Trangula, let me know. Grandpa will be here soon and I'll go home with him," Jamie said, as he shooed his borjo away.

Two units of ten Plotals ran to where Orongo and Jakla were.

A small fleet of crestriders approached the Plotal city. Colorful banners rose and flapped in the wind on each ship identifying the ships from Ebscalon. One of the Plotals left the group. He waved his hand in the air and directed the Ciertrons to land the ships in the open field east of the Plotal city.

Jamie joined Jakla and his soldiers while they waited for the contingent from Ebscalon to land and disembark their ships.

"I told Ekka to keep an eye out for more Trangula or doski," Jamie said.

"He won't eat them, will he?" Jakla asked.

"No, he knows we want to talk to them first. He'll only eat them if we give him permission," Jamie explained.

Trakon, D'laine, Lee and Stanley ran across the moss to join Jakla and Jamie. Jor-Dan, Dannin and several soldiers landed their ships and made haste to join the group.

The Trangula was bleeding from the borjo claws, and bruises rose on his face and hands from when Ekka dropped him to the ground. Two Plotals had a firm grip on the doski—he wasn't going anywhere.

"Where did you find him?" Trakon asked.

Jakla turned to Jamie. "Where was Ekka flying when he saw him?"

Jamie and Orongo, Jor-Dan's Plotal friend, pointed and spoke at the same time. "Over there!"

It was around two-hundred feet from the edge of the Ikley forest.

"When the borjo spotted him and dove, the doski started to run back to the forest," Orongo said, as he turned to his troops. "I want you to go through that forest. See if this doski had company. If so, hunt them down and bring them in."

The Plotal troops fanned out and headed for the forest. Plotals ran remarkably fast for their huge bulk, with their long tails trailing out behind them and their deadly pods closed tight.

"Bring the prisoner inside," Jakla demanded. He turned to the Ciertrons. "Come, we'll sort this out."

They all went inside the building, turned to the left and went through an open door and descended two flights of wide stairs. The lead Plotals tossed the doski inside a cage and shut the door. Jakla, Jor-Dan, Orongo, Trakon, D'laine and Stanley lined up in front of the cage and stared at the Trangulan. Jamie got right up to the bars and studied the creature.

"Is it my imagination, or is this one more like an animal than the other one?" Jamie asked.

The doski appeared hunched over and its knuckles rested on the floor.

"This one is more doski than Trangulan," Trakon observed. "Jamie, when Ekka grabbed him, did he say anything? Yell words or scream or anything at all?"

Jamie thought about it. "He screeched like a wild animal. I haven't heard him talk."

Stanley took a step forward. "Let me look inside his brain." The scientist stared at the creature's head, then turned to the leaders.

"Very basic language skills, so I'm not sure how he communicates," Stanley explained.

The creature grunted. Then he pointed directly at Lee. "You die!"

"How do we interrogate him? He seems to be more intelligent than the Fod," Jor-Dan asked.

"I can try to talk to him in his head," Jamie suggested.

Jor-Dan, Jakla, Lee and Trakon looked among themselves.

Lee noticed Orongo's questioning expression. "My youngest son, Jamie, communicates with animals. He can figure out any problem you have with pakows or anything else."

"He helped a farmer with his bobboes," Dannin explained.

Jakla nodded. "Jamie instructed us on the way to communicate with our pakows so that we have a better relationship with the beasts."

Orongo looked from Lee to Jamie. "So, you're the one? Our pakows are much happier now that we know what they want from us and the way they expect to be treated."

"Sometimes it's just simple things. The bobboes didn't want to see the farmer's axe in the tree stump. They called it the *death thing,* and they stopped laying eggs until I persuaded the farmer to move it," Jamie explained.

"Why don't you give it a try," Lee suggested.

Jamie stood in front of the doski. His mind arranged words in a form that the doski might understand. Jamie tapped his chest. *Hi. My name is Jamie.*

Then Jamie pointed to the doski. *What's your name?*

The doski stared at Jamie. *Wad.*

Wad, who sent you here?

The doski looked confused, so Jamie regrouped.

Wad, who is your king?

Custuf.

Did King Custuf send you here?

Custuf come. Kill many. Kill homan. He pointed to Lee.

Jamie turned to the group. "His name is Wad. King Custuf sent him. He said Custuf is coming and will kill a lot of people. Then he said kill homan. I think he means human, but I'm not sure. I guess he means you, daddy."

"Okay, ask him if the king is on the way," Jor-Dan added.

"How did he get here?" Jakla asked. "Did he walk? Do they have ships? Did he come by pakow?"

Orongo looked the doski over. "He doesn't appear to be wearing a military uniform, so I'm going to assume he's a scout."

Trakon nodded. "That sounds right."

Jamie presented the questions, but it was more than Wad could understand. The group went upstairs. Jakla led them to a meeting room where they all sat on the rather large furniture.

31

"Are you going to give him some water?" Jamie asked. "He's probably thirsty."

"He's a prisoner of war," Orongo said, snidely.

"Yeah, but he's like a pakow or an og," Jamie suggested. "He can only follow very basic orders. He'll never be as smart as me, and I'm just a little kid!"

Orongo looked to Lee. "Your son puts me to shame. Is he always like this?"

Lee smiled and tussled Jamie's hair. "More or less."

Orongo pressed his communicator and called one of his troops. "Bring the prisoner a bowl of water."

Orongo's communicator chirped an incoming call. "Yes?"

"We found several sets of doski tracks and followed them to the north-east side of the forest, where they exited into a clearing," the soldier announced.

"Have you located them?" Orongo asked.

"We're keeping to the edge of the forest. There's a couple of borjos flying around. One grabbed a doski and ate him," the soldier announced.

Jamie shot out of his chair and ran for the door. "I'll bet that's Foota!"

"Stay out of the way, but monitor the scene. Are there other doski's you can see?" Orongo asked.

"There's two that are afraid to move," the soldier said. "They're huddled on the ground trying to look like rocks."

Lee stood along with the others. He hit his communicator. "Jamie, tell the borjo not to eat any more doski!"

"I did, daddy. It's Foota. She said she was sorry. We never said she couldn't eat doski," Jamie said over his communicator.

"I guess we need to list everyone and everything," Lee muttered.

"You know, daddy, she's been behaving," D'laine said. "She hasn't tried to cause any harm since she grabbed Chacoodi."

Trakon took off running after Jamie. The others spilled out of the building and headed across the way to the ships.

"Foota!" Jamie called.

The borjo circled overhead then glided to the ground, chewing. Jamie ran up to her with Trakon catching up.

A boot with a severed foot fell to the ground in front of Jamie.

Foota ducked her head, scooped up the boot and tossed it in the air. She caught it and crunched it.

"Gross! What a show-off!" Jamie declared. "Come on, Trakon, we can fly over to the field and see those other doski."

Trakon and Jamie climbed aboard Foota and took to the air. Trakon hit his communicator. "We'll meet you there."

Ciertrons, Eartholians and Plotals clambered aboard the crestriders. The ships lifted into the air and followed the borjo. They all circled the field and landed close to where the Plotals had two Trangula in custody.

The Trangula shrieked when Foota landed. Their eyes about bugged out of their heads when Jamie and Trakon climbed off her back. The Plotals had a difficult time holding onto the doski.

"These two are military," Orongo announced. "See the difference in the clothing?"

D'laine, Stanley and Lee noticed the helmets that seemed more like little bowls on their heads with a strap under their chin. Their uniforms were brown with green and gold patches.

"Camouflage," Lee and Stanley said at the same time.

"So, they must have some training," Lee assumed.

Jor-Dan nodded. "It appears so, or at least whoever is in charge of their military operations understands how camouflage works in the field."

"You there... Trangula," Orongo called out. "What are you doing in Plotal territory?"

A prisoner pointed at Lee and said something in a language no one understood.

"Jamie, think you can talk to him and see what he said?" Jakla asked.

Jamie shrugged. "I'll give it a try, but I have no idea what he just said." He approached the Trangula that spoke. *No one can understand your language. What did you say?*

The Trangula tilted his head and stared at Jamie when he heard him in his head. *We come for him.* The Trangula nodded toward Lee.

"He said, we come for him, meaning my father," Jamie explained.

"Ask him how they travelled here," Orongo asked.

Did you walk here from your kingdom? Or did you ride a pakow? The Trangula Jamie talked to shook his head. *We run.*

"He said they ran," Jamie explained, somewhat confused.

Jamie took it upon himself to communicate with the Trangula soldier. *My father is a good man. The female that came to you—Augenta—is an evil person. She will get you all in big trouble and start a war. Is that what you want?*

The soldier nodded. *We come. Many, many of us. We steal your females! We kill your soldiers!*

"Well, I tried to talk some sense to him. I told him Augenta was a bad person and she'd cause a war. He said a lot of them were coming. They would steal our females and kill our soldiers."

Jakla, Jor-Dan, Orongo and Trakon conferred.

"Do we want to send him back with a message?" Jor-Dan asked.

"Tell them if they want war, we will be happy to oblige," Jakla about roared out.

"Augenta doesn't know we have more hungry borjos," Trakon reminded them. "And let's not forget the diwal dogs."

"We have a pack of diwals we've been feeding," Jakla added.

"They aren't as well trained as your dogs, but so far, we've had no accidents."

"What do we want to do? Return the one and keep the other?" Orongo asked.

The men nodded.

"Jamie, tell that one if they want war, we will be ready for them," Jor-Dan offered.

Jamie started. He had never been close to a war, or even a fight, back home. "Are you sure?"

"I'm afraid so," Jor-Dan said, with a nod.

Jamie turned to the Trangula he spoke with. *Tell your king if he wants a war, we will be ready for him.*

"Release that one," Orongo told the Plotals holding the two prisoners.

They let the Trangula go, and he ran swiftly into the forest. The other tried to join his partner, but the Plotal soldiers held him firmly.

"Put him in the cage with the other one," Orongo instructed.

The soldiers dragged the Trangula away.

"Send an image of the Trangula to all the kingdoms so the people can be on the lookout for them," Jor-Dan explained.

D'laine, Lee, Dannin and Stanley approached the military group. Trakon squeezed D'laine's shoulder.

"We prepare for war," Trakon announced.

CHAPTER FOUR

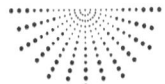

Sander, a weaver in the hosk building, took it upon herself to make beautiful collars for the borjos with their names embroidered on the fabric. Ekka's collar was a brilliant blue. Foota's was orange. Ehtuta's was silver. Grasko's was green, and Dundo's was purple.

The weaver came to the palace to request an audience with the royal family and was led to the salon where the family met. She stopped several feet inside the doorway after the guard presented her. She tapped her heart in respect, and handed out the collars while she explained what she did.

"Your majesties. The royal borjos are part of the army, are they not? I felt that you needed a distinct way to identify them from the ground," Sander explained. "I hope you approve of my craftsmanship."

"Sander, these are lovely!" Kitry exclaimed.

"Thank you, my queen! While you may not be able to read their names from the ground, their colors can identify them," the weaver surmised.

Trakon rubbed his fingers over Ehtuta's collar. "I would like an armband with my borjo's color for when we go into battle."

Jor-Dan nodded. "Yes. I like that idea." He turned to Sander. "Do you think you could make arm bands, Sander?"

"Certainly, sire. Those would be very easy to create. I'll make them in various sizes for different riders," she announced. "I also thought of the same color wraps for the borjos legs, and a wrap for around their bellies to protect them from ground laser fire and other projectiles. Do you think they would wear them?"

"Yes! They would love them!" Jamie exclaimed. "When I explain what they're for, they will be thrilled."

Sander took her leave, and the family passed around the collars.

"I like it when people take the initiative," Kitry said.

Three days later, Sander and two other women from the weaving building delivered the borjos' apparel.

"Jamie, call Ekka to the courtyard. Let's have a dress rehearsal," D'laine said, with glee.

They all walked to the courtyard and Jamie called his borjo. Ekka circled overhead and came in for a soft landing, wrapping his wings into his body.

Jamie held out the collar. "Ekka. Sander made you this collar. It has your name on it." He pointed out the embroidering. "She also made you some protective wear." He pointed to Sander.

The borjo sniffed the collar.

"Let's put it on you. Can you lower your head for me?" Jamie asked.

Ekka lowered his head and Jamie flung one end of the collar over Ekka's neck and grabbed for the end under his neck.

"How do I make it stay on?"

Sander came forward, a little nervous. She had never been this close to one of the creatures. "I wove smart buttons into the cloth. Do you see them?" She pointed them out to Jamie.

"Oh, yeah." Jamie pressed the smart button, and the collar fastened around the borjos neck. "Wow, Ekka. That's beautiful! Let's try these other things on you. There're these wraps for your legs and one that goes around your back and covers your belly. That way it protects you from anyone shooting at you from the ground."

Ekka looked over at Sander and snuffed.

Jamie looked at the weaver. "Ekka said he's honored to wear your cloths."

Sander patted her heart, a little flustered at the beast's acknowledgment.

They finished dressing Ekka in his finery. It took a little finagling to get the rear leg wraps in place because his back legs were shorter than the front.

"When I make new leg wraps, I'll create the back ones a little smaller than the front ones," Sander said, as she took a mental picture of how they fit the borjo and made a note of how to adjust future back leg wraps.

Trakon helped get the belly wrap put in place. He climbed up on the borjos' back and draped the material so that both ends hung down at Ekka's sides. He slid off the borjo and helped Sander secure the wrap at Ekka's belly. The weaver tugged on the fastened wrap and it held secure.

"Wow!" Jamie yelled. "Go fly so we can see what you look like from the ground."

The borjo leapt into the air and flew over the kingdom, wide and far. He returned to the courtyard and flew overhead.

Sander studied the borjo and nodded. "Looks like a good design. I don't think there's any way the cloths would fall off him."

The entire family and extended family stood in the court-yard, hands shielding their eyes, and watched the colorful borjo glide through the air.

"Call the others, Jamie. Let's get them all in their collars and wraps and see how they all look together," Kitry suggested. She turned to Sander. "You should be proud of your work, Sander."

The weaver's face brightened to a rosy glow. "Thank you, your highness!"

Ekka settled in the courtyard. Foota flew overhead. She saw all the family members and someone she didn't recognize.

"Come down here," Jamie yelled. "See Ekka's new battle gear? Don't you want to be like him with your own color?"

After a few circle glides, the wayward borjo landed. She sniffed at Ekka's wraps then turned to Jamie.

"This is your color, Foota. You'll be in orange—like the color for fire," Jamie explained. "Lower your head so we can put this on your neck."

Foota actually cooperated through the entire dressing of all the wraps.

"I think she's sitting taller," Kara observed. "Like she's proud of what she looks like."

"You're right," D'laine said. "We can only hope it improves her disposition."

When the other borjos landed, La'gar'ish's teeth clacked a warning.

Jor-Dan patted his dog. "It's okay, La'gar'ish."

The dog eyed the borjos. Grasko spewed smoke and a tiny flame toward the dog.

"Stop it!" Jamie thumped Grasko's snout. "Be friends. Borjos and diwals are protectors of Ebscalon."

After the animals calmed down, they dressed Ehtuta, Dundo and Grasko. Then all five borjos took to the sky and flew overhead.

"This was a good idea," Jor-Dan said, while nodding his approval.

Marrak came out of the palace and looked up. "The borjos have clothes?"

"Yes. Now we will be able to tell them apart," Jor-Dan said.

"Just don't decide to dress up the pakows!" Marrak joked.

EVERYONE PILED INTO THE DINING SALON AT DINNERTIME AND the majordomo summoned the servers. After their plates were piled with food and the eating began, the conversation rolled out.

"I've met with my advisors. We decided it would be a good idea to send a squadron of crestriders across the kingdom on rotation. We don't want to get caught off-guard with these doski and Trangulans," Jor-Dan announced.

"That's a good idea," Victor said. "I have seen nothing in the immediate future, but I may be unreliable until I get a better idea how my gift works."

"What about at night? It gets so dark at night you might not see anything on the ground," Lee asked.

"Have the borjos be the night scouts," Stanley suggested. "They have excellent night vision."

"They sleep at night, don't they?" Kitry asked.

"Not always," Jamie said.

"Now that we know what the Trangula and the doski look like, we can share their images with the borjos," Trakon determined. "We could rotate the borjos so that the five of them are on nighttime watch duty on different nights."

"I like that idea," Jor-Dan said, with enthusiasm.

"What about if we're attacked?" D'laine asked. "We know nothing about the doski or the Trangula. Do they have weapons? Ships? How do we defend ourselves by not knowing?"

"We have the army, the dogs, the borjos, and good weapons," Lee stated. "It's too soon to worry."

"We've never been in a war," Brian pronounced. His eyes sympathized with his sister.

"We haven't either," Stanley remarked. "None of the Eartholians here have been in any war, unless Ben was and we don't know about it. I'm willing to open the gate on my mind and annihilate the Trangula."

"Unfortunately, you'd most likely wipe us all out," Treikie declared, as she elbowed Stanley in the ribs.

"I'd like to take a quick trip to the cave and do a little more searching," D'laine informed them. "Now that I can read old Tholian, and who knows what else, I'd like to go back and see what we can find. Maybe there's more information tucked away."

"I'd like to go back also," Stanley pointed out.

"Let's see if there's anything else with my picture on it," Lee stated.

"When do you want to go?" Trakon asked.

"Why not right after breakfast tomorrow?" D'laine asked.

"Can I come with you?" Brian asked.

"Me too?" Victor asked.

AFTER BREAKFAST THE NEXT MORNING, STANLEY *STEPPED* THE group to the cave.

"Why don't we spread out, and each take a section?" D'laine suggested. She did this thing in her head, wiggled her fingers, and the dark corners of the cave lit up like daylight.

"How'd you do that?" Trakon asked.

She shrugged. "I don't know. Things just come to me."

Everyone spread out and began looking through artifacts, scrolls and everything in their section.

"Will you look at this?" Lee exclaimed, surprised at his find. A bust on a pedestal looked like him, only with a close-cropped beard. He ran his hand over the face of the bust, then over his own face. "It's like my face."

"Don't let it go to your head, daddy," Brian joked. "Not everyone is fit to be a king."

They went about their business. After about a hour, a pile of items were in the center of the cave. D'laine was going through a basket of scrolls, unrolling them one at a time and skimming the contents. Anytime she found something interesting, she tossed it toward the pile.

"Wow! Look at this! It's me and Jamie! I'm positive!" Brian declared. He rushed over to his sister with a silver-lidded box.

Everyone gathered around and looked the box over as D'laine turned it in her hands. "Nope, that's not the twins. I think that's you and Jamie," she replied.

"There has to be scrolls in this cave that explains this prophecy," Trakon insisted. "Where'd you find that, Brian?"

Trakon joined Brian in his section, and they carefully picked through artifacts.

After another hour, they headed back to the palace with their finds. After everyone picked up the items they found, Stanley brought them back to the main salon. They spread out their discoveries on the coffee table for everyone else to see.

The servers came into the room bearing little pots of pudding. They passed them out among the family members.

"No, thank you," Brian asserted, his lips curled in disgust.

"You're being ridiculous, Brian. It's not THAT pudding," Jamie joked. He eyed Trakon, but his brother-in-law seemed okay.

Lee summoned the server. "I'll take his, wench."

"Wench?" Ethaderia stammered. "Did you just call her wench?" She stared at her husband as if he had grown a second nose.

Lee blinked. "Of course not. I'd never debase a woman like that."

"Oh, yes you did, daddy," D'laine pronounced. "I can't believe that word came out of your mouth."

Lee appeared confused. "I swear, I don't recall ever saying that!"

Stanley stared at Lee, not saying a word.

D'LAINE GRABBED UP THE SCROLLS, THEN HEADED TO THE LIBRARY, where she spread them out on the table. With her new ability to read old Tholian, going through the scrolls was much easier. It was a much more dense language compared to modern Tholian, much like the old language in the Bible back on Earth.

"More scrolls from the caves?" Ugo asked, excited. The old scholar pulled up a chair and sat beside D'laine.

"Yes. There are so many scrolls in the cave, but it would take forever to go through them all. Why don't you come with us the next time? You read old Tholian, and we could pick what we should bring back."

Ugo rubbed his hands together. "I would love the opportunity to visit the cave with you."

D'laine unrolled a scroll. They placed lightweight books on the corners to hold it down. She and Ugo carefully read through the beautifully scripted lines. It was slow going trying to make sense of the old language.

"This mentions *the two*, but it isn't clear what two they wrote about. It could be you and your husband-prince, your twins, or your brothers," Ugo remarked.

"At least we found something. We just need to find more references, then we might be able to piece something together that we could understand," D'laine insisted.

"Remember, we need to piece it together in the correct order, or it could be all for naught," Ugo proclaimed.

CHAPTER FIVE

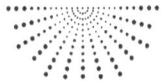

*E*thaderia woke up, stretched and yawned. She turned on her side and faced Lee. She was startled at the uncharacteristic change of her husband and scooted away, squeaking in fear as she got out of bed. She grabbed her robe and stabbed her arms into the sleeves before stepping into her house shoes to make distance between her and the bed.

There's something wrong with Lee! She broadcast to the family. She stared down at the man in her bed with the trimmed beard.

Brian and Jamie crashed into the room.

"What..." Brian stopped beside the bed and stared at his father. At least he thought it was his father.

"Daddy?" Jamie asked.

Ethaderia heard pounding at the front door and Eglabado questioning who was there. He opened the door, letting in visitors.

D'laine ran into the bedroom with Trakon, Pup and Chatter on her heels. She stared at the man in the bed who resembled her father. "Daddy?"

The room filled with the rest of the family members and close friends; Eglabado stood in the doorway.

Lee stirred in the bed, his eyes blinked open. He sat and stared at the gawking eyes.

"Be gone with you! Where's Chamblin? Send him in to attend to me at once!" Lee demanded. He looked around the room as if seeing it for the first time. "Where am I? These are not my quarters in the palace! How dare you stand before your king! Take to your knees!"

D'laine grabbed Trakon and Ethaderia's hands and backed away from the bed, then dragged them out of the room. Everyone else followed.

"What happened?" D'laine whispered.

"I'm not sure. I woke up just before I called out to you. He didn't have a beard last night!" Ethaderia whispered.

"That bust of King Jangston triggered something," Stanley pointed out. "Where is it?"

"In the salon, on a side table," Ethaderia stated.

"Remember the "wench" comment?" Stanley asked.

"Something about that cave triggered this other life," Victor babbled.

"Chamblin!" Lee called out. "Assist me!"

"What do we do?" D'laine asked.

Eglabado cleared his throat. "I could pretend to be Chamblin."

"I don't think King Jangston will approve of his clothes. They are not befitting a king," Ethaderia exclaimed.

"Let me have someone bring a full set of Jor-Dan's official robes," Kitry said. She called out silently to her assistant.

"I'll assist in his morning preparations," Eglabado explained.

The manservant entered the bedroom. "I'm sorry to be tardy, your highness."

Lee eyed Eglabado. "Where are we, Chamblin? I don't recognize this place. Are we visiting one of the lesser kingdoms?"

"Yes, your majesty. We are visiting King Jor-Dan and Queen Kitry in Ebscalon," Eglabado assured the king.

"Ebscalon? Never heard of it. Is it a new kingdom?"

"No sire, it used to be Ciert, before the Great War of Taylon," Eglabado explained.

"Ciert? Yes… yes. I recall Ciert. Why did they change the name? Did I give them permission? What is this about a war?" Lee asked. He clearly was confused.

"The war was over fifty years ago, sire," Eglabado replied. "You have been in a silent stilling for several years and just now woke up. I'm sorry to inform you that Chamblin is dead. My name is Eglabado."

"Silent stilling? Chamblin dead? What of my queen?"

"She is with her cousin, Queen Kitry," Eglabado said.

Lee nodded. "My beautiful queen. What of my son? My heir?"

Eglabado kept his worries hidden. He called out in a semi-panic. *Who is his son and heir? He's asking about him?*

Trakon will have to play that role, D'laine sent.

Trakon entered the room. "Father! You are awake!"

Lee stared at Trakon. "Iverdon! Why are we here and not at the palace?"

"The palace was damaged. We thought it best to transport you here, to mother's cousin for protection," Trakon explained.

There was a tap at the door. Ethaderia entered wearing one of Kitry's royal outfits. She carried one of Jor-Dan's ceremonial robes.

"Darling! I'm so happy to see you alert this morning. Why don't we get you prepared for breakfast? We can walk over to the palace and join my cousin and her family," Ethaderia exclaimed.

ETHADERIA AND LEE WALKED OVER TO THE PALACE AND ENTERED

the dining salon. No one knew what to expect. When they entered the room, everyone looked up and stared at Lee.

"To your knees!" he boomed out. "I may have been in a silent sleep, but I am still the King of Thol!"

Jor-Dan stood. "We no longer do that, your highness. This is the custom now." He thumped his heart with his fist.

They all stood and performed the royal acknowledgment.

"Why did that change? This chest thumping is not respectful," Lee pronounced.

"Your elderly advisors could no longer safely kneel and return to their feet, so you declared this new custom," Jor-Dan explained.

Lee thought about it. "Yes, that makes sense. You may sit."

Everyone sat. They truly tried to keep the worry off their faces. No one knew how this role change would play out. As each new layer presented itself and the occupants of the room took on new roles, it was a challenge to keep up. Brian and Jamie appeared stricken that their father didn't know who they were.

One of the palace guards appeared in the dining salon doorway. He thumped his chest. "Prince Herish and Commander Bosakin," he announced.

Herish rushed into the room. "Is everything okay?"

Jakla stepped into the dining salon. "I heard a distress call..."

Lee flinched. "Invader!" He reached out and mentally grasped Jakla by the neck and lifted him clear off the floor.

Everyone was in a momentary state of shock. They snapped out of it as Jakla's choking caught their attention.

"Daddy!" D'laine caught herself using the wrong name. "King Jangston! The Plotals are our allies now!"

"Father, this is Commander Jakla Bosakin. He is a friend," Trakon yelled. He looked around wildly, at a loss about what to do.

"What in the world is going on?" Herish yelled.

Stanley swiftly approached Lee. He pressed a finger into Lee's temple and the man crumbled to the floor.

Jakla thudded to the floor, rubbing his neck.

Jor-Dan rushed to his friend. "Jakla, please don't take this as an act of war."

They spent the next several minute explaining what happened, while Stanley levitated Lee, brought him into the main salon and settled him on a sofa. Everyone followed. Ethaderia fretted. She sat on the edge of the sofa and brushed some hair off Lee's forehead.

"What if Lee doesn't return?" she asked, as her eyes watered.

Kitry hugged her cousin to her. "We'll find a way."

"King Jangston seems to have powers that normal Tholians don't have," Victor expressed. He looked at the Tholians in the room, including Jakla. "Does anyone recall Tholians having powers like this?"

"No!" Jor-Dan insisted. "Most Tholians are normal people. The Kudaja morph, but that's about it where powers are concerned, isn't it?" He looked at Kitry, then Ethaderia, Herish then Jakla.

"I have never heard of any humans having powers," Jakla commented.

Herish shook his head. "Our morphing isn't a special power, it's more a trait some of our people have."

Lee stirred on the sofa. His eyes blinked open, and he saw Ethaderia's worried face. "Ethy, I've got a blinding headache."

She threw herself onto his chest. "Oh, Lee. I'm so glad you're back!" Ethaderia sobbed.

He hugged her to him. "Where'd I go? Was I gone long? What's wrong?" He nudged her to move and he sat up. He glanced around the room at all the worried faces. Then he noticed his clothing.

"Why in the world am I wearing Jor-Dan's ceremonial robes?"

D'laine slipped onto the sofa on the other side of him and patted his back. "It's a long story, daddy."

Everyone settled into the chairs and sofas. Lee got the whole picture in spurts. "I lifted Jakla off the floor?" He looked at the Plotal, not believing a word of it. Jakla was at the very least, eight feet tall, and he couldn't even guess at how much the Plotal weighed. Lee shook his head.

"This appears to be intermittent," Stanley observe. "It began with the *wench* episode. That was shortly after we returned from the cave. Is there anything in your house you brought back from the cave?"

Lee shook his head.

"I suggest we gather all containers and objects, except the scrolls, and lock them away in case there is some influence that calls to the old king," Stanley suggested.

Lee wiped a hand down his face. He stopped when he felt the beard. "What the...? Do I have a beard? Have I been unconscious for several days?"

"That was the first sign that something was wrong," Ethaderia recalled. "When I woke up this morning and saw your beard, it was very disturbing."

"Did I do... or say anything unforgivable... other than try to kill Jakla, that is?

"We had to role-play," Trakon shared. "I'm now King Jangston's son, Iverdon."

"Eglabado is your manservant. He replaced Chamblin," Ethaderia added.

Lee stood. He approached the Plotal. "I'm so sorry, Jakla. I have no memory of what I did."

The Plotal Commander grasped Lee's arm in the Tholian welcome. "It was not you, Lee."

D'laine approached Stanley. "Tell me what you did so I can step in if you're not immediately available."

"It's an Egrom thing, so I'm not sure you could replicate it," Stanley said. "I need to discuss this situation with the Egroms."

Stanley stepped out of the room.

"Let's go home so you can shave off that beard," Ethaderia insisted. She hooked her hand through Lee's arm and steered him to the salon doorway.

When they left, everyone let out a heavy breath and sat down.

"I could use a glass of kahl," Jor-Dan stated.

The majordomo entered upon the silent request with a decanter of the Tholian equivalent of wine. He was followed by a server who carried a tray of glasses and a larger vessel for Jakla.

Once everyone had their beverage, they sipped in silence.

"We had to separate the Trangulan from the doski," Jakla announced.

"Were they fighting?" Trakon asked.

"There seems to be class distinctions between them. The soldier would not tolerate being in the same cage as the other one," Jakla explained. "The guards had to pull him off the scout before he killed him."

"This keeps getting more and more strange," Kara said.

"So far, there have been no sightings of Trangula or doski," Trakon announced. "We have crestriders covering not only Ebscalon, but all the kingdom's, including Ta'Byu'Vohon, the Cember Forest and beyond the Ikley Forest."

"We are grateful for your vigilance," Jakla declared.

"All five of the borjos cover the same area at different times throughout the night," Trakon explained. "We just have to make sure they don't eat them if they find them. D'laine and Jamie explained that they need to come back here if they see any Trangula or doski, but I'm not sure about Ekka's mate. Foota still has a wild streak."

D'laine grumbled. "She's doing remarkably better, especially since she received her colors."

"Colors?" Jakla asked.

"Come see," Kitry suggested. "A weaver made colored cloths so we can distinguish one from the other while they are flying."

"I can't believe you dressed your borjos," Herish joked. "Ours better not want clothes when they see your borjos!"

They all left the palace and went to the courtyard.

Lee stood in the bathing room with a towel wrapped around his waist. He stared at the bearded face in the mirror above the sink. "Who are you?"

"He definitely wasn't the man I married," Ethaderia said, as she walked into the room to check on him.

Lee shifted his eyes to the floor. "I'm so sorry about all this."

"Not your fault. It must be some descendant thing because those pictures on the items we found look just like you," Ethaderia reminded him.

"While that may be true, I don't know how that can produce a beard overnight, and having me ranting about being king. I hope Jor-Dan, Kitry and Trakon aren't sorry I'm here, or married into the family," Lee uttered.

Ethaderia wrapped her arms around him. "Oh, Lee. Don't say such things. This is a strange situation—something I hope is behind us now that those items are stored in a vault somewhere."

"Knock, knock," Brian called from the doorway. "Are you okay, daddy? We just wanted to make sure everything is back to normal again."

"I don't like that King Jangston," Jamie said. "It was scary... we were like orphans for a while."

"You'll never be orphans," Lee declared. "Ethaderia will

always be here for you, and you have your sister, Trakon, and your royal grandparents."

"Yeah, but you're our father," Brian insisted. "No one can replace you."

Lee hugged his boys while shutting his eyes tightly. He prayed he never reverted to the old king again.

THE MARKETPLACE WAS CROWDED WITH SHOPPERS FROM NEARBY kingdoms, along with some nomadic Safri creatures, and wandering Plotals that didn't belong to an army. Bartering and haggling took place at booths and shops alike. Suddenly, a woman screamed long and hard when a hand dropped from the sky right in front of her. Blood splattered up onto her dress from the severed wrist. A man grabbed her when she fainted dead away.

A Ciertron guard who had been shopping ran to the scene. His eyes took in the hand on the ground, and he tapped his communicator. "Prince Trakon! A Trangula hand is in the marketplace." He listened. "Not the body, just a hand. Dropped out of the sky."

The guard's eyes scanned the crowd. "I need a sack or a basket." Someone procured a piece of cloth and it was handed through the crowd to the guard. He placed the cloth on the ground and used his boot to move the hand to the center of the material.

"Thank you. Someone help this woman to her home when she comes to," he ordered. Then he scooped up the cloth and left the marketplace.

Jor-Dan, Trakon, Dannin, D'laine and Victor stood in the courtyard looking up. The four dogs were standing by, not sure what was going on. No borjos were in sight, but that meant nothing. Enough time had passed for the animal to fly away.

The guard approached, fisted his chest, then the diwals were on him.

"DOWN!" D'laine commanded, using The Voice.

La'gar'ish and Chatter dropped to their bellies, eyes closed, submissive.

Pup was in bloodlust.

Guards came running from all directions, lasers drawn and ready.

Jor-Dan held up his hand to stop everyone from distracting D'laine in the tense moment.

D'laine grabbed her diwal dog by his scruff and forced him to the ground with a constant reverberation of The Voice rolling off her. Pup snapped out of it and cowered as flat as he could get to the ground. After a minute, he lifted his eyes to D'laine's face to check the atmosphere of his beloved human.

The men surrounded the guard who was attacked.

"Hovery, are you all right?" Trakon asked. He looked the man over and balked when he saw blood on his uniform. Then he noticed the severed hand had fallen loose from the cloth. He let out a huge sigh of relief.

"That was a close call," Dannin voiced.

"Too close for comfort," Jor-Dan stated.

"I'm okay. Wasn't expecting that," Hovery babbled. He was clearly shaken up.

The diwals teeth chattered because of the bloody appendage.

They all looked down at the hand.

"Yes, Trangulan," Dannin declared. "Someone dispose of that before we have an incident with the dogs."

A guard stepped forward, retrieved the cloth from Hovery and picked up the hand.

"Make sure you wash your hands and anywhere else you get blood on you," Trakon reminded the man. He focused on Hovery. "You were in the marketplace when this happened?"

"Yes, but I didn't see it drop from the sky, only where it landed, that's all," Hovery reported.

"Go change your uniform, and wash up," Trakon ordered.

Buffy stood beside Victor, her tail tucked between her legs. He reached down and patted her back. "It's okay, Buffy."

She looked up at his face for verification and relaxed a bit.

"Up," D'laine ordered. "Sit."

The diwal dogs got to their feet, then sat. Buffy plopped her butt to the ground. The dog's eyes darted around, nervous.

"I'm going to summon the borjos," D'laine announced. "Did anyone notice if that Trangula hand had any material to identify whether it was a scout or a soldier?"

"There wasn't enough left to hold any material," Trakon explained.

Come to me! D'laine sent to the skies.

Everyone's eyes were skyward. The five borjos showed up, one by one.

Down, D'laine ordered, more gently so they would not drop from the sky.

They spiraled down and congregated in the courtyard, all sporting their cloth finery.

Everyone spotted the blood on Grasko's front leg guards.

"Okay, how do we want to go about this?" D'laine asked the men. "I can ask him to take us back to where he grabbed the Trangula. But I've got to remind them that while they can eat them, they need to let us know immediately when they see them, otherwise, they won't be good spotters."

"Remind them of their duties first," Jor-Dan suggested. "Then question Grasko."

"Do we need Jamie?" Trakon asked.

D'laine hesitated for a moment. "Yeah, he should fly Grasko to reinforce the rules. Ekka will understand."

Jamie came running down the walking year from his new home. "What happened?"

They explained what happened in the marketplace. Jamie noticed the blood on Grasko's leg wraps.

Did you eat a Trangula?

The borjo dipped his head slightly as if he suddenly remembered the rules.

Can you take us to where you grabbed him?

The borjo snuffed out a reply.

Did you see other Trangula?

The dragon-like beast shook his head.

"Okay, he admits to eating a Trangula, but didn't see any others. He'll take us to where he grabbed him," Jamie reported.

"Okay, have him lead," Jor-Dan stated.

"Grasko would be honored if you rode him, Jor-Dan," Jamie declared.

"You don't think you should ride him?" the king asked.

"No, he's okay," Jamie answered.

Jor-Dan turned to the guards that remained in the courtyard. "Follow us in crestriders. When we get to where this incident occurred, fan-out and scour the area far and wide."

The guards pounded their chests and took off running to the ships. Jamie, D'laine, Trakon, Dannin and Jor-Dan climbed on the backs of the borjos. They lifted off the ground and Ekka allowed Grasko in the lead position.

CHAPTER SIX

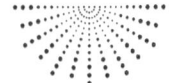

*S*tanley lounged back in the chair swing he rigged and had installed in his suite. His big brain churned through scenario after scenario, charting different outcomes. After more than a hour of contemplation, he slid out of the chair and stepped to the vast cave, then silently stood there.

His brain sent out feelers until it found what he searched for. Stanley walked toward the recesses within the cave.

"Light," he uttered.

The cave lit up as if both the suns were overhead.

He studied the contents in the corner. There was a large carved cabinet against the wall. He approached the cabinet and studied it, opened the door and stared at the shelves of priceless heirlooms. Stanley closed the doors, looked around the back edges of the cabinet and tugged the right side.

The cabinet slid smoothly away from the wall, exposing a dark inner chamber. The scientist stepped over the dark threshold and brought the light with him. The hidden cavity housed trunks filled with precious stones and jewels. Pots filled with what looked like gold and silver coins, and maybe some bronze coins, filled shelves along a wall.

Stanley wandered among the bounty no one knew existed. The large inner cave was filled to overflowing with priceless Tholian antiques. There were technological objects among the treasures.

"I would not be surprised if I found Jimmy Hoffa in here," Stanley joked.

He continued to peruse the contents of the room until he found what he searched for: King Jangston's crown. The gold crown had six points decorated with jewels he thought must be rubies. It sat in a clear case. He knew it wasn't glass, but suspected it was created from agrin tree resin. He used his knuckles to tap on the case. It was thick and seemed impregnable.

To be on the safe side, he manifested a container from the Earth world—a bomb container used to transport a bomb away from the public safely. He figured it would help shield the crown and suited his purpose.

Stanley opened the bomb container. He carefully lifted the crown in its clear case and set it inside the container. Once satisfied, he closed the container and latched it. He then stepped back to his suite in the palace to wait for Jor-Dan to return from the military reconnaissance he was conducting.

THE BORJOS FLEW ACROSS FIELDS OF MOSS, FOLLOWED BY A FLEET of crestriders. Grasko veered off to the Northeast, skirting around Ta'Byu'Vohon. The Ikley Forest was thinning out when Grasko dipped and spiraled down. Jor-Dan covered his face with his arms as the borjo headed straight for a tree. Grasko snatched a Trangula out of the tree.

Jor-Dan hit his communicator and broadcast to everyone in the flying party. "Trangula are hidden in the trees!" Jor-Dan patted Grasko. "Good boy, Grasko!"

The borjo dropped the Trangula. They heard his screech all the way to the ground, then a thump. The creature did not move.

Laser fire came from the trees. The crestriders returned fire with lasers from the front of their crafts. Several doski scouts and Trangulan soldiers dropped to the ground, dead.

Trakon, flying on the back of Ehtuta, approached an agrin tree from the top, looking down into the heavy branches laden with leaves. As they flew over it, Ehtuta's hind feet grazed the topmost branches. Suddenly, a head popped out. The Trangulan fired his laser as the borjo passed over the tree into free space.

The wild shot hit Trakon. He flipped over the borjo's head and free-fell, the ground coming up quickly.

D'laine screamed as she witnessed her husband fall, surely to his death.

Ehtuta dove. He tucked his wings tight to his sides, and snatched the prince of Ebscalon out of the air, only feet from the ground. He changed his trajectory and smoothly unfurled his wings, then came in for a smooth landing on the ground where he gently deposited Trakon.

"Trakon!" D'laine screamed.

The other four borjos landed and everyone ran over to Trakon. He was out cold. At first, D'laine thought he was dead, and could not stop hyperventilating as she sobbed loudly. She dragged his head onto her lap.

Jamie ran to his sister. "It's going to be okay, D'laine."

Dannin knelt beside Trakon and checked him out. "He's alive. Probably fainted during the fall, or could have been knocked out by the shot." He rocked him onto his side so he could see where the prince was injured.

The laser shot hit him squarely. Dannin found the point of contact between Trakon's shoulder blades. His suit smoldered, but the shot did not penetrate the indestructible material. The force of the blow was enough to unseat him from the borjo.

Jor-Dan knelt beside D'laine. "Are you okay? Can you heal him? He will be in a lot of pain when he awakes."

D'laine wiped her face with her hands. "I'm sorry, I thought I lost him. All brains went out the window. I didn't even stop to think I could fix him."

Jor-Dan patted her shoulder. "Shock does terrible things to a person."

"Okay, let's lay him flat on his stomach," D'laine said.

Jamie moved out of the way.

First, Dannin pressed the smart buttons, and the material clacked back to a regular uniform. Then he and Jor-Dan held Trakon up while D'laine scooted back. They settled him onto the moss with his head turned to the side.

D'laine stood on her knees at his head and hovered over him. She spread her hands on the scorched material and sent healing heat into the area under the uniform. Her hands triggered the uniform to self-heal. D'laine lifted her hands so the material could finish its procedure. The scorched mark was replaced with newly woven material. In the end, there was no sign whatsoever that the uniform was anything but brand new.

A tuft of moss just a few feet from Jamie, flew up in the air as a Trangulan fired his laser weapon and missed.

"Get Trakon out of here!" D'laine screamed.

Ehtuta roared out a blast of fire, followed by Ekka and Grasko getting into the revenge. The agrin tree went up in flames, along with the Trangulan who screamed as he burnt to a crisp.

Jor-Dan and Dannin grabbed Trakon under his arms and pulled him over to the borjos. Dannin hefted Trakon over Ehtuta's back. D'laine climbed up behind her husband and held onto him.

Everyone else climbed onto their borjos. Dundo was riderless, so he stayed behind and circle the trees.

Ehtuta flew like a speed demon back to the palace. He

spiraled down to the ground right in front of the palace entrance, while the other borjos landed in the courtyard.

Palace guards came running. They grabbed a hold of Trakon and got him off the borjo. D'laine slid to the ground, patted Ehtuta and kissed his velvety snout.

"Good borjo, Ehtuta. You saved your prince."

The borjo nudged her.

Stanley appeared at the entrance, took in the scene and stepped up to Trakon and the guards. "Here, let me. Where should I take him, D'laine?"

"Our suite. I have a little more work to do on him, then he can rest," she explained.

Stanley levitated Trakon up the stairs and down the corridor to their suite. D'laine scooted ahead and opened the door as Kitry ran up to them, followed by Lee, Brian, Victor, Kara and Darren.

"He's going to be okay?" Kitry asked, fraught with worry. "Jor-Dan said he was shot."

Jor-Dan and Dannin approached along with the family members.

"The Trangulan weapons can't penetrate the war uniforms, thank Thol!" Jor-Dan declared.

"Even with the healing, I suspect he will be very sore for a few days," Dannin mentioned.

Stanley settled Trakon onto the bed after D'laine and Kitry turned down the covers. They pressed the release buttons and tugged the suit off him. D'laine crawled onto the bed and knelt in front of his head. She placed her hands firmly onto the area between his shoulder blades, and heat penetrated deeply. She moved her hands out further and treated the area to his sides, then his shoulders and the back of his neck.

"I think that should do it," she said.

"Okay, we'll let him rest for now. He's in your capable hands," Kitry claimed.

"Let's have a military meeting downstairs in the salon," Jor-Dan suggested. With that, everyone but D'laine left the suite. The door closed quietly behind them.

D'laine pressed the release buttons on her suit, undressed and climbed back into bed. She pulled up the covers and cuddled Trakon.

"Never again!" she muttered, before she fell into a deep sleep.

EVERYONE CONGREGATED IN THE LARGE SALON. JOR-DAN PRESSED his smart buttons and his war uniform transformed back into a normal uniform. Dannin followed suit. Jamie needed a little help, then everyone was back to normal.

"We have to warn all the neighboring kingdoms that the Trangula take to the trees like their tree people ancestors. We would not have been aware of this if it hadn't been for Grasko. He dove into a tree with me on his back, ripped a Trangulan out of the tree and dropped him to the ground," Jor-Dan reported.

A murmur of great concern washed through the room.

"And, if it hadn't been for Ehtuta acting fast, Trakon would have fallen to his death. These borjos are to be celebrated as the greatest intuitive beasts of all time," the king declared.

"I'm glad I wasn't there," Kitry exclaimed. "I would have died on the spot from seeing Trakon shot and falling through the sky."

"We have a lot to do," Dannin said. "I'll fly to Ta'Byu'Vohon, then the Cember Forest and warn the Plotals, Egroms and the Kudaja, so they will be on the lookout for any doski scouts or the military Trangula."

Jor-Dan rapped Dannin on the shoulder. "Thank you, Dannin. I'll strategize with my advisors on how to move forward."

"Do you want me to go to the Cember Forest?" Lee asked.

"That would be great," Dannin replied. "I'll share the visuals with you so you can pass them on."

Dannin and Lee left the palace.

"I'll be with the Visionary," Victor announced. "Hopefully, I'll be able to see an outcome."

Stanley made eye contact with Jor-Dan and spoke into his head. *I need to see you in private. Tell no one. I'll be in my suite.*

The king started, then nodded. He turned to Kitry. "It would be best if you reminded the guards at the nursery about the protocols for an attack. We don't want to be surprised." He gave her a peck on the lips and left the room.

JOR-DAN TOOK THE STAIRS TWO AT A TIME AND CLIMBED TO Stanley's suite. He was curious and worried at the same time. The scientist wasn't known for theatrics, so Jor-Dan mulled over what could be wrong.

He tapped on the closed door, and Stanley opened it before Jor-Dan could tap again.

"Come in." Stanley stepped aside to let the king enter his suite, then he closed the door. He led Jor-Dan into the living area and invited him to sit opposite him.

"Something's wrong, isn't it?" Jor-Dan asked, as he settled into a comfortable chair.

Stanley tilted his head slightly. "Not exactly wrong. Let's just say I think I have a solution should war come to the gates of Ebscalon."

"What's the solution," Jor-Dan asked.

"Today I went to the cave to search for something. I knew it was there, but I wasn't sure if I could find it or not," Stanley started. "Do you recall that large cabinet in the dark corner at the rear of the cave?"

Stanley could see Jor-Dan thinking about the cave, going

through the vast expanse of it, then his mind's eye found the cabinet.

"If you stand on the right side of the cabinet and grab the back of it, you can swing it out. There's a secret chamber that contains an immeasurable amount of wealth," Stanley explained. He shared a mind-picture.

Jor-Dan gasped. "It's difficult to understand why all this was gathered there. The outer cave contains priceless artifacts from fifty years ago, and I don't understand why they weren't missed —why scholars didn't document the mysterious disappearances of these things."

"We may get to the bottom of that mystery one day, but for now, we have a key that may turn the tides of this anticipated war," Stanley stated. He stood, walked to his bookcases, stooped down and opened a cabinet on the bottom shelf. He withdrew the bomb container, walked back to the sofa and placed the container on the table between himself and Jor-Dan.

Stanley unlatched the container, opened it and pulled out the clear case with the crown.

Jor-Dan gasped. His eyes widened as he met the scientist's eyes. "Is this what I think it is?"

Stanley nodded. "This outer case is from Earth. It's what they use to contain bombs when they are discovered so they can transport the bomb away from civilians and buildings. I figured it would be the best device to contain any powers we aren't aware of. We can't have Lee turning into the king at a moment's notice."

Jor-Dan visually inspected the crown. "I wonder what causes the transformation."

"There's no telling, but I know that Lee can't return to the cave. There are most likely any number of things that could trigger an episode. But, I seriously feel that this crown will more than transform Lee. I'll bet there's some magic in this thing that will save the kingdom."

Jor-Dan nodded. "Yes, I agree. Keep it hidden away. Even though you have it double protected, I would not invite Lee to your suite as long as it is in residence here."

"Perhaps it would be better off in your treasure room?" Stanley asked.

"I'll guide you," Jor-Dan stated.

Stanley grabbed the container and tucked it under an arm, then placed a hand on Jor-Dan's shoulder and *stepped* them to the fortified chamber.

"This is Ebscalon... and Ciert's treasures. Once every ten years we have a celebratory event where we will display some of the treasures. No one but the royal family and the Visionary have access to the room, so it is safe from temptation," the king explied.

Stanley set the box on the table and looked around. "I don't want it to be obvious, just in case." He noticed a shelf that contained a dark corner, even with the glow lights at full strength. "There. That's where it will be safest." He carried the box over to the shelf and set it down. He stepped back to check it out.

"That's a perfect place," Jor-Dan agreed.

They both nodded, then Stanley stepped them back to the ground floor so that the king could gather his advisers.

CHAPTER SEVEN

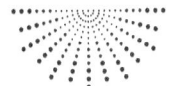

*A*ugenta sat on a throne beside King Custuf in a large round room. Their thrones were made of wood, with wooden seats padded with plain hosk fabric in a drab green and brown. The sides and backs were made of branches that came up from the floor and curved outward. The room itself was created with split agrin tree trunks that were connected together with agrin sap. She thought that they'd crafted the roof from a thick canvass, but wasn't sure.

Dozens of yort-like buildings were connected to the Trangula palace where citizens lived. Military Trangula were abundant, along with doski scouts. Periodically, Augenta spotted a human woman. They were hard to miss in their skimpy Trangulan clothing, which she knew would have made Kitry turn crimson. These Tholian women wore shiny metal collars with a chain that attached to the wrist of a male Trangulan. They were held captive for breeding purposes.

Augenta didn't like what she saw, but as the new queen, she would wait until her influence over Custuf was complete. Then she would make changes, beginning with the ridiculous crown of twigs on her head. As she looked around at the subjects, the yort itself, and even the king, she imagined jewel-toned rugs, pillows—even walls. Those silly helmets the military and doski wore, looked more like bowls than protective headgear. And they obviously did not have the modern military uniforms that transformed into impenetrable war gear with communication devices built in.

She had made some minor changes since she showed up at the Trangulan kingdom, which was walled with what looked like thin branches. A rampaging pakow wouldn't even hesitate to plow through the gates.

The king hadn't had a throne or ceremonial robes when she arrived before him. Augenta cleverly showed how she could help him elevate himself. Granted, thrones made of sticks was not her idea of anything kingly, but it was a start. And Custuf now wore garments that separated himself from his military subjects. Still, she had a lot of work to do to get this place turned into what she considered livable.

The first thing that helped her establish herself was the fact she stood more than a head taller than the king, and she appeared regal. And her brusque way of communicating, which everyone frowned upon in Ebscalon, had Custuf eating out of her hand. She explained to the king how badly she was treated by the royals. Then she told him how her daughter had turned her back on her, and her soon-to-be son-in-law had completely taken over. Augenta rapidly blinked her eyes to hold back tears, unsuccessfully. She practically had the Trangulan king on the floor showing his belly to her.

Augenta was not happy that her devoted Joseffa had abandoned her and had run off with Guerson, the caravan leader. Those two were most likely dead by now. She could not imagine them surviving the trip back to Ebscalon without her supervision.

CHAPTER EIGHT

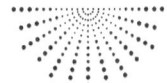

A couple of hours later, Trakon stirred. He groaned and rotated his neck and shoulders. D'laine woke, fuzzy-headed, then remembered what happened. She rolled to her side, got on her knees and looked her husband over.

"How do you feel?" she asked.

"Stiff... sore," Trakon stated. "What happened?"

"Do you remember getting shot and falling off Ehtuta?"

"I remember thinking I was going to die as the ground got closer," Trakon recalled.

"Your borjo saved you," D'laine said. Her eyes misted. "I thought you were gone, Trakon."

He grunted as he turned to his side, got on his knees and pulled her into a hug. "Looks like I have another day, wife." He kissed her with passion.

When they parted, D'laine ran her hand over his back. "Let me tend to your muscles. They're tight right now, and unless I get your muscles to relax, you're going to be in agony later."

Trakon laid down on his stomach.

"Put your arms by your sides," D'laine instructed. Then she scooted up behind his head and spread her hands onto his back.

JOR-DAN SUMMONED THE FAMILY TO THE DINING SALON FROM their various places. He tapped his communicator and hailed Dannin. "Where are you right now?"

I'm just returning from Ta'Byu'Vohon, he said over his communicator.

"Come to the dining salon and join us for dinner," Jor-Dan requested. "We can each provide updates so we don't have to repeat the information."

I'll be right there, Dannin answered.

Trakon and D'laine took their seats at the table.

"How are you doing, son?" Jor-Dan asked.

Dannin hurried to a vacant place at the table and sat.

"I'm much better. If D'laine hadn't worked on my muscles, I would most likely not be out of bed," Trakon answered.

Lee, Ethaderia and the boys entered the room and took their seats.

"Sorry we're late, I had an extensive meeting with the Egroms," Lee replied.

"We'll discuss this situation in between bites," Jor-Dan said.

The servers entered with the offerings for dinner: roasted par, braised sidel, three different vegetables, and round discs of bread. After everyone helped themselves from the platters and bowls, the majordomo and servers retreated.

Ethaderia noted that Jamie took his vegetables. Now that he understood the vegetables weren't the cause of the stomach rumblings, he dove in.

"We discovered an important strategy of the Trangula today," Jor-Dan explained. "I never would have expected them to hide out in the trees, for one. And we discovered that their weapons are inferior."

Stanley slid into his chair. The majordomo noted his appearance and disappeared into the kitchen. He returned moments later with a plate of the scientist's preferred foods and set it on the table in front of him.

"Thank you. I'm sorry I was late," Stanley whispered.

The majordomo nodded, then retreated.

"They are only inferior if they aim for the battle uniform. If they got lucky and hit a part of the body that wasn't covered, their lasers would do the job," Stanley stated.

"We will have to make sure everyone suits up from head to toe," Trakon declared. "They can't wait until the last minute to activate their headgear, including the face shields."

"Dannin, what did you accomplish at Ta'Byu'Vohon?" Jor-Dan asked.

"I met with Commander Bosakin and his generals. They studied the mind-movies I shared showing the doski being snatched out of the tree by the borjo," Dannin explained. "They're concerned that they might not be able to discern the enemy in the Ikley Forest at the back of their city. The doski's uniforms blend into the colors of the trees and moss."

"Back home, camouflage uniforms are used by all branches of the military," Lee shared. "They create them just for that purpose, so the enemy has a difficult time noticing the military."

"It sounds like they need some tech equipment up in the trees to detect intruders," Victor voiced.

"It's a large forest," Jor-Dan said, doubtfully.

"That may be so, but a device could be placed every so many feet apart and staggered several rows of trees back to cover a wide expanse," Victor explained.

"A motion detector that could specifically pick up their doski or Trangula signature would be ideal," Lee suggested. "Do you have anything like that?"

Trakon, Dannin and Jor-Dan nodded almost as one.

"We have some old technology that we haven't used in a long time," Trakon recalled.

"We'd have to make some upgrades," Dannin suggested.

"We could help with that," Lee said. "The Kudaja would benefit from those as well. While they live in the trees, they might be caught off guard to an attack on the same level as their houses because of the camouflage."

"I spoke with Herish, King Cagmondoore and his advisors," Lee continued. "They will install trip vines that will alert them to an invasion."

"The Plotals could use those in their forest," Dannin explained.

"I'm not sure what good that would do," Lee wondered out loud. "Remember, the Kudaja are sensitive to everything in their environment. Living in the trees gives them almost a psychic connection to the trees."

"For the Plotals, why don't you hang bells on the vines?" Kara asked.

Trakon, Dannin and Stanley shook their heads.

"Too many woodland creatures in the trees, like Brownie, Ben's pet gippe," Stanley recalled. "They'd be curious about anything new, and would most likely set the bells off."

"Oh, well, it was a thought," Kara said.

Lee made a face at Stanley, trying to stop him from saying anything more about the gippe, but Stanley was oblivious.

"A gippe?" Jamie asked. "What's that?"

Lee hung his head. "Stan, I beg you... stop while you're ahead."

The scientist realized his faux pas. He turned to Jamie. "Just one of the many creatures that live in the forests around here." Stanley turned to Trakon. "That old technology sounds like the best bet for the Plotals. Do you have enough of them?"

Trakon hit his communicator. "Hexlon, where are those old tracking devices? Do you know how many we have?"

What do you want those old things for? That's old technology, Hexlon replied.

Trakon explained the problem to Hexlon.

We have more than enough to plant along the Ikley Forest, but we're going to have to test them. Probably do an upgrade. Do we have time?

The men around the table thought about it, then nodded.

"Yeah. Lee, Stanley and Victor will help with the upgrades. We need them as soon as possible. Can you dig them out of storage?" Trakon asked.

Sure thing. I'll have them in the middle shop tomorrow.

Jor-Dan nodded. "Okay, that's partially taken care of. Lee, what about the Egroms?"

Lee leaned his forearms on the table, ignoring his dinner. "They seem to think the Trangula military aren't good at strategizing, and the doski scouts follow only simple directions from their military superiors. They drifted off into that inner dialogue they do with each other when I showed them the visuals of the doski in the trees. They're not sure where they got the laser weapons."

Jor-Dan appeared thoughtful. "I'm not too worried about the Plotals or the Kudaja. The Trangula argument is with you, Lee, because of Augenta's influence. Then again, we don't know what she's told them. They are our friends, so to her skewed way of thinking, they could also be considered her enemy."

"But wouldn't she think all the kingdoms that rejected her are her enemy?" Kitry asked.

"It's hard to tell what the Trangula will focus on. We don't know the size of their army, or anything about their leadership," Jor-Dan stated.

Stanley felt a summons. He stood. "Be right back." He *stepped* from the room and vanished. Moments later, he returned. He emptied the contents of his hands onto the table to show four translators. "The Egroms upgraded the translators. D'laine, here's yours." He handed it over.

Stanley picked up a translator and walked over to Darren.

"Let's switch yours out." He pressed on the translator that was behind Darren's ear. It wiggled loose.

Darren squirmed and laughed. "That feels so weird!"

Stanley pocketed the old translator, picked up the new device and pressed it to Darren's head. It settled into place. "Trakon, say something. Let's make sure Darren can still understand Tholian."

"What should I say?" Trakon asked.

"I understand you," Darren answered. "What's new with the translators?"

"You know those Egroms. Always keeping secrets," Victor mentioned.

Stanley replaced Brian and Jamie's translators. "There, all done."

The boys didn't miss that the adults were trying to control their smiles. They suspected the new translators were vastly different.

"Are you going to track us now? Is that what these new translators are for?" Brian asked, with a hint of attitude.

"All translators have location information," Trakon said. "It's a built-in feature in case someone gets lost."

"Oh, I didn't know that," Brian replied. "So, what's so special about these?"

"Your translators were old technology. Absadul tweaked some things so the movies would be more panoramic, and that languages would be easier to learn," Stanley announced.

"That's good," Jamie declared. "I like learning different languages."

"You do?" Lee asked, surprised. As far as he recalled, Jamie never even attempted Spanish back home.

"If you're finished eating, you can either join us in the salon, or go play," Ethaderia commented.

"Why don't you go outside," Kara suggested. "It's a nice day."

The boys needed no more encouragement. It wasn't

everyday they were excused from the table so easily. Once they were out of earshot, more conversations continued.

"School is on," Stanley snickered. He turned to D'laine. "You have the advanced courses."

"How will we know they're learning?" Kara asked.

"Make an outline for each grade, then after a while, ask each of them something that would be new to them. If they answered the question correctly, the educational movies are doing their job," Victor explained.

They all smiled with glee.

THE NEXT MORNING BETWEEN BREAKFAST AND LUNCH, DARREN, Jamie and Brian carried what looked like a cantaloupe, as they jogged into the palace. No one was in the salon or the dining area.

"Let's go see if Grandma is weaving in her room," Brian said.

They jogged down the hallway and turned the corner to Jor-Dan and Kitry's suite. Jamie knocked on the door, then just went inside.

"Grandma, are you here?" he called out.

"Back here!" Kitry called out. He could hear the smile in her voice. She liked being called grandma.

They walked through the rooms to where her weaving loom stood. Shelves held different colored skeins of yarn in different strand thickness.

"We found one of daddy's favorite fruits, grandma!" Jamie blurted.

Kitry looked up from her current work, a huge smile on her face. Suddenly, an alarmed expression crossed her face. "Brian! Do not accidentally drop that pod!" She tapped her communicator. "Bring a three-man ship to the palace immediately!"

She stood, her flowing gown swirling around her legs and

feet. She slipped into a pair of palace slippers and headed for the door. "Come with me. Be very, very careful with that pod. Do not drop it or make it crack in any way!"

"What's wrong?" Brian asked. He pressed his nose to the pod and sniffed. He didn't smell the fruit of the cantaloupe like he would have back home. "This doesn't smell like a cantaloupe. Maybe it's just not ripe enough." Brian turned to the boys. "We probably shouldn't have picked it yet."

They rushed after Kitry, out of the palace to where a crestrider hovered, waiting. They followed her up the escalator stairs and she took the controls. The escalator lifted and tucked itself away. The ship rose into the air and zoomed over the city gates.

"I didn't know you could fly a ship, grandma!" Brian proclaimed. "Awesome!"

"Where did you find that pod?" Kitry asked. "Can you direct me there?"

"They're to the West," Darren pointed. He showed her with his mind.

"What is this pod, if it isn't fruit?" Brian asked.

"It's a spider pod," Kitry explained. "When the spiders crack them open, they rush out and go about their business, which is good for Thol. They keep the balance between good and bad insects, and even small rodents. But, there are thousands of spiders inside that pod."

It alarmed Brian. He gripped the pod and swallowed a loud gulp. "Oh, no."

Jamie and Darren backed away from Brian.

The ship rushed through the air to the location Darren shared with Kitry. After several seconds, Jamie and Darren pointed.

"Over there," they both pointed out.

At the edge of the forest, vining foliage spread across the moss. Pods were attached to the vines with thick stems. Some vines had attached to the trees, and the pods hung suspended in the air. It was a bizarre sight.

Kitry hovered the ship. She turned to Brian. "Okay, carefully lean way over the edge of the ship and drop the pod."

Brian followed the queen's directions. The three boys clutched the railing and leaned over the side. The pod splattered on the ground. Thousands of spiders rushed from the pod.

The spiders jumped!

They jumped very high.

Kitry raised the ship, but not before a spider jumped up and gripped the edge of the railing.

The boys screamed!

Kitry opened cabinets and searched for something.

"Brian, raise the ship higher," she yelled.

Brian used his mind to elevate the ship.

Kitry found what she was looking for—what looked like a piece of board—wider than a ruler and thicker. She rushed to the railing where the spider clung, trying to attach more of its legs to the rail to hoist itself up. She whacked it repeatedly until it gave up and fell to the ground.

Kitry let out a sigh of relief.

The boys watched the scene way below them, which was like something out of a horror movie, but in real life. Spiders were fanned out across the moss.

They jumped.

They fought each other.

They raced away in different directions.

"What are they doing? Are they crazy?" Jamie asked.

"Some of them will travel a long distance away to establish their territory. They usually create their community with ten to twenty of their kind," Kitry explained.

"They won't hurt the hosks, will they?" Brian asked.

"No, they actually help the hosks by eating any bugs that would otherwise infest the hosks' fur," Kitry said. "Same with the pakows. You should always check your pakow for spiders before mounting, especially if you were riding in a field."

Darren shuddered. "Do they bite people?"

"Only if you show aggression towards them," Kitry reported. "Typically, if one climbs up your suit, it will nibble on your hand to identify you. Then he'll jump down and leave you alone. If you're friendly, he'll transmit your identity to the rest of his nest. Likewise, though, if you're mean, he'll send out a warning."

"Very scary," Darren muttered.

Kitry set the crestrider to the direction back to the palace. She turned to the three boys. "Remember everyone telling you how dangerous this environment is, and to proceed with caution?"

They nodded, wide-eyes staring at her face.

"There's a reason for the warning. If you come across some-thing you are unfamiliar with, take precautions. Reach out and ask someone before you approach whatever it is," Kitry lectured. "If you had dropped the pod and the spiders swarmed all over you, and the three of you started whacking them off, they would tell each other you were an enemy."

"Are they poisonous?" Jamie asked, his voice squeaking in fright.

"No, but if you got bitten twenty or thirty times, you'd be a big swollen mess, wouldn't you?"

They nodded, shocked.

The ship approached Ebscalon. They sailed over the gates and Kitry landed the ship in the courtyard. She tapped her communicator. "The ship is ready to be housed. Do a thorough check for spiders."

They all walked inside the palace.

CHAPTER NINE

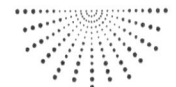

*J*or-Dan invited his friend Orongo and his family for dinner. It had been close to forty years since the men had socialized, and he was eager to reestablish their friendship. The entire Bramstone clan and extended members were in the large salon awaiting the arrival of the guests. The guards pinged the king when they arrived. He and Kitry left the room and went to the palace entrance.

They got there just as Orongo's pakows were handed over to the attendants.

Jor-Dan stepped forward. "Welcome, Orongo! I'm very pleased to meet your family!" He and Orongo firmly clasped arms.

"It is good to be here," Orongo declared. "May I present my mate, Naphelia; my son Plodu, and my daughters, Fingo and Zerke."

Orongo's mate and daughters nodded respectfully to Jor-Dan. His son clasped the king's arm in greeting.

"May I present my wife, Queen Kitry," Jor-Dan said.

"It is so nice to meet you, Orongo. Jor-Dan hasn't stopped talking about you since he reconnected with you at Ta'Byu'Vohon. Naphelia, I see you have your hands full with three children. Plodu, Fingo and Zerke, you will discover some playmates in the salon," Kitry said, as she shooed the children inside. "Why don't we go inside and you can meet our family members and close friends."

Kitry led the way inside with Jor-Dan and Orongo following the group, their voices booming laughter. She ushered everyone into the large salon where everyone stood upon their entrance.

Jor-Dan stepped forward. "This is my friend Orongo Draganza, his mate Naphelia and their children Plodu, Fingo and Zerke."

Kitry took the helm. "This is our son Trakon, his wife D'laine, her father Lee Jackson and his sons Brian and Jamie. They are Eartholians, along with Stanley Daigle and Victor Bennet, Eartholian scientists; Victor's wife Kara and their son Darren, Stanley's girlfriend, another scientist, Treikie Soluveia, and Lee's wife, my cousin Ethaderia."

There was a riot of conversations as everyone mingled. Kitry was happy to see the boys including the Plotal girls in their conversations. The men huddled, and the women grouped together. Naphelia was a little shy at first, but warmed up once she realized that no one seemed to stand on formalities regarding royalty. After that, she had a good time getting to know the human women.

D'laine and Kara were intrigued to discover that female Plotals wore similar clothing that flowed like Kitry's sari-type clothing on their large scaly bodies. Their small breasts were barely visible under the clothing.

The majordomo entered the doorway. "Dinner is ready." He led them to the larger dining hall, more conducive to sit their party. When Plotal or Egroms dined with them they required larger chairs, place settings and drinking vessels.

The women approved the seating of the children at the far end of the table. The adults settled themselves, partnered up.

Shortly thereafter, the servers brought the food, already plated, and settled the plates on the table in front of each guest and family member.

"I can't believe you found such a beautiful woman to marry you," Orongo kidded Jor-Dan.

"Ha! Look who's talking!" Jor-Dan laughed. He looked across the table to Naphelia. "Your mate was a big mess in his younger days. Were you forced into this mating?"

Naphelia chuckled, which sounded like coughs. "He says the same about you. Actually, that the two of you sought trouble all the time, and were taken to task for it by your commanders."

"Those were the days," Jor-Dan recalled, grinning from ear to ear.

"I'm surprised we lived through some of them," Orongo admitted.

"Why don't the Plotals have crestriders?" Stanley asked.

"We're slowly getting technologically savvy," Orongo said. "After all these years wandering with our tent cities, we have settled down and are building a city for our people. We hope to have all the modern conveniences soon enough."

"There are still Plotals that can't make the change to living in buildings," Naphelia explained, sadly. "We are trying to be as gentle as possible with the transition, but not everyone agrees with the modernization."

"Will they go nomad?" Trakon asked.

Orongo thought about the question. "I don't think so. They know what it's like from all the years we wandered. They may change their minds the more they are around the development of the city. If we pull them into meetings and social events, they may give it a try."

"We are creating a marketplace, gardens—so many new things we never experienced before," Naphelia exclaimed, excited. "Once a Plotal gets used to civilized living, they will never want to revert to our former way of life. I would not want to tromp around Thol on a pakow and live in a tent again."

"Our people are eager to take part in the marketplace, and welcome visitors from all the kingdoms," Orongo shared. "It is a new experience for us as we show the world our friendlier side, and prove that we, too, have much to offer."

Dinner ended, and the party moved back to the salon.

"Can we go to our house? I want to show Plodu and his sisters my room," Brian asked.

Lee turned to Orongo and Naphelia. "Ethaderia and I have a house nearby. They won't get into any trouble, Eglabado, our manservant will see to that."

Naphelia gave a stern look at her children. "You may go, but you behave like good Plotal children."

Fingo, Zerke and Plodu nodded to their mother, wide-eyed.

"We promise to be good children," Fingo declared. "I'll be in charge."

Naphelia nodded.

With that, the six youngsters raced from the room, not quite running so they would get in trouble, but still at a brisk pace. They exited the palace and ran down the way to Brian and Jamie's new house. Evidently, Lee or Ethaderia had pinged Eglabado, because he opened the door when he heard the feet stomping on the walkway leading up to the house.

"Young masters, and mistresses, I will provide provisions when you are ready for them," Eglabado informed them.

"Thank you," Jamie said, as he breezed past the manservant following his brother, Darren and their guests.

They ran up the stairs to Brian's room and the door slammed shut after them.

Eglabado opened his senses to monitor the young ones under his charge. After a while, Brian's door opened, then the group traipsed to Jamie's room. After ten minutes or so, they all returned to Brian's room. He prepared an assortment of goodies for the group, keeping things simple because of the large hands of the Plotal children.

He figured they would like the Eartholian food, particularly the pizza that the palace chefs had perfected. Besides the pizza, he placed bowls of different toppings they could add to the prepared crust.

The manservant hefted the large tray and climbed the stairs. He sent a mind message to Brian to open his door.

"Oh, wow, Eglabado!" Brian exclaimed. "That looks great. Thank you so much."

Eglabado entered the room and placed the tray on the small table in the middle of the room. "Enjoy!" He exited the room and left the children to enjoy their time together.

"What is that?" Zerke asked. She sniffed the baked pizza crust that was topped with a spiced tomato sauce.

"This is pizza. You'll love it. You can add anything you want to it. Back home on Earth, these toppings would be added to the pizza pie before they baked it in an oven," Darren explained.

Jamie grabbed a slice of pizza and plopped it on a plate. He added some chopped vegetables and meats, then took a huge bite and chewed.

Plodu wasn't shy. He followed Jamie's lead. He cautiously took a smaller bite. His eyes widened, and he made a sort of a low roar. His sisters, not to be left behind, created their own delicacy. After one bite, they were making sounds that showed their appreciation of the new food.

After everyone had finished, Brian stacked all the empty bowls and plates. He grabbed the tray and left the room and brought it back to the kitchen where he found Eglabado.

"Everyone loved their pizza," Brian announced. "The Plotal children never had pizza before and they really liked it."

"I figured it would be a hit. Prince Trakon can't get enough of pizza!" Eglabado joked.

"Do we have any chocolate? I'll bet they've never had chocolate before," Brian thought out loud.

Eglabado opened a cabinet and placed six moderate sized chocolate pieces on a plate. "That's all you get. And, whatever you do, do not tell the prince we have any!"

Brian took the plate and left the kitchen, laughing. His brother-in-law had a serious chocolate addiction and had to be rationed. He climbed the stairs to his room and presented the treat.

"Have you ever had chocolate before?" Brian asked the Plotals.

"No, what is it?" Plodu asked.

"It's like a dessert," Jamie explained. "It's sweet. Everyone on Earth, and a lot of Tholian humans love chocolate."

He grabbed a piece and bit into it.

Plodu took a piece and tried a tiny bite. Once again, he was amazed at the Earth food. He shoved the entire piece in his mouth and mumbled with his mouth full. "I like this chocolate!"

Everyone else dug in. The Plotal children were more than a little enthusiastic over the treat.

"We should make Smores!" Darren announced.

Brian and Jamie's faces lit up.

"That's a great idea! We should meet when it's dark and make a campfire!" Brian said. "Let's invite Cadj, Fazi, Vila and Chacoodi!"

"Do you play with Commander Bosakin's children?" Jamie asked Zerke.

"No," Zerke said. "We do not socialize with them; we only play with our mother's closest friend's children."

"You'd like them. We play with them when we visit Ta'Byu'Vohon," Brian explained.

They all huddled in a circle and whispered secret plans.

THE EBSCALON NIGHT PATROL FLEW CRESTRIDERS WITH lowlights, or they eliminated them altogether as they prowled across the kingdom on the lookout for trouble from the doski and Trangula. Every once in a while, they spotted a borjo soaring over the land.

A crestrider captain spotted suspicious activity and reported in. "This is patrol 2145. Request reconnaissance over sector F-22NW. I detect a campfire and several small individuals. Could be Safri or doski."

"Understood, 2145. Sending a squadron of five your way, flying dark," the command center returned.

2145 waited until the squadron joined him, then he shut down his lowlights and they proceeded silently and cautiously. Once they arrived at F-22NW and saw what was going on, they followed military protocols. They knew they'd cause trouble, but determined it was for the best.

The six ships formed a circle, turned on their spotlights and directed them to the ground. They caught the group of children jumping in circles, laughing and having a wild, good time around the campfire. They screamed at being caught—they weren't too sure who caught them and they were scared on many levels.

2145 decided to have some fun with the situation. "Invaders! You are under arrest! You will board the ships and we will take you to our commander! You, Egrom invader, do not *step* away. We will report you to the Egrom elders! We have your auric signature!"

Escalators lowered. Ebscalon guards in full battle gear raced down from each ship. One doused the fire. One gathered up what was left of evidence. The others escorted the frightened children to the ships. Then all the ships rose into the air and raced back to the gates to where the commander waited.

The ships landed and unloaded their captives. They all huddled in front of the stern-faced commander. Even though he knew the human children, and recognized the Egrom child, he still made their lives miserable.

"State your names and where you are from!" the commander thundered. He eyed Brian.

"You know who I am!" Brian snarked out, filled with an attitude.

"We are following wartime military protocol. State your name and where you are from!"

Brian gulped when he heard *wartime*. "Brian Jackson; Ebascalon."

The commander eyeballed Cadj. He knew full well who he belonged to.

"Cadj Bosakin from Ta'Byu'Vohon!"

All the children were identified. As the proceedings were taking place, a heavy-duty crestrider raced across the sky and disappeared into the darkness of the night.

They marched the children into the palace, which was lit up like daylight.

"You and your stupid idea," Jamie hissed to his brother.

"I don't remember you not agreeing to the plan!" Brian hissed right back.

"I'll be on latrine duty for the rest of my life," Chacoodi whispered.

"My father will enlist me in the army!" Cadj whispered.

"I'll be picking up pakow dung forever!" Plodu whispered.

The girls sniveled their misery as they were marched into the large salon.

Jor-Dan, Kitry, Kestrum, Lee, Ethaderia, Indii (Vila's mother), Victor, Kara and Ghury glowered as the youngsters stopped in front of them. A few moments later, loud footsteps approached the salon.

Jakla, Neska, Orongo and Naphelia entered the room and joined the other adults.

"What do you have to say for yourselves?" Jor-Dan asked.

"This is wartime. You have heard of the threats from the Trangula. You know about the dangers outside of Ebscalon's gates, Ta'Byu'Vohon's periphery, and the Cember Forest. Look at all the trouble you have caused!"

The clear looks of disapproval on the faces of all adults, and the king's words had the children shaking. They knew they were in for it.

"It was harmless fun," Brian declared, meeting his king-grandfather's eyes. The disappointment staring back at him upset him more than any punishment that would be dished out.

"You are grounded, Brian. As are you, Jamie." Lee stewed, afraid to say much more.

"What is grounded?" Indii asked.

"That means no more fun for a specified amount of time. No more running wild through Ebscalon, outside the gates or anywhere else. No flying on borjos all over the place. That also means that Eglabado will have a nice, easy time for several weeks while Brian and Jamie take over the household chores," Lee spat out.

Jakla turned to his children. "You are grounded as well. Fazi, your mother will be relieved that she can focus on the building interiors now that she doesn't have to run the household. You will assume those duties which includes cleaning of the containers for the waste we excrete. Cadj, you will take over the maintenance of the pakow pens, the slop buckets, and grooming the pakows."

Orongo and Naphelia silently conferred for a moment, then Orongo spoke.

"You have dishonored our family and our tribe," he started out. "Fingo, you will be on tent cleaning duty."

Fingo acted like they jolted her with electricity. "But Father, there are hundreds and hundreds of tents..."

"Zerke, you will feed the old ones. Plodu, you will dig and plant the gardens," Orongo lectured.

Zerke was appalled. No young Plotal wanted to feed the old ones. They no longer had teeth and their food needed to be ground into mush, then spoon-fed to them.

Plodu mentally felt blisters forming on his large hands.

Indii was up next. "Vila, you will work in the kitchens in the food prep area until further notice."

The Kudaja girl knew what that entailed. Peeling hundreds of vegetables untold number of times every day to feed the entire city.

Kestrum drilled her eyes into Chacoodi. "You are a disgrace and deserve full-time latrine duty. In addition to that, you will prepare the fires, then scour the village cook-pots after meals."

Ghury stared down Chacoodi. "Every morning you will begin your day with a full hour of meditation. Evidently, you have forgotten the role of the Egroms on Thol."

Victor and Kara scowled at Darren.

"How could you, Darren?" Victor asked. "Consider yourself on full-time kitchen duty."

When all the punishments had been doled out, parents and guardians left with their children in tow.

CHAPTER TEN

$\mathcal{T}$he next morning D'laine noticed that the breakfast crowd was lacking jocular conversations. She, Trakon and Stanley looked over the others at the table, wondering what was going on.

"Did we miss something?" she asked, as she looked around the table.

"Last night, the patrol caught several individuals out in the middle of the field having a celebration, without their parents' permission," Kitry explained.

D'laine, Trakon and Stanley stared at Darren, then they noticed Victor and Kara's tight eyes.

"They did? Who?" Trakon asked.

Kara let out a sigh. "Commander Bosakin and Orongo's children, Brian, Jamie, Darren, Chacoodi, and Vila."

"The patrols caught them dancing around a fire, hopped up on Smores," Victor reported.

"Whose bright idea was this?" D'laine asked.

"Brian's," Jor-Dan announced with a shake of his head.

"I'll bet he's grounded until he turns eighteen," D'laine joked.

"Oh, they're all grounded," Kitry remarked. "Your father

explained exactly what that meant, and all the parents agreed as they sentenced the offenders to the worst punishments they could imagine."

After everyone finished eating, they dismissed Darren to the kitchen. Jor-Dan told how the patrol handled the situation, and how the gate commander took over. They all chuckled, but everyone understood the seriousness of the situation.

"Thank Thol they weren't attacked by diwals, or captured by the doski!" Trakon snarled, as he shook his head.

"I can't believe Brian and Jamie got all their friends into trouble," D'laine said. "Poor Ethaderia. She probably regrets marrying my father. He tried to warn her that the boys were a handful."

"Look on the bright side," Stanley suggested. "The system you have in place worked. This was a good test."

Jor-Dan nodded. "Yes, I see your point. And it was a good thing this was a test run. Now we know how to adjust for a real life-threatening reconnaissance."

Lee and Stanley were discussing the latest documentation they had received from Al Jordan, the reporter from Houston who was now living in Victor and Kara's house. Suddenly, Lee received a hysterical message from Ethaderia. He jumped to his feet with, "I have to go home immediately."

He practically flew down the stairs and stampeded out of the palace. He ran down the walkway to Ethaderia's house and entered to a spectacle. Brian and Jamie were rolling across the floor, pounding on each other. Eglabado tried to pull the boys apart, while Ethaderia freaked out.

With his right hand, Lee grabbed Brian by the neck ridge of his uniform and pulled him off Jamie. "Sit down and don't move a muscle!" With his left, he grabbed Jamie by one of his arms and flopped him over and up so that he was on his butt. "What is the meaning of this?"

He looked Ethaderia and Eglabado over. "Are either of you hurt?"

They shook their heads.

"Who started this fight?" Lee demanded.

"Jamie!" Brian spat out.

Lee glanced over to his younger son. "Well?"

"It's all Brian's fault! No one would be punished if it weren't for his bright idea for everyone to sneak out," Jamie snarled.

"Did he tie you up and drag you out of the house with your mouth gagged?" Lee asked. Jamie said nothing. "I didn't think so. Accept responsibility for your decisions, son. You were taught to comprehend right from wrong. You also know the difference between a prank and a wrongdoing. Additionally, you understand what trust means. Right now, no one trusts any of you kids."

Lee surveyed the room. "Alright, neutral corners! Brian, you stand over there and face the wall. Jamie, you stand over there in that corner. You are not to speak or utter one sound, understand? When your time is up, I'll tell you."

He motioned for the adults to leave the room. They adjourned to the kitchen. Eglabado's face sported two bruises, but luckily, not a black eye. Ethaderia had a scratch on her arm because she was wearing a domestic sari-type garment.

"I'm so sorry, Ethy," Lee expressed. "Are you okay, Eglabado?"

"Nothing like a good brawl to get the heart rate up," the manservant chuckled.

"I'm sure this won't be repeated," Ethaderia said. Then she giggled. "When we have children, I will be fully prepared."

"The boys rarely fight," Lee said. "They should count themselves lucky that they don't have some of the punishments that were handed out by the other parents."

They heard a couple of raps, then the front door opened and closed. Trakon and D'laine entered the house. They saw the boys standing facing their corners. Trakon was going to say something, but stopped when D'laine elbowed him to keep quiet.

Ethaderia stuck her head out of the kitchen doorway and motioned for them to join them.

"Why are the boys in corners? Did they get into a fight or something?" D'laine whispered.

The story was relayed. D'laine noticed the manservant's bruises.

"Let me heal those bruises," she said. She placed her fingers on Eglabado's face, and within a blink, the bruising disappeared.

"Thank you," the manservant said. "That feels much better."

"I can't believe we missed all the action from last night, and now this," Trakon alleged.

"Just wait until your children are born," Lee warned.

Trakon scoffed. "Our children will be disciplined from Tholian genetics."

"What about my genetics?" D'laine asked. "We're not having little robots, or Youngmen. We're having real kids."

"Your genetics will be balanced," Ethaderia pointed out. "Your children will receive good and bad genetic qualities from each of you, Trakon. There's no telling how they'll be, or who they will take after."

"I have to go to the bathroom," Jamie called out.

"You can go to the bathroom, then return to your chores," Ethaderia called back. "Brian, you can return to your chores now."

"I should talk with Kitry about when she plans the celebration to introduce our children," D'laine commented.

"Everyone has recovered from the churling storm by now," Trakon pointed out. "Well, everyone except Patrosym—they'll be rebuilding for several years."

"Has anyone checked to see if Princess Yalalore is still under house arrest?" Lee asked. "Makes me uncomfortable knowing she would probably join the Trangula to escape her circumstances."

"She might escape, but she can't escape the silencing helmet," D'laine noted.

Eglabado excused himself. "I will supervise the young ones since they don't have any experience in their chores."

"I think you should have made their punishment worse than what it is," D'laine pointed out. "When I consider what the others are doing, my brothers have gotten off easier."

"What do you suggest?" Lee asked.

"Brian can help polish the crystals on the ships. They get dirty and there's a team that maintains them," Trakon suggested.

"Jamie's never had to shovel out the pakow pens, or groom them," D'laine noted. "His only interaction is training them and talking to them."

Lee and Ethaderia exchanged a silent discussion.

"We think those are much better ideas, and more fitting to the punishment of the others," Ethaderia said. She turned to Trakon. "Why don't you arrange that for tomorrow?"

"I'm sure Eglabado will breathe a lot easier with them not underfoot and just waiting for a chance to argue with one another," Lee teased.

"Good. Then it's settled. The house will be peaceful once again, and our wayward boys will see what the real world is like," Ethaderia advised.

THE NEXT MORNING STARTED THE WAY THEY TYPICALLY DID AT Lee and Ethaderia's house. Bathe, dress, eat breakfast. After they finished the meal, loud raps sounded at the front door.

Eglabado tried hard to keep the smile from bursting out as he opened the door to the two expected visitors.

Jugdaak and Hexlon stood on the door stoop, smirks on their faces.

"Come in, we've been expecting you," Eglabado said. He opened the door wider to allow the men to enter.

Ethaderia and Lee walked to the entryway and greeted the men.

"Brian! Jamie! Come here," Lee called out.

The sullen boys came to the doorway. Jamie carried a furniture polishing wand, and Brian carried a broom so he could sweep the exterior front doorway. They perked up when they saw who was at the door.

"Jugdaak, what are you doing here?" Jamie asked, squealing with glee. He envisioned working with the pakows, riding and having a good time.

"You're to come with me to help with the pakows," Jugdaak announced.

Jamie looked over to his father and stepmother. "Can I go?"

"You most certainly can," Ethaderia said, overly happy.

Jamie didn't think anything about their responses. He left the polishing wand on the table by the door and raced outside to freedom.

Brian eyed Hexlon. He had met the metalworker before. He was the one who had crafted Stanley's first helmet when the scientist needed his brain shielded, so he wouldn't unintentionally fry anyone close by. That was before Greg Claymore, the Eartholian who traveled back and forth from Earth to Thol more than once, solved the problem. Greg was a healer and lived with the Oolarooloo people near the Aguberro Mountains.

"Your parents have agreed to let you come to the shops to help out," Hexlon said, eyeing Brian.

"Great!" Brian exclaimed. "Let me put this back first." He ran back to the kitchen where the big closet was. On Earth, it was called a butler's pantry. He shoved the broom inside the area for brooms and mops, then took off for the front door, relieved that housework was over with.

"I'm ready," Brian said, filled with jubilation.

"I'll send him back at the end of the workday," Hexlon announced, nodding to Lee and Ethaderia.

They left and the front door closed.

JAMIE AND JUGDAAK ARRIVED AT THE PAKOW PENS. JAMIE VEERED off to the gate and Jugdaak continued on. He stopped, whistled and waved his hand for Jamie to follow him. The seven-year-old wondered where the pakow handler was headed. They walked to an area Jamie had never been to before.

He saw over fifty pakows in their individual pens where they slept at night. The pens did not confine the beasts, and some pakows were leaving to go wander the mossy fields over to the trees where they could get in a good back scratch.

Manure was plentiful in the pens. All told, there were over two-hundred pens. Jamie noticed two of the pakow workers shoveling the manure into containers that hovered off the ground several inches.

Jugdaak approached the pens on this side of the open area. He picked up a shovel and handed it to Jamie.

"You start on this end. I'll show you how to use the hover container so you can move it to where you like it," Jugdaak explained.

Jamie's mouth dropped open in shock. He looked from the sea of pens to the pakow handler in disbelief. How he longed for that furniture polishing wand right about then.

Brian and Hexlon walked over to the shops, but they didn't stop there. They came to a large surface area where the fleet of crestriders charged crystals from the strong sun rays.

"Here's where you'll be working," Hexlon noted. He walked over to a shed and opened it. A table held stacks and stacks of 12 x 12 cloths. A different type of smart closet than what Brian was familiar with, took up a portion of the back of the shed.

"The crystals on each ship need to be wiped down daily, so the dirt doesn't interfere with them charging," Hexlon explained. "When your cloth gets dirty, you need to hang it in the smart closet like this." He showed how to hold one edge of a cloth up to a rod. It sucked the very edge of the cloth into the rod where it was held firmly. There were rows and rows of rods.

Brian looked from the smart closet to the table filled with stacks of cloths to the sea of crestriders. He would never complain about housework ever again.

Jamie trudged through the city gates at the end of a long day. He wasn't sure he could make it to the house. He ached everywhere. His fingers ached. His shoulders were particularly stiff. He couldn't believe the work he did that day. He arrived at the house and slipped inside. He glanced at the staircase and silently groaned. He stunk like pakow dung, so he knew he needed to clean up for supper.

The young boy climbed the stairs to his room. He stripped out of his uniform and immediately hung it in the smart closet so he wouldn't have to smell it anymore. He slogged over to the bathroom he and his brother shared and walked down the stairs into the bathing pool.

He fell face-first into the water. The perfect temperature reinvigorated him. He went over to the edge of the pool and pumped shampoo into his hand, then scrubbed his hair and scalp. This was one of the few times he washed behind his ears without being scolded into doing it. Then he scrubbed up his body with the other soap. He climbed out of the pool and grabbed a towel and fastened it around his waist, then took a smaller towel and wiped his face and rubbed his hair.

By the time he was finished, his brother entered the room. They looked at each other.

"You'll feel better after your bath," Jamie mentioned. He knew exactly how worn out Brian was. He didn't think he could hold a fork—his fingers were so stiff from gripping the shovel.

Without speaking, Brian walked down the stairs into the pool and ducked down underwater. He pushed himself up, then floated on his back.

Lee and Ethaderia were sitting at the table when the boys stumbled into the room and took their seats. Lee tried not to grin like a demented clown, but he couldn't help it. He had never seen his sons so exhausted before.

Eglabado served the meal.

"So, how did your day go?" Ethaderia asked the boys. She quirked up an eyebrow as she glanced from Brian to Jamie, then back to Brian again.

"Who knew pakows dumped so much poopy in those pens! I'm glad that's over with!" Jamie declared, with a huge sigh of relief.

"Over with?" Lee asked. "That's your job for the next six weeks." He turned to Brian. "Did you finish cleaning the crystals on all the ships?"

"No, I didn't finish all the ships! There's only one of me," Brian exclaimed, his eyes wide as he realized his true punishment.

"I blame myself for not starting you off working on the ranch back home," Lee said. "You've lived privileged lives that don't benefit anyone, especially yourselves. How do you think you will develop good work ethics if you've never worked a day in your life?"

He ate quietly for a little while, then set his fork down on his plate. "I expect each of you to do your jobs to the best of your abilities. If you have questions, ask your supervisor. Contribute to the kingdom so the king and queen are proud when they introduce you to anyone who visits the palace. You will develop physical muscles along with mental muscles, and hopefully, you will learn what it means to take responsibility for your decisions and actions."

They finished their meal in silence. The boys climbed the stairs and dropped into their beds, grateful that the day was over with.

Ethaderia patted Lee's arm. "Don't be so hard on yourself, Lee. You went through a difficult time with losing your wife, not knowing if your daughter would survive the accident, and raising the boys while working full time."

He huffed out a sigh. "I know, but the fact is, I dove headfirst into my career, practically abandoning my children for the housekeeper to raise."

CHAPTER ELEVEN

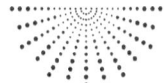

$\mathcal{F}$our days passed with the boys not contributing to conversations during meals. Finally, on the fifth day, Jamie popped up.

"I learned how to take care of the pakows' feet today!" he boasted. "I'm pretty sure their feet must be like elephant's feet, but I'll ask Stanley to find me a book that shows caring for elephant's feet."

"What does that entail?" Lee asked. He had no idea someone had to care for their feet.

"Jugdaak said that wild pakows sometimes suffer from foot problems. Their toenails grow too long if they don't rub them against rocks, and the pads of their feet can get stuff stuck in them and cause infections." Jamie explained in between spearing food and chewing. "I'm not strong enough to trim their toenails, but I learned how to use this wire brush to clean off their foot pads and the top of their feet."

"That must take a long time," Ethaderia said. "With six big feet on one animal—how many pakows are in the pens?"

"Over two hundred," Jamie announced. "Did you know the bottom of their feet had gullies? You have to dig stuff out of them, and their toenails need to be trimmed so they aren't longer than the edge of the footpad. I use a file on their toenails. You have to make sure they're rounded after they're trimmed, not square."

He looked at his father and stepmother with an all-knowing expression. "I'm going to be able to trim their toenails soon."

"Wow, I want to see you doing that," Brian said.

"It takes a team of people to care for just their feet," Jamie explained. He gazed off for a minute. "I wonder if the borjos' nails need trimming?"

"They have talons, not nails," Lee said. He turned to his oldest son. "How is your job?"

"Cleaning those crystals is delicate work," Brian explained. "Hexlon showed me how to use this air blower to clean in between the crystals before I wipe them down with a cloth. Sometimes we have to reattach a crystal that becomes loose."

"How do you do that?" Jamie asked.

"There's this function on the laser weapons that acts like a welding machine," Brian said.

"I remember that from when we had to attach the mirror to the periscope on the palace roof when we were preparing for the churling," Lee said. "You use the eye shield when you do that, right?"

"Yes, otherwise you can burn your eyes, or go blind," Brian said.

"Should you be doing that? It sounds dangerous," Ethaderia exclaimed, as her voice hitched with anxiety.

"It's no more dangerous than cooking," Brian said. "There're directions and rules to follow for everything, for a reason."

At the end of dinner, the boys ran up the stairs.

Lee and Ethaderia looked at each other.

"I guess they're no longer mad at us," Ethaderia whispered.

"Sounds like they're owning their jobs and understanding what being responsible for something really means," Lee noted.

D'LAINE SAT ON THE LUMPY SOFA IN THE TURRET WITH THE darker brown egg on the floor between her feet. She stroked the shell and hummed a nameless tune.

Coming up, Trakon sent, as the door downstairs opened.

Pup jumped out of his dog bed and trotted to the top of the stairs, his tail wagging in greeting.

The guards tapped their chests, and he nodded to them as he took the stairs two at a time.

Trakon patted Pup on the butt, then he walked over to the sofa. He bent down and kissed D'laine on the forehead, carefully lifted the lighter egg out of the nest and settled on the sofa beside his wife.

"The shells are to the point where we shouldn't lift them anymore," D'laine revealed. "They're getting big, and heavy."

"You know, I'd much rather hold them in my arms," Trakon said, with longing. "Leave the shells in the nest."

"Put the shell on the floor," D'laine said. She grabbed a cloth from the arm of the sofa and draped it across her lap, then she reached inside the shell at her feet and gently lifted out their baby daughter.

"Hello, baby," D'laine imparted. She placed the baby on the cloth and wrapped her. She handed their daughter to Trakon.

"It's time to choose their names," Trakon announced. "Traditionally, the male child's name within a royal family should end with the family designated extension. While my parents didn't follow that tradition, I'd like to pick it up with our son."

"What do you want to name him?" D'laine asked.

"Kal-Dan," Trakon stated.

"Kal-Dan." D'laine let the name flow over her tongue. "Yes, I like the sound of that. How about Jesslin for our daughter?"

"Hello, Jesslin," Trakon said, as he carefully cradled the baby in his arms. "Daddy loves you."

D'laine draped the second cloth across her lap, bent over and retrieved their son from his lighter shell. "Oh, Kal-Dan, what a handsome boy you are. Momma loves you very much."

Pup stood before them, tail wagging overtime. He licked the bottom of the baby's feet. The dog's eyes shined, and he wore a happy expression on his normally fierce face.

"Your mother is planning a party to announce our children in ten days, barring we aren't at war," D'laine recalled.

"Might as well. We can't hold our breaths waiting for these doski and Trangula to attack," Trakon admitted.

"Want to switch?" D'laine asked. She gently settled her son in Trakon's lap, and she retrieved her daughter. "Oh, baby daughter, you're going to steal all the boys' hearts when you're a big girl."

"If you think we had it bad with Biggan following us around, our daughter will have a squadron protecting her," Trakon joked. He looked down at his son. "And as for you, no arranged marriage! No one will force our children into a marriage just to please the crown."

"We have a long way to go before we need to think about that," D'laine said.

Trakon shook his head sadly. "Parents plan these arrangements shortly after their children hatch. We will be the first royal couple to stop that nonsense."

D'laine kissed their daughter on her forehead, unwrapped her, and settled her back into her shell. Trakon unwrapped their son, kissed him and handed him to D'laine.

"Grow big and strong so you can protect your sister," Trakon stated.

D'laine cuddled Kal-Dan for a moment, then returned him to his shell.

Trakon stood and placed the shells in their nests, then sat beside his wife. "It doesn't look like they've grown anymore."

"I wondered if you would notice," D'laine said. "I'm certain that their cycle is more Earth-like than Tholian."

"If that's the case, I better start making them beds," Trakon stated, somewhat alarmed.

"They need more than beds," D'laine informed him. She shared pictures of cribs, highchairs, changing tables, and playpens, and explained the functions of each item. "Two of each!"

"I'll have to enlist help from some tradespeople," Trakon declared. "When will we need all these things?"

She could see him mentally evaluating each item, then calculating materials and time. D'laine laid a hand on his thigh to get his focus out of its swirling numbers. "Let's pay a visit to Ben, swear him to secrecy, and have him work with Al to buy these things on Earth. Let's go look at our suite and see where we can set up the nursery."

"That's a good idea—sending for everything. The nests and stands were easy to make. These pieces of furniture are more complex, and I have nothing to go by here on Thol," Trakon noted.

He turned to Pup. "Take care of our children, Pup."

The dog wagged his tail. He was on duty.

D'laine and Trakon filed out of the room and down the turret stairs, walked through the corridors, down the regular staircase to their floor, then entered their suite.

"We have this area back here, but I don't think it will be large enough. We will also need a cabinet for baby clothes," D'laine remembered. "Babies are messy. They need a lot of onesies, and other pieces of clothing as they grow. Then there's the bedding, burp towels—we need furniture, and they'll need a larger smart closet."

"Two of everything takes up a lot of room," Trakon said, resting his chin in a hand. He walked to the wall and tapped it. "There's most likely another suite adjacent to ours. Stay here and I'll go knock on the wall. Tell me if you hear it right here, then let's look it over."

He left the room. D'laine pressed her ear to the wall. She thought she heard a door open, then she heard his tapping. She tapped back, then hurried from their suite.

"Where are you?" she called out as she walked down the corridor.

"In here," Trakon called out. He stuck his head out the door of the suite, grabbed her hand and pulled her through the doorway.

The suite comprised several rooms, similar to theirs. It would provide the twins their own private rooms when they no longer wanted to be attached at the hip.

"Yes, this will do," she nodded.

"I can cut a door through here," he stated. He dug a tool out of his pocket and outlined where the door should go. D'laine stared, amazed that his lines were so precise and straight. She didn't think she was capable of doing that.

"They won't use the highchairs right away, because I'll have to breastfeed them for a while," D'laine explained. "That worries me, because I don't know whether or not I'll have milk. Growing in the shells may have disrupted my natural ability to produce milk. Once they are ready to eat solid food, we can move the highchairs down to the dining salon."

"One thing at a time," Trakon suggested. "When should we have everything in place?"

"Ten days," D'laine said. "Let's go see Ben."

BEN WAS SNEAKY. AND HE KEPT SECRETS. D'LAINE HAD thousands of dollars in her college fund savings account, which was the money source of the debit card. She hoped and prayed that no one had an alert on her account, since she was officially a missing person.

Al had helped with a baby catalog. D'laine and Trakon poured through the pictures and descriptions and ordered two of each, delivered to Victor and Kara's house where Al lived. The spare room filled, then Ben brought it directly over to the palace.

D'laine had ordered clothing, accessories, bottles, nipples, blankets–the "whole nine yards" of everything she wouldn't be able to find in the marketplace. She included cases of formula, just in case.

Luckily, the nursery was secreted away. Trakon had Dreboo cut the doorway between their suite and the twins' rooms. He explained that they were expanding so that D'laine could have a place where she could do her crafts and things.

Dreboo never batted an eye. He knew how these young people were with all the things they liked to create. His daughter had a loom which required a large area that included space for all the supplies. He instructed his team to make a double door for a wider entrance.

When they finished, D'laine marveled that there wasn't even a speck of dust from the construction. Shortly thereafter, the rooms filled with all the boxes Ben had *stepped* over to them. Trakon and D'laine were ready to pull everything out of boxes to assemble what needed to be put together, when Ben held up a hand.

"Allow me," Ben suggested, a large smirk on his face. With a swish of his hand, one box evaporated, leaving a mess of parts on the floor.

Trakon looked at the pile of parts and the written instructions, overwhelmed. He glanced over the sea of boxes. "I'll need you to translate these instructions for me, D'laine. I sure hope I can get all of these things put together in time."

Ben practically cackled. "Stand back." After another swish of his hand, the crib was fully assembled.

"Oh, My Thol! You really ARE a wizard!" D'laine exclaimed. She grabbed Ben in a hug.

Within ten moments, not a box was present. D'laine directed where everything should go. Then she, Trakon and Ben stood back to admire the rooms full of furniture and supplies.

"Ben, I don't know how we would have accomplished this without your help. Thanks so much for keeping the secret, and swearing Al to secrecy as well," D'laine said.

"It was my pleasure. I can't wait until the event," Ben exclaimed.

SOMETIME DURING THE MIDDLE OF THE NIGHT, JAMIE WOKE TO AN alarming noise. He heard scrabbling and scraping outside his window and saw a gigantic dark shape, looming there. He held back a scream, illuminated the bedside lamp and was shocked to see Foota hanging onto the windowsill. He bounced out of bed and ran to the window.

"Foota, what are you doing? What's wrong?"

Baby. Baby help. Help baby.

"One of D'laine's babies needs help?" Jamie asked.

Foota nudged Jamie, acknowledging his correct guess.

"Okay. I'll meet you there. Be quiet, okay?"

The borjo lifted off from the side of the house and flew toward the tower.

Jamie took a moment to shake the cobwebs out of his mind. In an instant, he slipped into his house shoes and robe, before quietly sneaking out of the house. He ran into the palace, up the stairs and around to D'laine and Trakon's rooms. He tapped on the door softly, while calling out in his mind.

D'laine! It's me, Jamie.

The door opened, and Trakon and D'laine stood there, blinking back sleep.

"What's wrong?" D'laine asked, her voice rough from sleep.

"Foota came to my room and said one of the twins needed help," Jamie announced.

Trakon and D'laine flew out the door and ran down the hall to the door to the turret, with Jamie on their heels.

They startled the guards, who pulled their laser weapons out of their holsters.

"Has there been a breech?" Halvid asked. Her wild eyes widened as she grabbed the door handle and yanked it open. She and Amoroso ran up the stairs. Cendi and Zedonia, on watch duty in the turret room, had weapons drawn at the commotion.

Pup never left his bed.

Foota clung to the window, but didn't crawl into the room.

Trakon, D'laine and Jamie ran into the room on the guard's heels. D'laine hurried around the warrior women to the nests. She and Trakon looked over the shells.

"I don't see anything wrong," Trakon noted.

D'laine glanced around the room at the warrior women. "I am swearing you all to secrecy, understand?" She met each of their eyes, including her brother's. "You cannot tell anyone what you see take place here. Do you understand?"

They nodded, nervous.

D'laine ran her hand about an inch over the eggs, trying to determine what the problem was. She felt a flicker inside the dark shell. Without hesitation, she reached inside the egg and pulled her daughter out of the shell.

Jesslin cried and fretted.

The warrior women and Jamie gasped. They surrounded D'laine, Trakon and the baby, staring at the infant in wonderment.

"Oh, D'laine, she's beautiful," Jamie exclaimed.

"This is an Earthling baby?" Keeshi asked. She reached out and traced the tiny fingers.

"Eartholian," Trakon told her.

"What's wrong, Jesslin?" D'laine asked.

She held the baby against her chest and patted her back. The crying slowed to sniffles, then ceased altogether. D'laine adjusted the baby to cradle her in her arms.

The baby smiled up at her, then yawned.

D'laine turned to Trakon. "It seems she wants out of the shell."

Trakon frowned. "Can you persuade her to wait a little while longer? After tomorrow, no more shells."

D'laine stared down at her daughter. "Did you hear daddy? After tomorrow, no more shell. Will you be a good girl and wait patiently?"

"Can she understand you?" Jamie asked, squinting in question. "She's a newborn baby, D'laine. I wonder if she understands language yet."

"Remember where you are, Jamie? Things are much different here, and no one really knows how these children will develop," D'laine explained.

D'laine handed Jesslin to Trakon. She reached into the other shell and pulled out Kal-Dan, their son.

The guards cooed at the baby prince. This was an enormous secret.

CHAPTER TWELVE

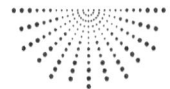

*E*veryone was dressed in their official kingdom finery, and inspected for flaws, or even a speck of lint. Ethaderia fluttered around Lee and the boys. She made sure their emblems were in the correct positions on their uniforms. When she was satisfied, they left the house and walked the short distance to the palace.

Kitry fussed about the throne room, making sure everything was ready. Lee and the boys joined Jor-Dan and Trakon, while Ethaderia rushed to her cousin to assist with last-minute preparations for the gala.

Stanley transported the two nests, along with D'laine, the warrior women, and Pup. The fierce women stood armed around the nests, scanning the nearly empty room.

Pup's teeth clacked when one of the palace staff came too close to the elevated platform, even though he knew who they were. Those men and women rushed away, fear plastered across their faces. No one wanted any type of incident with the dog. They knew it would be over within minutes.

D'laine and Lee had explained to Kitry and Ethaderia a while back that on Earth, blue stood for a baby boy, and pink was for a girl. The exterior of the palace, and throughout the kingdom were decorated with blue and pink bows created from spun hosk silk and agrin sap. The beautiful bows with their trailing ribbons wouldn't even droop in the daily rain showers. The theme continued inside with pink and blue decorations.

The guest arrival time approached. The attendant at the throne room door announced the first attendees: The king and queen of Aveldon, bearing a gift, along with their six delegates. From that point on, the room filled with the six other king-doms, the Plotals from Ta'Byu'Vohon, the Kudaja from the Cember Forest, the Egroms, and the Oolarooloo. The palace staff carried trays of abrajaii in champagne flutes for the guests, and larger mugs for their Egrom and Plotal guests.

Surprise arrivals included the Sagritols. No one had ever seen or heard of a Sagritol until D'laine had been abducted by Tetoni to help them survive as a species.

When the announcer called out the king and queen of the Raagor, a wide path opened down the room. For to touch one of the ice people with the shocking white skin and blue veins, would be deadly. They rode their chuns into the room.

Jamie approached and stood regally before them. He tapped his heart, then made a half bow. The queen's chun remembered him and rubbed its muzzle against Jamie's head.

Jamie couldn't help it. He laughed as he ruffled the chun's fur on its neck.

"Yes, I remember you, too," he said.

The queen stared at Jamie, hissing in their language, trans-mitting a message.

"The King and Queen of Raagor are sorry they can't stay for the festivities, but they fear they would perish in the heat," Jamie announced in a clear voice.

Jor-Dan and Kitry approached Jamie. D'laine grabbed Trakon's hand and moved them in front of her in-laws. They approached the Raagor royals.

"Please stay for a few more minutes while we present our children," she begged, and Jamie translated quietly.

D'laine whispered to Trakon that they should go to the platform, so his parents would follow.

When everyone was in place, Jor-Dan began the formalities with introducing the royals of Ebscalon and their family members.

Victor and Kara stood among the audience, when Ben suddenly appeared beside them with a shocked and excited Al Jordan in tow, and wearing a suit and tie. The journalist's eyes couldn't open any wider if he tried. He took in all the different peoples of Thol in all their finery, the palace—everything, in complete amazement.

The Bennets held off asking questions, while they turned their attention back to the festivities.

Trakon and D'laine stood behind the identical nests which held their eggs.

"Trakon and I would like to present Princess Jesslin," she announced, then she withdrew their daughter out of the shell with shocked gasps from family and attendants. Louder, she announced their son. "And Prince Kal-Dan."

D'laine met the Raagor queen's eyes. The ice-white woman smiled joyfully at D'laine and nodded. Then, she and the king turned their chuns, and they stalked out the door.

Kitry was at a loss for words. As a typical Tholian mother, she had never seen an infant. Her motherhood boiled down to training a fully matured child, around the size of a two-year-old toddler. She now understood the significance of the conversation she recalled with her son and daughter-in-law in the turret room about breasts.

The family surrounded the nests.

"How did this happen?" Kitry asked.

"Instinct," D'laine said. She explained how Jesslin wanted out of the shell during the night.

Ethaderia was almost overcome with emotions as she gazed upon the babies. "Oh, Lee."

Lee squeezed her hand. "They are a lot of work this young."

"I don't care!" Ethaderia stated.

They suddenly remembered where they were and who was in attendance. Jor-Dan and Kitry resumed their places on the platform.

"Well, as you can clearly see, this was a total surprise to us as well as you," Jor-Dan announced. "It appears the prince and princess are excellent at keeping secrets."

There was a round of laughter throughout the room. People raised flutes to the king.

D'laine stepped forward. "My marriage to Trakon, and our joining has produced evolutionary and physiological changes no one expected."

The room fell silent as everyone listened with their full interest.

D'laine looked over the people in the room. "I don't know how many generations it will take, but I suspect that the human women of Thol will once again have live births. Or a combination of egg and live births, as I experienced."

"How can you be so sure?" someone called out.

"I had a conversation with my husband, then with the queen, asking why human women of Thol had breasts. On Earth, breasts are for breastfeeding infants. If Tholian women didn't breastfeed, why did they still have breasts?"

She saw the stumped faces of the guests as they worked through what she said. Then the room roared with conversations.

Trakon, with Kal-Dan in his arms, now swathed in a blue blanket, approached his parents. "Sorry, we wanted to tell you, but thought it best to keep it a secret until the unveiling."

Jor-Dan and Kitry couldn't take their eyes off their grandson.

"We have a suite all set up for them," Trakon said. "Ben helped us with the purchases for the required baby tools from Earth. Wait until you see everything. It takes quite a lot of furniture, clothing and different pieces of equipment to sustain babies."

"It appears that your secrets run deep, son," Kitry remarked. She stroked Kal-Dan's cheek with a finger.

The time approached for Trakon and D'laine to receive gifts. Trakon returned his son back to his nest, then joined his beautiful wife. They stood behind a table, while kings and queens approached. D'laine couldn't help comparing the presents with the priceless items in the cave in the Aguberro Mountains. She and Trakon gracefully accepted each gift and thanked the giver. She had no idea where they would put all these invaluable things.

"We have a treasure room," Trakon whispered into her ear.

When the formalities were done with, Trakon and D'laine retrieved their children and joined the party so that people could see the babies. The warrior women flanked them. Pup put himself between D'laine and Trakon. People gave a wide berth around the diwal dog.

Trakon grabbed a flute of the Abrajaii and handed it to D'laine.

"I can't have any," she told him.

"Why not?" he asked, his face scrunched with questions.

"What I take inside my body in the way of food and drink, is transferred to the babies through the breastmilk. So, it's best that I don't drink right now," she explained.

"We, as a people, have a lot to learn from this experience," Trakon said.

"Come on, let's go find Herish and Meeri," she suggested.

Lee and Stanley approached Ben, Al, Victor and Kara.

"Al! I had no idea you would be here. What do you think?" Lee asked the stunned reporter.

Al tentatively touched the translator behind his ear. "I can't believe it. Any of it. I'm going to be black and blue from pinching myself to make sure this isn't a bizarre dream."

"Al helped with the baby furniture," Ben explained. "It was a lot, let me clue you. Outfitting a room for twins isn't that simple. I figured he deserved a reward."

Al couldn't take his eyes off the Egroms, Plotals or Sagritols. He almost had a stroke when he saw the chuns, which looked exactly like he'd expect a saber-toothed tiger would have looked like.

"He has to return tomorrow night, so I want him to experience as much as possible in a short period of time," Ben announced.

"Will my camera work here?" Al asked. "I want to take pictures so I can sketch out everything for an artist for the book. I won't be able to let the artist see the photos, so I'll have to trace them or something."

Stanley thought about that. "I don't think your camera will work, but we can test it out—only on people. Can't let real photos of the creature-people get out. Come to think of it, I may be able to use my mind to create a portrait that will look drawn."

Trakon and D'laine, and their entourage, approached Herish and Meeri.

"You are so full of surprises," Meeri stated, gently bumping against D'laine. She stared down at the sleeping baby in her friend's arm. "Oh, D'laine... she's so sweet. So beautiful. Now I understand what women of Thol are missing."

Pup's teeth clicked.

Meeri looked down at the dog. "Are you nervous with all these people, Pup?"

He wagged his tail at her.

Several guests approached to see the babies, but kept their distance from the dog and the warrior women.

"When will they walk?" someone asked.

"Not for several months. Babies start moving by crawling on the floor. Then they learn to pull themselves up to stand. They'll practice walking around something they're holding onto. Their first steps are rather wobbly, then they walk and get into everything," D'laine explained.

She looked at the guest. "You should talk to my father. He raised three children, so he can tell you a lot more than I can."

Trakon nudged D'laine. "Why don't we put the babies to bed in their new suite?"

"Okay," she said. She nudged Meeri. "Want to see their suite?"

Meeri's eyes widened. "Yes! I want to see the furniture and everything."

Trakon pinged his father. "We're going to bring our children upstairs and put them to bed. Do you want to see the suite?"

Jor-Dan pinged back, *Yes!* He and Kitry excused themselves from the couple they were talking to and found their son. The group left the throne room and climbed the stairs. Trakon led them past their suite to the twins' suite.

Everyone noticed the dog door cut into the bottom of the door.

"Aren't you worried about someone crawling through that door? It's big enough for a human," Herish exclaimed, with worry.

"Anyone familiar with diwal dogs would have to have a death wish to even think of crawling through there," Trakon suggested. "Besides, the guards will be out here."

He opened the door, and they all entered the suite. The warrior women stayed outside, covering the hallways.

Kitry and Meeri were all over the room inspecting the furniture.

"Your children will sleep in cages?" Jor-Dan asked, dumbfounded.

"They're not cages, they're called cribs," D'laine snickered as she explained. She showed how to lower the one side, then she placed Jesslin in her crib. "When they get bigger, they'll use the bars to pull themselves up to stand. Eventually, they'll be able to crawl over the top of the railing and get loose!"

Jor-Dan tapped the mobile that was attached to the headboard of the crib. The yellow ducks, orange giraffes, and purple elephants bounced and music played.

"That's a mobile," D'laine explained. "It gives the baby something to look at. I can wind it up and it will play a tune and the little animals will move."

"But first, we need to dress our children for bed," D'laine told them. She scooped up Jesslin and carried her over to a dressing table. There was a blanket on the table already, so she laid the baby down. "I had Ben send me human baby diapers. They're disposable, but I'm hoping to find someone in the marketplace to make some cloth diapers. They need to be leakproof."

Kitry studied a diaper and watched as D'laine put one on Jesslin. "Son, are you going to diaper your son?"

Trakon nodded. "My wife has shown me how to do this." He placed Kal-Dan on his dressing table, grabbed a diaper and wrecked it when he was too forceful pulling to expand it. Frustrated, he threw that to the floor and grabbed another.

His mother took it from his hands and demonstrated.

"Son, pay attention." She gently expanded the diaper and slipped it under her grandson. "Think you can do the rest by yourself?"

"I'm a new father, and this is all strange and different from what I expected," Trakon declared, a bit huffy.

Herish watched over his shoulder.

"Put a onesie on him," D'laine told him, as she dressed Jesslin.

"What's a onesie?" Meeri and Kitry asked at the same time.

Trakon pulled open a drawer and held up a onesie. He dressed his son as if he would break, but got the onesie on him without incident.

In the meantime, Pup trotted from one dressing table to the other, watchful of his new charges.

D'laine and Trakon settled the babies in their cribs and covered them each with a soft blanket.

"Show us these other things and tell us what they're for," Kitry said.

D'laine walked up to the playpen. "This is a playpen. The baby can go from the bed to the playpen, or, we can put them in a swing." She showed them the swings. Then the highchairs, then the bouncy swings. Finally, she explained what the rocking chairs were for.

"Just about every mother on Earth has a rocking chair. When a baby is cranky, crying and won't go back to sleep, it helps to sit in the rocking chair, holding the baby. The motion helps them fall asleep," D'laine explained.

Kitry made a mental list: diapers, blankets, onesies. "How will you feed them?"

"I'm going to try breastfeeding them, but I don't know if I will have milk," D'laine said, worried.

Kitry looked alarmed. "They'll starve outside of the shell!"

"Jesslin rejected the shell last night," Trakon explained.

"I have some baby formula in case my breastmilk doesn't come in. I don't know if they will take a bottle," D'laine said. She walked over to a counter that contained a sink and cabinets. She opened one of the cabinets and pulled out a bottle, the nipple and the cap. Then she pulled out a container of the formula. "I can make this one bottle at a time, or two or three in advance, as long as we keep them cool. Then I have to heat the formula before I feed them so it isn't cold."

"There's so much to do with a newborn baby," Kitry noted.

Meeri was dumbfounded, taking in everything—all that D'laine would have to do.

"I'm going to require different outfits while I'm breastfeeding," D'laine remarked. "The babies will need access to my breasts, and nothing I have right now is appropriate."

Kitry added D'laine's clothes to her mental list.

Jor-Dan walked up to his wife. "We should get back to the party."

Kitry nodded. They left the suite with Herish and Meeri following.

CHAPTER THIRTEEN

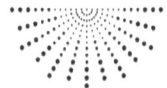

D'laine and Trakon stayed behind, along with Pup. D'laine led her husband over to the rocking chairs. She sat in the first one and he took to the other. He still was not used to the Earth furniture, but the whole parenting experience was new, and he figured he'd catch on soon enough.

"One thing we don't have is a baby monitor," D'laine explained.

"What's that?" Trakon asked.

"It's a device you can carry to any room that lets you listen to what's going on in the nursery," D'laine explained. She noticed her husband wasn't catching on. "If I'm not in the nursery and the babies cry, the baby monitor lets me hear them crying. Then I can come up here to see what's wrong. They may be hungry, or need their diaper changed."

"Oh," Trakon said. He fiddled with his virtual communication controls for several moments. "Problem solved." He showed her the virtual controls for her to set up. "When you hear something, you can look into the room with your mind and see what's going on, and whether to stop everything and rush there. Or someone else could check in on them."

D'laine fiddled with controls and set things up. "We should share this with our guards, and our parents. I think we should assign someone to watch over the twins when I'm not available. They would need training to understand how to feed them the formula, how to change their diapers and clothing, and how the furniture works."

"Good idea. Marrak probably knows someone." Trakon sent a message to start the search.

There was a tap on the door, then it opened. Zedonia entered with Pup's dog bed in hand, and his water bowl. "Where should I put these?"

Pup rushed up to her, tail wagging. He was happy to see his belongings.

"How about putting his bed right here, between their cribs?" D'laine suggested. She took the bowl and filled it with water at the sink. She looked around and saw an indention in a wall and set the bowl down. "Pup, your water is right here."

The dog trotted over to his water bowl and lapped up some water. He rested his dripping chin on D'laine's thigh.

"Glad you approve," she joked, as she wiped her thigh, then scratched his head.

"Instruct the team to adjust their settings to this frequency," Trakon told the warrior woman. "You'll be able to listen to the sounds from the room."

"We are going to keep the door open while we are on duty. Some of us will be in the rooms, others in the hallway. We are adding four more guards to the team to monitor the hallways. When you visit with your children, you can close the door for privacy," Zedonia explained. "Don't worry, we'll introduce them to Pup."

AFTER THE PARTY, WHEN ALL THE GUESTS HAD GONE, TRAKON showed everyone how to adjust their virtual settings for the baby monitor. Then everyone went to bed.

Sometime in the middle of the night, Kal-Dan fretted. Trakon jumped out of bed, grabbed his laser weapon from the side table and rushed through the doorway to the twins' suite. He mentally raised the lights to day-bright.

Pup blinked, then yawned.

D'laine joined him, less fearful. She knew their son most likely needed a diaper change, or was finally hungry from the separation of the shell nutrients.

She adjusted the lights down to where she could see what she was doing. Then she lowered the crib railing and lifted the baby boy out of the crib.

"What's wrong, Kal-Dan? Are you hungry?"

Trakon hovered, stressed, waiting for some crisis to occur.

D'laine brought the baby over to the changing table. Sure enough, his diaper was wet. She changed the diaper, and settled into a rocker to try to breastfeed. Kal-Dan latched onto her nipple. She felt a sensation and realized she had milk. *My milk is flowing* she sent to Trakon.

Trakon positioned his rocker so he faced her. As he watched his son nursing, tears came to his eyes.

When the baby stopped sucking, D'laine mentally nudged Trakon.

Get me one of the cloths, she sent. *I need to burp him.*

Burp him? What do you mean? He found the cloth at the changing table.

After babies eat, you need to put a cloth over your shoulder, pick them up and pat their backs until they burp. Otherwise they might get gassy and cranky.

Oh. He watched as D'laine put the cloth over her shoulder and positioned the baby. She patted his back while she rocked the chair. After three or four rocks in the chair, the baby burped.

As if she felt left out, Jesslin wailed. She was a full-lunged baby girl. Trakon was a nervous wreck as he lowered the crib rail and picked up his daughter.

"Are you okay? What's wrong?" He carried the baby over to the changing table, felt her diaper and changed her. It relieved him that the diaper stayed in place.

D'laine put Kal-Dan back in his crib and raised the rail. She returned to the rocker and Trakon handed Jesslin over. The baby nursed for at least ten minutes. *Do you want to burp her?*

Trakon looked startled. *Me? Don't you have to do that?*

No. If you were feeding her with a bottle, you'd do the whole thing by yourself. Come on, give it a try. As their father, you need to know how to do everything for our children.

D'laine handed over the burping cloth. Trakon put it on his shoulder. *Is this okay?*

Yes. She handed over Jesslin, and Trakon rested her against his shoulder and patted her back. He rocked the chair, and after a little while, the baby burped, and spit up a little on the cloth.

Is she throwing up? He all but panicked.

No, that's normal. Babies spit up. She may have taken in too much milk. This is why you always need a cloth nearby. They can get messy.

Trakon kissed the baby on the head, holding her protectively. *Oh, baby daughter. How I love you so.* After a few more minutes, he stood and returned her to her crib, covering her up and lifting the rail back into place.

You did good, husband.

Breakfast was a chatty affair. Everyone asked questions about the babies.

Why did they reject the shells?

Would they develop like Earth babies?

Did the new parents have everything they needed for their newborns?

"The only thing I can answer with any certainty is if we have everything," D'laine said. "We'll find out as we go along. I'm thinking about documenting the entire process of caring for a baby, the furniture and equipment we have, how to use everything. This way, if Tholian women's birthing process changes, they'll know what to do and what they need."

"I think that's a good idea," Kitry stated. "Our furniture makers could easily replicate everything you brought from Earth, and most likely things you don't have that you discover you require."

Ethaderia wandered in. "Good morning."

"Where's Lee and the boys?" Kitry asked.

"They're still sleeping. I thought I'd come over and see how the babies were doing this morning," Ethaderia replied.

"We are discussing all the needs a baby has," Kitry ventured.

"We have a catalog," Trakon stated, his eyes alight. "It has thousands of things for babies. Diapers, clothing, blankets, sheets, toys—many of the things are duplicated to show different designs, but this is something our craftsmen and seamstresses could use. The dimensions and different sizes would have to be translated though."

"Oh, I want to see the catalog!" Ethaderia exclaimed.

"Why don't we have Ben get several catalogs?" D'laine suggested.

"I'll ask him," Trakon said, sending a message to their wizard.

Ben was their very own Harry Potter. D'laine wished Trakon could watch the movies or read the books so he'd understand exactly what they meant by assigning that wizard title to their friend.

Within a few seconds, a stack of baby catalogs thumped onto the dining table. Duncts later, Ben materialized.

"Are there enough? I can get more," he stated.

Ethaderia and Kitry each took one, then Kara snagged one.

"I'm going to the salon," Kara announced. She and the other women stood. D'laine grabbed a catalog and joined them.

"Want a cup of coffee, Ben?" Jor-Dan asked.

"I always have time for a coffee," Ben joked.

Trakon regaled them with his parenting experiences from the night before.

Victor smiled widely. "Just wait until you have to change a poopy diaper." He roared with laughter.

The prince's forehead creased, along with his father's.

"What exactly do you mean?" Trakon asked.

Lee wandered into the room. "Good morning. Did I miss anything?"

"Grab some coffee," Stanley stated. "We're discussing disgusting baby things."

Lee laughed as he made a cup of coffee and joined the other men at the table.

"Think about it. So far, you've only changed wet diapers. Pretty soon, one of your children will need to do the other— eliminate their bowels," Victor noted. "I remember my first time. Kara was sleeping. I got up and attended to Darren. What a mess. I made more of a mess than what was necessary, because of my inexperience. Thank our Earthly lord, my wife came to my rescue—and Darren's."

"What was so difficult?" Trakon wanted to understand. He had to prepare himself for this seemingly unpleasant task.

"One. Never remove the messy diaper until the baby is cleaned up. Otherwise you make a bigger mess, waste a clean diaper, and even the cloth on the changing table," Victor explained. "Two. You need to wipe the mess off their bottoms the right way, otherwise you're just spreading it around."

The Tholian men appeared shell-shocked.

"We all need lessons," Jor-Dan stated.

Trakon looked mutely from his father to Victor and all the other men around the table.

Stanley shook his head. "I'm not having children."

All eyes swiveled to the scientist.

"You'd better inform Treikie of that. I think she expects a wedding soon," Lee stated. "Stand in line for lessons, Stanley."

The scientist looked frightened at the prospect. Wedding. Children. Messy diapers.

THE WOMEN SAT IN A ROW ON A SOFA IN THE SALON, FLIPPING pages. Some pages didn't flip by as fast as others.

"You're going to need small feeding spoons eventually," Kara suggested. "If Grubio has condiment spoons, those might do, but they have to be small for a baby's mouth."

Kitry added that to her mental list.

"Oh, and a potty chair for each of them, when the time comes," Kara added.

"Potty chair?" Kitry asked.

"Babies need to be trained to go to the bathroom in a smaller version of a toilet," Kara explained. "It takes time to transition them out of diapers to underpants, and even at that point, they may have an accident and wet their pants."

"I remember potty training Brian," D'laine remarked. She turned to the Tholian women. "When babies get to be toddlers —that's when they're walking and beginning to talk—they're too small to get up on a big toilet. They are trained on a potty chair that sits on the floor, and it makes it easier for them. Eventually, they'll transition to the regular facilities. But in the meantime, their potty chair has to be emptied out and cleaned."

Ethaderia's face cringed. "Babies are a challenge, aren't they!"

"For the most part, things will come naturally to you. But, for a race that hasn't experienced live births, or what D'laine experienced with her eggs, it will take time to adjust," Kara said. "I think D'laine's idea of documenting the process is a good idea."

Back in the dining salon, the men still chatted over coffee.

"Our trip vines are in place, and we have tested them," Ben explained. "So far, only one gippe has bothered with them."

"If Jamie could talk to the gippe's in the Ikley Forest so they'd leave the trip vines alone, that would work out for the Plotals," Stanley noted. "It's a good pre-warning system to keep the doski from spying on the Plotals, or attacking from the trees."

Jor-Dan nodded, thoughtful. "We don't have a forest problem. Our main problem is the expansive fields surrounding Ebscalon. Maybe Jamie could talk to the hosks and request they alert us to a doski creeping across the moss?"

Lee shrugged. "He's amazing with communicating with the animals, and they seem to understand what he wants them to do."

Jamie stood in front of Lulu, D'laine's pakow cow. "Just lay down so I can clean your feet."

The pakow cow gave a huff, then knelt down and flopped to her side. Jamie patted her. "This isn't going to hurt. You've seen me work on other pakows before, so what's the big deal?"

He took the wire brush and brushed the top of one of her six feet, and the ankle area. When he finished all six feet, he picked up a hooked knife and started working on the gullies of her footpads. They contained packed moss, dirt, pebbles and tiny pieces of twigs. If they weren't attended to, her feet could swell and become painful, which might lead to crippling.

As Jamie worked on the first foot pad, Jugdaak watched from nearby. A couple of hosks scampered over the pakow. One stood on its tiny hind feet and squeaked at Jamie.

Jamie listened, brows creasing. "You don't know what it is?"

More squeaks.

Jamie jumped to his feet. He manipulated his virtual communication system. "Jor-Dan! A hosk told me something was in the field and he didn't know what it was!"

There was static for a bit, then Jor-Dan's voice boomed out. "Where in the field? Can you show the hosk a picture of a doski?"

Jamie looked at the hosk. "Does it look like this, or this?"

The hosk squeaked its reply.

"I showed him the two pictures. One of the military ones, and the other scout doski. He recognized the scout," Jamie explained.

"Good work, Jamie. Thank the hosk for his action," Jor-Dan said.

Duncts later, a squadron of crestriders silently glided over the fields and spread out. Trakon and soldiers leaned over the railings on the ship, searching the ground. They had several miles to search, but the good thing was, the brown doski scout outfit stood out in the bright field of moss. Trakon and several soldiers beamed down surrounding the scout and captured him.

CHAPTER FOURTEEN

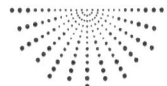

'laine was at Ethaderia's house with her step-mother, Kara and Kitry. Their catalogs, all dog-eared, were in the middle of the dining table.

"I would like to engage Ulavia, the seamstress, for the diapers and the baby clothes," Kitry noted. "I think it would be a good idea for her to see how the current diaper and onesie fits. She may be able to improve the design."

"That's a good idea," D'laine said. "Let's see if she's busy."

Kitry contacted the seamstress. "She'll meet us in front of the palace."

They all left Ethaderia's house with their catalogs in hand, and walked to the palace. They waited at the entrance for the seamstress and watched her approach.

Ulavia tapped her chest to the queen and princess. "Thank you for thinking of me for your project."

"There's nothing remarkable about these diapers and onesies," D'laine noted. "My wedding dress was so beautiful; I feel this is a huge step down for you."

"Nonsense," Ethaderia said. "You realize that Ulavia will be the first to create these things. The twins will require a lot of diapers and clothing. And who knows? Maybe other women will eventually give birth to babies, instead of hatching fully developed and functional children."

They entered the palace and climbed the stairs. As they rounded the corner where the guards were stationed, Pup raced out of the twins' suite with his teeth clacking in full attack mode.

Ulavia screamed.

Guards came running with lasers drawn and fire-ready.

"Pup! Down!" D'laine commanded, with her hand out in front of her. "It's okay, boy. Come. Meet Ulavia. She's a friend." She glanced at the seamstress. "I need you to hold out a hand so the dog can sniff you."

Ulavia squeaked in alarm, but after a moment, she managed to hold out a shaky hand.

The diwal dog's teeth still chattered as he calmed down. He approached the stranger and sniffed her hand. He gave her a little lick and a wag of his tail.

"Okay, I'm glad that's over with," D'laine exclaimed. "Let's go see the kids."

"What's a kid?" Ethaderia asked.

"It's a nickname for children," Kara explained. "I can't remember its origin, but everyone calls the children, kids."

They entered the suite where two of the warrior women stood guard.

"Everything okay?" D'laine asked.

"No problems, princess," Amoroso said.

D'laine lifted Jesslin from her crib and carried her to the changing table. The women had a long discussion about the diapers, the need for leakproof diapers, and the onesies. D'laine showed the seamstress how the disposable diaper expanded at the sides and how the tabs worked to fasten the sides to the front. They left after half an hour, giving Ulavia a diaper and a onesie so she could experiment.

"I'm taking Ugo, the scholar, to visit Ghury," D'laine told the women. "We shouldn't be gone long."

"Go. You need to keep hunting for information on the prophecy," Kitry said.

D'laine walked into the library and found the scholar. "Ready to go talk to Ghury?"

"Yes, princess. Let me gather some things," Ugo said.

They walked outside to a waiting crestrider. Ugo stored his bag of scrolls in a cubbyhole, and D'laine piloted the craft.

TRAKON, THE GUARDS, HIS FATHER, LEE, STANLEY AND VICTOR were down in the catacombs where they had the captive doski in a cell. It was impossible to talk to the creature unless Jamie was present.

Stanley looked into the doski's brain, then shook his head. "What's the point in using these creatures as scouts when they have so little communication skills?"

Jor-Dan shrugged. "I don't understand how this scout is supposed to gather any tactical information and report back to the military or his king."

Suddenly, a loud howl penetrated the basement.

"What's making that noise?" Trakon asked, alarmed. "Is that Pup?" He turned and ran up the stairs, raced to the main staircase with his laser lit in one hand, and his hunting knife ready to gut an intruder in the other hand. The howling grew louder and louder with every step of his approach.

Trakon thundered down the corridor toward the twins' suite. The guards were on high alert. He raced into the room. The guards had every door and cabinet drawer open, searching for an unknown enemy.

Pup stood by Jesslin's crib, mouth open, howling. He shut his mouth when Trakon arrived.

Trakon ran from one crib to the other, looking over his children. He couldn't see any problem. He sank to the floor in front of the dog.

"What is it, Pup? What's wrong?" Trakon asked.

The guards were breathing hard, eyes wide with fear.

Jor-Dan and the others raced inside the room. They looked around expecting to see someone dead, or in custody.

Moments later, Kitry, Kara and Ethaderia ran into the room.

"What happened?" Kitry shouted.

"We don't know," Jor-Dan said.

"Where's Jamie?" Lee said. "He needs to find out what happened."

"He's with Jugdaak at the pakow pens," Trakon said.

"I'll go get him," Stanley said. He disappeared, then returned moments later with Jamie.

Jamie ran up to Pup. "What were you howling about? What's wrong, Pup?"

The dog looked Jamie in the eye. Jamie patted his head. "Good boy."

Jamie stood. "Jesslin has a stinky diaper. You need to change it."

All eyes were on the dog.

Jamie shrugged. "He smelled the poop, and it alarmed him no one was here to change her."

Trakon holstered his knife, then his laser. He hung his head in relief. "Can you explain that next time he should come get someone and not act like someone was about to hurt one of the babies?"

Everyone's shoulders relaxed.

Trakon picked up his daughter and brought her to a changing table. "Oh, she does stink! I wish D'laine were here."

Jor-Dan placed a hand on his son's shoulder. "You should be glad she isn't here, because she would clobber you for saying that. Be a father... and a man and change that diaper."

Kara, Kitry and Ethaderia supervised.

"Use the clean part of that diaper to wipe her bottom," Kitry said.

"Wipe from front to back," Kara said.

"Here's a wet cloth," Ethaderia said, as she wrung out a cloth.

Trakon finally got the diaper changed to the women's satisfaction. He snapped the onesie back into place, cuddled his little girl, then handed her off to his mother. He turned to Jamie. "Does Pup understand not to do that again unless it is a dire emergency?"

"Yeah. I explained it."

Pup returned to his bed, now that things had been handled properly. He yawned widely, turned in a circle and flopped down.

"You'd better get back to work," Lee told Jamie.

"Can I get a snack first?" Jamie asked.

"Be quick about it. Jugdaak is depending on you," Lee said.

Jamie flew out of the room and thundered down the hallway, then the stairs.

Lee shook his head.

"I've had nothing but great reviews from Jugdaak," Jor-Dan told Lee. "He's said that Jamie is one of the best workers he has ever trained—after he settled into the work as work, not as a punishment."

"Well, that's good to know," Lee said. "Both boys have certainly turned their attitudes around. I'm glad they're learning something, and they enjoy the work."

Ethaderia joined them in their conversation. "Do you think their friends will still be friends with them after everyone's punishment ends?"

"That remains to be seen," Lee said.

Kitry waved her hand in the air, dismissing Lee's comment. "They all had a good time up until they were caught. I think they'll shrug it off to not the best-laid plans."

"I hope so," Ethaderia said. "We should check in with the parents and see how the other children are coming along."

THE MEN RETURNED TO THE CELL IN THE CATACOMBS, WHILE THE women retreated to the salon.

"Let's check in with Neska and see how her children are doing," Kitry said.

"Is that Jakla's wife... mate?" Kara asked.

"Yes." Kitry brought up the connection that showed an image of Neska. "Hello, Neska. I'm here with my cousin, Ethaderia, and Victor's wife, Kara. We wanted to find out how your children were doing with their punishments."

"Oh, Queen Kitry, my mate and I have discussed this and we think this was the best thing that could have happened," Neska said. "The first few days they were very ornery and argumentative, especially Cadj. His father intervened. Then, he seemed to own up to his responsibility and became a good worker."

"We are so happy to hear that. Brian and Jamie went through a similar transition, and now they are doing well in their jobs," Ethaderia piped in. "We decided housework was too easy for them, so Brian is now polishing the crystals on the crestriders, and Jamie is maintaining the pakow pens and helping groom the pakows."

"How is Fazi doing?" Kara asked. She liked the little Plotal girl.

"My daughter has surprised me. She has improved the organization in our household, and while doing her chores, she has supervised the staff on a better way of doing things," Neska said.

"That's wonderful!" Kitry said. They talked for a few more minutes, then ended the call.

Next, she called Naphelia, Orongo's mate. The conversation was similar to what they had with Neska. Fingo, Zerke and

Plodu had made improvements to the jobs assigned to them. When Kitry called Indii, she was happy to hear that the little Kudaja girl had the kitchen hopping.

Last up was Kestrum. "Oh, Queen Kitry, Chacoodi is back to being a good Egrom boy. It is amazing what pot scrubbing and latrine duties do to straighten out bad behavior."

They chatted a few more minutes, then they ended their call.

The women nodded knowingly.

D'LAINE AND UGO SAT AT GHURY'S TABLE WITH SCROLLS LAID OUT in the middle of the table. Adrum and Ghury studied the texts that Ugo brought with him.

"Yes, I understand your concern," Adrum said.

"Is the prophecy about me, Trakon and our children, or is it about my father as King Jangston?"

Ghury grumbled in thought. "Your father plays a part in the prophecy, but it is not about him. You, Trakon and your children are who is mentioned in the prophecy."

"What about my brothers?" D'laine asked. "Their faces are etched onto the lid of this silver box, but we couldn't find any scrolls that mentioned them."

One of Adrum's fingers moved down a scroll. "Eventually you will come across a scroll that mentions them. I feel certain they are involved, either directly, or indirectly, like your father, otherwise their likeliness would not be on that box."

"So, I guess we need to return to the cave and continue our search?" D'laine asked.

"That would be wise," Ghury said.

D'LAINE AND UGO FLEW BACK TO THE PALACE. THE ATTENDANT retrieved the crestrider and zoomed away. Ugo led the way inside to the library.

"Don't despair. We'll find something that ties everything together," the scholar said. "When you return to the cave, I'll go with you. Perhaps an examination of the layout of items will help me to understand if they were placed in specific areas indicating the completed path they were stored."

"We can bring other scholars with us," D'laine said.

They each went their separate ways. D'laine took to the stairs and entered her suite. She wanted to take a bath before dinnertime. She continued to the twins' suite to check in on her children.

The guards hit their hearts.

"Princess D'laine!" Amoroso said. "You missed all the excitement."

D'laine became alarmed. She rushed over to Jesslin's crib, then to Kal-Dan's. "What happened?" She didn't sense blood on the floor, and Pup appeared comfortable in his bed.

Three of the women warriors competed to tell the story.

D'laine stared at the dog. "Huh. I had no idea he would do that!"

"Your younger brother, the animal communicator, requested that the dog not do that again," Keeshi said.

D'laine flopped down by Pup's bed. "What a good boy you were today! But you sure scared Trakon and everyone else."

Pup licked D'laine's hand. His expression looked apologetic.

She stood. "I'm going to the bath. Do you have everything you need?"

"Oh, yes, princess. The chef keeps us supplied with food and drinks," Amoroso said.

D'laine nodded, then crossed through the connecting door and closed it behind her. She entered the bathroom, undressed and stepped down the stairs into the blissful warm water. Just as she reached the middle where the water reached her collar-bones, Trakon entered the room.

"Ah, you beat me to the bath," he said.

"I understand you had quite a stressful day," she said.

"That dog!" Trakon shook his head, while he undressed. He entered the pool and floated on his back for a minute. When he stood, he flung his hair back, splashing D'laine intentionally. He grinned.

She curved both her arms and let him have it, dousing him with a wave of water. Then, for several long minutes, they acted like teenagers and enjoyed a water fight. They ended up laughing and kissing in the pool.

CHAPTER FIFTEEN

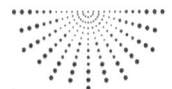

l Jordan could barely keep his eyes shut, he was so excited to be visiting Thol. Ben had contacted his friends Corl and Gafn, the men who had built his bookcases, to find out if there was a spare bed he could borrow overnight. They lugged over a huge, rolled-up mattress, the size of a double bed, but stuffed with hosk silk.

During and after the festivities, Al talked with Lee, Stanley, Victor, Kara, Ethaderia, the king and queen, Trakon and D'laine, some Kudaja, Plotals and Egroms. Al wanted to stay forever.

When the journalist sank down onto the mattress on the floor, he couldn't believe how comfortable it was. The mattress seemed to conform to his body. It was the most comfortable bed, even compared to the one luxury, high-end hotel he had stayed at in the Galleria in Houston.

Ben had a list of things for Al to do, including flying on his borjo, riding a pakow, flying in a crestrider, visiting the field of moss and petting a hosk. He wanted Al to lie down at the edge of the forest to see how high the agrin trees were, visit Ta'Byu'Vohon, visit the Egroms, and visit Ebscalon. There were so many things to experience, but Ben wanted Al to take away a real look at his new home world. The scientist would never voluntarily return to Earth. Thol was his paradise.

When morning finally arrived, Ben and Al got cleaned up. Ben had secured a Ciertron suit for Al and showed him how to inflate the suit and the boots. Then they walked over to the dining hall.

"I can't get over how this material feels. I'm not sweltering," Al said.

"The clothing is amazing," Ben said.

The Kudaja dining hall was the closest thing to a cafeteria that Ben could compare it to. But the difference between a Kudaja and Earth restaurant was that all food prepared in the Kudaja eatery was prepared from scratch.

No giant cans of vegetables, canned gravy or anything else. No processed foods. Just wholesome foods from a world that was not tainted the way Earth was. Pure soil, water and air was the difference in food growth and production.

After a hearty breakfast of delicious food, and a cup of coffee from the supply that Al had sent over from Earth, they were ready to start their day.

"I want you to experience flying on a borjo," Ben said. "Borjos pick their rider. Aob picked me right away. It was one of the most thrilling experiences to be chosen."

"Are they dragons?" Al asked. He wasn't sure. He remembered the picture Ben had shared with him, but the creature looked a little strange.

"They're sort of like dragonflies and dragons combined, but with these weird eyes that see in all directions," Ben said. "Plus, Kudaja borjos can morph from the size of a dragonfly to a full-sized dragon when the Kudaja require them to change size. It's one of the most interesting things about this world."

They walked back toward Ben's house. He looked up in the tree and spotted Aob perched across several large branches.

"Aob, let's take Al for a ride!" Ben called out.

The borjo's eyes popped open. He spread his wings and glided down to the walkway where the men stood.

"Aob, this is my friend Al Jordon from Earth." Ben turned to Al. "You can pat or rub his snout. It's like velvet."

Al stuck his hand out and touched the borjo's snout. "Oh! That's so soft. You're right, it is similar to velvet. Hello Aob. It's nice to meet you."

"Come on, let's go for a ride," Ben said.

Aob hunched down. Ben swung a leg over the borjo's back and waited for Al to climb up. When the journalist was seated, Ben instructed the borjo. "Aob, go easy. Al has never flown before."

Aob lifted off the boardwalk and flew up through the trees. Once he peaked the canopy of the agrin trees, he soared over the Cember Forest. Ben asked Aob to fly to Ebscalon. The borjo headed toward the city.

"I'd better call Jamie and let him know we're coming for a visit so their borjos don't attack Aob," Ben yelled to Al.

"Please... let's not be attacked!" Al pleaded.

Ben worked his communicator. "Jamie, I'm flying Aob over there. Let your borjos know, okay?"

Ben turned to Al. "We shouldn't have any problems. Borjo males are very territorial, but they listen to Jamie. The Ebscalon borjos are full-sized beasts that were never neutered. They are, in effect, fire-breathing dragons, and you sure don't want to start male posturing. They could burn down the forest!"

As they approached Ebscalon, Ekka, Foota and the other borjos flew out of their towers and approached Aob. They seemed to take in his scent and didn't appear to be hostile. Ben guided Aob to the courtyard, and the borjo spiraled down to the ground.

Ben and Al dismounted. Ben patted Aob's neck. "Good boy, Aob. Why don't you go get to know those borjos? Or, you can go hunt, or go back home."

Aob nudged Ben, then leapt into the air. His mighty wings caught an updraft, and he was airborne within minutes. He joined the borjos flying overhead, and they all flew across the city gates.

Al stared after the creatures, shielding his eyes from the flashing sky. "Wow."

Stanley instantly appeared beside them, and spooked Al. "Sorry, that might have been too close for comfort."

"Stan, let's give Al a crestrider flying lesson," Ben said.

"Good idea," Stanley said. "You've seen a ship, right?"

"Not in reality," Al said.

They all walked in the direction of the crestrider storage facilities.

"Let's detour and go to the marketplace first," Ben said. He turned to Al. "You are in for a treat. Wait until you get a load of this place. It's like walking onto a *Star Wars* movie set."

They rounded a corner and the huge marketplace sprawled before the journalist's eyes. He took in the wondrous array of booths, tables, stalls, stores. He marveled at the different people and creature-people in unimaginable varieties, while merchants called out to passersby.

"You're wearing a translator, right?" Stanley asked, as he bent Al's ear forward. "Good. I'd hate you to miss out on the haggling that goes on here. Talk about fun."

Al nodded, dumbfounded. There was jewelry, leather goods, and bolts of beautiful shimmering cloth. One booth held gigantic boots, vests, and enormous long shirts where some Plotals were judging the quality of the goods.

He watched several Safris looking over what seemed to be camping gear. One examined a cookpot, while another looked over some leather pouches.

There were women in their sari-type dresses with their hair piled on top of their heads, who picked through racks of jewelry. Others in the typical warrior outfits right out of a science fiction movie, examined sandals and other soft footwear.

"Stanley!" Treikie Soluveia called out. The lovely scientist rushed over to the men, while a younger woman followed.

"You're back!" Stanley said.

They kissed—just a peck on the lips. They held hands and gave each other moon eyes.

"Treikie, this is our friend Al Jordan from Earth. He's only here for a short time," Stanley said.

Ben nudged Al. "She's the female version of Stanley—all science."

"Nice to meet you," Al said, but his eyes were on her companion.

"This is my friend Jewellex," Treikie said, as she presented the younger woman.

Al felt as if his heart was going to thud out of his chest when he gazed upon the beautiful woman. He thought she was about his age, but wasn't sure if visual looks were any indication of age on Thol.

"Hi," Jewellex said, a little shy. She knew the Eartholians were important people in Ebscalon.

"Are you a scientist as well?" Al asked.

"Oh, no. I'm a documentarian," Jewellex said.

Al screwed up his brows. He looked to Ben and Stanley for clarification.

"She documents things," Stanley explained. He turned to Jewellex. "What is your area of expertise?"

"I'm one of the documentarians in charge of restoring all our lost technology instructions," Jewellex said. "I've been capturing how to build the crestriders, including the recent upgrades to the solar crystals on the wings."

Al looked from Jewellex to the men and Treikie. "Oh! You're a technical writer! I'm a journalist!"

Jewellex tried the word out. "Journalist. What does that mean?"

"I report news on Earth. We don't quite have the sophisticated communication systems that you have on Thol," Al said. "My editor at the newspaper assigns me a story to cover, and I interview everyone involved so I can write the details and present them in a factual manner."

"Oh!" Jewellex said. "Are you going to live here? You could be a documentarian. There are so many subjects to be captured."

Al shook his head. "I wish I could stay, but I have to go back to Earth and finish a big project."

Jewellex looked disappointed. "Maybe I'll see you when you visit again." She gave a little wave to the group and hurried away.

Al's eyes followed her until she disappeared into the crowd. He huffed out a sigh.

"Hon," Stanley said to Treikie. "We're going to take Al up in a crestrider. I'll catch you later, okay?"

Treikie nodded as she watched Al watch her friend. "Sure. We'll talk later."

"Come on, let's go check out a crestrider," Stanley said.

They left the marketplace and continued on to the buildings that stored the ships, and the huge ground area where the crystals charged. Brian was wiping down the crystals on a five-man flyer when the men approached.

"Hey, Brian. This is Al Jordan, the reporter from Earth," Ben called out.

Brian hopped down to the ground, stuck the cleaning cloth half into a pocket in his uniform, and held out his hand. "Nice to meet you. You going for a ride?"

"Yeah, Ben and Stanley are going to show me how a crestrider works," Al said, excited. His eyes took in the sea of ships, all in different sizes. "You clean all these yourself?"

"No, it would be impossible for one person to clean all these crystals," Brian said. "There's a team of eight of us." As he finished talking, a group of workers came out of a building and returned to their areas. They all began cleaning the ships where they had left off earlier.

"Well, we'll see you later," Stanley said. "I've reserved a three-man flyer."

They waved at Brian, then walked over to a different building. The ship hovered several feet off the ground. Stanley pressed a button near the bottom of the ship, and the escalator came down.

"Up you go," Stanley urged Al.

Al climbed up the stairs, followed by Ben. He looked over the open-sided ship. A railing went from one side of the bridge to around the rest of the ship back to the bridge again. Below the railing was enclosed, but above the railing was the wild sky.

Stanley took to the bridge. He explained the hovering, raising and lowering of the ship, the escalator, the communication devices, mapping systems. Everything the journalist would need to understand if he were going to write about those things in the book.

"Let me take the ship out to the field so you can try to fly it," Stanley said.

The ship rose, and they zoomed over the city, while the journalist turned right and left, taking in the sights. The ship flew over the city gates to the open field. Then the scientist hovered the crestrider in place.

"Give it a try."

Al nervously took the helm. He recalled the instructions and played with rising the ship, and lowering it. Then he made it go forward. Once he felt comfortable with the process, he had the ship gliding across the sky over the colorful moss field.

"Oh, wow! I love flying this thing!" Al said.

Stanley and Ben grinned at the journalist. They were giving

him the best experiences they could think of for his short stay on Thol.

"Better than cars rolling across the ground!" Stanley said.

"Stanley, let's head over to the pakow pens. I want Al to experience riding one of the giant beasts," Ben said.

Stanley took back the controls and made a wide turn. They zoomed over the fields to the other side of the city.

Al's mouth dropped open as his eyes took in the large animals grazing in the fenced-in area. "We're going to ride one of those animals?"

"Yeah. Wait until you experience six legs underneath you, running across the field!" Ben said.

Stanley landed the ship on the mossy field, away from the pens so that the pakows weren't spooked. No one wanted a stampede.

They walked over to the big pen where Jugdaak was grooming a pakow.

"Want to go for a ride?" the pakow keeper asked.

"Yes," Ben said. "We want our friend to experience riding a pakow."

"Hold on a minute," Jugdaak patted the pakow on the rump and gave three bursts of whistles.

Three beasts approached him. He patted each of them, saddled them, then brought them to the men outside the pens.

"Here you go," Jugdaak said. "These are nice pakows, they'll go slow or fast, whatever pace you ask of them."

"Thanks so much," Stanley said.

"Don't forget to be on the lookout for any doski or Trangula," Jugdaak said.

"Hopefully, we won't have to worry about that for the time being," Stanley said. He turned toward his friends. "All you do is ask your pakow to kneel so you can climb aboard."

He turned to his pakow and rubbed its snout. "Let's go for a ride. Please kneel so I can mount you, okay?" Stanley turned to Al."Watch how it's done."

The pakow knelt and Stanley climbed up the thick front leg. He swung his leg over the saddle and settled in. Ben was experienced already, so he clambered up his pakow's leg.

"Hello," Al said, a bit nervous as he patted the beast's strange, wide face, which seemed to be a cross between a cow and a goat. The two large fly-type eyes were disconcerting to watch. They seemed to move in all different directions simultaneously.

The ten-ton beast stood twenty-five-foot-high at its withers, supported by six thick legs and gigantic elephant-like feet. The pakow had long muddy brown hair, and a long, thin, cow-like tail that swished its back.

Al screwed up his courage. He wasn't going to pass up a chance to ride this creature. "Let's go for a ride with our friends, okay? Will you let me mount you?"

The pakow licked the side of Al's face with its gritty, cat-like tongue, then knelt.

The journalist wiped his face, laughed and rubbed the pakow's nose. He climbed the huge offered leg, not quite on his hands and knees, and monkeyed his way up to the pakow's back, then threw his leg over the saddle. He grabbed the saddle horn before he flung himself off the other side of the beast in his exuberance to get started.

Al let out a yelp when his pakow stood. It was a long, long way down to the ground. The movement felt strange with the six legs underneath. He had never ridden a camel back home, but he had seen how they stood. This experience would have been similar, but with a different rocking motion because of the middle legs.

"Wow!" he said.

"Yeah," Stanley said. "Wait until we ride."

Ben grinned like a Cheshire cat. "I'm so glad you're getting to experience these things. The book is going to be fabulous, Al."

They rode side by side at a slow trot, across the moss fields with hosks scurrying out of the way.

"You comfortable to go a little faster?" Stanley asked.

"Heck yeah," Al said.

Stanley urged his pakow into a canter. He didn't think Al could handle a full gallop, but a cantor was comfortable. When he glanced sideways at the journalist, he found him in with a full-faced smile. He was having the time of his life.

Let's show Al how tall the agrin trees are, Ben sent to Stanley.

Good idea. I remember when Trakon showed me. I could hardly get my head around how gigantic the trees were, compared to the redwoods back home, Stanley sent back.

Stanley sent his pakow a direction, to head over to the edge of the forest. They crossed the field in no time flat, then Stanley slowed his pakow, which the others followed suit. He dismounted down his pakow's front leg and waited for his companions.

"This is something you've just got to experience, Al," Stanley said. The scientist laid down on the ground, feet toward the forest.

Ben and Al followed his lead.

"What am I looking for?" Al asked.

"The top of the agrin trees," Stanley said.

Ben chuckled.

Al settled on his back on the comfortable mossy ground cover. He cupped his hands around his eyes to shield them from the dual suns and the ever-present flashing skies. He looked up, and up, and up to no avail. The tops of the trees disappeared into the clouds. "I can't see the treetops."

Stanley and Ben laughed.

"You can't. Trakon did a little experiment for us. The tallest of the California Redwoods is the Hyperion Coast Redwood. It's taller than the Statue of Liberty by seventy-four feet. The agrin trees are around eight-hundred feet tall," Stanley said.

"Holy cannoli! I've always thought the redwoods were immense trees. These agrin trees are something else," Al said.

Suddenly, three baby hosks climbed up on him. One on his head, one on his left arm, and one on his chest. He laughed as their tiny spider-like legs tickled him.

"What are these little guys called again?" Al asked. When he moved, the hosks jumped off him and scooted under the moss.

"Hosks," Ben said. "The males spin a silk that's used in practically everything you can think of material-wise. The clothes, bedding—the list is too long to go into. When it's combined with the sap from the agrin trees, whatever it creates is nearly indestructible."

"Has anyone shown you what Ben's talking about?" Stanley asked.

"No, not that I can recall," Al said.

"Oh, this is not something you'd ever forget if you saw it," Stanley said.

They stood up, and Stanley demonstrated. "Ben, take your knife and cut my suit."

Ben found his knife in one of the hidden pockets. He approached the scientist and stuck the point of the knife into the fabric on Stanley's arm. He cut a three-inch slit and put his knife away.

They all watched as the fabric repaired itself. In slightly longer than a slow blink, the fabric was seamless once again.

Al's mouth hung open. "I can't believe it. This material would last beyond the grave." He thought for a moment. "What about the women's clothes—those that look like saris?"

"Same thing. A snag, tear—anything—is repaired instantly. Then there's the smart closets," Stanley said. "Has Ben showed you his?"

Ben's eyes gave him away. "I forgot all about that. There's so many wonders in this dimension, it's hard to remember everything that we experience and use every day."

"Let's go back to Ebscalon. We can go to my suite and I'll show Al how it works," Stanley said.

They returned to their pakows and rode back to the pens. Then they climbed aboard the crestrider, lifted off with Stanley at the helm, and Al holding onto the rail and looking at the ground. Stanley maneuvered the ship to the place where they reserved it. They walked back through the city to the palace.

THEY ENTERED THE PALACE AND CLIMBED THE STAIRS TO Stanley's suite. The first thing Al saw when he walked through the door was the helmets on a shelf. He crossed the floor and gawked at them.

"Are these military helmets?"

Stanley chuckled as he nodded slowly. "They might be considered military." He explained how his brain had expanded and all the problems it had caused. He shared mind pictures of how grotesque he looked with his misshapen head, extended forehead and round shape.

"Before Greg Claymore worked on my head, I had to wear this first helmet all the time." He picked up the softer bonnet. "This is what I had to wear to bed, but if you look around the room, you'll see the special wall panels. The Egroms helped the architect reinforce the walls, ceiling and floor of my suite so I wouldn't kill anyone downstairs while I slept."

Al looked around at the material on every surface of the rooms in Stanley's suite. "Wow. I can't imagine what that was like."

"We decided to keep my rooms the way they are, just in case whatever Greg fixed, breaks," Stanley said. "I don't think it will, but I almost killed Adrum during my first lesson with the Egroms."

"Yeah, Stanley's brain issues are legendary in the Cember

Forest, here in Ebscalon, and probably beyond," Ben said. "Show Al your smart closet."

They walked into the bedroom, and Stanley stopped in front of the closet. He pressed buttons, and the door opened. Three uniforms and some robes hung in the closet. Stanley looked around, got down on the floor and looked under his bed. He found a deflated boot caked with mud.

"Here we go, this boot will have to do," the scientist said. He showed the boot to Al, as it was, then inflated it. It looked like a heavy-duty military boot. There were bits of moss and chunks of dirt stuck in the boot's sole. He placed the boot on a floor shelf in the smart closet, and shut the door. He pressed a button.

Nothing appeared to happen, so Al shuffled from one foot to the other, waiting. "What's it doing? I don't see anything happening."

Ben and Stanley smiled.

"Give it another minute," Ben said. "This thing takes cleaning and mending to the next level—or, a level we've never experienced on Earth."

Stanley opened the closet door and picked up the boot. He handed it over to Al. The journalist turned the boot over and inspected the sole. It looked as if it were brand new. No dirt, no moss bits—it was spotless.

"How did it clean this? Where did the dirt go?" He stuck his head in the closet and stared at the shelf, then the floor. No dirt.

"Can't answer that. Have no idea how it works. Like many things here, the technology has stumped Lee, Victor, Ben and me," Stanley said.

CHAPTER SIXTEEN

*A*l changed into his white button-up shirt, suit, socks and shoes. He stuffed his tie in his pocket. The journalist was sad to leave Thol, but he had a responsibility to the Eartholians. He was eager to get back to work on the book. His head spun with information he couldn't wait to get on paper. He folded the Ciertron clothing and placed it on Ben's bathroom counter, then he returned to the other room.

Ben stood. "All set?"

Al looked sad. "Yeah."

"Oh! Almost forgot. Have to remove the translator!" Ben said. He walked up to Al and pressed the translator the way Stanley showed him. The device wiggled out of the skin and bone behind Al's ear. Ben grabbed it, strode to the bathroom and laid it on top of the clothes Al had placed on the counter.

"That felt so weird," Al said, as he rubbed behind his ear.

"Come on, I'll take you back," Ben said. "You ready?"

Al looked around Ben's place. "I'm as ready as I'll ever be."

Ben gripped Al's arm, and stepped forward. They manifested in Victor's spare room in California.

"Is there anything I should take back with me?" Ben asked.

"I don't think so," Al said.

They walked out of the spare room, down the hallway to the kitchen. Al noticed the landline answering machine had messages. He pressed the Play Messages button and listened.

His neighbor from across the street called to tell him someone was knocking on doors asking about him.

Al and Ben shared a look.

Al listened to the next call, again from his neighbor, Jerry. "Al, I tried your cellphone but it kept going to voicemail and I think I filled your inbox. These guys are from the government. I told them you were out of town. Call me when you get back."

"The government?" Al said. He looked at Ben. "What would the government want with me?"

"I sure hope they haven't connected any dots," Ben said.

"I'll find out and let you know," Al said.

Ben patted Al on the back. "I'd better get going. I hope to see you again soon."

"Thanks for everything, Ben. This was the most exciting event in my life, and I'm sad that I had to return to this," Al said. He held his arms out to show not only Victor and Kara's house, which was fabulous, but to indicate Earth.

"Write the book. Make your mark on the publishing world. The sci-fi market will love the story," Ben said. "You deserve some success."

They walked back down the hall to the spare room, and Ben disappeared. Al stood there for a moment, hands in his pockets looking a little hang-dogged. He huffed out a sigh and walked to his bedroom to change clothes, thinking about how he would explain where he was to Jerry, across the street.

He pulled on a pair of the baggy shorts he always wore, then a t-shirt and his sandals. He retrieved his cellphone from the kitchen charger and listened to messages. Jerry was freaking out. He grabbed the house keys and stuffed them in his pocket, and walked out the door.

AL CHECKED THE MAILBOX AND REMOVED WHAT LOOKED LIKE several day's-worth of mail. His head was doing a number on him. He looked at the dates on the postage stamps, pulled out his phone and checked the current date. It looked like he had been gone for three days Earth time, when it was actually overnight and a day on Thol.

Screwy.

He crossed the street and knocked on Jerry's door. The door flew open, Jerry grabbed Al's arm and yanked him inside.

"What the…"? Al squealed out.

"Where have you been?" Jerry whispered.

"Why are you whispering?" Al asked.

Jerry cleared his throat. "Sorry, I've been really worried about you. These government guys have been here…"

"Did they tell you they were government guys? What branch?" Al asked.

"Well, of course they didn't say they were from the government, but it was obvious," Jerry said. "Where were you?"

"I went out of town for a baby announcement event," Al said. "My friends had twins, and it was a big thing."

"Oh," Jerry said, as his bubble burst.

"Did these guys leave a business card or anything? Did they get into the house?" Al asked.

"No, and not as far as I can tell," Jerry said.

"Well, in any case, I'm back," Al said. "I've got a ton of writing to do, and I have to check my email."

"How come you didn't at least text me?" Jerry asked.

"I forgot my phone on the kitchen charger," Al said. "Hope I never do that again!"

They walked to the front door.

"Okay, glad you're back and you're okay," Jerry said.

Al opened the door and left.

BEN MANIFESTED HIMSELF IN STANLEY'S ROOM AT THE PALACE. HE called out, announcing himself. "Stan, you here?"

Stanley popped his head around the corner from the other room and saw Ben.

"Did you take Al back home?" Stanley asked.

"Yeah. His neighbor left a message on the answering machine saying some government guys were looking for Al. I'm worried they might *disappear him*, Stan."

Stanley stared at Ben for a solid minute. "We're going to have to keep close tabs on him, to make sure nothing like that happens."

"He didn't break any laws, but if they want to question him about purchases he's made from any of the accounts, that might be difficult to explain," Ben said. "Do you think they're trying to find out about where all of us disappeared to? Or something else?"

The scientist was quiet a moment while his mind chased through scenarios. "We'd better talk this through with Lee and Victor. I'll call Lee." Stanley tapped his communicator and asked Lee to come upstairs immediately, while Ben called Victor.

Ben paced while they waited on their friends.

Lee arrived first, then Victor showed up moments later.

"What's wrong?" Lee asked. "Was there a problem sending Al back home?"

"The government may be on to us," Stanley said. "Tell them, Ben."

Ben reiterated the phone call Al received.

"Everyone calm down," Victor said. "We don't know for sure if this is like the FBI or the CIA—or a census taker!"

"I still say we need to keep watch on Al," Ben said. "You know damn well that the government can swoop in, and suddenly you find yourself in custody."

"All those baby items will be hard to explain, especially since they're not at my house," Victor said. "There's no way Al can prove where they went, which makes things really suspicious."

"We didn't think things through," Lee said. "I sure hope we didn't mess up Al's life."

"I'm wondering if there's a way I can rig his translator so he can communicate with us," Stanley said.

"Didn't we try to do this before?" Ben asked.

"No, we were messing with the laptops and cellphones, remember?" Victor said.

"Be right back," Ben said. He stepped back to his house, retrieved Al's translator and his Tholian clothes, then stepped back to Stanley's suite in the palace. "Figured I'd bring his suit as well. Should we leave it in the spare room for when he comes back?"

"Yes and no," Lee said. "If those government guys get into the house, we don't want them to see this suit."

"Maybe we can hide it," Victor said. "Have Al be able to retrieve it, but make it invisible to anyone else."

Stanley picked up the translator and went into a trance-like state for a moment. "Be right back." He *stepped* over to the Egroms around the fire.

"Yes, we understand the need for Al to be able to communicate with you," Adrum said. He took the translator and passed it over to Drusta.

The younger Egrom stared at the translator intently. He passed it back to Adrum. "There should not be any problems, but if you discover something not quite right, I'll make adjustments. Tell Al to press the device when he wants to contact you. There should be a direct connection."

Stanley took back the translator. "Thanks, Drusta. I owe you one."

"What is it you owe me?" the Egrom asked.

"That's an Earth expression. It's another way of saying I owe you a favor," Stanley said. He nodded, then *stepped* back to his suite.

"Okay, Drusta made an adjustment to Al's translator. Let's pay him a visit," Stanley said.

They banded together and Stanley *stepped* the group to Victor's house.

"Al?" Ben called out.

Al jumped out of his office chair and ran into the living room. "Oh, wow! I wasn't expecting to see all of you! Is everything okay?"

Lee held up a hand in the Stop position. He raised a finger to his lips and pointed up and around.

They understood what he meant—is the place bugged?

Stanley held his hands up in the air. He walked around the room, then walked from room to room. He returned to the living room. "The place is clean."

"How'd you... never mind," Lee said.

They all let out their breath in relief.

"What did you find out about those government guys?" Ben asked.

"No one's showed up at my door yet, so I'm not sure what to make of that," Al said.

"Just in case there's trouble, keep this translator installed," Stanley said. "One of the Egroms modified it and we need to test it." He walked up to Al, bent his ear forward and pressed the translator into the skin behind the ear. It wiggled into the skin and bone.

Al chuckled. "That's one of the weirdest feelings. How's this going to work between here and Thol? Is that even possible?"

"You don't know the Egroms. They're beyond wizards, or even Yoda," Lee said.

Stanley tapped his communications patch on his suit, brought up Al's name and chose his translator instead of his cellphone. He tapped the link. "Can you hear me through your translator?"

Al jumped. "Yes! Loud and clear."

"Okay. Now, I want you to wait a minute, I'm going to go back to Thol, then I want you to tap your translator. Drusta said it would connect directly to me," Stanley said.

"Just tap it?" Al asked.

"Yes." Stanley disappeared.

"Here goes," Al said. He tapped his translator once. "Hello? Stanley, are you there?" He received Stanley's message through his device. "Yes, I can hear you."

Stanley returned to the room. "Okay. Our failsafe is in place. If for any reason whatsoever you feel like you're in danger, you tap that translator and tell me what's going on. If I have to, I'll come and extract you."

They all looked worried.

"In the meantime, keep working on the book," Ben said. "You have connections in the media, so you might be able to get one of those New York book publishers to read it. It seems like journalists get published easier than your run-of-the-mill writers do."

Victor looked around. "I should have asked Kara if she wanted anything from here."

"What about the suit? What are we going to do with it?" Lee asked.

"You brought my Thol suit?" Al asked.

"Figured it might be a good idea to leave it here, but I'm not so sure now," Stanley said. "If I had to extract you in a hurry, I wouldn't want to leave it behind."

"We'd better take it back home," Victor said.

Lee looked the journalist over. "Start letting your hair grow. It'll be a good cover for the translator."

"Plus, you'll look more like a hip writer," Ben said, with a huge grin.

STANLEY, LEE, VICTOR AND BEN MANIFESTED BACK TO THOL.

"Ben and I can do spot checks," Stanley said. He turned to Ben. "Go to the room, and don't call out. Listen to make sure everything is okay. Once you think it's okay, you can call out, but let's not be pests."

"How often should we check on Al?" Ben asked.

"Every couple of days," Lee suggested.

There was a tap at the door. Everyone jumped. Stanley crossed the room and opened the door to D'laine. She looked inside and saw the men standing in a group.

"What are you all doing? Is this a secret club or something?" she asked.

"Oh, you know, scientist geeks getting together," Lee said. "What's up?"

"I was burnt out on the scrolls, so I thought I'd visit with my pal Stanley for a minute," D'laine said.

"Oh, we're done here," Victor said. "He's all yours."

Victor marched to the door. Lee stopped to give her a kiss on the cheek. Ben *stepped* back to his Kudaja house.

Stanley bowed low with an arm extended. "Entrez."

CHAPTER SEVENTEEN

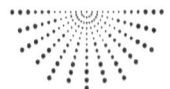

$\mathcal{F}$azi Bosakin turned out to be such a good household manager that Neska and Jakla determined she should teach others. Their household had never run so smoothly. Their daughter studied how the staff moved about doing things. Then she performed those duties herself—to her satisfaction, which at first, took multiple times while she learned how to do things efficiently.

She rearranged the order of chores. For instance, she noticed that the staff cleaned the carpets before they batted dust off the wall hangings. That would require cleaning the carpets again. She wondered why they did this over and over, day in and day out without figuring out they were doing the same chore twice.

Fazi progressed from room to room, implementing changes to how the staff did things. At first there were grumblings. No one wanted to take instructions from a CHILD. But after a while, the workers understood they were actually doing things quicker, and finishing all their chores earlier, which meant they could go home sooner.

Her brother, Cadj, didn't fare so well. He was so angry at his punishment, that he flung shovels full of pakow dung everywhere, including getting the beasts covered with their own poo. He learned that lesson quickly, since he was the one who had to clean off the pakows.

Jakla watched his son's behavior from the shadows of an agrin tree, while he shook his head. He determined he would have to take matters into his own hands by toning down Cadj's attitude. The Commander stepped out from behind the tree as the boy went on a rampage with the pakow dung. He gripped Cadj by the neck of his vest, grabbed the shovel and flung it to the ground. Jakla opened the pod at the end of his tail, exposing the deadly barbs.

He swiftly whacked his son on the rump with his pod—not using his full strength, but enough that it would send a message.

Cadj howled.

"You will pick up that shovel and complete your chores with no further show of temper, do you understand?" Jakla growled.

Cadj rubbed his rump while staring at his father in shock. He had never been whacked so hard before—ever.

Jakla shook him by the vest again, waiting for an acknowledgment.

"Yes, father. I understand," Cadj mumbled.

"Good. I expect you to excel at maintaining the pakow pens, and honoring the beasts by grooming them," Jakla said. He strode away, leaving his son to ponder on the lesson.

Orongo and Naphelia were amazed at how Plodu took to the gardening project. Instead of slaving away with a shovel and digging trenches for planting, he fiddled with his laser settings, stood where he wanted a row, held the laser toward the ground and pressed a button. The dirt blew up to the top of the row, leaving a small trench where he could drop the seeds and cover them with the dirt. It took several tries to get the right depth for the trench, but it was an amazing time-saver they would share with other neighboring kingdoms, especially their friends at Ebscalon.

AFTER CLEANING THE FIRST TWO TENTS, WHICH TOOK FOREVER because of their enormous size, Fingo's attitude turned from bad to worse. She started thinking about the problem. It was inefficient to clean the tents on the moss. As soon as she finished one side and folded the rather large section, the bottom side was covered in bits of moss and dirt.

She asked an elder where the old tents were stored, retrieved four with the help of a co-worker, and laid them out in a gigantic square on the moss. She cleaned the surfaces of the four old tents, let them dry, staked them down, and used that as her cleaning platform. She enlisted Plotal females to help with the scrubbing, rinsing and folding after the tent dried.

ZERKE HAD THE WORST OF THE HORRIBLE JOBS THAT HER PARENTS doled out. Feeding the old ones was an unpleasant way to spend any time. Their food had to be mushed, and someone had to spoon-feed them. Plus, who would want to eat food that was several different food types smushed into one blob? It not only looked disgusting, it had no appeal whatsoever. Zerke determined it was no wonder why they lost their appetites.

She decided the old ones deserved better, and while it might take longer to feed them, they would be happier and everyone would benefit. Zerke mashed each food group separately and arranged them into their own bowls. She discovered that several of the old ones wanted to try to feed themselves. They discovered they could hold the spoon and the bowl and didn't need help. It was a big jolt to their self-esteem to be self-sufficient.

Zerke went one step further. She had one of the craftspeople create a plate similar to an Earth deviled egg plate, but on a much larger scale, which would hold the different food groups. After she tried it out, she had the Plotal craftsperson create several dozen so there would be enough to go around for all the old ones.

INDII WAS PROUD OF HER DAUGHTER. THE POOR KUDAJA GIRL HAD blisters on her fingers and hands after two days of peeling root vegetables. She drilled down into the menu of her communications program, searching for something helpful. After what seemed an exorbitant amount of time, she discovered an application she thought she could modify.

Vila dug through a bin of old, discarded cups and mugs until she found what she was looking for. She used her laser tool to cut a length out of the metal material. She dropped a vegetable into the cup, balanced her laser tool on a stack of napkins, and started the cutting process with the laser. The first vegetable peeled too deeply and ended up the size of a pea.

After several tries, she had complete success: a perfectly peeled vegetable, and a spiral of peels. To be on the safe side, she peeled several more to make sure that her invention worked precisely, every time. It did. She determined that the new machine could peel a dozen vegetables in the time it would take her to peel one, manually.

Zabadoro, the Kudaja head chef, was impressed at the young girl's innovation. He brought Vila, her new-fangled invention, and her mother before King Uladosa Cagmondoore for a demonstration. It impressed the king.

"I want to barter with Grubio, the Ebscalon Chef," Zabadoro said.

"What does he have that you prize so highly?" the king asked.

"Some prize recipes that are better than what I have come up with," Zabadoro said.

"They are worth sharing this time-saving tool?" the king asked.

"When you taste both pizza and chocolate bites, you will ask me why I didn't have these recipes sooner," Zabadoro said.

The king stared at the chef for a long moment. "Have our craftsmen perfect the tool and thoroughly test it before you approach Chef Grubio."

Zabadoro beat his chest. "Thank you!"

The king looked at Vila. "This is a very important tool you have designed, young Vila. Your name will be on it so all of our people can praise you, deservedly so."

"Oh, thank you, King Cagmondoore!" Vila said reverently.

Indii was so proud of her daughter that she thought her heart would burst from her chest.

Chef Zabadoro hurried them away from the king back to the kitchen. "I will summon our craftsmen, Vila. You will demonstrate how the device works, how many napkins for the correct height of the laser tool, and the exact frequency of the laser to peel the vegetables precisely."

Indii looked at her daughter. "This is a lot of responsibility, but I know you are capable of it. After all, look what you came up with! All because of blisters on your hands."

"I'm so happy that everyone sees the benefit from my invention," Vila said. Her face was somewhat flushed from so much praise.

KESTRUM WAS TO THE POINT WHERE SHE WANTED TO CLOBBER Chacoodi. He was underperforming all of his duties. The cookpots did not pass her inspection, the latrine trenches were a stinking mess, and everyone on the planet heard his complaints who couldn't tune him out.

She was grumbling to herself when Adrum approached.

"Your charge can't seem to move beyond anger," Adrum said.

"That is true," Kestrum acknowledged. "What are your suggestions?"

"Begin with the meditations. Once those calm him down, everything else will fall into place," Adrum said. "A calm mind opens for innovation. Evidently, Chacoodi has forgotten he is an Egrom who has powers. Those powers remove the drudgery from his chores."

"Yes, that is what I shall do," Kestrum said. She nodded to Adrum, and approached Chacoodi, who was doing a pitiful job manually scrubbing one of the large cooking cauldrons as one of the cooks watched, puzzled.

"Chacoodi!" Kestrum called out.

The Egrom boy jumped, startled.

"Come with me," Kestrum said.

"Where are we going?" Chacoodi asked.

"You will see when we get there," Kestrum said.

Chacoodi abandoned his cooking pot and followed Kestrum. They walked through the forest to the pond where D'laine and her family bathed. The quokin bobbed through the steamy water.

"What are we doing here?" Chacoodi asked.

"Sit down," Kestrum said, as she settled on the bank of the pond on the moss. She folded her legs into what the Eartholians would call a half lotus position, which was normal for an Egrom.

Chacoodi sat close by, watching her.

She rested her hands on her thighs, and turned to her young charge. "Let us meditate on the serenity of the pond. On the steam rising into the air and the quokin gliding through the water, ever so happy and peaceful."

She closed her eyes, Chacoodi followed suit.

Meditating is better than cleaning those pots!

I wonder what Brian, Jamie and Darren are doing?

Vila hasn't called to me today. Is she mad at me?

I'm going to ask the cooks to add more adpe to the pot!

My butt itches.

Chacoodi's mind would not shut up. Kestrum nudged him with her mind.

"Quiet your mind, Chacoodi. Put aside all your chatter and find peace in the setting where we sit," Kestrum said. "Anytime you feel something pop into your mind that draws you away from peaceful meditation, tap one of your fingers with another one. Train yourself to do that to become peaceful."

Chacoodi nodded, knowing Kestrum would feel it. He began meditation again. He breathed in and out, freeing his mind. Latrine duty zoomed into his head. He tapped a finger, and the chore slid away. He continued on like this until he fully harnessed a quiet mind.

After a good, solid hour, Kestrum stretched her four arms over her head. Then she unfolded her body and stood.

Chacoodi came out of his meditation, calm, peaceful. He stood.

"You are to begin each day with a serene meditation. This will lead the way to a good day," Kestrum said.

Chacoodi nodded. "Yes, I understand. I feel the difference. My brain is calmer."

"As it should be," Kestrum said.

DARREN HAD A BAD CASE OF DISHPAN HANDS, EVEN WITH USING the gloves the palace kitchen staff provided. Every day there were stacks and stacks of plates, cups, goblets, pots and pans, serving dishes and platters. They never seemed to stop.

On the fourth day, he had a meltdown. Granted, it was a mini-meltdown, but nevertheless, he went a little out of control. He removed the gloves from his reddened hands, threw them down on the counter. He held his hands out in front of him and zapped a counter full of caked and encrusted pots and pans.

To his amazement, along with everyone else's in the kitchen, the filthy cookware suddenly shined as if brand new. After Darren closed his gaping jaw, he picked up a pan, looked at the inside, then turned it over in his hands.

"It's clean," he whispered reverently.

Grubio grabbed the pan out of his hands and inspected it. "How did you do that?"

"I got mad and used my powers. I thought it would destroy the pans, but looks like I have this ability to make things like new again!" Darren said.

Everyone took turns inspecting all the previously discolored, dinged, scratched and very used cookware. It was so shiny, they saw their reflections in the pan.

"What else do you think you can do with these powers of yours?" Grubio asked.

Darren shrugged. "I have no idea."

Grubio looked around the kitchen. He spotted a chipped serving bowl. He pointed it out to Darren. "Think you can repair this?"

"I'll give it a try," Darren said. He zeroed in on only the bowl and held out a finger. There was a little *zing* sound. He approached the bowl, picked it up and turned it around in his hands.

Grubio took the now restored bowl. "This is an amazing talent! We must tell the royals! Come!"

The chef took off out of the kitchen with Darren in tow. They walked to the main salon where everyone typically gathered after meals. Sure enough, everyone was in attendance. Grubio entered the room, tapping his chest to the royals.

"My king and queen," Grubio began. "I have wonderful news. We've discovered a great new power that our young Darren possesses."

Victor's eyebrow hitched as his eyes appraised his son. He wondered *what now?* Kara shared his questioning expression.

Grubio explained what Darren did. He mentally called out for Hruk to bring one of the pans and the bowl. Moments later, the assistant walked into the room with the items. He handed them over to Grubio, tapped his chest to the king and queen, and waited for further instructions.

"The whole set of pots and pans were very worn. All were discolored, dented—from years and years of use. This bowl was chipped. Darren zapped them with his powers and now all the cookware looks brand new," Grubio exclaimed.

Everyone was on their feet examining the two items.

"Well, Darren, looks like you have a remarkable talent," Jor-Dan said.

"I imagine you will be in hot demand," Stanley said, as he examined the bowl for any sign of a chip. The surface was as smooth as if the bowl had just been created.

"This is amazing, son," Victor said.

"I wonder what else you could repair?" Kara asked.

"He turned at least a hour's worth of scrubbing and cleaning into an instantaneous event!" Grubio said. He still could not get over it. He waved to the room, nudged Darren, then they returned to the kitchen.

Darren studied the kitchen. "Let me experiment with something." He focused on the walls, surfaces and cabinets. He spread his fingers on both hands. Within minutes, the entire kitchen looked brand new. There was a roar of exclamations from the entire kitchen staff.

CHAPTER EIGHTEEN

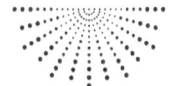

*C*hef Grubio paid another visit to the king in the throne room, unbeknownst to Darren. He shared before and after pictures of the kitchen. "Your highness, Darren's talents should be utilized within the kingdom. Think of the good he could do for some of the oldest residents of Ebscalon!"

Jor-Dan, Marrak and the advisers exclaimed when they saw how Darren had transformed the kitchen.

"We should start a renewal initiative," Marrak said.

"That would be a good use for Darren's gift," Jor-Dan said. He turned to Grubio. "Well done, Chef Grubio. We will act on this."

Grubio left the throne room beaming satisfaction.

"Let's have Victor and Kara join us," Jor-Dan said.

Marrak pulled up his communicator and contacted Darren's parents.

Kara entered the room wondering what was wrong, if they required her lie detector ability to handle a dispute, but there weren't any petitioners around.

Duncts later, Victor walked into the room. He raised an

eyebrow, wondering what was up when he noticed Kara present and just as curious.

"Victor, Kara, not to worry, nothing is wrong," Jor-Dan said. "Things have escalated from Darren's little display in the salon."

The Eartholians were clueless.

Marrak showed them before and after pictures of the kitchen. While it had recently had some structural changes because of the churling, the before picture still looked like a well-worn kitchen. The after picture was such a change, it didn't even look like the same space.

"Darren did that?" Kara spurted out.

"Yes. This all started with him hating his punishment," Marrak said. "Some way, his powers triggered this ability. After he and Grubio showed us the new cooking pot, and the repaired bowl, Darren experimented. The after picture is the end result."

Victor and Kara could hardly believe the transformation.

Jor-Dan patted Kara on the shoulder. "Chef Grubio suggested we start an initiative to restore older residents' homes. We think that would be a good way for Darren to contribute to the kingdom."

"That's a wonderful idea," Victor said.

"I'll send a message to all the citizens asking them to identify not only homes, but businesses that could use some uplifting," Marrak said. "When we have a list in place, we can send someone to verify the need, then have Darren restore the place."

Everyone agreed to the plan.

They began with the poorest of the poor hovels. It shocked Jor-Dan when the discovery of the half-dozen residences on the list were verified. One of the worst hovels belonged to Ja-Toy-Anic, the former traitor who was now a member of the Ebscalon army, and his mother. Laoife worked in the palace kitchen as a sauce expert.

While they had brought themselves back up into society, their house was no better than a lean-to. The committee began with that house. Darren stood before the wretched house with Laoife. She provided a mental picture of the house when she and her late husband had first moved in. That's all the young boy needed. Within a quick blink, the exterior of the house was unblemished sandstone material.

Laoife squealed in surprise.

They all walked inside. The place was a disaster, and not from bad housekeeping, but from wear and tear. Darren didn't need any pictures to restore the place. He did his magic and the whole structure seemed to stand straighter. He restored walls to their original color and perfection; the floors were sparkling clean, and he restored even the furniture.

Ja-Toy-Anic walked down his lane to his house and passed it up. He stopped, recognized his neighbor's house, then walked back to the newly restored house where he was positive his mother's house used to stand. He walked up to the door and knocked, unsure of what to say.

Laoife yanked open the door and grabbed her son in a hug, sobbing.

Ja-Toy-Anic couldn't believe their good fortune, given his traitorous behavior when he was nothing more than a drunk.

The neighbors joined them in their celebration. Now, the lane no longer appeared downtrodden. The simple restoration uplifted their morale.

Darren moved on to the next property location with an advisor.

THE PLOTALS SIZE MADE IT A CHALLENGE FOR THEM TO SQUEEZE between the branches to help with the motion detector installations, so the Ciertrons did the work using the old technology. The Eartholians had worked with Trakon's team to update the detectors. Now, the doski and Trangula "signatures" would be the only things that would trip the detectors to alert the Plotals to an attack.

Lee prayed that Jamie didn't have to talk to the gippes. He imagined their house, and possibly the palace, overrun with the cute creatures. He was grateful that his son hadn't discovered the animals yet.

They performed a test using the captive doski scout and the military Trangulan. Plotal guards walked the captives along large agrin tree branches in two different areas in the forest, setting off the motion detectors, which in turn, sent silent alarms to Jakla, Orongo and Trakon.

They ran several tests, with and without the captives. The only time the detector's alarms blared on their communicators was when the captives were present in the trees. That was a relief to both the Plotals and the Ciertrons.

"We have the sensors set to report to you, Jakla, Orongo, and to me," Trakon said. "If the alarm goes off, you need to let us know whether this a true attack, or if there are doski scouts spying on you."

"Are there locations for each motion detector?" Jakla asked.

"We will need to know the location of the alarm in the forest," Orongo said.

"Yes," Lee said. "We have a schematic for you that shows each detector and its alarm location. After you have checked it out and found the infiltrator, you can shut down the alarm on your communicator."

"That's good. It seems that you have thought of everything," Orongo said.

"We're engineers. That's what we do," Lee said.

Suddenly, an alarm in the far north area of the Ikley Forest lit up their communicators. Automatically, the schematic map popped up and showed the exact location of the motion detector.

Orongo tapped his communicator. "Send two patrols to this location immediately. There is a doski scout in the trees! Try to be as quiet as possible."

"Let's take a crestrider," Trakon suggested. He, Lee, Jakla and Orongo ran to a five-man crestrider, then boarded.

Trakon got the ship in the air and they silently flew to the coordinates of the breach. They spied the Plotal patrols on the ground. Suddenly, there were shouts from the ground as they watched a doski running along the thick branches over the patrol's heads.

"Hang on," Trakon called out. He maneuvered the ship and skimmed the top of the trees, following the doski. The scout was quick!

"Let me stun it," Jakla called out. He set his laser weapon to stun and leaned over the side of the ship. The doski jumped from branch to branch trying to stay ahead of the ship. After a couple of failed tries, Jakla finally hit the creature, and it toppled through the trees.

The Plotal patrols kept up with the doski's flight through the trees and caught the scout as he plummeted toward the ground. They all headed back to the edge of the forest in the rear of Jakla's new city, Ta'Byu'Vohon. Trakon landed the crestrider and they disembarked, waiting for the ground patrol to return.

Several minutes later, the Plotals emerged through the trees with a squirming doski trying to escape.

"This certainly was good timing," Jakla said.

"Maybe it would be a good idea for your people to build stairs on the sides of the trees like they have in the Kudaja city?" Trakon suggested.

"Would your soldiers be able to run through the trees like that doski?" Lee asked. He wasn't sure that would work.

"We will have to practice," Orongo said. He turned to Jakla. "We need Bist to meet with the Kudaja and find out exactly how they constructed their stairs, and what measures he would have to take for our size and weight."

"Jakla, I think it's time for you to consider crestriders," Trakon said. "We could easily purpose a five-man ship for you."

Jakla and Orongo nodded.

"Yes, the time has come for us to embrace more of modern technology," Jakla said. "We will start with one ship and flying lessons, and will purchase more as the need arises."

Everyone nodded at the plan.

"Take that doski to the holding cells and put him with the other scout," Orongo instructed.

BOTH TRAKON AND D'LAINE WERE SOUND ASLEEP WHEN JESSLIN woke up in the middle of the night. She wasn't crying, but fretting. Pup got out of his dog bed and stuck his nose in between the crib railings. He trotted into the bedroom and nudged D'laine. She was out for the count. The dog scurried to the other side of the bed and nudged Trakon.

Trakon started awake with a snort, focused his eyes and noticed the dog. He whispered. "What's the matter, Pup?" Then he heard the baby. He quietly got up and went into the other room with the dog on his heels.

"What's wrong, Jesslin?" Trakon asked. He lowered the railing, picked up his baby daughter and kissed her forehead. He brought her over to the changing table and checked to see if she was wet. She was. He changed her diaper like an expert. He wrapped her in a baby blanket, retrieved one of the prepared bottles and a burb towel, and walked over to the rocker with the baby. He settled into the chair.

Jesslin latched onto the bottle nipple and ate her formula. Trakon rocked in the rocking chair and rocked both of them to sleep.

Pup watched from his dog bed. He got up and walked to the chair and watched them sleep. The baby was snug in her father's arms. The dog returned to his bed, turned in a half circle, plopped down and yawned.

Sometime later, Pup woke again, one eye taking in the room. He saw Trakon, head flung back against the chair, mouth agape, sleeping soundly. Baby Jesslin had slid out of his arms and was sleeping soundly at the edge of Trakon's knees.

Pup trotted into the bedroom and nudged D'laine. She was still out for the count. He returned to the twins' room and took charge. He opened his mouth. His smaller inner teeth came forward and clenched the baby blanket, then his larger outer teeth clenched more of the blanket over his inner teeth.

The dog slowly and gently lifted the baby, backed away from the chair and trotted over to her crib. He stepped onto the bottom railing to boost himself up, and hoisted the baby over the lowered railing. He settled her onto the mattress. The diwal sniffed her from head to toe. When he was satisfied that all was well, he returned to his bed and fell back to sleep.

Close to dawn, Trakon woke with a snort. The burp towel was still in place. The empty bottle was on the floor. The baby was no longer with him. He sprang out of the chair and rushed over to the crib, where he discovered his daughter still wrapped in the blanket, sound asleep. He raised the railing and stumbled into the bedroom and quietly slipped into bed, dropping off into a deep sleep.

D'LAINE WOKE FIRST. SHE COULDN'T BELIEVE SHE SLEPT THROUGH the entire night. She turned and found Trakon sound asleep on his back, mouth hanging open, softly snoring. She got out of bed and walked into the twins' bedroom. Pup's tail thumped against his bed in greeting. The dog stood, stretched, and trotted to his beloved human.

She scratched him behind his ears and tickled him under his chin. Anyone who said dogs didn't smile, obviously didn't spend any time with them—on either world.

D'laine stood over Jesslin's crib. Her brows creased as she saw the baby blanket surrounding her daughter. What caught her attention was the way it peaked up in the center of Jesslin's chest. She stooped for a closer inspection and discovered distinctive tooth markings. She glanced down at the dog.

"Did daddy fall asleep with Jess on his lap?" she asked. "Did Pup put the baby back to bed?"

Pup's facial expression was one of guilt and worry. He wagged his tail tentatively.

"What a good boy!" D'laine said. She got on the floor and pulled the dog into a full-body hug. "Good boy! Mommy and daddy appreciate your help."

Trakon stumbled into the room. "Whose help?" He was not quite awake.

D'laine stood and wrapped her arms around her husband. "Pup put Jesslin back to bed. You must have fallen asleep in the chair."

Trakon jerked awake. "When I woke in the chair, she was not in my arms. I figured I must have put her back to bed then returned to the chair."

"Nope. You can see Pup's two sets of toothmarks in the blanket." She pointed them out.

Trakon hung his head. "I can't believe I almost hurt our baby girl!"

"I feel bad because I'm sure Pup tried to wake me," D'laine

said. "This is the first real deep sleep I've had since their births." She walked over to Kal-Dan's crib. The baby boy yawned and wiggled.

"Good morning, Kal-Dan," she said. She picked him up, changed him and settled in the rocker to breastfeed him.

Buffy and Chatter barreled through the dog door into the nursery.

Trakon squatted and rubbed both dogs' heads. The dogs sent a silent message to Pup, and all three plowed through the dog door and out of the suite to beg for food from the chef.

THE FAMILY SAT AROUND THE PALACE BREAKFAST TABLE, SETTLING in. Kitry noticed her daughter-in-law's happy demeanor.

"You look well-rested," Kitry said.

"Last night I slept through the entire night," D'laine said. "Pup tried to wake me, but I never heard him."

Trakon yawned.

"Son, you look like you could use more sleep," Jor-Dan said.

Trakon yawned again. "Jesslin woke up; Pup came and got me. She needed a diaper change and milk."

"They fell asleep in the rocking chair," D'laine said. "Pup is the ultimate babysitter." She explained what the dog did, the teeth marks on the blanket, and how she slept through the entire experience.

"Those dogs are totally misunderstood," Jor-Dan said.

"How are the Plotals doing with that pack they feed?" Victor asked.

"They said they haven't had any accidents, so that goes to show you that the dogs are adaptable to their environment," Trakon said.

"We owe it all to D'laine for showing us how to live with animals, even our pakows," Kitry said.

Stanley shuffled into the room, looking a little worse for wear. "Morning." He muttered his greeting, waved with a little effort and plunked down into his chair.

"Why do you look so exhausted?" Jor-Dan asked. "Are you sick?"

The majordomo disappeared into the kitchen and returned moments later with a plate for the scientist.

"I was with the Egroms almost all night," Stanley said. He thanked the majordomo, picked up his fork and shoveled food into his mouth, chewing by habit.

Everyone waited for an explanation. When he finally noticed their stares, he abandoned his fork.

"They have felt a disturbance and we are trying to determine what is causing it," Stanley said.

D'laine and Victor perked up.

"Disturbance? What, exactly? Another churling?" D'laine asked.

"No, not a storm," Stanley said.

"I have detected nothing across Thol," Victor said, looking to D'laine. "The dome shows that all is calm in our dimensional world right now."

"We could not identify it," Stanley said. "There's something just on the edge of our knowing, but it hasn't come forth to speak to us."

Everyone stared at the scientist. They all let their minds ponder *speak to us*. The Egrom ways were a mystery to normal Tholians, and Stanley was very much like the human version of the white creatures with his big, contained brain.

Jor-Dan let out a long-held breath. "This does not bode well. We have our hands full with the doski and Trangula situation, waiting for them to make their move."

"We must alert the kingdoms, the Plotals and Kudaja," Trakon said.

"Alert them to what, though?" Victor asked.

"Son, we can't really do that. As Victor pointed out, it would be senseless to put everyone on edge about an unknown event, or enemy," Jor-Dan said.

"Believe me, as soon as I get a glimpse of what's coming, I'll alert you," Stanley said. "I shouldn't have mentioned anything until I had solid information."

"No, don't feel like that," Kitry said. She patted the scientist's hand. "When you determine what the disturbance is, we will be ready to take any action that is required."

CHAPTER NINETEEN

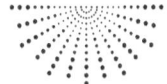

*L*ee and Ethaderia finished up breakfast after the boys had left for their jobs.

"It's downright amazing how Jamie and Brian are so eager to go to their new jobs," Ethaderia said. She stacked the dishes and carried them to the kitchen, Lee on her heels with drinking vessels in his hands.

Eglabado was putting the food away as they came into the room. "You don't have to do that, mistress, sir."

"We know that," Ethaderia said. She patted the manservant on the back after she placed the dishes into the empty sink.

"I wonder if we should send Brian back to the palace to help Marrak?" Lee asked.

"You should talk it over with Jor-Dan and Trakon," Ethaderia said. "He seems to enjoy cleaning the crystals on the ships."

"I'll talk to them today," Lee said.

Lee entered the throne room where Jor-Dan and his

advisors were just getting situated for petitioners. Trakon was discussing something with Dannin at the end of the long table.

"Good morning," Lee said. He tapped his chest in respect to the king.

"We miss you at breakfast," Jor-Dan said. "How are the boys doing? Since their punishments, I rarely see them." He looked a little forlorn.

"It's amazing how they have turned into productive citizens, instead of running wild through the kingdom without a care in the world," Lee said.

Trakon and Dannin joined them.

"Do you think Brian should return to helping Marrak?" Lee asked. "Keeping the crystals clean is important, but you already had a team of people doing that."

"Oh, Brian's not on crystal cleaning duty anymore," Trakon said.

"He's not? What's he doing then? He leaves the house every morning eager to go to work," Lee said. He was furious thinking his son had duped them.

"Huh. I figured he would have told you," Trakon said. "We discovered he has a real talent for the mechanical aspects of building and restoring the ships."

Lee stared at his son-in-law. "I wonder why he hasn't mentioned it?"

Trakon shrugged. "He's been working on the ship for the Plotals. He's done the math for the extra weight that's required to have five fully grown Plotals on the ship. Plus, we've discussed the larger controls for the Plotals' enormous hands."

"Looks like he's following in his father's footsteps," Dannin said.

"I never expected this," Lee said, dumbfounded. "He's never expressed any interest in engineering or design before. I fully expected him to be a documentarian, like Marrak."

"He has good instincts," Trakon said. "You'd be proud of his work ethics."

"You should all come to dinner tonight," Jor-Dan said.

Brian arrived home after his day at the shop and headed up the stairs to clean up for dinner. A few minutes later, the door opened again and Jamie entered the house.

Eglabado barely got out of his way as Jamie thundered up the stairs.

"Sorry!" the boy yelled out. "I have to go to the bathroom."

About twenty minutes later, both boys were downstairs, heading to the dining room.

"We're going to the palace for dinner," Ethaderia told them.

Brian and Jamie high-fived each other.

"We haven't seen anyone in days!" Jamie said.

"As soon as your father is ready, we'll walk over there," Ethaderia said. She no sooner got the words out, when Lee came down the stairs.

"I'm ready!" he said.

The boys took off out the door and thundered down the walkway.

Lee and Ethaderia held hands as they walked at a leisurely pace, then entered the palace. They walked to the large salon where the family met before and after mealtimes.

Brian, Jamie and Darren huddled in a corner, telling each other about their accomplishments.

D'laine and Trakon each held a baby. The adults swarmed around the infants. Ethaderia made a beeline straight for the babies.

"Oh, they are just precious," she said. "May I?" She held her hands out toward D'laine.

"You sure can," D'laine said. She handed Kal-Dan over to her step-mother.

Ethaderia's face had a soft look as she gazed down at the baby. He smiled up at her and grabbed her finger.

"You're setting yourself up for heartbreak," Lee warned her. "We don't know if it's possible for a Tholian woman to have a real live baby."

"Well, we can try and see," Ethaderia said. She so wanted a real-life infant instead of the fully mature children Tholian people were so used to raising. Supervising was more like it though. They emerged from the shell fully mature with everything loaded in their brains.

The majordomo got Trakon's attention.

"We should bring the kids back upstairs. Dinner is ready," Trakon said.

Pup jumped to his feet, ready for duty.

Ethaderia reluctantly handed over the baby.

D'laine and Trakon, with Pup on their heels, then scooting around them to lead the way, climbed the stairs to their domain.

AFTER EVERYONE SETTLED AT THE TABLE, THE MAJORDOMO LED HIS entourage of servers into the room. The aroma of succulent sidel, braised par, roasted vegetables, and crunchy dinner rolls was mouthwatering.

La'gar'ish lifted his nose to the edge of the table and took a sniff. Jor-Dan flicked a finger at the dog's nose.

"Bad dog," Jor-Dan said. "Lay down right now or you will be barred from the dining salon."

The dog grumbled and flopped down by his human's feet.

"He seems to be testing me," Jor-Dan said.

"Don't give in," Victor said.

As everyone dug into the food on their plates, Lee couldn't

stop himself. "So, Brian, how's the crystal cleaning coming along?"

Without batting an eye, his oldest son delved into his job. "I can average two ships per hour."

Lee stared at him. "Really? Is that as many as the rest of the team? How do you compare to them?"

Trakon and Jor-Dan averted their eyes to their plates of food. They realized where Lee was going with the conversation.

"I think I'm average," Brian said. "There's a lot to cleaning the crystals, you know. It's not just rubbing a cloth over them. They get embedded with dirt, and we have to use the air blower machine to get into the cracks."

Lee huffed out exasperated. "Son, why is it you don't want to tell me about your new job?"

Ethaderia gave a quizzical look toward her husband.

Stanley's fork stopped midway to his mouth.

"Brian's no longer on crystal cleaning duty. He's helping to upgrade the ship that's going to the Plotals," Lee said.

Victor and Kara exchanged curious glances.

Brian's face dropped from smiling to apologetic. "Daddy, I wanted to wait until the ship was finished before I told you."

"Why? You're doing mechanical engineering, and I couldn't be prouder!" Lee bellowed. "I never realized you were interested in design."

Brian shrugged. "I didn't know either until I was watching guys in the shop trying to work out a problem with the weights of the Plotals. It all just seemed so natural to me."

Jor-Dan pointed his fork at Lee. "Let's just be grateful he discovered this talent and the shop crew recognized and accepted his meddling."

Lee nodded. "You're right. I'm overreacting."

Kitry shook her head. "No, I understand fully why this upset you. I would be wounded if Trakon developed a skill that I heard about from someone else."

"Come over to the shop tomorrow," Trakon said.

"I think I worked out the controls for their big hands," Brian said. "I'll show you tomorrow."

Stanley turned to Darren. "So, what's the latest restoration project?"

Darren perked up. "Dannin and I are going around the countryside and perking up old barns and farmhouses." He turned to Jamie. "I fixed up that farmer's barn who had a problem with his bobboes."

"You did? I'll have to go talk to the bobboes and see what they think about it," Jamie said, between mouthfuls of food. "They're very opinionated."

"Bobboes have opinions?" Jor-Dan asked. "I didn't think they had the intelligence to communicate."

Jamie snorted. "You should be in my head sometime. All these animals have a lot of conversations about their lives. They talk about the humans who care for them, they complain about each other, have arguments—they're just like us. Think of them like Egroms and Plotals, or those Safri creatures, just not as smart."

"If they're like those creatures, as you say, should we be eating them?" Kitry asked, alarmed.

"Humans are carnivores," Jamie said. "Some only eat vegetables and fruit and stuff, but mostly everyone eats meat. If God didn't want us to eat meat, he wouldn't have put us among creatures. We're part of the problem, and part of the solution for species control."

Everyone stared at Jamie as if he were a complete stranger.

Stanley cleared his throat to move the conversation to a different direction. "I'm considering going to Patrosym to monitor the silencing helmet. I'd like to cross that off my list of things to keep track of for now."

"That sounds like a good idea," Jor-Dan said. "Would you like someone to accompany you?"

"If there's other business to attend to, that would be good," Stanley said. "We could see what progress they've made restoring their city."

"I'll go with you," Lee said. "I'd like to see if they've upgraded to the best materials, or if they're small-minded again."

"Surely they wouldn't want to build hazardous buildings again," Kitry said.

No one would ever forget the devastating affects the churling had on Patrosym.

"What else are you going to monitor?" Victor asked Stanley.

"I'm going to step to random places I've been before, and see how things feel," Stanley said.

"This is about that disturbance, isn't it?" Victor asked.

Stanley nodded. "Something's coming and we can't determine what. There's not even another hint of it, but it's *out there* if you know what I mean. The Egroms don't jump to conclusions. They're not wired the same way we humans are—they go on instinct alone."

"That, along with their ability to see through dimensions, makes them so completely different from the rest of us," D'laine said.

"D'laine, you're not exactly like the rest of us," Lee said. "You're almost in the same category as Stanley—very Egrom-like."

D'laine waved her father's comments aside. "Honestly, give a girl some unusual attributes and she's not human anymore."

"You know good and well that if you were back on Earth, the military would weaponize you," Lee said.

"But I'm not, and they can't," D'laine said. "Surely they would realize I could destroy them with a thought, if it came to that."

"How did a little family dinner turn into this meal of doom?" Kara asked.

"I agree," Kitry said. She turned to Stanley. "Where's Treikie? She hasn't been around in quite a while now."

"She's helping her friend Jewellex. Treikie is developing the schematics and drawings for everything Jewellex is documenting of the technology, so we don't lose anything in war again," Stanley said.

"Are they backing that information up some way?" Victor asked.

"It's in their systems," Stanley said.

"Remember, electronics and technology can get you into trouble," Lee said. "If there were an attack on those two fronts, everything would be lost. You have to make other types of backups that, say, an electromagnetic pulse could not destroy."

Jor-Dan pondered the discussion. "Lee is right. We don't want to ever experience the after effects of a war like Taylon."

THEY FINALLY MOVED AWAY FROM THE DINING TABLE TO THE family salon, where they discovered Buffy sound asleep on a sofa, with her feet in the air. Chatter was curled up on a sofa cushion that had fallen to the floor.

"Well, what do we have here?" Jor-Dan asked.

La'gar'ish's tail wagged against Jor-Dan's legs.

They watched as Buffy's feet slowly fell to the side and her tail thumped on the sofa. She stood and gracefully jumped down, almost on top of Chatter.

The diwal dog stood and shook himself, which wasn't even necessary since diwals don't have fur.

Kitry summoned a staff member. She picked up the cushion and handed it to the woman. "This needs to go into the linen smart closet."

The woman tapped her chest, took the cushion and left the room.

"What do you have to say for yourselves?" Kitry asked the dogs.

They both looked like pictures of innocence.

"Next thing you know, they'll be sleeping with you in your beds," Lee said. "Dogs are sneaky that way."

"My dog seems to be testing me," Jor-Dan said. He made his way over to a chair and settled in.

Everyone took a seat and got comfortable.

Pup wandered into the room. The other dogs were happy to see their absentee friend and leader. They all romped around the room.

"Pup must be hungry, or something," Trakon said. "He rarely leaves the twins' suite unless he has to go to the bathroom, or eat."

D'laine's diwal approached her and sat his chin on her thigh. She scratched his ears and rubbed the tufts of hair on his head. She wondered how their skin didn't get sunburned since they didn't have fur. The slick skin reminded her of a snake. It had an oily, cold feel to it that was hard to get used to. Just the idea of a dog without hair seemed wrong. It's not as if the diwals were like hairless dogs of Earth.

"Go hunt!" she said.

Pup raised his brows, wagged his tail, then took off with all the dogs on his heels.

"Buffy!" Lee, D'laine and Victor called out.

The Earth dog looked over her shoulder, barked, but reluctantly returned to the salon.

"You can't hunt with the diwals!" Lee scolded his old dog.

Buffy whined. She flopped down onto the floor and sulked.

CHAPTER TWENTY

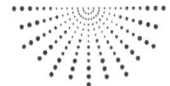

*T*rakon, Lee, and Stanley were at the shop looking over the Plotal crestrider that Brian was working on with Hexlon. Brian projected a large Plotal hand in various positions of the control panel.

"See, that won't work, because their fingers and hands are too big for that space," Brian explained, visually.

"How'd you do that?" Trakon asked.

Brian shrugged. "I just thought it, and it was there."

Stanley leaned in and studied what seemed like a disembodied hand, scales and all. "Interesting."

Suddenly, the scientist straightened. His eyes glazed out of focus and he nodded.

Hexlon and the shop guys stared at Stanley, their brows wrinkled with curiosity.

"Is he okay?" Hexlon asked.

Trakon, Lee and Brian checked out Stanley.

"Yeah, it's an Egrom thing," Brian said.

"He's not an Egrom," one of the guys said.

Stanley snapped out of it. "I've been summoned." He *stepped* away and vanished.

It spooked the shop workers. They had never witnessed the scientist's activities.

After several moments, Stanley returned with Ghury.

"Let's return to the palace for a meeting," Stanley said. "You too, Brian."

Lee raised his eyebrows at that, but kept his mouth shut.

The men and Brian marched through the city back to the palace into the large salon.

"Gather Jor-Dan, Victor, all the boys, and D'laine," Ghury said.

Trakon ran out of the room down to the throne room. Stanley *stepped out* of the room and returned with Jamie. Victor hurried to the kitchen and returned with Darren.

Jor-Dan entered the salon. A few minutes later, Trakon and D'laine came into the room.

"What's going on?" D'laine asked.

"Stanley mentioned the disturbance we are monitoring?" Ghury asked.

Everyone nodded, silent.

"We have detected a jarvust," the Egrom said.

"Jarvust?" Jor-Dan asked. "I've never heard of that. What is it?"

"We do not know very much about what we assumed was a myth, or a bedtime story to keep little children from being bad. This seems to be a discontented being created from someone who has lingered behind after they have died," Ghury said.

"An evil spirit?" Jamie asked.

Ghury stared at Jamie in that odd Egrom way. Eventually, he nodded.

D'laine and Victor shared a questioning expression.

"This is a soul that has not returned to the light, like Swezek did?" Victor asked. He was grasping to understand.

"That is somewhat correct," Ghury said.

Everyone waited for further explanation, but none was forthcoming.

"The jarvust will make its presence known soon, at which time we will determine what action is required," Ghury said. "I gathered you because of your specific powers which may help diffuse whatever situation presents itself. According to the myths that Drusta uncovered, jarvusts can be very powerful; caution is of the utmost with them."

Lee screwed up his face. "I don't have any helpful powers."

The Egrom elder studied Lee's face. "Yes, you do."

Lee's eyes travelled to Stanley, then his daughter, and finally to Victor. Everyone but Stanley shrugged. The scientist smiled wanly.

"How will we know when this jarvust makes its move?" D'laine asked.

"We will feel it," Ghury said. "When that happens, we will gather."

Kitry and Kara entered the salon and noticed the tense group.

Both Jor-Dan and Victor sent silent messages to their wives. *We will talk later.*

Kitry watched the faces of everyone present. She felt something had disturbed them. Kara picked up on the same emotion. The two women exchanged a look, then left the room. They went to Kitry's suite.

"There are no precautions to take?" Jor-Dan asked. The pressure of the situation weighed on him. He could handle an attack, such as the doski and Trangula with the army, borjos and diwals. He couldn't prepare for something that hadn't presented itself yet. He didn't want the citizens of his kingdom or the other kingdoms to be unprepared and defenseless.

Ghury stared at the king. "Your army cannot help in this situation." Ghury nodded to Stanley. "I will return to the village. We will sit in our circle and wait."

With that, the leader of the Cember Forest Egrom tribe disappeared.

Stanley cleared his throat. "He doesn't mean they will sit around twiddling their thumbs. They will cast out mental feelers to discover the threat."

The boys looked scared. Brian didn't know if this was a worse sense than the upcoming war with the doski and Trangula. He felt helpless and scared.

The adults urged the boys to return to work, to keep their minds occupied. Once they left the palace, everyone sat and stared at each other for a few minutes.

"Seems bizarre that we'll be dealing with evil spirits," Victor said. "Never, ever came across that back home, except in horror movies or books."

"There's a lot of things I've experienced here that I never would have even dreamt of in my former life," Lee said.

"Me too," D'laine said.

"We can't even warn anyone." Trakon worried.

Jor-Dan huffed out in exasperation. "There's no point in overreacting to this unseen threat. We can't do a thing about it, so we should go about our business."

"We should have the scholars search the library for this myth," Stanley said. "Maybe ask the citizens of Ebscalon whether they have heard these bedtime stories."

"Good idea," Trakon said.

THE NEXT DAY, STANLEY *STEPPED* LEE AND HIMSELF TO PATROSYM. They found Queen Egraphor and King Emeric in the Plotal tents.

Lee looked around. The beauty, luxury and comfort contained in the huge tents stunned him.

"Hello, King Emeric," Stanley said, when presented before

the king. "Hello, Queen Egraphor. We come as emissaries from Ebscalon to see how your reconstruction is progressing."

"If there is anything we can do to help, we would gladly offer our assistance," Lee said.

"Thank you," Emeric said, as he stood and grasped arms with each man, in the Tholian custom. "There will be no skimping on agrin sap to cut corners. Our previous building master pocketed money instead of buying materials. We are still searching for him."

"And what of your daughter?" Stanley asked. "Is she in a secure place?"

Egraphor stiffened her posture.

Both Lee and Stanley stayed quiet, unsure of what was to come.

"Do not call that vile woman our daughter! We have disowned her," the queen finally said.

"She is imprisoned in one of the turret tower rooms far away from the damage," Emeric said. "We allow none of her detail to guard her for more than one day every month. We wanted to make sure that she couldn't sway any of the guard with her pleading eyes."

"What about her servants, or the people who bring her food?" Lee asked.

"No one person is alone with her. Any visit is for no longer than ten or fifteen minutes, even to change bedding," Egraphor said. "We know how easy it would be to pass a note. We scan everyone and everything that goes into or out of that room."

Emeric sighed and shook his head sadly. "We honestly don't have any idea why she turned out this way."

Lee placed his hand on the king's shoulder. "No one can determine the path their child takes. You are not responsible for her decisions, so don't blame yourselves. It is painful to see you suffering from your daughter's treason, but at some point, you have to let it go."

Emeric nodded sadly. Egraphor had a difficult time letting it go.

Lee and Stanley walked the premises with Emeric pointing things out. Egroms demolished the entire palace, and the debris "evaporated". The new foundation had been prepared and structural beams were being installed. They impressed Lee with their innovative methods and materials.

They walked over to the turret housing the princess. The guards saluted with their fists to their hearts.

"We have to scan the visitors," a guard stated.

Emeric waved his hand in a dismissal, but Stanley spoke up.

"It's quite all right to scan us, King Emeric. You don't want to make allowances," the scientist said. "Once you dismiss one person, someone else wants the same privilege, or they will find inequity in being treated differently."

"Yes, yes, you're right," Emeric said. "Go ahead, scan the Eartholians."

The guard pulled his laser tool from its holder and scanned Lee, then Stanley. They followed Emeric and the guard inside. There was another door and another set of guards, but no scanning at the second point of entry. The guards opened the door and King Emeric, Lee and Stanley walked into an empty, dank area. The guard approached a panel on the wall, keyed in a code and waited a second. Another panel popped out of thin air, and the guard entered another key.

A staircase to the top of the tower materialized.

"Another failsafe," Emeric said.

"That's quite handy," Lee said as he walked over to the stairs and stared up at several lengths of stairs and landings going up the height of the tower.

Emeric led the way. Stanley's brain determined that they were climbing what would be equivalent to three or four stories of a building of only stairs—no living areas.

Around what would normally be the fifth floor, a living area appeared. They continued to climb up. They passed two more floors, then Emeric stopped on the eighth floor. He pressed his fingers to the panel on the walkway. A room appeared.

Lee and Stanley shared a surprised glance. The cloaking technology intrigued them. They looked over a modestly furnished room for a regular citizen. No luxuries were visible. Tight bars were on all the windows. It would be impossible to slip an arm out of the window through the bars, unless it was a slender arm.

Lee determined even an elbow on a slender arm would not make it past the bars.

They noticed a dark form sitting in a chair in front of a window.

"Yalalore!" Emeric called out. There was no love in his voice.

The dark form turned. The silencing helmet fully encased the crown of the head. Only her face was visible. Her lips curled into a sneer.

What do you want? Princess Yalalore mouthed the silent words with a silent snarl.

"We're here to assess your prison," Stanley said. He crossed the room and stood in front of the princess. He gripped the helmet and tried to remove it. The device held firm.

Lee studied the bars on the windows, inspected the entire room, then entered the inner room which consisted of a bedroom and bathroom. Satisfied with the security of the place, he returned to the living area.

"Everything seems secure," Lee said.

"The helmet appears locked in place safely," Stanley said.

Emeric nodded. They turned and exited the room, and the king pressed his fingers to the panel. The room faded from view. They made the long climb down the stairs and left the building.

"I don't know how you do it," Lee said. "If I had to disown one of my boys, it would crush my spirit."

"The only thing that is keeping us going is what the Eartholian, Victor said. Egraphor has passed an egg. We pray that our son will be a good and just person," Emeric said.

"Congratulations!" Lee said, with Stanley echoing him. "Victor sees the future. He would not have spoken up if he wasn't one-hundred-percent sure of the results."

They said their goodbyes, and Stanley *stepped* them back to Ebscalon.

LEE JOINED EVERYONE IN THE DINING SALON FOR LUNCH AT THE palace. He and Stanley discussed what they found in Patrosym.

"The tower has good security," Stanley said. "Are you aware of the cloaking technology they use to hide the stairs and walkways?"

"Cloaking?" Trakon asked. "What do you mean?"

They explained how the stairs appeared, and how the room appeared and disappeared.

"I wasn't aware of that," Jor-Dan said.

Brian watched the grownups discussing the technology the Patrosyms had. "That could be handy for the crestriders."

All eyes focused on Brian, with interest. He pushed his chair back and stood. "I've got to get back to the shop."

Heads nodded to the boy.

"That's a common feature in many science fiction books and movies back on Earth," Lee said. "It would be very beneficial in a lot of different scenarios."

"Stealth," Trakon said. "Could you show us what you saw?"

Stanley presented a step-by-step repeat of how they approached the tower, the scanning, the second set of doors, the blank space, the wall panel, and the stairs appearing. Next up, he showed the empty hallway, then the room appearing, and vanishing when they exited.

Trakon stared at his father. "Do you have any recollection of anything like this prior to the Great War?"

Victor zoned out.

Kara and Kitry noticed something going on with him.

Kitry was about to say something, but Kara shook her head and held up her index finger.

Several quiet moments passed, when Victor's eyes refocused.

"Horld," Victor said.

Everyone waited for more to follow, but Victor looked around the table, waiting for someone to recognize what he said.

"Is that a name of a person, place or thing?" D'laine asked. She had been quiet through the discussion, pulling all the details inside her head.

Victor thought about it for a minute. "I'm sure it's the name of a man."

"Let's get Treikie and Jewellex over here. Maybe they would recognize the name from all the documentation they've created," Jor-Dan said.

Stanley sent a message to his girlfriend. "They'll be here in a little while."

Kitry summoned the majordomo. He set two more places at the table. She thanked him.

The two women entered the salon.

"Please join us for lunch," Kitry said.

They were barely in their seats when Jor-Dan picked up the conversation. "Have either of you come across the name Horld?"

"Horld was the inventor of the lasers we use," Treikie said.

"He contributed many, many technological inventions to our society before the war," Jewellex said. "I've documented several things."

The men shared a knowledgeable look. D'laine followed them with her eyes.

"Have you uncovered anything pertaining to cloaking?" Trakon asked.

"Cloaking? Like in making something invisible?" Treikie asked. She scanned the faces around the table.

"Yes," Jor-Dan said. He nodded at Stanley and Lee.

Stanley led the discussion and showed what he and Lee had experienced at Patrosym.

Jewellex frowned. "Where would they have come across the technology to develop working models?"

"We don't know," Jor-Dan said. "It's interesting that they would have this advanced technology, but their city crumbled in the churling."

They all fell silent, contemplating, as they ate their food.

Treikie couldn't let it go. She pulled up the search engine in her communicator and typed the name Horld into the search box.

"Horld was a Ciertron!" Treikie said. "He passed on thirty paths before the war. He had so many medals on his uniform!" She showed everyone a picture of the stately man from the file Jewellex had found in some old archives.

"If he was a Ciertron, how did Patrosym get his inventions?" Victor asked.

"Maybe his inventions were commonplace in those days?" Kara asked. She looked around the table to shrugs and nodding.

"Keep digging into the files, and keep documenting procedures," Jor-Dan said.

"We certainly don't want to lose any recently recovered technology," Kitry said. "Especially with this threat of war from the Trangula."

Lee was quietly thinking. "I want to show this technology to Brian."

Trakon nodded. "That would be wise. He has this uncanny ability to see things the rest of us don't."

"Just think what he'll be like when he's an adult," Stanley said.

"Should we consider having the kingdoms and villages come together to discuss the recovery of this lost technology?" D'laine asked.

"Treikie and I could present what we are doing. Perhaps that would encourage the other kingdoms to do the same thing, and we can all share our findings, or create a library," Jewellex said.

"I like the idea of a library," Kitry said. "Didn't Jakla suggest we build something in that area between all the kingdoms?"

"Yes. Yes, he did," Jor-Dan said. "A library would be excellent for all generations, and might even encourage people to become documentarians or researchers."

Trakon, Lee and Stanley nodded.

Jor-Dan thought for a moment, then shook his head. "Let's not jump on this quite yet. I think we have enough to focus on with the threat of war, and this jarvust. Find out what you can, see what Brian makes of this, and after things calm down, we will tackle this situation."

CHAPTER TWENTY-ONE

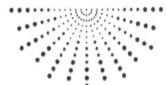

*A*fter lunch, Lee walked with Trakon, Victor, and Stanley back to the shop. Brian was just getting out from underneath a crestrider when they arrived.

"Brian!" Lee called out.

Brian turned to see his father and the men approaching. He did a rapid assessment of anything he could have done wrong, either at home, or anywhere else and came up blank.

"Hi, Dad," Brian said. He eyed the men warily.

"We need to show you something and see if you know what it is or how it works," Trakon said.

Brian relaxed. Since his punishment for his part in the wild fling with his brother and their friends, he was touchy whenever someone called him out for anything.

"Okay," Brian said.

Stanley played the sequence of events.

"Stop!" Brian said, as he watched the guard key in the first sequence at the wall panel. "Go slow."

Stanley showed the guard entering the second sequence.

"Hold on a sec. Can you back up just at the beginning of that?" Brian asked.

Stanley eased his memory backward.

Brian turned his head this way and that—almost like a dog. "I'm ready."

Stanley showed the staircase appearing and their ascent. Brian watched the rest without another word. Duncts passed without him saying anything. Suddenly, data and pictures streamed in front of their eyes, in thin air. More data than even Stanley could keep up with.

"Whoa! What is this?" Lee asked.

"It's the entire coding for the cloaking!" Stanley said, so loud that others turned to look at the group. "How did you do that? Where did it come from?"

Brian shrugged. "These things just sort of come to me. When someone keys in those sequences, it triggers an enfolding. I'll bet those people don't even know or understand that, but I captured the entire process which I guess is the whole cloaking invention. It's sort of like how I learned how to fly a crestrider when Trakon gave us those lessons."

Lee nodded. "I remember that. You used your mind to man the controls. You didn't need to hold them or touch them like the rest of us."

"Let me run this by Treikie and Jewellex," Stanley said. "They can document this procedure and share it in words and pictures for the rest of us."

"Good idea," Trakon said.

Victor zoned out. He was *gone* far longer than usual. Everyone was getting nervous when he finally *returned*. He turned to Brian, then made eye contact with the group. "Brian's role is similar to Horld. He will be a great inventor."

Everyone was startled with that announcement, even Brian.

"You saw that in his future?" Lee asked.

Victor nodded. "It was a blessing when you switched his punishment from household chores to working with the crys-tals. The natural progression was solving the problem with the

Plotals' ship. That was the correct course for things to fall into place for his future."

"Let's go talk to my father and his advisors," Trakon said. He pointed to Brian. "Not you… you can return to work."

The group walked back to the palace.

THAT NIGHT AT THE DINNER TABLE, LEE TOLD ETHADERIA WHAT had occurred that day, and what Victor said.

"Oh, my Great Thol! What a gift you have, Brian!" she exclaimed.

Brian shrugged. He didn't see why everyone was making such a big deal of it. "A lot of people come up with things every day."

Lee let out an exasperated huff. "Son, you're right. Many people come up with ideas. Only a tiny percent of those people ever DO anything with their ideas. I saw it repeatedly through my career with NASA."

"I have stuff buzzing through my brain all the time," Brian said. "It's no big deal."

Lee opened his mouth, but Ethaderia laid her hand on his arm to hush him.

"It would be a very good idea for you to document those things," she said. "No matter how small and insignificant they seem. You can never tell who would value those tiny inventive ideas of yours."

Brian looked from his step-mother to his father. "You really think I should do that?"

They both nodded enthusiastically.

"Okay," he said. He stabbed a vegetable with his fork and shoved it in his mouth, without grace.

"Wow, Brian. You sure are smart!" Jamie said. He had watched and listened to the exchange between the three of them with interest. "Grandpa Jor-Dan and the rest of the kings sure could use your help in getting things back to where they used to be before that big war."

"Tell us about your day, Jamie," Ethaderia said.

"Dannin came and got me. An og's been hanging around near the chocolate tree forest, and he was worried the kitchen people might get hurt," Jamie said.

"Was it your og?" Lee asked.

"No, it wasn't Oggy. This is a wild og that seems lost. He couldn't find his family and wouldn't move away from the gardens," Jamie said. "I talked to him and he showed me where he was from. He swears he doesn't know how he got to the garden, and I believe him."

Lee's brows furrowed. "Is he still there?"

Jamie nodded while chewing his food.

"We'd better contact Stanley so he can look into his head. Something doesn't sound right," Lee said, worried.

"What could possibly be wrong?" Ethaderia asked.

"Either there's something wrong with his memory, from an accident—maybe he hit his head? Or, someone or something has manipulated something in his mind and removed a memory," Lee said.

"Would this have something to do with the Trangula?" Ethaderia asked.

Lee shook his head. "No, but it might have something to do with this other issue that we're waiting for—the jarvust. We'd better go to the palace after we finish eating."

Lee, Ethaderia and the boys entered the palace and headed to the big salon. They found the family discussing the daily events.

"Hello!" Jor-Dan bellowed out as Lee and his family entered the room. "It is good to see our future inventor!"

Brian blushed at the attention. He hurried over to where Darren sat on the floor with Buffy.

"Jor-Dan, Jamie had a strange situation today, and we need Stanley to check this out," Lee said. He explained what Jamie told him.

"Is the og still in the garden?" Stanley asked.

"As far as I know," Jamie said. "He didn't want to leave. I don't think he'll hurt anyone."

Jor-Dan, Victor, Trakon and D'laine stood.

"Let's have Stanley take a look and see if he can determine what's going on," Jor-Dan said.

The group left the palace and trekked to the gardens. Sure enough, the og was curled up on the ground at the base of one of the chocolate trees. It grunted a warning, but Jamie and D'laine soothed it so that Stanley could delve into the animal's brain.

"Huh. There's a whole blank area. No wonder this fella doesn't want to leave. He doesn't know where he's been, or where he's supposed to be," Stanley said. He dug further into the creature's head and did some repair work. "I've found his most recent memories before this one block was erased. He has a mate and piglets—is that what they're called?"

"Og's are sort of like pigs, so I guess piglets is right," Jamie said. "Will he be able to find his family now?"

"Yes, but I'm concerned whether or not he will be welcomed," D'laine said. "It seems like his memory of the family is damaged." She turned to Stanley. "Was this intentional?"

"Why would anyone want to distort an og's memory?" Jor-Dan asked.

"He must have seen something he wasn't supposed to," Trakon said.

"That's not good," Jor-Dan said. "That leads me to believe

that who or whatever did this knows animals can communicate with humans."

Stanley focused more deeply on the animal. He did something in the og's head, and the beast squealed, turned and was going to attack.

D'laine used The Voice to subdue the animal. "What did you do?"

Stanley studied the brain more intently. "I found what he saw." He projected what he assumed was the jarvust.

"What is that?" Lee asked.

"I'm guessing this is that jarvust," Stanley said.

"We should call Ghury," Trakon said.

As soon as the words left his mouth, the Egrom, along with the rest of the elders, appeared.

The Egroms studied what Stanley extracted from the og's brain.

"Is that the Ikley Forest?" Drusta asked.

"No, it feels like the Tempe Forest," Adrum said.

"Tempe? Where's that?" Trakon asked.

"It's the span of forest between the Cember Forest and the Ikley," Jor-Dan said.

The shape of what scared the og, and what wiped his memory, was difficult to identify. It seemed like an illusion more than a solid figure. Tall, thin with roped hair hanging down the sides of a face with old, weathered eyes, a beaked nose and what appeared to be thin lips. The hair ropes hung below drooped shoulders. If they could identify any clothing, it would be a shroud or robe of some type.

"That's the jarvust?" Lee asked.

After a long moment of studying the vision, Ghury and the elders nodded.

"Yes," Ghury said. "I cannot determine if this was a human at one time, or another creature."

"This being has not decided whether or not to strike," Drusta said.

Everyone was nervous.

"What do we do with the og?" Trakon asked.

The Egroms scanned the beast, holding out their four hands in front of them. The og didn't seem to mind the attention.

Absadul tilted his head. "His brain is functioning. I will give him a boost to make him leave the garden and find his family. They are searching for him near where your pet stayed in the pen, Jamie."

"Should I bring him over there?" Jamie asked.

"No, it's best for him to make his own way back home," Absadul said.

Absadul's nudge had the og scurrying to its feet and running away at a brisk pace.

The Egroms nodded to the group.

"We will return to the tribe and continue to study this situation," Ghury said.

With that, the Egrom elders vanished.

LATE THAT NIGHT, JAMIE TOSSED AND TURNED IN HIS BED WHILE making little urgent noises. Suddenly, he sprang to a sitting position and screamed for all it was worth.

Lee and Ethaderia rushed into the room, followed by Eglabado and Brian, who was rubbing his eyes.

Jamie looked awake, but he kept screaming.

"Be gentle," Ethaderia said. "He's still sleeping, and you're not supposed to wake someone who is having a terrible dream."

There was a clattering at the window opening, and large claws anchored Ekka to the side of the house. The borjo stuck his head inside—there wasn't room for more of him.

Lee rushed to the borjo. "It's okay, Ekka. Jamie is dreaming."

The borjo wasn't at all satisfied. He huffed out a tiny bit of flames and smoke.

Lee jumped back. *D'laine! Jamie is having a nightmare and Ekka may burn the house down!*

After several long minutes, D'laine ran into the house, thundered up the stairs and took in the situation. She approached her brother and studied him. He looked awake, but it was obvious he was sleeping. She walked over to the borjo, hanging on the windowsill.

"It's okay, Ekka. Jamie is okay." She patted the borjo, rubbed his velvety snout and calmed the beast. "Your human is okay."

The borjo looked D'laine in the eye. He seemed to trust what she said to him, but he didn't leave.

Jamie stopped screaming, but his eyes were still wide open.

The downstairs door opened. Eglabado turned to attend to whoever was there, when Trakon called out. "D'laine? Lee? Is everything okay?"

"We're up in Jamie's room," Ethaderia called out, just as Eglabado had descended the stairs.

"Come, Prince Trakon," Eglabado said. "Master Jamie is having a nightmare, and it upset his borjo."

They climbed the stairs and joined the others in Jamie's room.

"What's wrong with him? He looks awake to me," Trakon said.

"He's still sleeping," Ethaderia said.

Suddenly, Jamie turned to his side, flopped back down again and resumed sleeping.

Everyone let out their breaths they had been holding. Ekka watched his human, then let go of the ledge and pushed off. He flew back to his tower.

"I thought Ekka was going to char me," Lee said. "That borjo definitely watches over Jamie." He turned to his daughter.

"Thanks for coming, D'laine. Ekka didn't trust me, and he let loose some flames and smoke."

"Everyone go back to bed," Ethaderia said, as she shooed everyone out of Jamie's room. She pulled the covers up, bent and kissed him on the head. "Have peaceful dreams."

THE NEXT MORNING AT BREAKFAST HAD PEOPLE SHUFFLING INTO the room. No one seemed perky, except for Jamie. His eyes took in all the tired faces, including Eglabado's.

"Why's everyone so tired?" Jamie asked.

Brian kicked his brother under the table.

"Ow! What'd you do that for?" Jamie asked.

"You woke up everyone in the middle of the night screaming your lungs out," Brian said.

"Did not!" Jamie sputtered.

"Did so!" Brian almost shouted, but calmed himself.

"Boys! Please, we don't need a shouting match at the table," Lee said. He turned to Jamie. "You were having a nightmare."

"You don't remember anything?" Ethaderia asked.

Jamie shook his head, then thought for a moment. He suddenly recalled something. "I saw that thing in my head! It scared me!"

"What thing? Can you be more specific?" Lee asked.

"That jarvust thing," Jamie said.

Ethaderia turned to Lee, then Brian. "What is this about?"

"The Egroms identified that disturbance as a jarvust," Lee said. "We saw a picture of it from an og's brain."

"Did it say anything to you?" Ethaderia asked, as she studied Jamie.

He shook his head slowly, but uncertainly. "I don't remember. I think it was just looking for something in my head."

"This doesn't sound good," Lee said.

"It doesn't seem to have hurt you as far as I can tell," Ethaderia said.

Jamie shrugged and shoved a forkful of scrambled bobboe eggs into his mouth.

"Honestly, when I want information, I can never get any. When I want peace and quiet, you can't shut up," Lee said, frustrated.

The boys finished eating and were out the door without being nagged to go to work.

Lee stood and stacked dishes. Eglabado grabbed them out of his hands.

"More coffee?" the manservant asked.

"No, thanks," Lee said. He kissed Ethaderia on the cheek. "I'm heading over to the palace to see what Stanley's up to."

"I'll see you later," she said.

LEE WALKED THROUGH THE PALACE ENTRANCE AND WAS HEADING toward the stairway when Jor-Dan left the dining salon.

"Good morning, Lee," Jor-Dan said. "I understand you lost sleep last night. Is everything okay now?"

"Jamie just left for the pakow pens, and seems to be okay, but I'm concerned," Lee said. "I'm going to ask Stan about it. Jamie said the jarvust was looking for something in his head."

"I don't like the sound of that," Jor-Dan said, his eyebrows scrunched up. "Let me know if Stanley has any insight."

"Will do," Lee said. He took the stairs two at a time up to Stanley's suite, then rapped on the door.

After several long minutes, his friend opened the door, hair mussed up and a goofy look on his face.

"Hey Stan, got a minute? There's been a development," Lee said.

"Ah… sure, Lee. Come on in." Stanley stepped aside and Lee entered the living area and plunked into a chair.

"That jarvust was in Jamie's head last night," Lee said. He heard a noise in the other room. "Oh, I'm sorry, is Treikie here? I can come back later." Lee stood abruptly, embarrassed at interrupting a possible love tryst.

Stanley waved a hand in front of him. "It's okay. What exactly happened?"

Lee explained how Jamie woke everyone with his screaming, and what he said happened this morning at breakfast.

Stanley pondered the news. The bedroom door opened and Treikie entered the living area.

"Good morning, Lee. I'm sorry to hear about Jamie's nightmare… I couldn't help overhearing what you said just now," Treikie said.

"It was awful," Lee said. "Ekka didn't trust me, and I was afraid he'd burn the house down—he puffed out fire and smoke!"

"Oh, no!" she turned to her boyfriend. "What do you make of this, Stanley?"

"I've been contemplating about the whole jarvust scenario. I can't help but wonder if this has something to do with the Trangula," he said.

"How is that possible?" Lee asked.

"Think about it. No matter what you want to call that thing —a ghost, spirit, evil entity—I'm positive it's something that evolved from hate," Stanley said. "The Trangula are a species that rule with a hard fist. From what the Plotals and the Egroms have said, the Trangulan subjects are the true downtrodden under this King Custuf. Add Augenta stirring the pot, and you've got a lot of negativity churning up."

Lee and Treikie nodded.

"That makes sense," Lee said. "So, you think that's what created this jarvust?"

"That's the only working theory I have," Stanley said. Suddenly he started and stared at Lee, as alarm crossed his face.

"What's wrong?" Lee asked.

"I just had an alert from Al! Be right back—need to make sure he's okay!" Stanley vanished as he *stepped* to Earth.

STANLEY APPEARED IN THE EMPTY SPARE ROOM. HE OVERHEARD normal, calm voices from the living room.

"Mr. Jordan, we'd like you to help us clear up some things regarding the disappearance of the Jacksons, professor Joplin, and the Bennet's," an agent said.

"I'm not sure what I can tell you that hasn't already been printed in the paper," Al said. He sounded steady, not alarmed. "Could I get you a cup of coffee, or some iced tea?"

A different voice responded with, "no thank you."

"My editor assigned me the story when D'laine Jackson first disappeared. I interviewed professor Joplin when he was still at Rice University, and I spoke with Mr. Jackson briefly," Al said. "Then I did a follow-up interview on the one-year anniversary of the disappearance. By that time, the Jackson's had vanished and professor Joplin was retiring from Rice."

"How did you come to be living in the Bennet's house?" the first agent asked.

"I interviewed Victor Bennet for the anniversary article. He and his wife... uh, Kara? seemed like nice people. I stayed for the weekend, headed back to Houston on Southwest Airlines and began work on the article. I tried calling them several times to clarify something, but I never heard back from them, which seemed odd. I called the local police department—that's all on record—and asked if they would check on them. They found food on the table, but no sign of the Bennet's. It's like they vanished into thin air."

Stanley smirked while he listened to Al's convincing tale.

"So, tell us how you came to be living here in the Bennet's house," the second agent asked.

"This lawyer contacted me and said they appointed me like a guardian for the house and property," Al said. "I don't understand how or why. I didn't know the Bennet's personally. They were subjects I interviewed, but I wasn't going to turn down an opportunity of a lifetime. It's not like I was making tons of money as a junior reporter, you know?"

Stanley listened to muted sounds from the living room, which he assumed came from the agents standing, then Al getting to his feet.

"Thank you for your time, Mr. Jordan," the first agent said. "If we have any more questions, we'll contact you."

"Sure thing. I'll be here working on my book," Al said. He walked them to the door, and they left.

Stanley tapped Al's name on his communicator. "Shhh. Do not talk yet." He walked into the living room and used his sensors to check for bugs. Sure enough, he found a listening device on the underside of the sofa, on the inside of the upholstered board. He disabled it with a thought. He found nothing else. "That went well."

"Thanks so much for coming. When they showed up I nearly freaked out, but kept it together," Al said.

"You did good. They seemed satisfied with your answers," Stanley said.

"Are you sure?" Al asked.

"They didn't haul you out the door in handcuffs," Stanley said.

Al let out a deep breath. "If they talk to my former boss and the attorney, it's all verifiable."

"Let me see if Kara wants anything before I go," Stanley said. He worked his communicator and sent Kara a message.

You're at my house? Kara sent.

Yes. Need anything?

Victor said to check his desk for a thumb drive. Can you grab Darren's baseball hat? It was in the mudroom. And for me, grab my apron that says Best Cook—I want to have Ulavia design something for Grubio.

Okay. I'll be back in a jiffy, Stanley sent.

He asked Al about the whereabouts of the things Kara requested.

Al walked into Victor's old office and opened the keyboard tray. The thumb drive was still there. Since Al only used a laptop, he never even bothered to pull the keyboard tray out.

They easily found Darren's ball cap and the apron.

"Call me if you need me," Stanley said. "I don't think those guys will show up again anytime soon, but you can never tell."

"Thanks for coming over," Al said. "They won't come back because of their bug?"

"If they do, it would be foolish on their part. Let's hope they assume it was defective and leave it at that," Stanley said. "I'd better go. Lee's waiting for me."

With that, Stanley *stepped* back to Thol.

LEE JUMPED TO HIS FEET WHEN STANLEY APPEARED IN THE ROOM. "Everything okay?"

"Yeah, there were some government agents questioning Al about why he was living in Victor and Kara's house. He kept his cool, and they seemed satisfied with his answers," Stanley said. "They left a bug under the sofa, but I disabled it."

Lee wiped a hand through his blond hair. "Why would they leave a bug? What could they assume Al was harboring?"

"They're the government. They can do whatever the hell

they want," Stanley said. "Let me go give these things to Kara. Where's Treikie?"

"Jewellex needed something. She said she'd catch up with you later," Lee said.

Lee and Stanley left to track down Kara. They found her in the small salon with Kitry and Ethaderia. Stanley handed over the three things he had collected for her.

"Oh, thank you so much, Stanley." She held up the apron. "I'm going to have Ulavia make Grubio an apron something like this. He's going to like it."

"Where's Victor, in the Visionary's temple?" Stanley asked.

"Yes, he headed over there after breakfast," Kara said.

"Okay. I'll tell him you have the thumb drive," Stanley said.

CHAPTER TWENTY-TWO

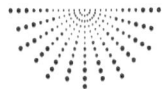

S tanley and Lee took off and headed out of the palace. They walked across the city to the Visionary's temple and stopped inside the archway.

"Are we supposed to remove our shoes?" Lee whispered.

Stanley shrugged. "Should we knock, or simply go inside?"

"Welcome," a voice called out. "Please enter. You may leave your shoes on."

Lee and Stanley exchanged a look, shrugged, and walked inside. They looked around the vast room and saw Victor and the Visionary, in their white robes and sandals, standing at the floating planet under the glass globe.

"Come... join us," the Visionary said.

They walked across the floor and joined the two men at the floating planet, suspended in the air and surrounded by clouds. The skies flashed under the globe, similar to how they did outside the temple.

Lee wasn't sure if he should bow, like to the Dalai Lama, or what, so he did nothing. He stood quietly and watched the fascinating scene before him. He didn't understand how the glass dome worked, how the scene replicated Thol right down to the flashing skies, which he hardly noticed anymore.

Victor hadn't greeted them. He was standing at the floating dome with his eyes closed and his hands stretched out in front of him.

Lee and Stanley stared at their friend, not sure what to do.

The Visionary turned to them, a smile on his serene face. "You have concerns?"

"Yes," Lee said, after a bit. "I'm worried about Jamie, my youngest son."

The Visionary nodded. "Yes, I understand. The jarvust was looking inside his head. This being was curious about the boy because he communicates with animals. Nothing more."

Lee wondered how the man knew about that event, but thought perhaps Victor mentioned it. Evidently it was a breakfast topic at the palace.

Next, the Visionary faced Stanley. "While your theory about discontent makes sense, that is not the case here. The jarvust has nothing to do with the Trangula."

Stanley was about to speak up when Victor *returned*.

"There has been no decision made. The jarvust is unsure why it's even here, back in the physical plane of existence. This was not the era it came from, and it doesn't recognize this Thol of today," Victor said. "What Alatheers said is true. This jarvust did not appear because of discontent. It seems it returned here for revenge from an unjust action that took its life force."

"I wonder if he was killed in the war?" Lee asked.

"I don't know, I have not seen its original form, which might lead to its identity," Victor said. "This being has not made its intentions clear either, so the outcomes for the future are murky."

"That could be good," Stanley said. "Maybe it won't stay here."

The Visionary shook his head. "No, according to the myths

we have studied, when they return like this, they stay until they have finished what they came to do."

"I only wish we knew what this being is here for," Stanley said. "It has everyone on edge."

Lee and Stanley determined there was no more to say on the subject, so they said their goodbyes and left the temple.

"Hopefully, it won't visit Jamie again," Lee said.

As they walked back toward the palace, Brian called out to Lee as he ran up to them, all smiles. "Guess what, Dad?" Brian said.

"What's going on?" Lee asked. "How come you're not at work?"

Brian could hardly contain his excitement. "I finished the Plotal ship! We're getting ready to deliver it to Commander Bosakin! Want to come for the ride?"

"Oh, wow!" Lee said. "I'll bet your sister would like to come along. Can I invite her?"

"Sure!" Brian said.

Lee sent her a message.

"That was pretty neat how you used a replica of a Plotal hand to create the right size controls," Stanley said. "Before you did that, I could not imagine Jakla manning a ship at all, unless he did everything mentally."

The men waited for D'laine. When she exited the palace, she looked around, spotted them and hurried over. She patted her brother on the back.

"This is exciting! You worked on the first ship for the Plotals," D'laine said.

"We'd better go, Trakon is eager to deliver the ship and have Jakla do a test flight," Brian said.

They all headed over to the shop where the rather large crestrider hovered off the ground. Trakon's head popped up. When he saw them, he waved. "Ready to head out?"

Brian, his father, sister and Stanley joined Trakon on the

ship. Lee and Stanley looked over the helm and all the oversized controls.

"This is amazing," Stanley said. "The next step in Plotal evolution. There's no turning back for them now. After flying, they'll be hooked on technology."

"Neska is hooked on the smart closet already," Lee said. "She will steer Jakla in the right direction if he needs a push toward this new way of life."

Trakon maneuvered the ship over the buildings and the city gates. Four crestriders followed, two on each side of the Plotal craft. They zoomed across the moss fields toward Ta'Byu'Vohon.

Stanley and Lee studied the forests that lay at the edges of the field of moss. They were vigilant in trying to discover the jarvust threat. All they saw were colonies of hosks going about their business, along with sighting sidels hopping about, and a nesting par. Lee pointed to two male mrucks that were battling for territorial rights.

He and Stanley watched their brutal dominance fight for a few minutes. When one of the mrucks fell down, the champion roared his success. They watched the loser limp away into the forest.

"Guess it's no different from Earth," Lee said. "That reminded me of African beasts fighting for their territories."

They approached Ta'Byu'Vohon, and Trakon steered the ship away from the pakow pens and landed, followed by the four other crestriders.

Jakla and Orongo led others from the stronghold. They approached the reinforced crestrider. Plotal mouths were like alligators, so there wasn't muscle movement to show a smile on the long, nubby snout. However, their eyes lit up in wonderment and happiness. All of the Plotals who approached the ships and the Ciertrons, had lit-up eyes.

This was an important day for Plotals world-wide.

Embracing technology had never seemed important to them when they were nomads living in their tents. Since the days following the Great War of Taylon, Plotals left behind their destroyed permanent city to wander the planet. They had turned into fierce warring creatures who enslaved anyone who crossed their paths.

D'laine had changed Jakla. She had saved him when a robot shot a direct hit of energy to Jakla's heart during the robot invasion from Zan, which should have killed him. From that point on, the Plotals evolved, changing the way others perceived them. They strived for non-aggressive friendliness. Jakla's motto with his people was *think before you act.*

Trakon, Brian, Lee, Stanley and D'laine walked down the stairs to greet the Plotals. Trakon spread an arm out toward the ship.

"Here it is. You can thank Brian for redesigning the control panels to accommodate the size of your hands," Trakon said.

Jakla stared at Brian. "You did that?"

Brian nodded. "I'm positive everything is to scale for you."

"Come on, I'll show you the control panel and everything else," Trakon said. He led Jakla and Orongo up the stairs to the deck of the ship.

The Plotals looked over the space.

"This is large enough for four or five Plotals," Jakla said.

He and Orongo followed Trakon to the helm.

"How do your hands fit with all the controls?" Trakon asked.

Jakla and Orongo took turns and wrapped a hand around a control stick, touched a finger to a button on the control panel —they tried everything while the ship was stationary.

"Yes, these controls are perfect for our hands," Orongo said. "That human boy has good instinct."

"Have three of your party board. We configured the ship for five of you," Trakon said.

Orongo lumbered over to the railing. He pointed to specific

Plotals and had them board the ship. When everyone onboarded, Trakon stood beside Jakla at the helm.

"This will raise the ship," he pointed out.

Jakla pressed the control, grabbed the joystick, and the ship rose slowly into the air.

"This is how you hover in place," Trakon said, as he pointed to a control.

Jakla tried it out.

"Okay, now move the stick forward and we'll go for a ride."

The ship took off. The humans and Plotals on the ground observed as the ship flew straight, banked, turned this way and that, then hovered in place.

Jakla called Orongo to the helm. "Your turn. You will enjoy this experience immensely!"

Orongo landed the ship, rose the ship in the air and followed all the steps that his commander did.

The new experience satisfied the Plotals, so Orongo returned to the starting point and landed the ship. They all disembarked and joined the others on the ground.

"Our children will be much more advanced than we old Plotals are," Orongo said.

Jakla grasped Trakon's forearm. "This is a glorious day for my species." Next, he grasped Brian's arm. "Brian, my people will remember your name as the Eartholian human boy who understood our needs."

Brian flushed. He felt his ears burning. "I'm grateful for my gifts from Thol to do the things I do. I hope your people get over their fear of technology."

Finally, Jakla approached D'laine. "I owe you a great debt, D'laine. If it hadn't been for you, Plotals would still roam Thol with our tent cities and act like monsters."

D'laine hugged the huge seven-and-a-half-feet tall creature. "Oh, Jakla. I'm so happy that we're friends."

He patted her on the back as gently as he could, which still felt like hard whacks to D'laine. "I have benefitted greatly from our friendship. The Ciertrons are now our friends, and our reputation is changing among the other kingdoms."

"We will try not to fight over who flies the ship," Orongo said, with a Plotal laugh, which was like loud coughing.

"We should probably order several one-man flyers—or rather one-Plotal flyers," Jakla said. "They would be good for patrols of our land, and normal activities that require traveling to distant kingdoms."

"We can accommodate your order," Trakon said. "When you decide on exactly what you want, we will build them to your specifications. You might consider ships for multiple riders. Two is a popular size."

Jakla and Orongo nodded. "We will discuss our needs with my advisors and let you know what we require."

D'LAINE ROCKED KAL-DAN, ENJOYING THE PEACEFUL AFTERNOON. She glanced over to Jesslin's crib and was shocked to witness her daughter sitting up, holding onto the crib rails.

"Jessie! When did you learn to sit up?" D'laine called out to Trakon. *Jesslin is sitting up!* She hit her communicator and called her father with the same message.

Pup got out of bed and approached the crib, his tail wagging. He licked the tiny fingers clutching the rail.

Jesslin gurgled baby talk and whacked Pup in the nose. He wagged harder, seeming to be happy with this new interaction.

The door opened and Trakon bounded in. He gave a big surprise face to his daughter. "Look at you! What a big girl!"

Lee entered the room shortly thereafter. "Well, I'll be darned."

"Is this a little early for sitting, or normal?" D'laine asked.

"Sitting and crawling happen around the same time," Lee

said. "Now that she knows how to sit, she's going to start crawling. After that, she'll be able to sit when her knees get tired. Has Kal-Dan sat up yet?"

"Not as far as I know," D'laine said. She finished burping her son and put him in his crib in a sitting position. He gave a big smile, grabbed the rails and pulled himself to his feet.

"He's standing!" D'laine was so surprised at this new progress.

"Pretty soon they'll be talking," Trakon said. He picked up his son and kissed him.

Both Lee and D'laine squinted at Trakon.

"That comes much later," Lee said.

"We can't be too sure about that," Trakon said, as he bounced his son in his arms.

Kitry and Jor-Dan entered the room. It was funny to see Jor-Dan get so animated around the babies. It was totally unexpected. He picked up Jesslin and danced around the room while babbling nonsense to her.

Kitry held out her hands for Trakon to hand over his son. "How is my grandson today?" She kissed his cheek, and he let out a giggle. "When will they begin to eat food?"

"I'm not sure. They seem to be developing faster than normal Earth babies," D'laine said. "We should probably move their highchairs to the dining room."

"Have any of their teeth come in yet?" Lee asked.

"No, and they haven't been fussy," D'laine said.

Kitry studied Kal-Dan's mouth. She stuck her finger in his mouth and he sucked. "No teeth here. How will they eat food?"

"They'll start off on soft food that doesn't require chewing," Lee said. "D'laine will have to talk to Chef Grubio about mashing vegetables and fruits for them. It's a slow progression, otherwise their stomachs might not adapt well to solid foods."

Trakon raised his eyebrows.

"Messy diapers," Lee said.

"Oh! We should be very careful about what they eat," Trakon said. He was not a fan of changing messy diapers.

"I think they should begin socializing in the dining room now that they can sit up," Jor-Dan said. He poked Jesslin in the side and got a giggle out of her. Everyone realized that he wanted as much time with his grandchildren as possible.

Trakon grabbed a highchair. "I'll bring this downstairs."

Lee grabbed the other one. "Let's go."

"I'll put them down for their nap, then I'll go to the kitchen and talk to the chef," D'laine said.

D'LAINE ENTERED THE KITCHEN, AND A WORKER RUSHED OVER TO her, all flustered at seeing her in the kitchen.

"How can I help you, Princess?"

"Is Chef Grubio here?" D'laine asked.

"Yes, let me get him for you," the worker said, and quickly scooted away.

Grubio came through the doorway from the inner room, wiping his hands on his chef's apron. "What could I do for you, Princess D'laine?"

"We would like to try feeding the babies mashed vegetables," D'laine said. "They sat up today for the first time, but they don't have teeth, so their food has to be mashed—no lumps at all."

"What should they start with?" the chef asked. He didn't have a clue about the eating habits of babies.

D'laine noticed several kitchen workers listening in on the conversation. "We should begin with something mild. And they won't eat a lot in the beginning until they are used to table food, so only this much for each of them." She held her finger and thumb in an O.

A worker came forward. "Bagos are mild. We can mash some up with a little pakow milk or buttercream."

D'laine thought about the vegetable, then nodded. "That should work. Bagos are like potatoes on Earth."

Grubio nodded. "We shall prepare some for the evening meal." He turned to the worker. "Good suggestion."

"Their highchairs are in the dining room, and I'm afraid they may make a mess," D'laine said.

Grubio laughed a big belly roar. "We can't wait to see your children in their chairs. Never worry about any messes. We're experts at cleaning up anything regarding food."

"By any chance do you have small spoons?" D'laine asked.

"Yes, Kara told us you might need condiment spoons. She said they were the right size for the twins," Grubio said.

"Oh, great! We should be all set," D'laine said. "I'm a new mother, so we'll all learn together!"

BEFORE DINNER, D'LAINE SHOWED THE FAMILY, AND HER HUSBAND how to remove the highchair trays. The majordomo observed the procedure, fascinated at this new experience. He and the staff needed to know how the tray was removed so they could give it a good cleaning after meals.

Victor, Kara and Darren joined everyone at the table.

"Oh, fun time begins," Kara said.

D'laine showed them how to unlatch the tray and pull it back and seat a squirming baby. She made everyone take a turn with the chairs so they understood, in the event D'laine wasn't there at a mealtime.

"Luckily, you have a few backups. Victor and I, and your father. We are all experienced with everything regarding babies, their furniture, and all the rest of it," Kara said.

D'laine and Trakon brought the twins downstairs. Their wide eyes took in everything. They had not been out of the nursery since their infancy, and they were intrigued with all they saw, reaching out and trying to grab things.

Kitry rushed over to a chair and loosened the tray. D'laine lowered Jesslin into a sitting position, and Kitry maneuvered the tray back into place.

"Is this too tight, or too loose?" Kitry asked.

"No, that looks good," D'laine said. She went to the other chair and pulled back the tray. Trakon lowered Kal-Dan, but the baby held his leg out to the tray, making it difficult for Trakon to lower him into the chair.

"Kal-Dan, no," D'laine said. She took hold of the baby's leg and removed it from the edge of the tray. Trakon managed to sit his son in the chair while D'laine adjusted the tray.

"I can see we're going to have a challenging time with your son, Trakon," she said.

"So, he's *my son* when he's acting up, but *your son* when he's sweet?" Trakon asked.

D'laine snickered, then poked her husband in the ribs. "That's the way it works."

Kal-Dan discovered his tray was his own personal drum. He slapped the surface, proud of himself.

Jesslin wasn't happy. She pouted, and wailed.

Jor-Dan was upset that his little princess of a granddaughter, the apple of his eye, was crying. "What's wrong? What does she need?"

The kitchen staff poked their heads around the corner. They saw the one baby having a good time, and the other crying.

"What's wrong, Jessie?" D'laine asked. She sat in her chair and pulled her daughter's highchair closer to her. She tried to distract her from whatever it was that was making her sad.

Jesslin rubbed her tiny fists over her eyes, stuck out her bottom lip and sniffled.

Everyone made an Oooo sound. Jesslin noticed, then smiled big.

"Oh, no. You're not going to be one of those children who tries to get her way by crying, little girl," D'laine said.

Everyone sat at the table, then the staff brought the food out. Grubio brought out the twins' food and their special spoons. He handed one little dessert bowl to D'laine and one to Trakon.

"I don't know what to do!" Trakon said. It alarmed him that he might do something wrong and hurt his son.

"It isn't difficult, Trakon, you can't hurt him," D'laine said. She picked up the little spoon, dipped it into the mashed bago and held it to Jesslin's mouth.

Her daughter opened her mouth, D'laine pushed the spoon in a tiny bit, and lifted up, scraping the food into the baby's mouth.

Jesslin smacked her lips together in her very first attempt to eat real food.

Trakon watched like a hawk. He dipped the spoon into the mush, presented it to Kal-Dan, and successfully mastered his first feeding attempt.

"See, that wasn't so difficult, was it?" D'laine asked.

Both babies seemed okay with the food. By the time they finished, they were both sticky with mashed bago on their faces, in their hair, all over their hands, and the highchair tray.

"Are they always so messy?" Trakon asked.

Kara and Victor laughed.

"This is just the beginning," Victor said.

The majordomo rushed from the room and returned with wet cloths. He handed one to Trakon and one to D'laine.

"Thank you! I forgot about this part," D'laine said. She wiped Jesslin's face, the hair by her forehead, and her fingers. She wiped up the tray as best as she could.

Trakon tried his best, but Kitry stood and came around the table to take over.

"Son, you are many things, but this seems to be out of your scope of understanding," she said.

"Don't everyone gang up on me," Trakon said. "I'm a new father."

"You're doing okay," D'laine said. "Look at how good you are with changing a diaper, feeding them when I'm not around, or asleep, and rocking them. I'm proud of you."

Trakon leaned over and gave his wife a sweet smooch on the lips. He appreciated her praise when he was so unsure of himself. He felt out of his comfort zone when it came to caring for his children. He didn't want to hurt them due to his ignorance.

CHAPTER TWENTY-THREE

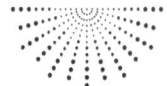

*T*he next day they had a visit from Jakla and Neska. Jakla flew the crestrider over the city gates, waved at the gate guards with his large, scaly hands and maneuvered the crestrider to the plaza area. He carefully landed the ship, lowered the stairs, and half-climbed, half-rode down the escalator stairs to the ground, followed by his mate.

Jor-Dan, Kitry, Lee, Trakon, D'laine, Dannin, Stanley, Victor and Kara greeted them. Kitry and Kara could see the excitement in Neska's eyes. Everyone else focused on Jakla. He beamed with pride at his newfound skills and having the means to fly the ship.

Ethaderia and the boys hurried to the plaza to join the group. "Well, Mr. Bosakin, it looks like you can zip around a lot quicker than riding a pakow."

"We still love our pakows, but this technology makes life much easier. In an emergency, it is an efficient way of escaping, or getting help," Jakla said. He focused on Brian for a minute. "There's one adjustment you should make on the other ships we order. The short switches that I'm required to flick either up or down... they are a little short for my large fingers."

Brian nodded. "That shouldn't be a problem." He turned to Trakon. "Do those switches come in a larger size? I could change them out right now."

"Let me call Hexlon. I believe we have them in stock." Trakon brought up Hexlon's name in his communicator. "Hex, the switches on the dash are too short for the Plotals. Do we have longer ones in stock? If so, Brian can change them out while Jakla and Neska visit."

Hexlon's voice came through loud and clear. "Yes, we have just enough. I'd better order more if we'll be retrofitting more ships for them."

"Okay, Brian will be right there. And, yes, order enough for several ships," Trakon said.

"Come inside so we can visit," Jor-Dan said. "Brian will take care of the ship for you, and your return trip home will be better."

Brian flew the ship over to the shop, while everyone else went inside the palace.

Neska looked around the salon. "Where are your children?"

"They're in their nursery upstairs. Would you like to see them?" D'laine asked.

"Very much so. I have never seen what you call, babies," Neska said.

As they climbed the stairs, Kitry regaled the baby food experience at breakfast.

Neska turned to D'laine. "Your prince helps?"

They stopped on the stairs for a few moments.

D'laine chuckled. "He's afraid he's going to do something wrong and hurt them, but he has been wonderful through all the learning phases."

Neska chuckled, which sounded like something was stuck in her throat. "I remember one of us telling you about Jakla having to place guards around my egg plot of ground. I was afraid someone would step on the eggs and break them. But, what we didn't tell you was how worried he was about me being worried."

"Men," Kara said.

"Jakla did not know what to do when they hatched. Two of our hatchlings died within a few days—this sometimes happens," Neska said, a little sadly. "It upset him more than he admitted, so he went into protector mode for Cadj and Fazi. A male Plotal in protector mode is a dangerous creature."

"I'm so sorry about your hatchlings," D'laine said, as she patted Neska's arm. They continued their climb up the stairs, and D'laine led them to the twins' suite. The guards were startled at Neska's unexpected arrival, but relaxed when they saw the other women.

Pup, on the other hand, jumped up from his bed and stood in the center of the room, teeth clacking.

"Your dog is a good protector," Neska said.

"Pup, come," D'laine said.

The dog eyed Neska. He gave one louder clack of his teeth, but approached D'laine.

"Neska, let him sniff your hand, then he'll be okay," she said.

Neska bent so that the dog could sniff her hand.

Pup sniffed all over, more than what was necessary.

"He probably smells his relatives. We have a pack of diwals we have adopted," Neska said.

After Pup had her scent, he wagged his tail and returned to his bed, his job done.

Neska looked around, eyes wide. "There are many things required to raise your children."

Kitry nodded. "Ethaderia and I were amazed at the helplessness of human babies. They are very fragile when first born and rely on their mother for all their needs."

"They do not arrive with all the knowledge and skills of your Youngmen?" Neska asked.

"No, typically, it takes a great many paths until they are self-sufficient," Kara said. "Human Earth babies are born without teeth. They can't talk, walk or run for many months. We have to teach them how to dress and feed themselves."

Neska's eyes widened. "That is a lot of work! Tell me what these things are that you have here. This is all required equipment?"

D'laine and Kara explained each of the items in the suite.

Downstairs in the salon, the men discussed ships, the doski and Trangula, the trip vines and other things that seemed to work. Lee and Stanley reported what they discovered at Patrosym regarding the building materials, and that Princess Yalalore was indeed secured. They did not mention the cloaking device.

Jakla reported that the main building was complete, and two other buildings were almost complete. Individual housing was in progress throughout his territory, and Cadj was assisting Plodu with the gardens. He also mentioned they would build a building for the ships.

"You, or whoever you assign, should spend a day here to learn basic ship maintenance," Trakon said.

"That is a good suggestion. When we determine who that will be, I will contact you and make arrangements," Jakla said. "Neska wants her own ship and informed me she has certain requirements she will discuss with you."

The men raised their eyebrows at that, but no one was brave enough to question, or even guess what that meant.

CHAPTER TWENTY-FOUR

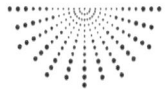

*T*he women joined the men in the salon. Trakon cleared his throat and focused on Neska.

"I understand you have requirements for your personal ship?" he asked.

"Yes. I would like the ship's color to be the same as the flashing sky, to blend in from below, as a concealment," Neska said.

Every male in the room wished at that moment they had thought of the brilliant idea. The perfect camouflage!

"I would also like mirrors mounted at the helm so I can see what approaches from behind," Neska said.

Trakon nodded. "Neska, these are very good ideas that we will incorporate in all future ship designs. Is there anything else?"

"Not at this time. If I think of anything else that would be useful, I will share my thoughts with you," Neska said.

Jakla's chest puffed in pride at his mate's foresight into what every male in the room thought of as important improvements to the crestrider designs. He had never taken his mate for granted, but after all these years, he was just starting to realize just how smart she was. From her interior designs in the palace and the other buildings in his territory, to the ship designs—this was far and above domestic management. At that moment he considered involving her in a larger-scaled role in community development... and beyond.

Victor and Stanley had a private conversation going. Stanley nodded ever so slightly.

"Jakla, have you ever heard of a jarvust?" Victor asked.

All eyes swung over to him. Everyone present thought that subject had been shelved until it was understood what they were dealing with. Both Victor and Stanley got stink eyes from certain others in the room.

Neska perked up. "Jarvusts can be nasty things! Do you have one?"

Stanley shook his head. "No, but the Egroms determined that one is lurking just on the outside of their periphery."

"My Nepsi and Nepsa told me a story of a jarvust in the village where they lived many years before the great war. It was a water jarvust and turned the pool where they swam into a pit of tainted water."

"I didn't realize Plotals swam," D'laine said. She wasn't the only one who was surprised.

"Where do you swim here?" Jor-Dan asked.

"Oh, we don't swim anymore," Neska said sadly. "That was during a time when our Plotal ancestors lived in villages across Thol. They always lived near bodies of water."

"I remember we mentioned that back on Earth, there are creatures called alligators and crocodiles whose forms are similar to yours, but they have not evolved past their animal characteristics. They always live near water," Lee said. "Do your scales dry out in this heat?"

"We adapted," Jakla said.

"You should build a bathing pool in your suite. Actually, in all the living quarters," Trakon said. "You could tap into the aquifers underground, as we do, and have water to soak in."

Both Jakla and Neska's eyes widened at the prospect of soaking in the water in their own suite.

"I'll ask Dreboo to contact Bist to discuss the plans," Jor-Dan said.

Kitry stood. "Why don't I show you our bathing pool?"

Jakla and Neska stood. "Yes, we would like to see how you accomplished this."

"I don't recall showing you the bathing room when you came to visit that first time," Kitry said.

She led them out of the room, down the hallway and around the corner to the suite she and Jor-Dan shared. When the Plotals saw the bathing room, they gasped.

"We will build this!" Neska exclaimed. "Do all the rooms include a private pool, or shared spaces?"

"When Lee and the boys lived here, the boys shared a connecting bathing pool," Kitry said. "You could do the same thing for your children, unless you want separate boy-girl pools."

Neska and Jakla nodded. "Adjoining pools for shared spaces makes sense."

They returned to the main salon and sat, Jakla's and Neska's minds wandering to so many thoughts.

"What happened to the jarvust?" Victor asked. "Did they get rid of it?"

"My Nepsi and Nepsa spun a lot of tales to frighten us. They said the villagers tried different things, but nothing seemed to work. My Nepsi said they noticed it always appeared in the same place, but no one knew if it came up from the ground, or down from the sky," Neska said. Everyone was spellbound with her story. "They tried digging a pit, but that couldn't contain the being. Then they created a large dome and lined it with crystals. No one mentioned what they made the dome from, and they didn't say whether the crystals were what worked, but the jarvust disappeared. They never were bothered by it again."

"I'll share your story with the Egroms," Stanley said. "Until we discover what type of jarvust is lurking, we won't know what to do about it."

"Remember, these were just stories old Plotals told to small Plotal children to scare them into behaving properly," Neska said.

D'laine pondered something. "To think the Great War of Taylon was all because of cultural misunderstandings and not talking openly about it."

Everyone looked to her, waiting for more.

She shook her head. "The Plotals banished someone from their tribe. Evidently, when your people banish someone, they run through a gauntlet of their peers prior to being cast out. They brutalized this Plotal to the point he could barely walk, but he got away from the tribe and out of their territory. Then a kindhearted human Tholian found him, cared for and healed him, which was taboo to the Plotals."

"That's what started the war?" Kara asked. "Sounds like Earth with all the different cultures, religions and beliefs. I try to stay out of the way of politics."

"Hopefully, we won't experience another war like the great war," Jor-Dan said. "The doski and Trangula situation may not even materialize. It's been a while since anyone has captured any scouts or military Trangulans."

"One of my ancient advisors has reminded us that Plotals used to be climbers," Jakla said. "Our claws became dulled over time, but they were once very sharp to dig into tree trunks as our kind scurried up the trees to the canopy."

"Looks like you won't need those stairs in the trees after all," Lee said.

"You are correct," Jakla said. "There are now mandatory practice sessions with our elders advising us on techniques."

"What was the purpose of scaling trees?" Stanley asked.

"This was hundreds of years before the war," Neska said. "It was even before Plotals adopted clothing, or rode pakows."

Jakla nodded. "This was from our primitive days when our kind would scurry up trees and pounce on prey. I can't imagine living like that anymore. We have come a long way in our development."

Stanley pondered that statement. "Don't you find it interesting how quickly evolutionary changes happen? Newborn Plotals and future generations of your kind will look back at riding pakows as the *old way* of travel."

"Unless they consider it a fun pastime," Victor said. "I think of it as similar to old time hayrides. Now, I wonder if even farm children in rural areas of the United States still do that. I'm not sure those types of wagons exist anymore."

The Plotals nodded.

"Yes, I understand what you are saying. We are turning towards technology—smart closets, crestriders, and whatever other things we discover that would save us time and energy," Neska said.

Trakon's communicator beeped an incoming message. He brought up the message. "Brian's finished replacing those switches. He'll return the ship to the plaza."

"Excellent," Neska said.

"Don't forget the military aspect of modernization. Paths ago, we used our teeth, claws and tail-pods as our weapons," Jakla said. "Now, we use lasers, knives, swords, and crestriders."

"The great war brought many things to a standstill. No one had technology for many years," Jor-Dan said.

Neska stood. "We must go back home. There are many things to attend to."

They all stood.

"I'll fly the ship back!" Neska said with glee.

Jakla met the stares of the males in the room. He felt a

sudden sense of his mate's independence. While he would never consider overriding her, in that moment, he felt he had lost some of his former overbearing hold on her. He noticed the slight nods from Victor, Lee, Jor-Dan, and Stanley. He wondered if Trakon had succumbed to D'laine's lead.

AFTER THE BOSAKIN'S CRESTRIDER LEFT EBSCALON, THE WOMEN went about their business, but the men stayed behind at the palace entrance.

"I didn't see that coming," Jor-Dan said.

Trakon scrunched up his brows. "What? I don't understand."

There were chuckles from the rest of the men.

Trakon didn't have a clue what they found so amusing.

"Jakla just realized he's losing his grip on his wife, and he'll never get it back," Lee said.

Jor-Dan stared at his son. "Just two years ago, the Plotals were nomads. Now, they live in a city. They are adopting technology. And, Neska has discovered she has power. Once you have power, you rarely give it up, unless you are a male who is bewitched by a female."

They all chuckled rather loudly, except for Trakon. He stared at his father and friends, feeling the sting of their words.

"Don't worry, Trakon. You're not alone in this. We have all discovered that we have wives who are quite independent, with minds of their own," Victor said. "Even Stanley, with Treikie, has most likely been put in his place once or twice."

The scientist frowned, but nodded, reluctantly admitting a small defeat. "If you want a woman, you have to learn to give in… not so much as to choose your battles, but to step away from your stubbornness. The days of *that's the way I've always done it* are gone… forever."

Trakon's shoulders drooped.

Darren and Dannin walked down an alley looking for the house that was nominated for a re-do. While this was an alley of backdoors, they came to the end where it veered off to the right and left of a cross street. They did not find the ramshackle place.

Dannin scratched his head. "I don't understand, Darren. We've been up and down this alley twice now."

"Let's go to the right; maybe it's over there. Maybe they gave the wrong address," Darren said.

They continued walking, turned right on the cross street, but didn't find any structure in need of a re-do. They turned around and walked in the other direction for a little while with the same results.

As they stood at the crossroad, looking up the alley, someone waved at them. They started walking to the man in the middle of the road.

"We can't find the house," Dannin said. "We've been up and down the alley twice now."

The man blushed. "I'm Yorkens. My neighbors nominated my house. It's this way."

He led them up between two nice looking houses to what looked like a one-car garage-sized shed.

Darren gulped silently and turned to Dannin with a questioning look.

"Yorkens, tell us about this place," Dannin said. "This isn't even really a house."

Poor Yorkens. His bronze skin turned more reddish. "Back in the times when homes were quite small, our home was the first one built here. Ma had to sell off property when Da passed on. People built these bigger homes all around us."

"It's okay, Yorkens," Darren said. "I'm going to walk around and look at all the sides of your house." Darren noted how the house was nestled in between four other properties. Two in the front and two in the back. He wasn't familiar with the property lines though. "Hey, Dannin, how do I find the property lines?"

Dannin looked in his communicator menu for the public records which Marrak kept up to date. He pulled up a survey of Yorkens' property, all the way back to when his mother had sold off lots. Then he worked the file forward to determine the delineation of the current houses surrounding the smaller house.

"This is how the property was divided. Yorkens' property is a narrow parcel," Dannin said, as he showed Darren the plots.

"Okay. I'm ready to get to work," Darren said. "Yorkens, is anyone inside the house right now?"

"Ma's in there. Should I bring her outside?" Yorkens asked.

"Yes, that's a good idea. She'll want to see what I do to the outside, then I'll go inside and do some work in there," Darren said.

Yorkens hustled inside the decrepit place and returned with his elderly mother in a Tholian version of a wheelchair. It was a padded chair with wheels that could climb stairs, or turn a corner on a dime.

"Ma, this here's the boy who's going to give our house a re-do," Yorkens said.

The old woman shook her head. "Not worth it anymore."

"Just you wait, ma'am," Darren said. He visualized a place that took up most of the plot of land, with a porch and doorway that was wheelchair accessible. Within a long blink, the structure reformed into a ranch-type house with a wide porch. He even included a porch swing.

Yorkens and his mother gasped. They couldn't believe what their eyes gazed upon.

Dannin smiled. The boy was amazing at what he could do.

"Let's go inside. I want you to show me what your old place looked like back when it was brand new," Darren said. He walked behind Yorkens and the wheelchair, with Dannin bringing up the rear.

The current interior was sad, with old, lopsided furniture that was barely standing, but what Darren found inside the mother's consciousness was homey and comfortable. He nodded, pulled in a breath, and within a minute, the place was furnished in a country style that reminded him of a magazine ad. He included wide hallways and doorways to accommodate the wheelchair.

Yorkens and his mother cried.

"Look, Ma. It's beautiful, just the way it used to be, only better," Yorkens said between bawling.

The old woman wheeled up to Darren. "Youngster, I never understood what they meant by having this boy re-do my house. What you did is miraculous. I hope Thol blesses you ten times over!"

Darren blushed. "I like helping people."

"Wait until the neighborhood sees our new home," Yorkens said.

"We'll be going now. Enjoy your new home," Dannin said.

They let themselves out the door.

"That was some change, Darren," Dannin said.

"They won't have much yard left, but I think that's okay. They deserve a nice, spacious place to live instead of that one big room," Darren said.

"Your family can be proud of you. I know the people of Ebscalon are proud of you," Dannin said.

CHAPTER TWENTY-FIVE

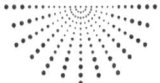

D'laine, Ugo, and three other scholars *stepped* into the cave with Stanley. The scholars stood in the center of the huge cave and took in the different placements of historical artifacts.

"The items seemed to show up in this order," Stanley said. He pointed to a part of the cavern. "We found two items that depicted Lee there." Next, he pointed to another area. "That's where we found a likeness to D'laine, Trakon and the twins." He looked toward the left. "I'm pretty sure that's where we discovered a reference to Brian and Jamie."

The scholars split up to those areas. They carefully looked over each artifact. They unrolled scrolls and skimmed for context. When they came across an artifact or a scroll that pertained to anyone they recognized visually, or in prose, they set those things aside for further consideration.

Stanley brought D'laine to the far corner where the huge cabinet stood against the wall. He pulled the cabinet back and brought the princess into the vast chamber filled with untold wealth.

D'laine gasped as her eyes swept the chamber. "This doesn't

make any sense whatsoever! How is it possible the royal treasurers did not miss this wealth over the years?"

Stanley shook his head. "I've wondered the same thing. Evidently, someone transported these things here when the first inkling of war manifested. I'm not sure whether a Visionary was in charge, or someone else, when the war was underway, but all the wealth of the kingdom was placed here for safekeeping."

D'laine nodded. "That makes sense. And, because so much was destroyed over the war years, I can understand how these missing treasures didn't cause any alarm. People probably thought they were destroyed or plundered. There wasn't much left of Ciert, other than rubble."

"What we don't know is, was this all Ciert's wealth, or several kingdoms?" Stanley asked.

"I wonder how Jor-Dan could make a claim on this?" D'laine asked.

"I'm not sure. It would help if we knew who moved everything here," Stanley said. "That would solve most of the mystery in regarding ownership. It might also answer some questions regarding the prophecy."

"Should we show this room to the scholars?" D'laine asked.

"They might be able to identify some of these things," Stanley said. "It's not like they would ever be able to get to this cave on their own and steal anything."

They walked out of the inner chamber. Small piles of scrolls and a few artifacts were piled near each scholar.

"Ugo," D'laine called out. "We want to show you and your team another room."

The scholars stopped their poking around and joined D'laine and Stanley toward the back of the cave.

"You cannot speak of what you are about to see," D'laine said. "Do you thoroughly understand?"

"Don't make me erase some part of your mind if you can't keep this secret," Stanley said.

Ugo raised his brows. "We are not yammering gossips. We take our work seriously."

"I don't mean to be obnoxious, but when you see what we are about to show you, you will understand my insistence on secrecy," Stanley said.

He led them through the dark opening to the lit room beyond.

The room echoed gasps from each of the scholars.

"There doesn't seem to be a way to identify who this belongs to. Stanley and I think it was Ciert's treasures, but unless we can prove that, we don't think Jor-Dan can claim it," D'laine said.

One of the scholars hurried over to a magnificent throne. "This was Jor-Dan's grandfather's throne! See the initials here? SD. That stands for Sar-Dan! And look!" He wildly pointed to another part of the room where another throne was laden with treasures. He bent and searched for identifying marks. "Hal-Dan! The king's father's throne! These ARE Ciert's treasures! They weren't lost in the war!"

The scholars split up and sorted through the artifacts. They called out to each other when they identified one of the price-less items.

"I wonder if there are any of King Jangston's treasures in here?" D'laine asked. She poked through items, but was unable to identify anything belonging to anyone specifically.

Keeping a straight face, Stanley shrugged. "It's difficult to tell. I wonder how his things could be identified. No one but the Egroms seemed to know there was a king of the entire planet."

After a hour in the treasure room, the scholars returned to their work of searching for the prophecy. Stanley pushed the cabinet against the wall, sealing up the opening.

Neska walked across the open area between two buildings. Off in the distance she noticed a female hauling away half of the large, empty shell her child emerged from. Suddenly, an idea bloomed in Neska's head. She jogged across the area and approached the female.

She gruffed a greeting to the female, which sounded like a short *bbbrrrppp*. "I would like to take that shell, if you are going to break it down. Did you destroy the other half?"

The female studied their leader's mate. "Surely, you don't want these old things?"

Neska nodded. "Yes, I want them. How many hatchlings are there?"

"I have three more egg shells," the female said.

"Good. Would someone deliver them to Dojesk's shop? Do you know where that is?" Neska asked.

The female shook her head.

"It is in the new marketplace. You will see his sign," Neska explained.

"Okay. My mate and our oldest child will bring them to that shop," the female said.

"Make sure they are not cracked or crushed." Neska nodded, then she took off toward the marketplace to tell the shopkeeper what she required.

Dojesk arranged some of his wares on shelves. He liked the new marketplace because the toys he crafted for Plotal children would get noticed now that he had a shop to display them in. He wiped his hands on his large shop apron and was about to go into the back room when Neska approached.

They gruffed greetings to each other.

"What brings you to my shop, Neska?" Dojesk asked.

"A family is bringing you their eggshells," Neska said.

Dojesk's brows between his Mohawk rose in question.

"I have a proposition for you. If you are interested, we can become business partners," she said.

"It would honor me to partner with you on your endeavor," Dojesk said. "What business are you considering?"

"I want you to create Wobbly toys for children throughout Thol. The pointy areas should be smoothed down where the shell split apart so a Plotal, human, Kudaja, or Egrom child would not get hurt by a sharp edge," Neska said. "The shells should be enforced with several layers of agrin sap to make sure they will not break. I envision a child holding the shell low to step into it. They would move from side to side and roll with it. This would be great fun and good exercise."

Dojesk nodded as he listened. "We will have to make sure we can supply these wobbly shells for the demand."

"The first will be a gift to the Eartholian twins. They are what they call babies, and are quite helpless," Neska explained. "Their Wobblies would have to be made from smaller shells. As they grow, they can use the larger Wobbly."

A Plotal male and a male child approached the marketplace carrying shells. They looked around. Neska waved a hand at them.

"Over here," she said.

They hauled the shells over to the shop.

"I am grateful for your labor of bringing the shells to the shop," Neska said. She reached into her dress and pulled out a pouch. She dug into it and retrieved some Sepiks. She gave one to the boy, and several more to the father. The boy's eyes lit up.

"We have two more for you, if you still want them?" the father asked.

"Yes, bring them here," Dojesk said.

The father and son left, happy to earn money from something that they would have crushed on their own, then spread the shell dust in the forest.

"I will use my children and their friends to test the first ones you create," Neska said. A thought crossed her mind. "You should paint these first two. One should be pink, which is for a female, and the other blue, for a male."

DOJESK STUDIED THE SHELL HALVES. HE DETERMINED IT WOULD take too long to apply agrin sap on the shells manually. He recalled seeing something at another shop, so he left his place and walked across the marketplace to where he thought he saw a large container. Sure enough, he spotted it outside, along with different sized pots and containers.

"How much do you want for this large container?" he asked the shopkeeper.

"Twelve Sepiks," the shopkeeper said.

"Would you take ten if I order more?" Dojesk asked.

"How many more?"

"I'll know in a week," Dojesk said.

"Okay. Ten it is," the shopkeeper said.

Dojesk handed over the money, picked up the large container and returned to his shop. He brought the container into the back room where he created things. He grabbed what looked like a handcart on Earth, but this one had a large, flat bed made from agrin wood, and it hovered over the ground. He steered the cart out of the back of his shop to where he had several casks of agrin sap. He loaded two onto the cart. It dipped with the weight, but adjusted the hovering height. He brought the casks into his shop. He pried off the cover of one cask, hauled it up into his powerful arms, and poured the sap into the new container.

He steered the cart over to the wall, replaced the cover on the cask, then started to work. Dojesk carefully separated two shells. He took one shell, turned it on its side and sunk it into the agrin sap.

"Maybe I should have softened those points first," he muttered to himself. He picked up a wooden pole and moved the shell to coat the other side. He realized he would need a drying rack. He looked around his workshop and saw a long, metal pole with a flat end.

Dojesk grabbed the metal pole, stepped out the back door and stuck the pointy end into the ground. He didn't want the flat end to stick to the inside of the shell, which would adhere like superglue ten times over.

He walked back over to the shopkeeper. "What repels agrin sap?"

"Grog's the only thing I know of. Spread a thin layer on what you don't want the sap to adhere to," the shopkeeper said.

"Do you sell that here?" Dojesk asked.

The shopkeeper shook his head. He pointed. "Go to the third shop opposite yours. They sell it there."

"Thanks," Dojesk said. He walked over to the shop, found the grog and made his purchase. He spread a thin layer on the flat piece of the metal pole, returned to the container and used the wooden pole to roll the shell again.

It was a long process, but finally satisfied that the shell was heavily coated with agrin sap, Dojesk slipped on a pair of gloves. He scooped out a small supply of the grog and rubbed his gloved hands together. He turned the shell on its side and lifted it out of the vat. He let it drip over the container for several minutes, then he brought it outside and gently lowered it over the pole.

He stripped off the gloves, careful to not tear them, and set them on his workbench. He ran a finger across the points on the second shell half. They were rather sharp and jagged in places. Dojesk walked over to the wall of hanging tools, spotted what he needed and grabbed it. He pressed a button and a blue light emitted from a conical end. He slowly moved the blue light over a point, down, up, down and up until he had smoothed the entire circumference.

The craftsman ran a finger up and down the points of the shell. He worried about the shape of the points, so he made an adjustment on his tool and started at the beginning again. He rounded all the points so that if a child fell, he would not accidentally mutilate himself. Satisfied with the results of the second round of smoothing over, he lifted the shell and lowered it into the vat of agrin sap.

The Plotal dinner table did not differ from a human Tholians table, except for the size of everything. Jakla sat at the head of the table, Cadj sat at the other end, being the second male in the family. Neska and Fazi sat across from each other.

Jakla eyed his son. Since the boy's meltdown, and subsequent discipline, he seemed somewhat better, but still resented the work they had issued him. He thought he had a solution to the problem.

"Cadj, tomorrow, I will fly you over to Ebscalon, where you will work beside Jamie at the pakow pens," Jakla said.

Cadj's eyes lit up. "I can go play with Jamie?"

Jakla huffed out, showing he was not happy with his son's assumption. "There will be no playing. The Eartholian boy has a method of how to care for the pakows. You will learn how he attends to the beasts, then you will come back home and provide that same level of care for our pakows, their pens and everything about them. Do you understand?"

Cadj's shoulders slumped. There didn't seem to be any way of getting out of this work.

"Fazi, you improved the management of our household and the attitudes of the workers," Jakla said. "I recently communicated with Vila's mother and you can spend the day in the Cember forest with Vila."

Fazi's eyes lit up. She could hardly believe what she heard. "Thank you, father!"

"Good work is always rewarded," Neska said.

"It wasn't always rewarded," Cadj spat. "I remember when we still lived in our tents and travelled around the countryside…"

"That was before we mended our ways," Jakla said, rather gruffly.

"D'laine healed your father when she could have let him die from that robot's attack," Neska said. She gave her son a stern eye. "Your father understood what kindness accomplished. After many, many discussions with me, and meetings with his advisors, the Plotals changed their ways and adjusted their outlook on life for the betterment of our species. Is your memory so short that you cannot tell the difference in your own life over the past two years?"

Fazi felt a pinch of vindictiveness. "We never stayed in one place long, and we couldn't play with other Plotal children that were below our class, remember, Cadj? Now we can play with Plodu, Fingo and Zerke."

Cadj figured he'd better keep his opinions to himself, otherwise he'd be in more trouble.

Jakla drew in a breath to calm himself. He gazed upon his mate. "How did your day go today?"

Neska reached her tail out and rubbed Jakla's tail. "I had the most satisfying day." She explained about her toy creation idea.

The Mohawk hair between Jakla's brows moved as he frowned with thought. "These wobbly things will be strong enough to hold a child?"

"Yes, they will be able to hold more than one child, even if they are roughhousing," Neska said. "Dojesk understands, and he will make sure the shells are so reinforced that they will never crack. I told him our children will be the test subjects."

Jakla nodded. "You think there is a need for these wobbly things? People will buy them?"

"Oh, yes. Wait until Dojesk is finished with the first two. You will see how much fun they will be for the children. And, it is good exercise as well," Neska said.

THE NEXT DAY, DOJESK REMOVED THE ONE DRIED SHELL FROM THE pole. He rapped it with his knuckles. He looked around, picked up a discarded piece of wood and whacked the shell on the bottom. Not even a scratch. His eyes lit in satisfaction.

He returned inside to his work area and perused the shelves of paint. No pink. He discovered red, and he found white paint. He opened the white container, then the red. He added a little red to the white. Dojesk looked around and grabbed a thin piece of wood and stirred until he was happy with the nice shade of pink it created.

He poured some paint into his spraying device, brought the device outside and mounted the shell back onto the pole. He pressed the power button and sprayed the egg as he walked around the circumference. The craftsman determined it would take two coats of paint for complete coverage. After the paint dried, he would add a topcoat that would make the egg shimmer in the light.

Dojesk stood back and observed his work. He nodded. This partnership with the leader's mate was a good idea.

THE CRAFTSMAN APPROACHED THE MAIN BUILDING WITH HIS hover cart. The shells were covered with a heavy tarp so no one would see his creations. Neska came outside and invited Dojesk into the building. She brought him into a meeting room and summoned her mate and her daughter. She also contacted Naphelia to bring her children to the room to get their input.

After everyone arrived, Dojesk unveiled the shells. They were beautiful with a light shimmer to the surface.

"What are those?" Zerke asked.

"Those are birthing shells, aren't they?" Naphelia asked.

"Yes," Neska said. "They are a new toy I named a Wobbly."

Jakla stared at the bright shells in dismay. He didn't understand how they could possibly be fun, but he didn't say anything.

"The pink is for a girl, and the blue is for a boy. Those are the colors from Earth," Neska said. She looked to the children. "Climb inside and make the shell roll around."

Since Plodu was the only boy present, he tilted the blue shell and stepped inside. Once he got the shell moving, he laughed uproariously.

Fazi scampered into the pink shell. She started the motion and squealed with delight. She stopped the shell. "Fingo! Come inside! This is fun!"

Zerke walked over to the blue shell. "I'm coming inside your shell!"

Plodu huffed, but allowed his sister to tilt the shell and climb inside. They discovered it was loads of fun with two people inside to cause the rocking, rolling motion to swing wilder.

Jakla turned to his mate. "You have done well, Neska. I didn't understand at first, but now I see how all children will want one of these innovative toys."

"I will send a bulletin out to all Plotals asking them for their shells," Neska said. "We will pay them a dinkst for each shell, and we will offer a discount on the price of the Wobbly if they purchase one."

"I may have to hire help," Dojesk said.

CHAPTER TWENTY-SIX

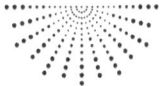

*T*he day after Neska and Dojesk's satisfactory testing of the Wobbly shells in Ta'Byu'Vohon, they loaded the bright shells along with the hover cart onto the crestrider. The ship sported the banner colors for the House of Bosakin.

"Queen Kitry, gather the children. I have created something for the twins, but the older children should test these toys first so the twins can understand how they work," Neska said. She flew the craft across the miles of mossy fields. "Perhaps invite that Egrom boy, and the Kudaja girl. We will be there shortly."

She was eager to check on the status of her personal crestrider while she visited Ebscalon. Neska had felt the emotions of every male in the room when she had announced what she required for her own craft. The sky camouflage was the perfect concealment. It would be difficult for anyone on the ground to spot a ship painted like the flashing sky.

Neska steered the craft towards Ebscalon. She flew over the gates, giving the guards a wave, and landed in the courtyard. The royals and their entourage of family and friends were awaiting her arrival. As the crestrider settled on the ground, she recognized the Egrom boy and the Kudaja girl among the small crowd. Cadj stood beside Jamie in the throng.

She waved as she came down the escalator, followed by Dojesk and his hover cart with the concealed Wobblies.

D'laine held Jesslin and Jor-Dan held Kal-Dan, while Trakon hovered close by.

"I have created something for your twins," Neska said. "Actually, I came up with the idea, and Dojesk created what you will see." She nodded to her craftsman partner. "Plotal children tested them yesterday, and they had wonderful fun. Even my mate was surprised, and I know he wasn't sure what to make of these Wobbly toys at first."

She reached out and grabbed the covering and yanked it off in one swift pull. The shells glimmered in the sunlight.

"Oh, those are beautiful!" Kitry and Kara said at the same time.

Ethaderia clapped her hands together. "What do they do?"

Dojesk carefully lifted the shells off the hover cart and settled them on the ground.

"You'll see shortly. Cadj, come here and climb into the blue shell," Neska said.

Cadj tilted the shiny blue shell and lifted one leg inside, holding his tail high. He stepped the other leg inside, then lowered his tail. "What do I do?"

Suddenly, when he moved, the shell moved. Cadj's face lit up. He grabbed ahold of the edge of the shell and made it roll and spin. He laughed up a storm at the fun he was having.

Vila approached the pink shell, tilted it and got inside it. She shrieked and laughed as the shell rolled.

Jesslin laughed as she watched the fun from D'laine's arms.

Vila slowed the shell. "Chacoodi! Come inside with me. It's fun!"

The Egrom boy scurried over to the pink shell and climbed

inside. He and Vila made it roll, tilt and spin. Their laughter filled the air.

Jamie joined Cadj. The two boys were much rougher than their playmates in the pink shell, but they didn't do any harm to it.

"You need to stop so the other children can have a turn," Neska said.

Cadj and Jamie grumbled, but climbed out of the shell and let Darren and Brian take a turn. The older boys rocked and rolled the shell and made it spin around.

"Neska, these are remarkable toys," Kitry said. "The children not only have fun, but they expend excess energy which will help them settle down."

"Do you think the twins are too young to play inside these shells?" Neska asked. "They were who I designed these toys for to begin with."

Kitry clapped her hands together. "Everyone out of the shells. It's time for the twins to experience some fun."

D'laine carried Jesslin over to the pink Wobbly and set her down inside. She stood beside the shell, and waited to see what her daughter would do.

Jesslin wiggled her fanny, and the shell moved. She shrieked out a loud laugh. Then she moved some more and giggled with each movement.

Jor-Dan settled Kal-Dan inside the shell. The little boy stood on his hands and knees and moved around. The shell wobbled as he moved and the motion scared him. He wailed out a distress signal to his father and grandfather.

"What's wrong with him?" Trakon asked, confused that his daughter was laughing crazily while his son was alarmed. He reached into the egg and picked up his son. He brought him over to the pink shell and showed him how his sister was playing and laughing.

"It's different, and he's unsure of himself," D'laine said.

Everyone gathered around the tiny boy, patting him, cooing at him, and trying to make him feel better.

Kal-Dan sniffled, stuck his thumb in his mouth, and watched his twin sister. He leaned over in Trakon's arms, making a grabbing sign with one hand toward his sister.

"Do you want to play with Jesslin?" Trakon asked.

Kal-Dan made the grabbing motion again.

"Okay, here goes." Trakon set his son in the pink shell with his sister.

Jesslin patted her brother's face with her tiny hand as she laughed. She wiggled her butt, and the shell moved. Her face was alight. Kal-Dan observed her, smiled, and laughed. He made a scooting motion, and the shell moved even more. They both laughed.

"I guess he's more comfortable being with his sister when it comes to doing new things," Trakon said.

"Remember, you were an only child, so you didn't have a close companion," Kitry said. "Being twins, they share a bond."

Jamie and Cadj crept back into the blue Wobbly and rolled the shell around, much to the chagrin of the other children.

"Okay, you two. Out of the shell and back to work. Playtime is over," Lee said.

The boys muttered to themselves, but got out of the shell and started walking away.

"I will see you back home tomorrow, Cadj," Neska said.

Cadj lifted his tail in acknowledgment.

Neska muttered to herself as she shook her head in exasperation.

"Your son has done well working with Jamie," Jor-Dan said. "Jugdaak, the pakow handler, said he was angry at first, but Cadj and Jamie bonded as they worked. I think Cadj has a better understanding of why it's important to care for livestock."

"My mate was positive Cadj would come around to the work if he worked with Jamie," Neska said. "He determined that the young animal communicator could partake some wisdom to our son."

"I'd say that worked," Jor-Dan said. "They are at that age where they are a challenge."

Neska nodded.

D'laine and Trakon lifted their twins out of the Wobbly.

"I think that's enough for one day. How about a nap?" D'laine asked, as she caught Jesslin yawning widely. She and Trakon left the group and entered the palace with the twins.

The women gathered around Neska.

"What a clever use for the shells!" Ethaderia said.

"Do you want smaller shells? We could save shells for you," Kitry said.

"We are paying people a dinkst for their shells, and will offer a discount if they order a Wobbly," Neska said.

"That's smart," Victor said. "Have you alerted the kingdoms of your new product?"

Dojesk joined into the conversation. "Neska will send out a bulletin to the Plotals and the kingdoms. I'll hire helpers if the demand is more than I can handle. They weren't difficult to make, just time-consuming."

"I really like the shimmering paint," Kara said.

Lee, Victor, Jor-Dan and Stanley examined the shells. The boys really gave them a good workout, along with Chacoodi and Vila in the pink shell. There wasn't even a mar on the bottom of the shell.

"Did you coat these with agrin sap?" Lee asked.

"I soaked each shell in a vat of the sap, then suspended them onto a pole to dry," Dojesk said.

"The shell didn't stick to the pole?" Victor asked, curious.

"No, I used grog on the flat part of the pole, and actually on my gloves as well. Agrin sap won't stick to grog," the craftsman explained.

"Never heard of it," Stanley said. He shot a look at Jor-Dan. "Do we use that around here for something?"

Jor-Dan nodded. "Over at the shop, and many other places. Like Dojesk said, it's the only thing that agrin sap won't stick to."

Neska, Kitry and the rest of the women went inside the palace. Dojesk followed with the shells on the handcart.

Something flickered through Stanley's thoughts. "I wonder... Could it be possible to test some of the rubble over at Patrosym to see if the builder used grog maliciously? I just can't get my head around how weak their buildings were."

The men shared a thoughtful look.

"That would be premeditated malicious intent," Jor-Dan said. A shocked expression was plastered on his face. His communicator dinged an incoming contact. He was astounded when he saw who was calling. "It's Emeric!"

Victor, Stanley and Lee shared surprised looks. Trakon joined their group.

"Emeric! Is everything okay?" Jor-Dan asked.

Trakon quirked an eyebrow.

Lee filled him in, silently.

We offered a reward for the whereabouts of Teego Boinoroko, our former builder, but gave up after all the time that has lapsed from the churling damage, Emeric said.

Everyone was quiet as they listened to the Patrosym king.

"Did someone turn him in?" Jor-Dan asked.

Yes! We have him in custody. We're going to have a tribunal, and I'd like you and your Eartholian engineers and Kara present. I will reach out to Jakla Bosakin and his architect, Emeric said.

"Excellent! When have you scheduled this tribunal?" Jor-Dan asked.

In two turns. Is that convenient for you, Jor-Dan? Emeric asked.

"Emeric, we were just discussing grog. Would it be possible

for your people to test some of that rubble to see if grog was used to weaken the structure?" Jor-Dan asked.

The communication went dead silent.

"Emeric?" Jor-Dan said.

When you asked me about grog, it stole all of my thoughts, Jor-Dan. I can't believe someone would actually plan to cause that damage, Emeric said. *But, it is obvious that the buildings were inferior. I will discuss this with my architectural committee and we will get to the bottom of this before the tribunal.*

"It's a terrible thing—to think someone would intentionally want to do you harm," Jor-Dan said. "We will see you in two days." He ended the communication. "Stanley, it's a good thing you thought about the grog regarding that disaster."

"It doesn't make any sense," Victor said. "Why would a builder even consider doing something like that? His name would be on the building plans. It's not like he could walk away from the destruction without being blamed."

"He would have been paid already, and had the money flowing for materials and expenses, plus labor," Trakon said.

They all hemmed and hawed about the act of sheer maliciousness and greed.

Neska and Dojesk exited the palace. She walked to the group of men while Dojesk headed to the crestrider.

"How is my craft coming along?" she asked Trakon.

"It should be completed within four days," he said.

Neska nodded. "I look forward to seeing how you have painted my vehicle." She nodded, then climbed aboard the five-man crestrider, and took off for home.

The men contemplated for a moment as the Plotals flew away in their ship.

"This tribunal will be interesting, all things considered," Lee said.

Jor-Dan was getting ready to comment when he detected

Neska's ship returning. "I hope there isn't a problem with the ship."

The ship hovered over the plaza and Neska leaned over the rail. "Fire!"

"Where?" Trakon shouted.

Neska pointed. "The forest is on fire!"

Everyone was on their communicators all at once.

D'laine ran out of the palace, followed by Brian and Darren. Jamie and Cadj ran through the gates to the plaza.

"There's a fire!" Jamie yelled.

"We know!" Lee said.

Victor had a tingling sensation. "It's the jarvust!"

Ships flew over the gates toward the forest. A mid-sized ship hovered over the plaza and the escalator descended. Everyone scampered up the stairs, and the craft took off toward the Tempe Forest.

As they flew near the fire, they observed a shimmering image hovering over the trees. It was the exact same image that they had seen in the Og's head.

Victor zoned out again. After several moments he spoke in a trance-like voice. "Sangdons."

"What's a Sangdon?" D'laine asked Jor-Dan.

"Extinct little forest people," he said.

"How long have they been extinct?" Lee asked. "I'll bet the jarvust doesn't realize they're no longer there."

"At least a hundred years, or more," Jor-Dan said. He looked to Trakon for validation.

"I think it's been longer than that," Trakon said. "I don't even remember what they looked like from our histories."

"I recall a lesson about them in one of the advanced Egrom movies," D'laine said. "They're tiny elf-like people with big pointy ears. Back on Earth they we would consider them elves or hobbits."

"Perhaps these Sangdon people treated this jarvust badly?

They probably kicked him out of the forest and he wants to take his anger out on them," Stanley said.

Trakon shrugged. "Difficult to say. Who knows when this happened, but it seems obvious the jarvust has a grudge against them."

As they got nearer, they spotted a line of Egroms spread across the moss with their four hands held out in front of them.

Ghury suddenly materialized on the ship. "We are not having any progress with trying to eliminate the fire. Evidently the jarvust is controlling this fire with his power."

He turned to D'laine. "You are correct in your assumption of the Sangdons. They are similar to those tiny people you mentioned that are no longer on Earth. Perhaps they came here, then they left here for another dimension."

"You mean elves were real? Not some made-up tale?" The scientific part of Stanley's brain needed proof, validation or some type of Egrom hard-core facts.

"Jogavungdal," Victor said, still in his trance.

Ghury shook his head. "I do not know what that is."

"Could that be the jarvust?" Jamie asked.

Victor startled out of his trance.

They landed the ship and everyone plowed out and down the stairs.

Another crestrider flew from the direction of Ta'Byu'Vohon. It landed nearby, and the Plotals rushed to join them.

"What can be done?" Jakla bellowed. He was freaked out that his brand-new territory would burn to the ground. If this fire in the Tempe Forest jumped over to the Ikley Forest, there would be no stopping it.

"The Egroms can't stop the fire, and they can't control the jarvust, since it's just a projection in the sky," Lee said.

Jakla, Orongo and the three Plotals they brought with them were close to panicking.

"Should I try to talk to it?" Jamie asked.

"Try it," Jor-Dan said.

Jamie stared at the vision over the forest and sent a silent communication. *Please stop burning the forest.*

The jarvust never even acknowledged Jamie.

"What if he can't see me down here?" Jamie asked.

Jakla grabbed a hold of Jamie and lifted him onto his broad shoulders.

"The jarvust is not a solid object over the forest," Ghury said. "It is a projection."

"What about when it was looking in my head? Where did that come from?" Jamie asked. It was odd to look down to the Egrom. From the Plotal's shoulders he was now a few feet taller than Ghury.

Ghury pondered. "That is a good question. I don't have an answer."

Everyone stared at the elder Egrom. If he didn't have the answer, how would they deal with this entity and stop the fire?

"It could be like that fairy tale about Rumpelstiltskin, and you need to guess its name?" Brian asked, with a shrug.

Full-sized borjos flew toward them. They landed, and Herish and a team ran over to them.

"Can you stop the fire before it reaches the Cember forest?" he asked, in somewhat of a panic.

"Jamie tried to talk to this jarvust, but it didn't answer him," D'laine said.

"Let me try again," Jamie said.

"Do you want to stay on my shoulders, or get down on the ground?" Jakla asked.

"You can put me down on the ground," Jamie said.

Jakla swung Jamie back to the moss.

Jamie stood, feet apart, hands on his hips. *Hey! You up there! Jarvust! I know you see me down here. You looked inside my head when I was sleeping!*

The image over the forest turned its eyes and looked down upon Jamie.

You are not the one I have come for! The words boomed out. Everyone felt the jarvust's communication like a vibration.

Jamie spoke out loud, and inside his head, not sure what the jarvust could hear.

"Those Sangdon people no longer live here. They disappeared hundreds of years ago, so if you're mad at them, leave the forest alone and stop burning the trees!"

The jarvust stared at Jamie.

They are here! I will destroy the entire forest!

Stanley huffed out in exasperation. "I'll see if I can find this creature's brain. Talk to it, Jamie, so I can try to follow the path back to it."

"Who is Jogavungdal?" Jamie asked. *"Is that who you're mad at?"*

Suddenly, a section of the forest in front of them seemed to erupt in a fierce fire. The flames rose into the sky.

Stanley stared straight ahead. He must have done something energetically, because suddenly Ghury turned his attention to the scientist, but no one else paid attention.

"That hit a nerve," Lee said. "We'd better move back!"

Herish grabbed his hair on the top of his head with both hands. "We have to stop this fire!"

Smoke made everyone's eyes sting. They coughed and covered their noses and mouths.

"We realize what's at stake," Trakon said. "The forests are connected, so the Cember and Ikley Forests are in great danger. The problem is, how do we make a jarvust stop what it's doing?"

"Jamie! Its name is Dighasogajal. Call it by its name. Tell him Jogavungdal left here with their tribe. Tell him there are no longer Sangdon on Thol," Stanley said.

"Dighasogajal! The Sangdon tribe no longer lives on Thol. Your enemy, Jogavungdal, may even be dead by now," Jamie said.

The jarvust stared at Jamie.

You called my name. You have given me form again!

Stanley held out a hand, pointed a finger at the being that wavered over the forest. "D'laine, use The Voice. I want you to say, *Dighasogajal be gone. Take your fire with you.*"

D'laine stood front and center. She pulled up her powers, and The Voice reverberated out.

DIGHASOGAJAL, BE GONE! TAKE YOUR FIRE WITH YOU!

They watched as an expression of surprise seemed to cross the being's face. Then, suddenly, the vision vanished, and the fire stopped.

Herish nearly passed out from relief. He bent forward and grasped his knees to stop himself from collapsing. "Thank Thol!"

The Plotals made a loud *bhah* sound through their long snouts.

"How did you figure out that would work?" Jor-Dan asked Stanley.

"I followed the energy sequence back to Dighasogajal, the entity that created the jarvust," Stanley said. "He was a Sangdon in his actual life form, but when he died, he was bitter at being kicked out of his tribe. His hate for Jogavungdal was palpable. I don't know why he was banished, and most likely he didn't even remember in this form. But all that bitterness roiled into this ball of discontent that was so powerful, it created the jarvust."

Darren and Brian whispered back and forth off to the side of the Egroms, Plotals, Kudaja, Ciertrons and Eartholians. When they came to an agreement, they trotted over to stand in front of the groups.

"I'd like to try to restore the forest," Darren said. "It can't be any different from restoring a house or building, right?"

Everyone stared at the boy. His gift was undeniably one of the best talents.

"What do you mean by restore?" Herish asked. "How would you do that?"

"Darren's gift is multifaceted," Victor said. "He discovered he can focus on something old and make it brand new again."

"It's much more than that," Jor-Dan said. "He has taken old barns, houses and buildings that were practically falling down, and restored them to different shapes and sizes, and made them beautiful again. Inside and outside."

"You can do that?" Orongo asked.

Darren nodded. "It first happened when I was on kitchen duty for my punishment. I had sore hands from scrubbing pots and pans, and piles of dishes."

"He got mad, which triggered something in his head, and suddenly the kitchen was sparkling, as if it were just constructed instead of years and years old," Lee said. "Pretty handy gift, I'd say."

"You Eartholians have made Thol and its peoples so much better," Jakla said. "I am very grateful for the day D'laine healed me on the battlefield. I should have died during the robot invasion. I owe it all to her, this great change the Plotals are going through to become civilized."

D'laine walked over to Jakla. She patted his arm. "I saw someone worth redeeming."

"Give it a try, Darren," Victor said.

"We've seen what you've done all throughout Ebscalon," Jor-Dan said. "This would truly be a gift if you could restore the forest from this devastating fire!"

Darren faced the gigantic trees. A vast swath of woodland was charred in the middle of the Tempe Forest. He held out a hand. His face showed his intense focus. Suddenly, the smoke and acrid air cleared. What was burnt and scorched, was now restored to big, beautiful agrin trees, with their deep purple bark, with branches that contained foliage that sparkled like glitter.

Multiple loud gasps sounded from the group.

CHAPTER TWENTY-SEVEN

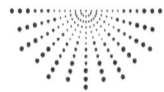

*J*oseffa knocked on Ethaderia's door. She fidgeted, wondering if they would turn her away. After all, she had served the vile Augenta for more than a dozen years. Eglabado opened the door and stared at the woman on the stoop, in shock.

"Joseffa?" Eglabado gasped. He stepped outside and looked around, fully expecting Augenta to come forward.

"She's not here," Joseffa said. "May I speak with Ethaderia?"

Eglabado held out his arm, hand extended toward the house. "Please, come in. I will contact the mistress for you." He showed Joseffa to the sitting room where non-family guests were escorted to wait. He disappeared to his kitchen where he could communicate in private.

Ethaderia, your mother's helper, Joseffa is here to talk to you.

ETHADERIA SAT WITH KITRY AND KARA IN HER COUSIN'S CRAFTING room. They were having a humorous conversation as they designed a new wall covering, when she received the ping from Eglabado.

"Joseffa?" Ethaderia sent to Eglabado. She turned to her cousin. "My mother's helper is at my house!"

Kitry and Kara stopped what they were doing and shared surprised faces.

"Is your mother back?" Kitry asked.

"I don't know!" Ethaderia said. She held up a finger. *Eglabado, is my mother with her?*

No, the woman is by herself and would like to speak with you.

"It's only Joseffa," Ethaderia shared.

"I think it would be prudent to have her come here so we can get any information about these Trangula," Kitry said. "I'll contact Jor-Dan and the others."

Eg, have her come to the palace.

I'll escort her myself.

The three women rushed from the queen's suite and headed to the large salon. They were joined by Jor-Dan, Marrak, Dannin, Trakon, Lee, Stanley, Trekie, Victor and D'laine.

"What is this all about?" Jor-Dan asked.

"We don't know," Kitry said. "Joseffa showed up on Ethaderia's doorstep. Eglabado is walking her to the palace."

They all settled into the room. Within a few moments, Eglabado bade Joseffa to enter the family salon. The woman was nervous. She tapped her fist to her heart, first to Jor-Dan, then to Kitry. She was about to greet Trakon formally, but Eglabado squeezed her elbow for her to stop.

"Joseffa!" Jor-Dan boomed out. "Where is your mistress?"

"King Jor-Dan, Guerson and I left the Valley of the Wailing Winds as soon as we delivered Augenta to the Trangula," Joseffa said. "When we saw what it was like, we didn't want to stay there. Please take us back! I didn't want to leave Ebscalon!"

"Who is Guerson?" Jor-Dan asked.

"He led our caravan from Ebscalon to the Trangula king-dom, if that's what you want to call it," the woman said.

Dannin leaned in and whispered to Jor-Dan. "People hire him to move them to their new location. He has a caravan of pakows."

Jor-Dan nodded. "Good to know."

"Why don't you start from the beginning and tell us what happened when you left Ebscalon," D'laine said.

"Let the poor woman sit down," Lee said.

"Of course," Jor-Dan said. "Please, be seated, Joseffa."

Eglabado escorted the nervous woman to a chair. He tapped his chest to the royals, and left the room quietly.

"You have been gone for several months," Stanley said. "Where have you been all this time?"

"When the mistress was banished from Ebscalon, we rushed to pack during that churling storm. She hired a caravan led by Guerson and we set out as soon as it was safe to travel," Joseffa said. "It took us four months to travel by pakow to the other side of Thol."

"This is to the Valley of the Wailing Winds?" Marrak asked. He recorded everything.

Joseffa nodded. "Yes. It was treacherous. The men fought off diwals, ogs, and a crazy pakow." She shook her head, as if reliving the experience. "Most of the time we didn't even erect a shelter, we slept on the ground. When we finally got there, we couldn't believe what we found."

"Describe what the Trangula kingdom looks like," Marrak said. "Do they have a large military force? Ships?"

Joseffa shared visuals with them. The gates and walls made from tree limbs. The yort-like palace and living places. King Custuf and his entourage of little Trangulans. The Tholian women held as captives.

"Guerson and I decided right away we were not staying. I refuse to live among sub-humans. If I were to stay there, I'd end up with a collar around my neck and chained to some male." She shuddered at the memory.

"Where is this Guerson now?" Trakon asked.

"He is at our room, or out trying to find work," Joseffa said.

Jor-Dan turned to Marrak and Dannin. "Find him and bring him here. We need to debrief him more thoroughly."

Dannin pulled up his communicator and searched for Guerson's name and location. When he zeroed in on the man's *signature*, he left the room, while Marrak worked his communicator.

"How long did it take you to return to Ebscalon?" D'laine asked.

"Two and a half months," Joseffa said. "We didn't have the burden of the caravan. Another man came with us, but a mruck gored him a half a month after we left that awful place, and he died."

The room became quiet as everyone was busy with their thoughts. Several moments later, Dannin returned with a tall warrior of a man beside him. They both tapped their chests.

"This is Guerson," Dannin reported. He took his place beside Marrak.

The man was nervous as he stood before the royals. His eyes wandered over to Joseffa, then back to his king.

"Guerson, explain your part in this business with Augenta," Jor-Dan commanded.

The man swallowed a loud gulp. "She paid me half a year's wages to escort her and her people to the Trangula territory."

"But you didn't see a reason to stay once you delivered her?" Trakon asked.

The man rotated his head to release neck tension. He let out a huge sigh. "I'm a caravan escort, for hire. I don't travel with people to live with them at their destination."

He shook his head as if trying to dispel a bad dream. "It was like going back to what I'd expect early Tholian humanity came up from. I couldn't believe my eyes. A gate and a wall made from sticks! They wear these little pots on their heads with a strap under their chins. The king didn't even look like a king. He wore the same clothes that those military Trangulans wore."

"Did you see any technology? Ships? Weapons?" Jor-Dan asked.

"Nothing. They didn't even have a pakow pen from what I set my eyes on," Guerson said. "We were lucky to get away with the three pakows we rode. The Trangulans couldn't even figure out how to mount the beasts. I'm wondering how they plan to keep them if they don't have a pen for them."

Joseffa nodded. "Probably in one of those round buildings."

"The Plotal tents were fancier than this place." He shared his visions with the room.

"We appreciate the intel," Dannin said. "What type of work are you looking for?"

"I'm getting out of the caravan business," Guerson said. "Pays well, but not worth it. I'll try to find some repair work. I'm handy with building and fixing places."

"I'll connect you with Dreboo, our city planner. He should be able to help you find work," Dannin said.

Guerson nodded. "Thank you. I appreciate it."

Joseffa turned her big eyes toward Jor-Dan. "So, we can stay in Ebscalon?"

"Of course," Jor-Dan said. "You did nothing wrong."

Guerson and Joseffa left the palace.

"Why would she stay there?" Ethaderia wailed. "Did you see the place? It's like Guerson said, early Tholian living standards!"

Lee patted her hand to calm his wife. "No one else would have her, and she probably thinks she'd be better off with a society below her."

"Knowing my aunt, she will try to bring them up to her standards," Kitry said.

Augenta had to draw out what she tried to explain. The language barrier was getting easier, but most of the Trangula had a peculiar way of saying things, or pronouncing things. She was never sure they were on the same page. The doski were far worse. They were able to memorize what she told them, but again, their language skills were not there.

She was finally about to get something done regarding the crowns she and Custuf should wear. She grabbed one of the tin plates used for eating and shoved it at the craftsman in front of her.

"Make this!" she said, holding the drawing up in front of him. "One for Custuf, one for Queen." She pointed to the king, then herself.

"I make this for king and queen!" the craftsman said. He smiled a wide, toothy grin at her.

Augenta clasped her hands together and looked skyward. "Yes!"

Jamie rode a pakow toward the Tempe Forest at a leisurely pace with Chatter and Buffy loping alongside. He was eager to find out how the forest was restoring itself after Darren's magic. He worried about the animals that might have lost their lives in the raging fire.

The forest loomed up ahead of him. He pulled up his communicator and found the coordinates of the fire damage. He nudged the pakow to change direction to the right. As the beast slowed down, Jamie watched the communicator guide him to the exact spot where Darren preformed his miracle.

"Okay, you can stop now," he told the beast. "Don't disappear, okay? I'll need a ride back to the pens in a little while." He patted the pakow as it knelt on the moss. Jamie swung himself out of the saddle, then carefully made his way down the tremendous leg of the beast and jumped to the ground.

"Buffy, why don't you take a break?" Jamie studied his old dog, who didn't even appear old anymore. He still worried that Buffy was overdoing everything. Back on Earth, she had been an old dog when he was living with Victor, Kara and Darren. Now, Buffy seemed more puppy-like. It was odd.

Jamie headed into the forest. Dappled sunlight spotted the forest floor. There was no sign of a fire having ever taken place where he walked, from only a few days ago. Still, he walked on, keeping to the periphery of the forest, searching for signs of dead animals. After a while, he walked several feet further into the forest to continue his search. He used the light from his communicator to shine the way.

"This is really weird," he said. "I wonder if Darren's gift restored the animals as well?"

Jamie maneuvered around the enormous agrin tree trunks. He stumbled over something. He shined the light to the forest floor and discovered a dead mruck. It wasn't blackened as if burnt. He wondered if it died from all the smoke in its lungs. Jamie was about to move on when he heard weak mewling sounds. He crouched down and discovered three baby mrucks trying to nurse at their dead mother's teats.

"Oh, no!" Jamie exclaimed. He figured they couldn't possibly be more than a couple of weeks old. He picked one up, and it squealed. He petted its crusty brown skin. "It's going to be okay. I'll find some way to take care of you until you grow up, okay?"

The baby mruck wrapped its short little trunk around Jamie's finger. He watched as its tiny pig ears twitched. He gathered the other two up in his arms and raced around tree trunks back to the pakow.

Buffy napped in the pakow's shade. The giant beasts were good for something besides work and transportation.

Chatter became alert to the possibility of a meal. He raced toward Jamie, teeth clacking.

"Don't even think about it," Jamie yelled at the diwal dog.

Chatter pranced around Jamie.

"No!" he yelled. "Do I have to call D'laine and have her get after you with The Voice?"

Chatter let out a huff. He definitely recognized and understood the word *D'laine*, and most likely processed he would be in big trouble if he acted inappropriately. He quieted his teeth and flopped down onto the moss and sighed loudly.

"Good dog," Jamie said. He approached the pakow. "Help me get these mruck babies back to the pakow pen, okay?"

The pakow knelt, and Jamie scooted up. He stared at the saddle and wondered how he would manage to get his leg across while holding the three baby mrucks.

"Don't move," he pleaded with the pakow. He got down on his knees and inched forward. Then he turned around and scooted backwards until he was abreast of the saddle. He eased his right leg over the seat and settled in. "Well, that was interesting." He nudged the pakow with his heels. "Let's go home."

The beast rose to its feet in a rocking motion, then it took off the way they had come. The dogs romped alongside at first, then in front of the pakow, and finally, following behind.

JAMIE RODE THE PAKOW UP TO THE PAKOW CORRAL. JUGDAAK waited for the beast to stop, then grabbed ahold of the reins as the pakow knelt. Getting down was a lot easier than climbing up the leg.

"What's that you've got there?" Jugdaak asked.

Jamie alighted on the ground, and the pakow handler came around to his side of the beast.

"Are those mruck babies?" Jugdaak asked.

"Yes. Their mother must have died from the smoke. She didn't seem burnt," Jamie said.

"What are you going to do with them? They'll die without their mother for the first month," Jugdaak said.

"I don't know what to do," Jamie said. "I'll put them in Oggy's old pen for now, then I'll go to the kitchen and find out what Grubio suggests. He knows a lot of things."

Jugdaak rubbed his chin. "Well, we could try to feed them pakow milk. I don't know if they'll like it or not."

"I'll ask D'laine if I could have one of the twins' baby bottles. She's got a bunch of them," Jamie said.

"That might work. I wonder if the nipples will be too big?" the pakow handler asked.

Jamie shrugged as he carried the three hungry babies to the og's old healing pen.

CHAPTER TWENTY-EIGHT

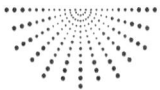

*J*amie climbed the palace stairs to Trakon and D'laine's suite, then detoured around to the twins' suite. The woman warriors greeted him.

"Hello, young Jamie," Amoroso said.

"Is D'laine here with the twins?" Jamie asked the guard.

"Yes, she's inside."

Jamie went through the open doorway. Kal-Dan was being bounced in Zedonia's arms while D'laine burped Jesslin.

"Hi, D'laine!" Jamie said. He walked up to Zedonia. "Hi, Kal-Dan. Uncle Jamie loves you!" He continued over to the rocking chair. He peeked at Jesslin on his sister's shoulder. She looked asleep. Jamie whispered, "Hi Jess!"

"It's okay, you don't have to whisper. She's tuckered out from feeding," D'laine said.

"D'laine, I found three baby mrucks in the forest," Jamie explained. "They were trying to nurse at their dead mother. They're really tiny. Do you think I could try one of the baby bottles and see if I can feed them? Jugdaak said we could try pakow milk."

"Oh, their poor mother. Was she burnt?" D'laine asked.

"No. Maybe her lungs couldn't recover from all that smoke," Jamie said.

D'laine got up and put Jesslin in her crib and lifted the rail. She walked over to the supply cabinet and looked at the various bottles they had in stock. She pulled one out.

"This looks like the smallest nipple," she said. "We got several different sizes to experiment with."

Jamie studied the bottle. "That might work."

"Are you keeping them in Oggy's old pen?" his sister asked.

He nodded. "I hope they don't die."

Jamie held the bottle steady, while Jugdaak poured pakow milk inside it. They heard the mewling baby mrucks in the pen. Mrucks had lidless eyes, but the babies had a membrane over their eyes, so they were still blind. They belly crawled around on the moss, not being fully ambulatory yet. They wouldn't see for a couple of weeks, and wouldn't start walking until their sight came into focus.

"Okay," Jamie said. He screwed on the top of the bottle. "Let's see how the feeding experiment goes."

He opened the gate and got on the ground. He picked up one of the mrucks. It squealed in fright until he nudged the nipple into its mouth, then the baby sucked contentedly.

"Looks like it's working," Jugdaak said. "Maybe you'd better see if you can get a couple more bottles and find someone to help with the feeding."

"Yeah, that's a good idea. Now that we know they'll eat from a bottle, I'll try to line up people to help with the feeding schedule," Jamie said.

"They should be able to drink milk from a bowl once their eye membranes lift," the pakow handler said.

The other two babies cried as they crawled blindly about on the moss, tumbling over, searching for their mother.

D'LAINE INFORMED EVERYONE ABOUT THE MRUCKS AT dinnertime. Darren's eyes lit up.

"Can I help feed them?" he begged his parents.

"Sure, I don't see why not," Kara said. "I'll even help. We'll have to coordinate with Jamie. I wonder if they're like kittens and have to eat every few hours."

"That boy," Jor-Dan said, with a shake of his head. "He has such an affinity with animals."

"I hope they don't turn on him when they mature," Kitry said. Worry creased her otherwise calm face.

"The og didn't," Trakon said.

"There's something about Jamie that animals trust," Victor said. "Remember, Oggy introduced his family to Jamie months after he was released to the wild."

Stanley stared at Darren. "Your restoration of the Tempe Forest may have restored some animal life. I want to find out how those restorations affect the lives of those animals—that's an Egrom question. I wonder exactly how the mother mruck died."

"Jamie said she didn't look burnt," D'laine said. "He assumed it was from smoke inhalation."

"Poor thing," Kara said.

ETHADERIA AND LEE STARED AT THEIR YOUNGER SON AS HE SPUN the tale about the mruck babies. Brian smirked. His brother had an animal menagerie that couldn't be beat. The borjos were the most beloved of all the beasts of Thol, but those mrucks were fierce. He hoped they would still love Jamie when they were older.

Jamie's communicator dinged. It startled him since the most obvious people to communicate with him were sitting at the dinner table.

"Hi Stanley. What's up?"

Would you be able to show me where you found those mruck babies? I want to examine the mother and see what she died from.

Jamie looked across the table to his father and stepmother.

"Sure," Lee said. "I'll tag along."

"Stanley, I can go. Daddy wants to come with us."

Okay. Be right there.

He wasn't kidding either. As soon as the words left his mouth, Stanley materialized in the dining salon at Ethaderia and Lee's house.

"Oops! I didn't realize you were having supper," Stanley said. He glanced at the table to see if what they were having was just as good, or better than what he just ate at the palace.

"Would you like something to eat or drink?" Ethaderia asked.

Stanley looked at Jamie's plate. "What is that?" He pointed to a vegetable he didn't recognize.

"Roasted hofo. It tastes like zucchini," Lee said.

Eglabado appeared with a plate for the scientist, along with a fork and knife.

"I wonder why we haven't had this at the palace?" Stanley said.

Ethaderia smirked. "Jor-Dan hates hofo. Even the smell of it gets to him, but not like Trakon with jiffaberra. He must have had to eat a lot of it when he was very young, and refuses to eat it now."

Stanley speared a piece from Jamie's plate, shoved it in his mouth and chewed. "Oh, this does taste like zucchini! I'll have to tell everyone about this. We'll have to bully Jor-Dan so the chef serves this."

When the Jackson's finished their meal Lee and Jamie took off with Stanley. The scientist placed his hand on Jamie's shoulder to get the location they needed to go, then he *stepped* them to the forest.

The dead mruck was still on the forest floor. Stanley did his thing with his hands and the heavily shaded area lit up.

"No burns," Stanley said.

Lee squatted beside the scientist. "Do you think it suffocated because of the smoke?"

Stanley stared at the animal for a long minute. Then he snapped back, alert. "Yeah, poor thing. She was trying to get her newborns out of the forest." He stood and brushed off his knees. "I just wanted to make sure nothing else was going on."

"We don't need anything else to worry about," Lee said.

"Do you think her babies will be okay without her?" Jamie asked.

"Let's go see them," Stanley said. Within a blink, they were standing beside Oggy's old pen.

Jugdaak was inside the pen feeding one of the mrucks.

Jamie scooted inside and dropped to his knees. "How are they doing?"

"They seem to be doing just fine," the pakow handler said.

"We need more bottles," Jamie said.

Lee hit his communicator. "D'laine? Can you spare two more bottles for the mruck babies?"

Sure. The twins don't like those small nipples. I've got three more if you want to come get them.

"I'll go get them, then all the mrucks can eat at the same time," Stanley said. With a blink, he was gone, and back again.

"Where's the pakow milk?" Jamie asked.

Jugdaak pointed with an elbow. "Over in the corner."

Jamie held the bottle, while his father carefully poured the milk. They filled two bottles and left the spare by the milk pail.

Jamie got comfortable on the ground and brought one of the babies into his lap. Lee followed suit. They were hungry little animals.

Jugdaak set his baby mruck on the moss and it curled up and went to sleep. "Looks like the pakow milk agrees with them." He stood, brushed his knees off and left the pen. He returned a few moments later with the bottle rinsed, and placed it in the corner with the other bottle and the milk.

"Will the milk spoil out here in this heat?" Stanley asked.

"Hadn't thought of that," Jugdaak said. "Better bring it into my shed." He reached down, grabbed the jug of milk and left the pen.

"Darren's going to help with the feeding, so's Kara," Stanley said.

TRAKON WAS KISSING D'LAINE'S CHIN, THEN KISSED HIS WAY DOWN her neck in the still of the night in their suite. The twins were fast asleep, and Trakon was taking advantage of the time with his wife. Suddenly, his communicator blared out an alarm. He practically jumped two feet in the air, his arms making swimming strokes as he scrambled across the enormous bed to reach his device.

The racket woke the twins, and they screamed in stereo. The women warriors were on high alert. Halvid knocked on the connecting door.

"Is everything all right, Prince Trakon?" she asked.

"Trangula set off the perimeter alarms at Ta'Byu'Vohon!" he called out.

D'laine got up, into her robe, and rushed into the other room to reassure her children that everything was okay. Cendi bounced Jesslin in her arms and made shhh noises. D'laine retrieved Kal-Dan from his crib and tried to comfort her son.

"Thanks so much, Cendi," D'laine said.

"This little girl has a pair of lungs on her!" Cendi said.

Trakon hurried into the room. "I've got to wake my father, then we'll contact Jakla."

"You should check in with Herish to make sure they are not under attack," D'laine said.

"Will do." He kissed her on the forehead and left the suite. She heard him running down the hallway, then the stairs.

Cendi called out to Amoroso. "Alert the nursery guards to be vigilant!"

They heard Amoroso communicating with the warrior women over at the hatching building.

"It's better to be safe than sorry," Cendi told D'laine.

"We used that expression on Earth, as well," D'laine said.

The twins settled down, yawning and dozing off in their arms. D'laine put Kal-Dan back to bed, while Cendi did the same with Jesslin.

TRAKON RAPPED ON THE DOOR TO HIS PARENTS' SUITE. NO ONE answered, so he quietly entered, went to their bedroom and repeated the rapping on the bedroom door.

Jor-Dan stumbled to the door tying his rope, hair askew. "What's happened?"

"The Ta'Byu'Vohon alert sounded. We need to contact Jakla to find out what's going on before I summon the fleet, and we need to contact Herish," Trakon said.

"I'll meet you in the salon," Jor-Dan said. He stepped back into his bedroom.

Trakon hurried to the salon and paced, waiting for his father. D'laine entered, fully dressed.

"My father will be here shortly," Trakon said.

Jor-Dan entered the room fully dressed. Two of his advisors entered the room in their bathrobes.

"Any word yet?" one of the advisors asked.

"No, I haven't taken any action; we're just now making the call," Trakon said. He pressed his communicator and pulled up Jakla's ID. "Jakla? I received the alert. Should we come with the fleet?"

Yes! There are Trangula all throughout the trees. We are dealing with them as best we can, but in the dark, it's a challenge.

"We'll be there shortly," Trakon said, then signed off. He pulled up Herish's ID. "Herish, sorry to wake you, but Ta'Byu'Vohon is under attack by the Trangula. Have any of your trip wires sounded off?" He listened. "Okay, good. We're heading over to the Plotal compound."

Stanley stepped into the room, rubbing sleep out of his eyes. "I'll come with you. D'laine and I can light up the forest."

Jor-Dan turned to his advisors. "Rouse Lee and Jamie. Have the borjos cruise around the fields to make sure this isn't a ploy to get the fleet away so they can attack Ebscalon."

"I hadn't thought about that," Stanley said.

Trakon was working his communicator, alerting the fleet commanders.

The second advisor was working his communicator. "I have warned the gate guards. They will send a squadron to the fields."

Stanley, Trakon, D'laine and Jor-Dan vanished. They appeared at the ship buildings just as several crestriders rose into the air and hovered over the buildings. They rushed up the stairs to one of the motherships. Within moments, the ship rose into the air, accompanied by three other motherships.

"Everyone gear up in full war mode," Jor-Dan sent to every ship in the fleet. He pressed the button on his suit, along with everyone else on the ship. Loud clacking of the suits transitioning to war mode, including helmets, shattered the quiet of the night.

D'laine's suit molded to her curves. She looked Stanley over to make sure he was fully suited up. The scientist knocked his knuckles against hers.

"Will someone tell my father and Jamie to suit up in war mode?" she asked.

"They should have been advised, but I'll send the warning to them to be sure," Jor-Dan said.

The fleet appeared as dark dots against the night sky. The ships took off in fast mode, heading toward Jakla's territory. They witnessed the borjos flying over the field. Some skimming the edge of the forest, some flying mere feet off the ground.

D'laine spotted Jamie on Ekka's back. His war uniform encased his body, including a helmet. She thought she saw her father, but couldn't be sure, and then the ship was too far away. She turned her focus toward Ta'Byu'Vohon.

THE SHIPS APPROACHED THE PLOTAL TERRITORY, WHICH WAS IN dark mode with only ambient light from the night sky.

"Klaxjor, keep the fleet overhead," Trakon spoke into his communicator. "We'll go to the surface to see what the Plotals have put into action."

They all pressed a button, then they were on the surface and running toward the Plotal commander.

Jakla was in full war gear with his plumed helmet, standing outside his stronghold building with Orongo at his side.

"What action have you taken?" Jor-Dan asked. "We don't want to send the fleet in shooting if your warriors are in the trees hunting down the invaders."

"We aren't very efficient in the dark, so I have not sent them into the trees," Jakla said.

"Stanley and D'laine can light up the forest," Trakon said. He turned to the scientist. "How should you approach this? On the ground or in the air?"

"Either way works," Stanley said. "It will look like the suns are shining through the trees."

Jor-Dan and Jakla nodded.

"We should send ground troops into the forest and have the fleet spread out over the entire area," Jor-Dan said. He turned to Orongo. "Do you have the exact coordinates of the alarms?"

"They are all spread out, east to west. Every single alarm went off silently, as planned, so they don't know we're onto them," Orongo said.

Trakon sent instructions to the fleet. "Set identifications in your communicators so you don't accidentally shoot at a Ciertron or Plotal."

Orongo talked into his communicator spreading the same instructions.

"We should wait until everyone is in place before we light the place up," Stanley said. "We don't want to be too abrupt, otherwise we lose the element of surprise."

They all nodded.

"We need to have several platoons at the edge of the forest where they entered before we begin any attack," Orongo said.

Trakon's communicator chirped like one of the Tholian bugs that was similar to a cricket. He looked to see who was contacting him in stealth mode and read the message. "The Kudaja are approaching." He thought for a minute. "They could quickly be in place on the east-west perimeter of the forest."

Jakla, Jor-Dan and Orongo nodded.

"Good plan," Jakla said.

Trakon worked the communicator and sent the instructions to Herish, along with having his warriors adjust the IDs to include the Kudaja so no one accidentally got killed.

"Everyone ready?" Jor-Dan asked.

Everyone in the group nodded.

"Who wants to beam up, and who wants to stay on the ground?" Trakon asked.

Jakla's five-man ship cruised over to the group. "I'll take my ship. Orongo, you stay on the ground."

"I'll go with you," Stanley told Jakla.

"Orongo, I'll tag along," D'laine said.

"Be careful, wife," Trakon said. He pulled her close and pecked her on the lips.

"I'll try not to kill everyone," D'laine said.

MULTIPLE CHIRPS WERE HEARD IN THE QUIET OF THE NIGHT AS the Plotals, Ciertrons and Kudaja arrived at their strategic locations. From the air, Stanley held out his hands and the forest lit up. From the ground, D'laine thought the word *light* and everything from the ground to the tops of the trees shone like midday.

They caught the Trangula and doski off guard. Hundreds of them scurried through the trees in retreat. Laser shots pinged from all directions. The Ciertrons were well-protected in their fortified war uniforms. The Kudaja had similar uniforms. The Plotals did not have protection covering their bodies. Their helmets were more ornamental than protective, and their long vests, shirts and boots were not meant to protect their heavily scaled bodies.

Herish communicated to everyone. "The Trangula are pouring out of the forest. We're missing a lot of them—they run very fast, and they're small, so they make difficult moving targets."

D'laine ran beside Orongo. They both returned fire on the Trangula and their doski scouts, as they ran on the ground. Orongo roared as one of the critters shot his left boot. He ratcheted up his laser weapons and made like Clint Eastwood in one of the spaghetti westerns, as he blazed away at the trees.

His boot smoldered and a large hole appeared. The boot didn't appear to self-heal.

"Is your foot okay? I can do a quick healing so it doesn't interfere with running or walking," D'laine said.

"I should be okay," the Plotal said. He took a step forward and almost dropped to the ground. "Maybe you should assist me with your healing."

D'laine controlled her face to stop a smile from emerging. She got on her hands and knees and examined the hole. She pulled one of her crystals out of her pockets, set it over the hole in Orongo's boot, then she closed her eyes. She held her hands above the crystal and let out a long-held breath.

Orongo made a gruff huffing sound. He wiggled his enormous toes inside his hefty boots.

D'laine lifted the crystal off the boot. The material completed the self-healing. "How does your foot feel?"

Orongo stared at her, mystified. "It is completely healed!" He reached down his huge hand and helped her to her feet. "Ready?"

D'laine smiled at her new friend. "You bet!"

LASERS LIT UP THE NIGHT SKY AS THE SHIPS RETURNED FIRE FROM the Trangula spread throughout the trees. With Stanley's light, they could easily see the little sub-humans jumping from limb to limb. They scurried to get out of the light, which was impossible, but they hadn't figured it out yet.

Even though the Trangula had inferior laser weaponry, they could still do damage to the Ciertrons, Plotals and Kudaja. Ciertrons who hadn't activated their face shields were vulnerable in that a lucky shot could be a direct kill.

One borjo was shot where its wing connected to its huge body. The rider held on while the beast howled in pain and tried to glide down to the field without killing both of them. For a borjo, this was a life-threatening injury. They could not survive on the ground.

Ships darted over the forest, firing at will. Trakon took out two Trangula at once—they were standing close together on a limb, firing at the ships nonstop. The entire fleet seemed to dodge each other while tracking down the enemy and eliminating as many as possible.

Some Plotals took to the trees, running down the Trangula. Stanley watched three Plotals as they raced across the enormous limbs, shooting their opponents. It amazed him at how the huge creatures easily jumped from limb to limb, tree to tree. They appeared to be very light on their feet.

Herish and his warriors flew down toward the ground above the escaping Trangula and eliminated as many of them as they could. There would not be any prisoners. What they all learned was that the creatures were little more than talking dogs, so there was no intel to be gained by holding them in cells. They didn't believe in feeding and supporting a prisoner who only took up space.

After over three arduous hours, the fight seemed to be over. Trangula and doski bodies littered the forest floor and the field.

D'laine hurried over to the wounded borjo. The beast bellowed in pain as he tried to flap his wings and take to the skies. She talked with his handler to see if she could approach the borjo.

"Napi! Be calm," the warrior said.

The borjo was in mental and physical agony over its inability to lift off the ground.

"I'm going to have to take drastic measures, so you should back away," D'laine told the warrior. She held out her hand and commanded The Voice.

Napi, be calm!

The borjo appeared to be more peaceful.

Down, to the ground, Napi.

The huge beast lay on its side with its damaged wing facing up.

"Good boy," D'laine said. She approached the borjo and patted its side. She pulled out her biggest crystal. She didn't dare set it on the skin where the wing was damaged, so she held the crystal in both hands, only inches from the surface of the wound. D'laine closed her eyes. She moved her hands in the general area of the raw, bloody skin where the wing was partially severed from the body. Within several moments, the wing reattached to the skin and looked like new, completely repaired.

D'laine patted the borjo. "You're good to go, boy."

The borjo lumbered to his feet. Napi experimented with flapping his wings. Pure joy emanated from the creature when he realized he was healed.

The warrior stood beside D'laine. "That was amazing. Thank you for saving my borjo. I raised him from when he was a week old, and we're inseparable. I don't know what I would have done if he had died."

"I'm glad I could help," D'laine said.

Puando, Herish's borjo, landed close by at the same time that Trakon beamed down to the moss. Napi proudly beat his wings without lifting off.

"Let's all head toward the stronghold to debrief," Trakon said.

Herish climbed aboard Puando. "Let's ride. It'll be quicker."

Trakon rode with Herish, while D'laine rode on Napi with his handler. They soared above the Ikley Forest and landed near the stronghold, where a large group of various warriors stood.

Jakla stood front and center, with Orongo on one side and

Jor-Dan on the other. Stanley stood close by. Trakon, D'laine and Herish joined the other leaders.

"We were fortunate to have the help of our friends from Ebscalon and the Cember Forest, and we all learned something new today. The Trangula and doski, while small, are extremely fast. If it hadn't been for the forest being lit up like a dozen suns, we would have lost the advantage of the attack," Jakla said.

Orongo whispered something to Jakla. "I was just informed that Orongo was wounded, and the princess healed him. I am grateful, D'laine. Orongo may be ugly, but he's one of my best friends."

"Did you just make a joke?" D'laine asked.

Jakla gruffed out a belly laugh. To the uninformed, it sounded as if an attack would begin immediately. The Eartholians were used to the sound, but the first time they heard a Plotal laugh, they were in fear of their lives.

Orongo stepped forward. "We are grateful for all the assistance we had. The alarm system was tedious to install, but it paid off. The enemy didn't even realize we had the upper hand." He nodded to Herish. "The Kudaja saved the night when they arrived and patrolled the back of the forest. It would have taken us too long to get platoons back there without giving away the plan to the enemy."

Jakla nodded his agreement. "We are forever in debt to the Eartholians with their special gifts. Lighting up the forest was the best-laid plan. Our Ebscalon friends were quick to jump to our aid. We now know how important it is to have a fleet of ships."

Jor-Dan stepped forward. He nodded to Jakla and Orongo, then the body of warriors in front of him. "Ebscalon will always help our friends in any way possible. We have all learned over the past two years that we are more powerful as friends than as enemies. When we join forces, we can accomplish anything. It started with the robot invasion when a young stranger to Thol healed what must have seemed like a gigantic monster to her. Then she vanquished the robots and pushed them back to their realm."

With that, the warrior groups broke up and headed back to their homes, or modes of transportation.

Jakla nodded to the leaders and royals who remained. "Loss of life was less than expected. Three Ciertrons died. A laser nicked one and he catapulted over the ship and fell to his death. One died from an unlucky Trangulan shot to his face, and the other had been caught in the firefight between the enemy and his own people. It was one of those unfortunate friendly fire incidents."

Jor-Dan shook his head. "It could have been a lot worse."

"Two Plotals died, and one Kudaja lost his life. A borjo was critically wounded, but thanks to the healing powers of Princess D'laine, that creature can fly again," Jakla said.

He affectionately nodded toward D'laine.

They all stood in a moment of silence digesting Jakla's words.

"Let's go home," Trakon said.

CHAPTER TWENTY-NINE

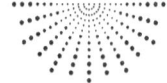

*T*rakon was practically sleeping on his feet when he pressed the deflating button on his uniform and fell onto the bed. D'laine nudged him. She shook her head at her husband, grabbed one of his boots, deflated it and tugged it off. She grabbed the other boot and removed it, then slid his uniform down his muscular form and threw it on the floor.

D'laine climbed onto the bed, bent over Trakon and rolled him completely onto the bed. She knee-walked to her side of the bed, removed her uniform and slipped into her nightwear. Within moments, sleep overtook her.

D'LAINE WOKE TO A LICK ON HER NOSE. SHE PEEKED THROUGH squinted eyes to see Pup with his two front feet on the bed, and a doggie smile on his otherwise frightful face. The suns were streaming into the room, and she heard cooing from the twins' suite.

"Hi, Pup. Did mommy sleep late?" she asked.

Trakon was still sound asleep, one of his arms thrown over his eyes, and soft snores barely discernible.

D'laine smiled wickedly. "Pup, go wake Trakon."

The diwal dog dropped to the floor and hurried to the other side of the bed. He tapped Trakon with a paw. When the prince didn't respond, Pup jumped up so his front paws were on the bed. He licked Trakon's open mouth.

D'laine's warrior husband sputtered, arms wavering over his head and his eyes blinking. He stared at the dog for a while.

"Is everything okay?" Trakon looked over at his wife and saw her holding back a laugh. He lunged for her. "You think that was funny?" He began tickling her, making her screech loudly in laughter.

Pup's tail beat against the bed. He jumped down and raced to the other side of the bed. He didn't want to be left out of the fun.

They settled down amid Trakon's gut grumbling loudly. "Did we miss breakfast? I have no idea what time of day it is."

"Let's go see the kids before we go get something to eat," D'laine suggested.

Trakon pulled her to his side and thoroughly kissed her. "I love you, wife."

"I love you, husband."

Pup made a happy whining sound.

"We love you too, Pup," D'laine said. She rubbed the little tuft of hair on top of the dog's head.

Trakon climbed over D'laine and slid off on his side of the bed. He snatched up his discarded uniform, brought it to the smart closet and hung it up. He looked around for both boots and placed them into the closet on the shoe shelf, then grabbed a clean uniform. He retrieved D'laine's uniform and boots from the foot of the bed, and placed them inside the closet and chose a uniform for her.

They dressed, pulled on and inflated boots, and opened the connecting door to their children's suite.

Kitry rocked Kal-Dan, while Jesslin swung in her favorite swing, and Keeshi, one of the warrior guards, played peek-a-boo with her. D'laine was amazed at how the small circle of people who were around her children every day, adapted to Earth-type baby language and games.

"Good morning," D'laine said. She stroked Kal-Dan's head, then kissed Jesslin on the forehead.

"Did we miss breakfast?" Trakon asked.

"We just finished," Kitry said.

Trakon grabbed D'laine's hand. "Come on, let's hurry before they put everything out for the poor."

D'laine hit her communicator. "Chef Grubio? Trakon and I are on our way down. He's starving."

Prince Trakon is always starving. I'll have the majordomo set two place settings at the table, Chef Grubio said.

"Thanks!" D'laine said. She disconnected her communicator.

Trakon hurried her out of the room, down the hall, and down the stairs to the dining salon.

"You'd think you haven't had a meal in days," D'laine grumbled.

"I'm bigger than you are, so I consume more," Trakon said.

She eyed him in disbelief.

"What? I use more energy than you do," Trakon said.

The majordomo carried two plates of food to the table. The plate he settled in front of Trakon contained a mound of different foods. D'laine's plate contained normal portions.

"Let me know if you require anything else," the majordomo said.

"Thank you!" D'laine said.

Trakon dug in with his fork. After several mouthfuls, he slowed down to a more normal pace. "I was starving! Must have been all that activity last night. All my stores of energy were depleted."

D'laine eyed his plate. "I'm pretty sure you've replaced those."

He patted his stomach. "Feels better." Trakon finished his breakfast.

The majordomo appeared. "Do you need more?"

Trakon shook his head. "No, that was very satisfying. I'll be okay until lunch."

The majordomo removed their plates and disappeared into the kitchen.

"You know, it would be nice if you said thank you," D'laine said.

"I thought I did," Trakon said, thinking about it.

Trakon and D'laine's communicators went off at the same time.

"Herish," Trakon said.

"Meeri's calling. Something must be wrong," D'laine said.

We're under attack! Herish said. *Can you help?*

D'laine! We need help, Meeri said.

"We'll gather everyone and be there shortly," D'laine said.

"What's the situation?" Trakon asked.

Looks like hundreds of those doski scouts and the military Trangula. They're all throughout the forest. The Egroms are zapping them with non-lethal energy, but it's not working, Herish said.

D'laine sent out an alert to Jor-Dan, her father, Victor, Stanley and Dannin. Next, she sent out an alert to Jakla and Orongo, asking for their help as well.

Thundering feet sounded down the hallways, stairs, and through the entrance to the palace. Everyone was suited in their war gear.

"We're on our way," Trakon said.

"We should send a ship to get the Plotals. It will take them too long to ride to the Cember forest," D'laine said.

Jor-Dan nodded. Dannin sent instructions for a warship to go collect them.

D'laine sent a message to both Orongo and Jakla to gather their forces, and they would be beamed onto the ship.

"Should we ride the borjos?" Lee asked.

"The Kudaja borjos can't fight with fire like our can," Stanley said. "We should ride ours. They can communicate with the other borjos."

Jor-Dan nodded. "We'll take the ships to transport the army, and all of you can ride borjos."

"Let's go," Trakon said.

They all ran out of the palace.

THE CEMBER FOREST WAS TEEMING WITH MILITARY FROM Ebscalon, Ta'Byu'Vohon, and Kudaja.

The Egroms, while not military, were walking weapons. They changed their strategy from stun to eliminate. They always tried the peaceful approach first, but they weren't bleeding hearts. They would not be overtaken by an enemy.

The Ebscalon borjos were distinguishable from the other borjos by their colored cloths and the steam escaping from their snouts. Evidently, there had been some communication between the two different breeds, because it seemed that the Cember Forest borjos followed their wild cousins' lead. They quite fancied munching on the enemy, now that they knew they could eat them.

Domestic women along with children were evacuated to the Egrom village.

Ben rode Aob alongside Trakon on Ehtuta. This was the first time the physicist engaged in war on Thol, so he studied how Trakon and his borjo dove through the trees, firing at the enemy.

Jor-Dan was aboard one of the warships, shooting from the sky. Plotals were up in the trees, running down the boardwalks, firing at the doski and Trangula who were also in the trees. Dannin flew on Grasko, shooting with two laser pistols as if he were in a gunfight in a western movie.

D'laine rode Ekka, and Stanley rode Foota. Victor was aboard Dundo.

Herish, flying Puando, and the Kudaja warriors aboard their borjos were something else to see. They flew with the structured precision of a well-choreographed performance to prevent any cross-fire upon each other.

The Plotals and Kudaja waited at the perimeter of the forest, where they determined the enemy had entered. As the tides turned in the fighting, the doski and Trangula poured out of the forest and ran. Many escaped due to their size and speed. In the end, the fighting ceased after two hours.

The leaders gathered on the boardwalk.

King Uladosa Cagmondoore triggered his war uniform back to normal forest-dwelling clothing. "I can't thank you enough for coming to our aid. We were overrun with doski and Trangula."

"That's what neighbors are for," Jor-Dan said. "Fatalities?"

The leaders checked their communicators. There were no expired contacts.

"We were lucky this time," Orongo said.

"This is the second attack," Trakon said. "I expect Ebscalon is next."

"Do you think they would attack tomorrow… or tonight?" Jakla asked.

"I can sense it," Victor said. "When they make a decision, I'll know and will send the alert."

Everyone nodded. They were all on edge.

"We need help with removing doski and Trangula bodies to the field," Herish said. "The borjos and wild diwals can feast."

The Egroms, Stanley and Ben made quick cleanup by transporting all the bodies to the field.

Trakon patted Ehtuta. "Don't eat so much that you can't fly!"

His borjo huffed out steam.

"Go on," Trakon said.

The borjos all flew to the field to assist in the cleanup. Two packs of wild diwals ate their fill, then went about their business.

CHAPTER THIRTY

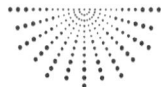

 guard ran from the gates through the city, across the courtyard and entered the palace at full speed. He went directly to the throne room, found it empty, then backtracked to the dining salon. There he found the royal family all accounted for, tired from the two recent battles.

The guard stepped just inside the room, pounded his chest. "Sire! Prince Trakon! The Trangula are storming across the field toward the palace. The borjos are overhead."

Everyone was out of their chairs and in action immediately.

"I'm going to our suite," D'laine said. "I will monitor the borjos from there and defend my children at the same time."

Trakon kissed her. "Be safe and keep our children safe." He bashed his communicator. "All troops to the crestrider buildings. Prepare to engage in battle." He sent another message out to the people of Ebscalon. "War is at our gates. Protect Ebscalon!"

He turned to his father. "Don't take unnecessary risks. Contact the Plotals and Kudaja!"

Jor-Dan nodded at him. Trakon turned and raced out of the room as his battle gear clacked into place.

Stanley and Jor-Dan shared a silent communication. They turned and met Lee's eyes.

"Lee, you're going to have to take one for the team," Stanley said.

Ethaderia's eyes bugged out. "What do you mean? Are you enlisting Lee in battle? He has no experience with war. He was lucky he didn't get killed defending the Plotals and Kudaja."

"Ethy, I'm a man. I will defend our kingdom in any way I know how," Lee said. "Thol is my homeland, and I chose this life over that of Earth. She has given me and my family incredible gifts. I owe her for that."

Brian, Jamie, Darren, Kitry, Victor and Kara stood frozen waiting for whatever was to come.

Stanley manifested the bomb container. He moved his hand over the top of the box and it unlatched. He reached in and removed the encased crown.

Everyone gasped.

"Is that King Jangston's crown?" Victor asked.

"Yes," Stanley said. He turned to Lee and Ethaderia. "I know you don't want to do this, but as the king, you have unprecedented powers. You can put a halt to this war."

OUTSIDE, THE BATTLE HAD ROARED TO LIFE. THE TRANGULA'S laser weapons were old technology, but effective nevertheless. Their sharpshooters aimed at the borjos, hoping to eliminate the beasts, but the cloth coverings the borjos wore protected them.

The borjos not only breathed fire down upon the enemy, but they also dropped through the air and snatched Trangula off the battlefield. Body parts fell to the ground.

The field was dark with tens of thousands of Trangula in their dark brown uniforms. The thunder from a thousand or more pakows carrying Plotals joined the melee. The Plotals were never happier than when in battle. The Kudaja joined them flying their borjos, their wyres killing the enemy left and right.

Suddenly, the field was white from an outpouring of Egroms stepping onto the field to do battle. They held no weapons... they were walking weapons.

Crestriders filled the skies sporting flags from the different kingdoms. Ground troops in hand-to-hand combat with the enemy, made a kaleidoscope of color from the neighboring monarchies.

D'laine had to remind the Ebscalon borjos that they could only attack or eat the Trangula. She feared the Kudaja borjos would engage with her borjos and not respond to their riders, but it all seemed to be okay.

Pup, Chatter and La'gar'ish implored her with their clacking teeth and their begging eyes. The women warriors kept their backs to the walls of the room and hallway, keeping out of the way of the bloodthirsty dogs.

D'laine made eye contact with the dogs. "Only kill Trangula and doski!" She projected a visual for them in their heads. When she uttered the word OKAY, the dogs ran down the stairs, and charged out of the palace.

Guards jumped out of the way when they saw the dogs tearing through the city toward the gates. One guard punched his communicator. "Open the small door and stand back! The dogs are coming!"

D'laine had her hands full with Buffy. The Earth dog wanted into the fray.

"No, Buffy. Stay here with me. Guard the twins! That's your job today. Do you understand?"

Buffy met D'laine's eyes. She walked over to the cribs where the twins slept and sat on Pup's bed, ears peaked, listening closely.

D'laine watched out a window as the dogs tore into the Trangula and the doski scouts.

LEE KNELT IN FRONT OF HIS SONS. "IT'S GOING TO BE OKAY. I want you to stay here, do you understand? Go to D'laine's suite and help from there."

Jamie sniveled and wiped his eyes with a hand. "I don't want anything to happen to you, daddy."

Brian laid a hand on his younger brother's shoulder. "This is war, Jamie. We're all going to have to make sacrifices for our way of life here on Thol. Daddy's going to be okay. He's going to be the King of Thol and he will defeat the enemy."

Jamie outright cried. "I know, but I'm scared."

Ethaderia knelt and hugged her stepson. "Let's go to D'laine's suite and help protect the twins. Your father has an important job to do." She stood, eyes shiny with tears. Lee wrapped his arms around her.

"I'll be back."

Stanley placed the clear container with the crown on the table. He closed his eyes and focused on the ancient words that had sealed the container hundreds of years ago. Within moments, the crown sat on the table, unprotected from its vessel for the first time since it was entombed.

"Jor-Dan, you should place the crown on Lee's head," Stanley said. "It's a king to king passing."

Jor-Dan picked up the crown that felt warm to the touch and stepped over to Lee. "May Thol protect you." With that, he placed the crown on Lee's head, then stepped back.

A transformation occurred before their eyes. Lee glowed. The beard was back. He was swathed in ancient royal clothes, including a thick, long red robe that contained blue stars on a white background at his shoulders.

Get down on one knee, Jor-Dan sent to everyone in the room.

They all dropped to one knee and bowed their heads.

"Stand!" Lee/King Jangston said. His voice seemed to reverberate off the walls.

They stood and faced him.

"Your majesty," Jor-Dan began. "The Trangula have committed an act of war. They are upon us, battling outside our gates. The Kudaja, Plotals, Egroms and all the neighboring nations have come to our aid."

"They have defied my edict of peace?" the king boomed out.

"Yes, your highness," Jor-Dan said.

"Take me to the wall!" Lee/King Jangston ordered.

Jor-Dan turned to the others. "Go to the tower."

Jor-Dan and Stanley led Lee out of the palace, across the city to the gates of the kingdom. They climbed the stairs and looked out over the battle across the field of moss.

The noise was deafening. The moss was littered with blood and bodies, in mostly brown uniforms.

Stanley hooked a hand through Jor-Dan's arm and tugged him away from Lee a few feet. Jor-Dan raised his eyebrows in question.

"Trust me," Stanley whispered.

Lee took in the battle scene before him, from the skies to the field. He grew to ten times his size. His crown glowed golden in the light of the two suns.

"STOP" he commanded in a voice booming similar to D'laine's when she used The Voice. He waved one hand flat, from left to right.

The battlefield participants froze. Even the borjos and crestriders were suspended in the air.

"Who defied their king and brought war to the gates?" his voice rang out.

His eyes zeroed in on the field where the Trangula ruler stood frozen in battle, his laser raised over his head. Beside him, dressed in a shiny, bronze colored battle uniform, stood Augenta.

Lee mentally latched out and grasped them and raised them above the field. "You would defy the King of Thol and take it upon yourself to declare war?" He released them and all the fighters from their suspended animation.

All eyes were fixed on the gigantic king on the wall. He stood as large as an agrin tree. The Ebscalon borjos glided through the air. The Kudaja borjos hovered like dragonflies. The crestriders from all the different kingdoms hovered. Soldiers on the field lowered weapons, waiting for an unknown command.

"Take to your knees!" Lee commanded.

On the battlefield and ships, soldiers dropped to one knee. The Kudaja on their borjos bent their heads.

"There will be no war on Thol, this I decree!" Lee boomed out. King Jangston had a hypnotic voice.

To the Trangulan ruler and Augenta, the king dealt a punishment worse than death.

"To the traitors before me, I banish you to the Nothingness." He waved his hand and the Trangulan king and Augenta vanished. Their tin crowns were all that was left of them.

"To the rest of you, return to your homelands. Put your battle gear away. Show kindness and be helpful to your neighbors."

The groups on the field broke away from each other. The kingdoms retrieved their dead and returned home. The Trangula abandoned their dead. A military Trangulan scooped up the crowns. The rest of them scurried back toward the direction they had come. Now that their wicked ruler and his queen were gone, they had work to do.

Lee's gigantic figure shrunk down to his normal size. He gazed upon the field with the various groups heading in different directions.

Jor-Dan faced Lee. "Thank you, your highness."

Stanley removed the crown from Lee's head. The golden glow disappeared, along with the robe, ancient clothes and Lee's beard. The container manifested in front of Stanley. He carefully placed the crown inside and sealed the box.

"Jor-Dan, I'm going to place this in your treasure room for now," Stanley said.

Lee *came to* and blinked several times. "Well? What happened?" He looked around and was surprised to see that he stood on top of the wall at the gates. He caught the end of the crestriders flying away, the pakows returning to the Plotal city, and the Kudaja borjos flying home to the Cember Forest. No Egroms were left on the field. They had *stepped* back home already.

The ground was littered with only the Trangula soldiers. The Ebscalon borjos were feasting on the field, along with the diwals. He noticed there were more than three diwal dogs.

"Must have been some battle!" Lee said.

"It was," Jor-Dan said. "We owe you a great debt, Lee."

Lee shook his head. "Wasn't me."

Stanley placed a hand on Lee's shoulder. "Yes, it was. Accept it."

"Let's go home," Jor-Dan said. He turned to the stairs, and they descended.

THEY RETURNED TO THE PALACE, TO THE DINING SALON. Everyone more or less dropped into their chairs and stared at each other across the table.

The majordomo approached them. "The evening meal will be served shortly. They are reheating the food. Would you like some Abrajaii?"

"That would be very welcome," Jor-Dan said.

Servers carried trays of flutes filled with the amber liquid. When everyone had a glass in front of them, Jor-Dan lifted his flute.

"To the end of war!" he said.

"To the end of the Trangula and their doski!" Trakon said.

Everyone lifted and drank, even the boys, who only had a swallow's worth of the champagne in their flutes.

"Let's hope we don't have to call upon King Jangston again," Kara said.

"His powers are unheard of," Kitry said. "I don't understand how he did the things he did. How did he become the size of a tree? How did he manage to stop everything in the air and on the ground?"

Victor shook his head. "Somewhere in those scrolls, there has to be a mention of this king. I can't find any information about when he ruled. How did the kingdoms form if he was the ruler of the entire planet?"

Stanley tapped his chin. "I wonder if the Oolarooloo or the Raagor have any information about him? We should also check with the Plakados. They left Thol for a reason."

"Don't forget the Sangdons," D'laine said. "They must have had a reason to leave this realm."

"That may be true, but we don't have any way to contact them. At least we know we can reach out to Maldi Amadal," Stanley said.

The servers brought out the food. Everyone quieted as they filled their plates, then started the meal.

Ethaderia looked across the table at Victor. "Where did my mother and the Trangula king disappear to?"

"The Nothingness," Victor said.

"Is that like Purgatory, or Hell?" Lee asked.

Victor shook his head. "The only way I can explain it is to say it's like between worlds where nothing exists. Life does not exist there, so when something goes to the Nothingness, their life either ends or is in some sort of suspended animation."

Ethaderia looked down at her plate. "I don't understand why she was the way she was. She never showed my sister or me a mother's love." She looked over to D'laine. "When I see how you look at your children, my heart aches. I would have loved to have you as a mother, and experienced the gift of a mother's love."

Lee patted his wife's hand. "You never have to worry about her again. She's gone, permanently."

Ethaderia raised her face and met her husband's glance with shimmering eyes. She nodded.

"All I want to do is enjoy my food, play with my twins for a little while, and have a good night's sleep," Trakon said.

La'gar'ish meandered into the room and flopped down at Jor-Dan's feet, looking quite satisfied. Chatter nudged Trakon to let him know he was back from the feast. They heard Pup scampering up the stairs back to his guard duty. Buffy stood in the doorway and huffed out a sigh.

D'laine patted her thigh. "Buffy feels left out. She can't hunt with the diwal dogs or go into battle. She probably wonders what her purpose is here."

"Other than Thol being her fountain of youth?" Lee said. He turned to Stanley. "Why don't we go see what Al is up to?"

The End - Never!

Creatures of Thol
© 2020 by Dawn Greenfield Ireland

Ghury
Egrom elder of the Cember Forest Tribe

Jakla Bosakin
Plotal Commander

Diwal Dog

Borjo

MAP OF THOL

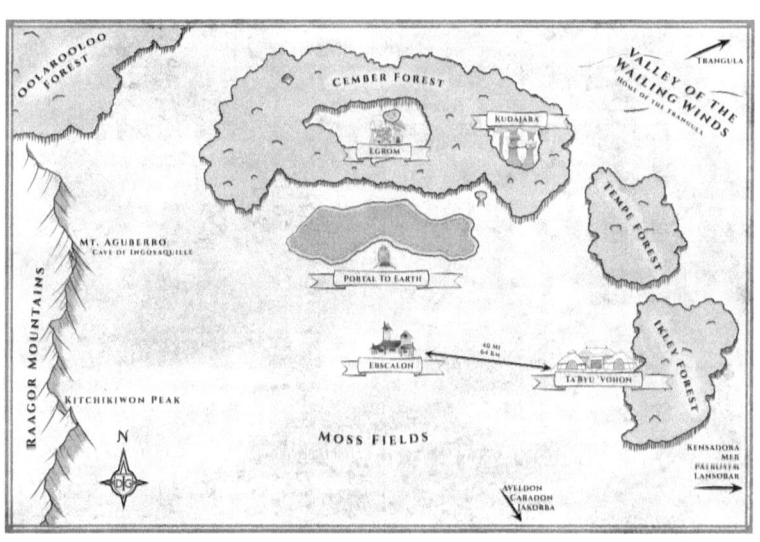

King of Thol: A Glossary

A * indicates a new character, creature, or thing introduced in King of Thol.

Characters

Absadul	One of the Egrom village elders.
Adrum	One of the Egrom village elders, he is tasked specifically with teaching D'laine the history of Thol.
Akubel	An ancient Egrom leader from long ago who received a prophecy.
Al Jordan	A junior staff member at Houston Daily News looking to make his big break, and a science fiction fan at heart. His plans to run a story on the anniversary of the Jackson family's disappearance turn into helping hide them. Later visits Thol when he sources baby supplies. Back on Earth, he begins writing a fiction book based on what happened to the Jackson family, amidst suspicious investigations from the government.
Amoroso	One of the women warriors assigned to guard D'laine and Trakon's children.
Anwak	The documentarian of the Plotals.
Aob	One of the Kudaja's borjos, he chooses Ben as his rider.
Augenta	Ethaderia's mother, she sorely disapproves of her daughter's match. After her exile from Ebscalon, she mysteriously vanishes. Having fled to the Trangula, she becomes their queen and manipulates their leader to urge them to war for the purpose of vengeance. It backfires with her getting banished to the Nothingness for her crimes.
Ben Joplin	The head of Rice University's physics department. He gets enlisted by Victor Bennett for a desperate plan to save the man's wife. The next to migrate to Thol after his retirement, he settles alongside the Kudaja and gains the gift of intertransport between Thol and Earth.
Bensol	One of the Egrom village elders tasked with helping and training D'laine to realize her destiny. He is the youngest of the Egrom elders.
Biggan	An Ebscalon guard assigned to D'laine and Trakon as the amorous couple's chaperone.
Bist	A city planner and one of several Plotals accompanying Jakla on his visit to Ebscalon.
Bok-Tor	A Safri prisoner D'laine saves from the Plotals.
Borg	One of the Kudaja, he helps Ben adjust to Tholian life.
Brenda	D'laine's childhood friend since 3rd grade.

Brian Jackson	D'laine's younger brother; at 10 years old, he played in the Little League, but health complications put a stop to it. Traveling to Thol after being healed, he was the last to come into his powers: detecting the portals between the alternate earths. He develops an interest in learning how the kingdom of Ebscalon is run. Inadvertently discovers his calling as an inventor and engineer when he is made to work on the crestriders to learn the value of labor and responsibility.
Brownie*	Ben's new pet, a gippe.
Buffy	The Jackson family's tan and white pit bull. Oddly, she seems to be getting younger on Thol despite her physical age.
Cadj	Jakla's son, he and his sister befriend Brian, Jamie, Chacoodi, and Darren, often getting into trouble with them. It takes a long time for him to accept both his punishment of shoveling pakow dung and the importance that his job provides.
Cagmondoore	King of the Kudaja; he is willing to let Ben settle in their village in Cember Forest.
Cendi	One of the women warriors assigned to guard D'laine and Trakon's children.
Chacoodi	A young Egrom from their village, he is quick to befriend both Brian and Jamie, becoming best friends with the former. He gets punished with scrubbing the village's cooking pots and cleaning the latrine trenches after causing too much mischief and havoc with his friends. Although a sullen attitude means he has to learn to properly clear his mind first.
Chamblin*	King Jangston's manservant.
Chatter	Trakon's pet diwal dog.
Connor	Tall, dark-haired, and D'laine's ex-boyfriend.
Corl	A furniture crafter; one of the Kudaja.
Custuf*	The leader of Trangula, he intends to kill many of the Tholian humans and raid them of their women. In the end, he is banished to the Nothingness alongside his co-conspirator.
Dannin	One of Ebscalon's council members, he is in charge of livestock, food and water, and hosk gathering.
Darren Bennett	Victor Bennett's son, this 8-year-old is both space obsessed and loves a good story. Enamored by Thol, he has no objections once his parents are convinced to move there. His gift is revealed to be electricity. Being put to work washing dishes in the palace kitchens has a surprising outcome when he discovers on top of electric powers, he can also restore things to make them good as new.
Dighasogajal*	The jarvust haunting the area. He was a Sangdon when he was alive, but became intensely bitter after being kicked out of his tribe.
Ditol	One of the Egrom village elders tasked with helping and training D'laine to realize her destiny.
D'laine Jackson	Smart and resourceful, D'laine was in for more than she could have ever imagined when her mysterious dream became reality. Now fully settled into Thol along with her family, learned advanced healing, and married to Trakon, the couple are in for a surprise when her body adapts to mimic Ciertron physiology.
Dojesk*	A Plotal who makes children's toys. With Neska's help, he creates a new type of toy called a Wobbly.

Dreboo	Ebscalon's architect.
Drusta	One of the Egrom village elders tasked with helping and training D'laine to realize her destiny. He has a close connection to plants.
Dundo	One of the borjos that come from Mt. Aguberro to live in Ebscalon. Wears a purple collar.
Dupree	An inventor defensive about his achievements; he comes up with a device to pick up spectral images.
Eglabado	The manservant at Ethaderia's home.
Egraphor	Queen of Patrosym.
Ehtuta	One of the borjos that come from Mt. Aguberro to live in Ebscalon; he becomes Trakon's mount. Wears a silver collar.
Ekal	One of the Visionary's only two disciples.
Ekka	A full-sized borjo gifted to Jaime by a mysterious traveler. Made the protector of Ebscalon, he lives at the top of one of the kingdom's towers. Wears a blue collar.
Emeric	The king of Patrosym, his life is saved thanks to D'laine's healing.
Eric Villarreal	Rosa's husband.
Ethaderia Justalon	Cousin to Kitry, she found shared feelings with one of the newcomers from Earth, and is now finally joined in happy matrimony with Lee Jackson.
Fazi	Jakla's daughter, she and her brother befriend Brian, Jamie, Chacoodi, and Darren, often getting into trouble with them. She straightens up and becomes more responsible, causing less mischief after being put to work managing housework.
Felid	One of the women warriors assigned to guard D'laine and Trakon's children.
Fingo*	One of Orongo's daughters. After causing too much mischief, she and her siblings are put to work to teach them responsibility. Fingo is told to clean the Plotal camp's many tents.
Fod	A mysterious figure and a member of the Fod race, a group of creatures who (due to a misunderstanding) intend to harm Marrak.
Foota	Ekka's new borjo friend and mate. Wears an orange collar.
Forador	The agriculturist of Ebscalon.
Gafn	A furniture crafter; one of the Kudaja.
Ghury	A key member of the Egrom village elders, Ghury becomes D'laine's mentor and guide for the path that lays ahead.
Grasko	One of the borjos that come from Mt. Aguberro to live in Ebscalon. Wears a green collar.
Greg Claymore	An Earthling sundered from his home and family many decades ago, Greg has come to terms with his new life on Thol; however, the newcomers to the planet find themselves suddenly in desperate need of his healing abilities.
Grubio	One of the palace's chefs.

Guerson*	The caravan escort who led Augenta and Joseffa to the Trangula. Later he fled the area with Joseffa.
Hal-sa-Bin	A member of the Ebscalon council, he is in charge of security.
Halvid	One of the women warriors assigned to guard D'laine and Trakon's children.
Herish Cagmondoore	A Kudaja warrior of Cember Forest. Revealed to be the prince of his race, Herish tries to make amends with D'laine; all while getting into the occasional tussle with Trakon.
Hexlon	Usually seen working on the crestriders, Hexlon's various skills came in handy when he received an unusual commission. Now, he is tasked with digging up and upgrading old trackers to use against the Trangula.
Horld*	A famous Ciertron who invented many technologies, including laser weapons.
Hovery*	A minor Ciertron guard who finds a severed Trangulan hand in the market.
Hruk	One of the palace chefs who specializes in desserts.
Ilanda	Ethaderia's sister; she is already married to the king of Kensadora.
Indii*	Vila's mother.
Iverdon*	King Jangston's son and heir.
Jakla Bosakin	Once a pillaging warlord, Jakla has since turned to more peaceful ways, his goals switching from using D'laine's powers to rebuilding his people's kingdom.
Jamie Jackson	At only 6 years old, he's D'laine's youngest brother. Always having a special kinship with animals, Jamie's talent gets taken to new heights once his Tholian powers are realized; however, his innocence may mean learning the hard way that not all animals are perfectly friendly. After causing too much mischief, he is made to work in the pakow pens to learn the value of labor and responsibility.
Jangston*	Once the king of all of Thol a long time ago, he possessed many unusual powers, including size growth, The Voice, and telekinesis.
Ja-Toy-Anic	Despite being a citizen of Ebscalon, his loyalties lay elsewhere. Now reformed, he is a member of the Ebscalon army.
Jawget	A Ciertron farmer infected by a mysterious ailment.
Jerry*	Al Jordan's neighbor.
Jesslin*	D'laine and Trakon's daughter.
Jewellex*	Treikie's friend and a documentarian, she is among those in charge of restoring lost technology.
Jor-dan Bramstone	Despite his age of sixty years, the King of Ebscalon doesn't shy from being both venerable ruler and fearless warrior.
Joseffa*	Augenta's maidservant; she fled the Trangula with Guerson after refusing to stay.
Jubulon	The ruler of Aveldon.
Jugdaak	The pakow handler of Ebscalon, he came to verbal blows with Jamie over an injured og. Later, he takes on Jamie as a worker in the pakow pens and is pleased with his work.
Jum	A young fhahadda saved and later relocated.
Kal-Dan*	D'laine and Trakon's son.

Kara Bennett	Victor Bennett's wife, and the receiver of a horrible medical diagnosis; the ripple effects of which will affect both Thol and Earth. Originally apprehensive about moving to Thol, she eventually agrees, gaining the gift of distinguishing lies and truth.
Keeshi	One of the women warriors assigned to guard D'laine and Trakon's children.
Kestrum	A female Egrom who lets D'laine stay at her mushroom house; the two quickly become fast friends.
Kitry Bramstone	The motherly Queen of Ebscalon, always looking to make those under her care as comfortable as possible.
Klaxjor	One of Ebscalon's flight lieutenants.
Kyo	Dannin's younger brother; he used to be Trakon's childhood friend before they grew apart.
Lansing	The widowed Queen of Jekorba.
Laoife	Mother to Ja-Toy-Anic, she shared both his leanings and vices. Now reformed, she works in the palace kitchens as a sauce expert.
Lee Jackson	Father of D'laine, Brian, and Jamie, this former NASA scientist's faith was tested when his eldest mysteriously vanished. Now reunited in a new world, Lee turns to using his career skills and his gift of holographic envisionings to help the Ciertrons with their technology. Though happily remarried and made an advisor to the king, there may be still more mysteries surrounding his ancestry. After coming in contact with the old king's crown, he begins remembering and acting like his past life, even transforming to resemble him.
Lorand	A member of Princess Yalalore's guard detail, he is sent to either kidnap or kill the royal eggs.
Lori Jackson	Lee Jackson's late wife, and the victim to a tragic accident.
Lulu	A female pakow that becomes D'laine's mount.
Maldi Amadal	A Plakado traveler and wanderer, he has found several secrets on his journeys, including a mysterious staff.
Mark	Victor and Stanley's tech assistant.
Marrak	A member of Jor-Dan's council, his role is that of a documentarian, recording petitions made to the king, the decisions taken, and applying the royal seal to the finished documents. Victim of a mysterious attacker, he hovered between life and death.
Mayaar	Jor-Dan's manservant.
Meeri Glascombe	One of the Kudaja, she becomes Herish's betrothed and later his wife, befriending D'laine along the way. She is now with child.
Naphelia*	Orongo's mate.
Neska	Jakla's mate.
Noona	Tetonie's mate. She and her partner are the last of their race, and desperate for any help they can find.
Oggy	An injured og rescued and later adopted by Jamie. Eventually reintroduced to the wild, he returned to introduce Jamie to his family.
Oogo	The leader of the Oolarooloo village who took in Greg Claymore.
Orongo	Jor-Dan's old Plotal friend.
Plodu*	Orongo's son. After causing too much mischief, he and his sisters are put to work to teach them responsibility. Plodu is tasked with working in the gardens.
Pra-yor	One of several Plotals accompanying Jakla on his visit to Ebscalon.

Puando	A neutered borjo serving as Herish's mount.
Pup	D'laine's diwal dog. Took up the self-appointed role of fiercely guarding D'laine and Trakon's children.
Quag	One of two farmers that come to Jor-Dan with a complaint over their shared well.
Quark Zerfre	One of Jor-Dan's advisors, he heads Ebscalon's crestrider fleet.
Rachel	D'laine's childhood friend since 3rd grade.
Rettu	The second disciple of the Visionary.
Rosa Villarreal	The Jackson family's housekeeper.
Sander*	A weaver employed in Ebscalon's hosk building.
Scooby	One of the diwal dogs tamed by D'laine. Upon becoming King Jor-Dan's guard dog, he is given the Ciertron name of "La'gar'ish."
Sorgus Blaski	The leader of the Plakados and the one to discover Asbram.
Stanley Daigle	Victor Bennett's old friend and fellow physicist, this genius's enthusiasm with the alternate dimension theory is unmatched. With his head shape entirely restored and his gift of telekinesis and telepathy under control, Stanley is chosen for an important role; and might find love along the way too. Retrieves the old king's crown from a hidden cave, and theorizes the artifact holds the key to turning the tide of the war.
Swezek	One of the Egrom village elders tasked with helping and training D'laine to realize her destiny. Even Egroms can only live for so long; and Swezek is past his time.
Teego Boinoroko*	A former builder of Patrosym, he deliberately used grog in the construction of the buildings to make them more unstable.
Tetonie	Noona's mate. The last of their race, Tetonie is willing to go to drastic measures to get help; though his horrendous social skills might hamper that.
The Visionary	Both healer and spiritual guide, the old Ciertron man is one of only three inhabiting Ebscalon's sacred temple. His true name is Alatheers.
Trabet	One of the Egrom village elders tasked with helping and training D'laine to realize her destiny.
Trakon Bramstone	The Prince of Ebscalon. Despite his hasty temper, Trakon is willing to befriend once adversaries; and maybe take his relationship with D'laine to the next level. He's recently developed an almost obsessive love for Earth food.
Treikie Soluvia	Stanley's girlfriend, a scientist just as obsessed with the subject as he is.
Twum	D'laine's handmaiden assigned to her during her stay at Ebscalon's palace.
Ugo*	The old Ebscalon scholar studying the cave's artifacts and scrolls.
Ulavia	A Ciertron seamstress, she made D'laine's wedding dress. Later, she is tasked with making the diapers and baby clothes for Ebscalon's royal twins.
Ulf	One of two farmers that come to Jor-Dan with a complaint over their shared well, the problem lies with him, though in a way many might not think.
Uni	One of the Kudaja, he helps Ben adjust to Tholian life.
Victor Bennett	An accomplished physicist and best friends with Stanley Daigle, he's one of few who found out what happened to D'laine Jackson. Later he moves along with his family to Thol, gaining the gift of foresight.
Vila	A Kudaja girl who befriends and plays with Darren and Chacoodi. After being put to work in the kitchens as punishment for causing too much mischief, she straightens out and becomes more responsible.

Wad*	The second *doski* captured, he and his fellow *doski* serve as scouts for the Trangula forces.
Wegore	One of several Plotals accompanying Jakla on his visit to Ebscalon.
Yalalore	The princess of Patrosym, she seems only concerned with herself, her father, and bettering her own social standing. Before D'laine's arrival to Thol, she was to be engaged to Trakon. Now disowned and imprisoned in a tower under heavy rotating guards, she can only communicate by mouthing her words.
Yorkens*	A Ciertron whose house is nominated for restoration by Darren.
Youndon	The ruler of Lansobar.
Ystap Olu	One of several Plotals sent as diplomats, she is a city planner with her sights set on helping her people rebuild.
Yucovia	A Ciertron girl who seems to be developing feelings for Brian.
Zabadoro*	The Kudaja head chef.
Zandal	The cruel leader of the robotics forces of Zan, he aimed to conquer any and all who stood in his way; and an unknown anomaly provided just that opportunity.
Zedonia	One of the women warriors assigned to guard D'laine and Trakon's children.
Zerke*	One of Orongo's daughters. After causing too much mischief, she and her siblings are put to work to teach them responsibility. Zerke is sent to help feed and care for the senior Plotals.

Locations & Places

Asbram	Another separate realm, and the place to which the Plakados migrated to, vanishing from the surface of Thol.
Aveldon	One of Thol's city-kingdoms.
Caradon	A city-kingdom, and home to the Caradonians.
Cave of Ingosaquille	A cave hidden on the crest of Mt. Aguberro, it contains many mysterious artifacts, scrolls, and treasures belonging to the old city of Ciert.
Cember Forest	Home to the Egroms and Kudaja, this giant, colorful forest is filled with massive, unknown flora and fauna.
Ebscalon	A Ciertron city of diamond-like roofs and colorful banners rebuilt in the wake of a devastating war, its name means "knowledge". Nests are being constructed on the city's towers to house the few full-sized borjos brought from Mt. Aguberro.
Egrom Village	Home of the Egroms of Cember Forest, visitors must be invited to it; else the village and inhabitants remain invisible to them.
Ikley Forest	A forest located nearby Ta'Byu'Vohon, the city-kingdom of the Plotals.
Ingosaquille	A crest on Mt. Aguberro, it is located one drok from the summit and hides a cave containing mysterious artifacts and scrolls from times lost.
Jekorba	A neighboring kingdom to Ebscalon.
Kensadora	A neighboring kingdom and the place where Ethaderia's sister lives.
Kitchikiwon	This mountain serves as home to the Raagor, the ice people living on the cold slopes and terrain.

Locations & Places, *Continued*

Kudajara	The home of the Kudaja, it is located deep in Cember Forest. The village itself is made up of boardwalks, with its homes and structures built into the large trees.
Lansobar	A neighboring kingdom to Ebscalon.
Mer	Kingdom of the Mers.
Mount Aguberro	The least explored mountain on Thol and the tallest at 6.75 droks, Mt. Aguberro is home to an impressive population of borjos, the untamed creatures able to reach their full-size without outside interference. It houses some form of ambient magic, allowing the Fod to assume different appearances as need be.
Oolarooloo Forest	Home to the Oolarooloo people's village. While this forest on the other side of Thol has no official name, it is certainly unforgettable, with lush flora and an abundance of fruits and vegetables like a garden.
Patrosym	A neighboring kingdom to Ebscalon.
Raagor Mountains	A large mountain range home to the Raagor Ice people.
Sagritol Valley	An unnamed valley hidden between the mountain ranges, it is odd by Tholian standards: grass instead of moss, small trees, and flora that appears to be from Earth.
Ta'Byu'Vohon	The city-kingdom of the Plotals, it was destroyed in the Great War, leaving nothing behind. However, nothing states that it must remain that way.
Tempe Forest	The stretch of forest linking the Cember Forest and Ikley Forest together.
The Nothingness	The void between worlds. Life does not exist there, and anything placed in it either dies or enters suspended animation.
The Visionary's Temple	The sacred Ciertron temple is set in the middle of Ebscalon.
Thol	An alternate Earth, Thol is the third planet in orbit; but this is where similarities end, with two suns, four large moons, vibrant landscapes, and a plethora of unique creatures and races.
Valley of Wailing Winds	Located on the opposite side of Thol, it is home to the Trangula people.
Zan	Another alternate Earth, this world has been reduced to a barren wasteland by its robotic inhabitants, humans made into slaves and prey.

Races

Caradonions	Another of the many races of Thol.
Ciertrons	Most resembling Earth's humans with their bronzed skin and dark hair, the Ciertrons are a technologically advanced society, defenders of justice who value honor despite their constant conflicts with Plotals. Their offspring are split between being born with childlike minds and those of adults. Ciertron women lay small eggs which slowly grow over several paths, reaching 2-3 feet in diameter before hatching.
Egroms	A wise, ancient race possessing wonderous abilities, the long-lived Egroms have since faded into myth and legend, isolating themselves in the Cember Forest while they continue to carry out their self-appointed duties. Recently, they have become more involved in the affairs of Thol's other races, interacting and aiding those they can. Egroms have an age limit of two thousand years; once it is reached they will pass on.
Fod	The sentinels of the cave on Mt. Aguberro. Resembling hunch-backed creatures covered in brown hair, they guard the cave's artifacts and treasures.
Kudaja	Described as tiny peoples who inhabit the Cember Forest, the Kudaja ride borjos as their mounts and wield wyres. Despite their stature, they possess a significant ability to morph to a larger form. However, not all Kudaja are able to do this. They reach full adulthood in two paths, and have a near-psychic connection to the trees.
Mer	A very similar race to the Ciertrons, Mers only differ by their square jaws and pronounced foreheads.

Races, Continued

Oolarooloo	Distinctive by their tall and thin appearance, dark bronzed skin, oblong heads and long ears, and lengthy necks, the Oolarooloo a people living on the opposite side of the Thol, renown for being great healers and keepers of the knowledge of many mysterious of Thol.
Plakado	Long thought extinct, the Plakado are distant relatives of the Plotals, differing slightly with their lack of a snout, along with other features. Interestingly, they are physically incapable of entering places or past thresholds without first being invited in.
Plotals	Tall reptilian bipeds that appear both human and alligator with the addition of hidden barbs on the ends of their tails, their society was destroyed by the Great War, leaving the survivors to live a nomadic life of plundering and slavery across Thol. Recently, they have switched to a more peaceful way of living, trying to rebuild their old kingdom. Similar to Ciertrons, Plotals also lay eggs, burying them until they hatch.
Raagor	Living in the mountain range of their namesake, the Raagor wear little clothing without fear of the cold. Also known as the "ghost people" because of their hairless pale skin and blue veins, the Raagor avoid socializing with other races. They are capable of freezing a person with a single touch, but cannot withstand high temperatures, preferring to live high in the frigid mountains.
Safri	An intelligent race of Thol, the Safri have friendly relations with the Ciertrons and trade with them. Their appearance resembles a blend of human and goat, with horns, pointed ears, and cloven hooves; the small wings and three-fingered hands being an exception.
Sagritols	Appearing as dark humanoid with fine, fuzzy hair all over their bodies, and a butterfly's orange and black wings, Sagritols are fast and agile flyers, capable of withstanding cold temperatures. They have a pair of antennas on their heads which they can use to communicate, and unusually, arms located much further down their torsos.
Sangdons	An extinct race of tiny people with large, pointed ears, they made their home in the trees, and have been extinct for about 100 paths.
Trangula	Inhabiting the Valley of Wailing Winds, the Trangula resemble humans with lengthy arms, large flat noses, and a small hump between their shoulder blades. They are seen as violent people, causing much problems and strife. Sharp teeth indicate their carnivorous diet, and they traverse and hide expertly in trees, using laser weapons to strike. The Trangula are "*doski*"; not fully human, nor as intelligent. They came about via a mating between an extinct race of tree people and the early version of Tholian humans. It is important to note *doski* does not equal Trangula; a *doski* can also refer to the simple-minded scouts, treated as lesser by others.
Triculated Cribustals	Tiny, parasitic organisms that feed off an individual's life force; they are foreign to Thol and come from another alternate Earth.
Zan Robots	These robots began as self-evolving technology built by the humans of the alternate Earth called Zan. Later, they took over the world and either enslaved or exterminated their creators.

Creatures

Augugal	A large spiked, hard-shelled animal, augugals are capable of blending into their environment, but these herbivores will prove to be both quick and dangerous when threatened.
Bobboes	Large, flightless birds raised by Ciertrons for their eggs, bobboes have large chests and a fluffy plumage of blue and purple.
Borjo	Resembling small dragons unable to breathe fire, the dragonfly-like borjo are used as mounts by the Kudaja. They are neutered upon hatching; otherwise, an unneutered borjo will grow to be large enough to ride by full-sized humans, capable of breathing fire with a wild temperament. These large borjos are unable to transform to a smaller size, unlike neutered ones. When ridden, they are steered using the fuzzy layers above their wings, but can also be communicated with using telepathic commands. They have excellent night vision.

Creatures, *Continued*

Diwal dogs	Roaming the sponge plains, diwal dogs are widely considered vicious carnivores, capable of stripping their prey in seconds with their layered, razor-sharp teeth. However, some find the gray-skinned, tufted canines to be misunderstood creatures.
Dooba	A bird-like beast with a bill instead of a beak, blue, orange, and purple feathers, short orange legs, and clawed feet. It lays colorful eggs and mates for life.
Fhahadda	A giant snake-like worm, the fhahadda burrows through the ground with the use of its many teeth. An odd creature, it is capable of both live births and egg-laying, with the number of offspring ranging widely in number. Despite this, no fhahadda has been sighted in over five centuries.
Floff	Despite its cute, wide-eyed appearance and fluffy limbs, this is a carnivore that hunts on the wing.
Gagu	Brightly colored feathers cover most of this flying creature, with its clawed membrane wings being the exception.
Gippe	A brown forest creature with furry hands and a long, semi-prehensile tail.
Grophie caterpillar	Living in the Cember Forest, its sting results in itchy purple spots that must be soothed with an Egrom antidote.
Hosk	This spider-creature's palm-sized, fluffy body varies in color, and contrasts its black legs and eyes. Living in colonies, the males spin plenty of silken webbing from the moss-like sponges of the plains; a material widely used by both Egroms and Ciertrons alike.
Jarvust	An evil spirit similar to a ghost or poltergeist, a jarvust is created when someone discontented lingers after dying, evolving from the intense hatred and negative energy. It appears as a tall and thin figure with hanging, straggly hair and robes like that of a burial shroud.
Kumbora bear	While usually brown and green-furred, kumbora bears can change their colors to blend into their surroundings. Their long tails and flexible digits allow it to traverse the trees with ease.
Mruck	Appearing a mishmash of creatures with its lidless eyes, long trunk, split hooves, and short ears, mrucks are surprisingly edible and enjoy water.
Og	Large, lumbering animals with blue-tinged fur and knobby heads that live on the sponge plains. Despite being prone to attacking other animals, ogs are in fact herbivores, their aggression stemming from being highly territorial.
Orich	A large flying creature with a heavily-built body and broad wings.
Pakow	The epitome of gentle giants, pakows are bulky, wooly beasts with six legs, wide faces, and compound eyes. They are used by several races as mounts, transportation, and labor. Their six legs create a characteristic rocking gait.
Par	A type of scarlet-winged bird.
Queper	While they can be touched without any issue, the real problem is when a predator makes the fatal mistake of trying to eat a queper. This cloven hooved animal's flesh is highly toxic and poisonous.

Creatures, *Continued*	
Quokin	This draconic creature makes its home in water, recognizable by its green-tipped black scales and curious personality. It is said a person touched by a quokin will find their true love.
Ragapunga	Resembling an anteater, the ragapunga should never be startled, as it sprays a deadly acid when frightened to protect itself.
Saber-toothed chun	Large, saber-toothed felines the size of horses that inhabit the Raagor mountains, they serve as comfortable mounts for the Raagor people, their thick manes and paws suited for the cold environment.
Sidel	A rabbit-sized creature that lives on the sponge plains; its meat is an easy source of food.
Xidilot	Now extinct, the xidilot was the natural predator of the Sagritols, hunting their eggs. It resembled a large eagle, and the effects of its hunting habits was enough to force its prey to seek out increasingly desperate measures to hide their unborn offspring.

Measurements

Chack	A Tholian hour
Closed Moon	New moon phase
Complete path	A Tholian year
Dinkst	A Tholian currency
Drok	Tholian unit of distance; equivalent to a mile
Dunct	A moment
Full turn	A Tholian day
Half Notch	Half-moon phase
Keld	A Tholian month
Notch	A Tholian week
Open Moon	Full moon phase
Quarter Notch	Quarter moon phase
Sepiks	Copper coins used by Ciertrons as currency.
Tuke	Tholian unit of distance; equivalent to a foot

Months

Janswary	First month of the Tholian year
Farvry	Second month of the Tholian year
Marsus	Third month of the Tholian year
Averil	Fourth month of the Tholian year
Mai	Fifth month of the Tholian year
Joono	Sixth month of the Tholian year
Jalie	Seventh month of the Tholian year
Austem	Eighth month of the Tholian year
Sustimbre	Ninth month of the Tholian year
Otocbrim	Tenth month of the Tholian year
Nosimbre	Eleventh month of the Tholian year
Docimbre	Twelfth month of the Tholian year

Technology

Cloaking	Technology used by the Patrosyms to hide the stairs and walkways of secured places, turning them invisible.

330

Technology, *Continued*

Crestriders	Flying ships invented by the Ciertrons for travel and city-wide defense against intruders. They are capable of "beaming up" objects and people inside, can both fly and hover, and are controlled with a series of levers, switches, and a joystick. With the crystal solar tech improved by aligning the charging crystals, they can now operate at night.
GSB	Short for "gravitational synchronizing beam," crestriders use it to enable flight and store solar energy in crystal cells.
Jumpsuit	A Ciertron type of clothing made from breathable fabric and worn by its warriors. It has multiple different "forms", including an armored one for combat.
Light healer	A Ciertron invention that uses a beam of light to heal injuries.
Restorative chamber	A glassed-in multi-purpose chamber serving as wardrobe, washer, and restorer for clothing. Also known as a Smart Closet.
Silencing helmet	A helmet secured to the head with a "cerebral key", rendering it unremovable; it cuts off the wearer's ability to communicate both verbally and mentally.
Sonicate box	A Ciertron invention used to assess injuries.
Translator	A small metal clip placed behind the ear which then settles into the flesh and serves as an automatic language translator.
Wyre	Bows used by the Kudaja, they form an arrow made of pure energy when the glowing string is drawn. Arrows can be set to either stun or kill.

Miscellaneous

Abrajaii	A golden Ciertron drink resembling champagne; it is drunk during celebrations.
Adpe	A Tholian vegetable, it resembles a wide Italian green bean.
Agrin trees	These trees produce large amounts of sap, which is tapped and blended with hosk webbing to create many durable items like footwear and banners. Entire forests can grow from one seed, reaching heights tall enough to touch the clouds. Its hard and dense bark can be carved to make durable toys.
Bago	A Tholian vegetable similar to a potato.
Bonding	The spiritual bond formed between partners in a Tholian marriage; once it has been broken, only time may heal it.
Churling	A devastating type of storm, with winds worse than a Category 5 hurricane.
Cribbage	A Plotal board game played with markers, octagonal dice, and dowels.
Eartholian	The term used to refer to those from Earth who moved to Thol and gained gifts.
Grog	A substance that repels agrin sap.
Hofo	A vegetable similar in taste to zucchini.
Jiffaberra tea	Made from jiffaberra leaves, it helps treat digestive parasites; despite its awful taste.
Kahl	A thick, sweet alcoholic drink consumed by Ciertrons.
Lantern-wick plant	The exact name of this plant is unknown. It grows in large clusters among shaded areas of the Cember Forest, and its thick, oily blue stalks are used in lanterns due to their slow-burning nature.
Lightning stones	A special type of rock that produces a purple flame when gently tapped against itself. Banging them together creates an explosion.
Nepsa	Plotal term for grandfather.
Nepsi	Plotal term for grandmother.
Silent stilling	A coma.
The Great War of Taylon	A lengthy Ciertron-Plotal war that left both sides decimated. It occurred fifty years ago and resulted in the loss of many technological advancements.
The Staff	A sacred relic thought to have been destroyed centuries ago.

Technology, *Continued*

The Voice	A mysterious ability that allows one to control others with verbal commands.
Youngmen	Not all Ciertron children are the same; Youngmen are those that emerge from their eggs in child-like bodies but with the minds of fully functioning adults.

A NOTE FROM THE AUTHOR

If you discover a missing element that should be included in the
Glossary or Errors in the book, please let me know at
dawn@degreenfeld.com

WANT MORE THOL?

Earth Calling Thol

Book 5 in the Thol Series

Stanley receives an alert from Al as government agents haul the former reporter into custody. A New York publishing giant published Al's book *Doorway to Thol* and agents read it. Now they're taking Al into custody to grill him about the portal at Coronado Beach in California.

While he sticks to the story that the book is make-believe out of his wild imagination, the agents aren't buying it. They send a team of scientists and physicists to the beach.

Luckily, Stanley listens to everything through the translator hidden behind Al's ear. He beckons everyone for an emergency meeting to determine what action they should take.

Everyone agrees that they must stop the government. Ghury, the Egrom leader of the Cember Forest tribe, posts several Egroms at the portal site to monitor any activity.

D'laine wants to extract Al. It would be easy for her, Stanley or Ben to *step* to Earth and step back with the reporter.

Unfortunately, the government agents, scientists and physicists open a portal, but not to Thol. An alien race breaks through the portal. The Xeddicts, frightful creatures, are killing machines. The government implores Al to contact D'laine for help.

Once again, D'laine uses her powers to save a world from death, destruction and slavery. Instead of thanking her, the US government tries to take her into custody. They want to use D'laine's powers for their own greed.

They can't imprison her in any bunker, cell or chamber. She walks through everything they try to seal her in. They finally understand her complete power. She leaves with Al, giving the government a clear warning: they are never to breach any portal ever again.

On another note, the Wobbly toys become a hit across the kingdoms.

The cloaking investigation resumes.

A Trangula with a white flag approaches the gates. They want to meet with Ebscalon, Kudaja and Ta-Byu-Vohon leaders to learn how to make their kingdom better.

The search for clues about the prophecy, and the treasures in the inner cave continues.

Those two babies are not your regular babies!

Stanley and Treikie tie the knot.

The adventure continues

Book 5 ~ Earth Calling Thol

Did you miss Book 1?
Prophecy of Thol
Book 3 ~ Love of Thol
Book 4 ~ King of Thol

ABOUT THE AUTHOR

D.E. Greenfield, aka Dawn Greenfield Ireland, is the award-winning author of 22 published novels which consists of 5 series: cozy mystery, sci fi/fantasy, billionaire shapeshifters, and dystopian. There's also a stand-alone sci-fi romantic adventure, 7 nonfiction books (1 hardcover), and she adapted 4 of her screen-plays into book format. She also has created over 50 themed notebooks.

Two of her screenplays were optioned, and she worked on a screenwriter-for-hire project. Dawn has a certificate from the Professional Program in Screenwriting from UCLA (2002) and with ScreenwritingU.

D.E. Greenfield's business, Artistic Origins, has been around since 1995. Besides writing, she coaches writers, edits, formats and publishes clients' books.

Her former day job as an award-winning technical writer played a major role in her fiction writing. She is detailed-oriented, the organizational queen of the known universe, and never misses a deadline.

ACTIONS APPRECIATED

How about leaving a review? Reviews help authors so much.

Sign up for the newsletter and get the inside scoop ahead of everyone else:

http://degreenfield.com

facebook.com/dawn.ireland.18
x.com/dawnireland
instagram.com/dawngreenfieldIreland
goodreads.com/dawnireland
linkedin.com/in/dawnireland